BAINE

AND THE OUTLAW OF CORWICK

Terry Cloutier

Copyright © 2023 TERRY CLOUTIER

All rights reserved. No part of this book may be reproduced,

in whole or in part, without prior written permission

from the copyright holder.

Also by Terry Cloutier

The Wolf of Corwick Castle Series

The Nine (2019)

The Wolf At Large (2020)

The Wolf On The Run (2020)

The Wolf At War (2021)

The Wolf And The Lamb (2022)

The Wolf And The Codex (2022)

Baine And The Outlaw of Corwick (2023)

The Wolf At The Door (Fall 2023)

The Past Lives Chronicles

Past Lives (2021)

Jack the Ripper (2022)

The Zone War Series

The Demon Inside (2008)

The Balance Of Power (2010)

Novella

Peter Pickler and the Cat That Talked Back (2010)

Contents

PROLOGUE 5
Chapter 1: Alone 15
Chapter 2: Sunna 21
Chapter 3: Raiders 32
Chapter 4: Time To Leave 42
Chapter 5: Tragedy 50
Chapter 6: Odiman 59
Chapter 7: Heading North 76
Chapter 8: Pembry Drake's Head 88
Chapter 9: The Boar That Starts It All 97
Chapter 10: Hadrack Will Understand 106
Chapter 11: The Hunt Begins 115
Chapter 12: Cairn 127
Chapter 13: Tadley Platt 135
Chapter 14: When Is A Juggler Not A Juggler? 149
Chapter 15: Rupert Frake And The Spy 162
Chapter 16: A Tired Jester? 175
Chapter 17: Bent And The Ugly Merchant 185
Chapter 18: Konway 198
Chapter 19: The Hungry Oak 210
Chapter 20: Alen Hawe 222
Chapter 21: Bones Or Knots? 234
Chapter 22: Ward Grich 246
Chapter 23: Pax 256

Chapter 24: Tasker Grich	268
Chapter 25: Ira	279
Chapter 26: Escape	292
Chapter 27: Pit Kelly And The Halfwit	303
Chapter 28: Heply Boll	313
Chapter 29: Alone For Eternity	322
Chapter 30: Everything Has Changed	335
EPILOGUE	345
Author's Note	349

PROLOGUE

February is easily the worst month of all, I thought dismally as I stared out the window of my solar. I could see little outside except for endless swirling snow and what might be the hint of the White Tower off in the distance. Winter had arrived early in Ganderland this year, with the first snows coming in mid-October, ruining my plans for an expedition to Mount Halas to recover Waldin's codex. Now I had no choice but to wait until spring, or worse, maybe even early summer before the mountain passes would be clear enough to travel. It was a thoroughly depressing thought.

I sighed, leaning my forehead against the cold glass of the window as a log in the new fireplace I'd built along the eastern wall shot sparks upward in a swarm of orange and red. *Face it*, I thought, closing my eyes. *You're bored, you old bastard.* There was little for me to do during these long days of winter except write, for my son, Hughe, had taken on more and more responsibilities ever since my unfortunate sickness. I'm sure the boy had expected me to die before the snows fell, as had everyone else in Corwick, myself included. Only my granddaughter, Lillia, had had faith in both me and the Three Gods—well, that and the brilliance of my physician, Kieran Acker, I suppose. It was he who had saved me from an invasive tapeworm that had tunneled into my brain. Though in truth, I still hadn't quite decided if removing the damn thing had been a blessing or a curse.

I turned as a knock sounded at the closed door. "What?" I grunted, perhaps a little more forcefully than was warranted. I tended to get irritable and moody when my writing wasn't going well. The long table in front of me was scattered with paper, ink, and quills, since I was once again trying to put down my life experiences for others to read. The boredom I was feeling stemmed from that, for the unenviable truth was I'd become sick and tired of writing about myself all day long. I needed something else to occupy my mind.

The door opened with a creak, revealing my steward, Walice. "Might I come in, my lord?"

I glanced down at the man's calfskin boots, the toes of which had already crossed the threshold by a good four inches. "I'd say you already are *in*, Walice."

The steward looked down, allowing his lips to twitch slightly in amusement, which was the extent of any emotion he usually allowed himself to show. Walice was a serious man, filled with the importance and purpose of his office—as had his father been before him. Walice's youngest son, Riffin, was apprenticing with his father even now to continue the family tradition, though I feared after I was gone that Hughe might not keep Walice or Riffin on. It was something that I knew I needed to talk to my son about before I died.

"Lady Lillia has just arrived in the outer bailey, my lord," Walice said.

I frowned in surprise, glancing toward the heavy snow slapping with enthusiasm against the glass windowpane. "In this?"

Walice shrugged. "Apparently, when the lady left Darkcliff three days ago, the weather showed little signs of turning, my lord."

"The impetuous little fool," I grumbled. I shook my head at the follies of youth. "A pregnant woman should not be moving about at this time of year."

"Quite right, my lord," Walice agreed. "But you know Lady Lillia and her ways."

"Indeed I do," I said with a resigned sigh. My granddaughter was as headstrong as her mother and grandmother had been before her—maybe more so, if that were even possible. "Did Lord Alder accompany Lillia?" Lord Alder was my granddaughter's husband. He was also a great-nephew of one of my dearest friends, Lord Fitzery, who had died more than ten years ago now. I blinked in surprise at that realization. Where had the time gone?

"No, my lord, he did not," the steward answered. His expression clouded, indicating there was something else—something I clearly was not going to like. "In fact, according to Lady Lillia, it seems Lord Alder forbade her to journey here, and he was not made aware that she'd left until it was too late."

I grunted in annoyance. Why were all the Corwick women so damn stubborn? "Did my granddaughter tell you why she rode all this way?"

Walice hesitated. "She did, my lord. Though perhaps it would be best if she told you herself."

"And perhaps you should stop wasting my time," I growled. I motioned with a hand. "Out with it, or I'll demote you to kitchen duty—or better yet, cleaning latrines."

Walice sighed, quite rightly not looking alarmed at my threat. I probably made the same one ten times a day to the man. "Lady Lillia came here accompanied by a young woman named Kather Merklar, my lord. They would both like a moment to speak with you."

I just stared at the steward, not recognizing the name. "And who might that be?" I finally asked, not hiding my impatience.

"She claims to be Baine's granddaughter, my lord."

I groaned and rolled my eyes. "By The Mother," I whispered. "Not another one?"

"I'm afraid so, my lord."

"How many is that now?"

"At last count, I would say this makes eleven children and five grandchildren that we have been made aware of, my lord. Knowing the man, I'm sure there are many more still to come."

I snorted in agreement. "So, let me guess. This *woman* expects some kind of stipend from me like the others, is that right?"

"That I cannot say, my lord," Walice responded, his features blank and unreadable. "I have shared with you the extent of my knowledge regarding this."

I started to pace, getting angry now. I wasn't sure why my blood was up, since Baine's many dalliances with the fairer sex were hardly news to anyone. I pointed a finger at my steward. "I did not lie with this woman's grandmother, whoever she might have been. Which means by the King's Law, I have no responsibility toward this person at all. The fact that Baine might or might not have done so is meaningless to me. I'm tired of these people taking advantage of my generosity. That ends now. So, you can tell this little charlatan that she won't get a single coin from me over—"

"Kather Merklar is not here for your money, my lord," a female voice cut in.

I glanced to the open doorway of the solar, where my granddaughter, Lillia, now stood. She wore a thick green cloak with a fur mantle, the cloth still dark and wet from melting snow. She also wore a matching beaded and feathered hat, though the decorations were drooping precariously at the moment. Lillia's blue eyes sparkled with welcome and love, although I also recognized a trace of irritation hiding in their depths that I knew well.

"Lillia, my dear," I said, setting aside my anger. Seeing the girl always brought joy to my heart, and this time was no different. I limped around the table, spreading my arms as my granddaughter hugged me.

"How have you been, my lord?"

"Well enough," I said, breaking the embrace. I took a step back, examining the girl's obvious swollen belly through her cloak with a critical eye. "You've gotten fat, child. They must feed you well at Darkcliff."

Lillia laughed. "And you're even balder and more wrinkled than I remember, my lord."

I chuckled, my good humor diminishing somewhat when I noticed a second figure standing in the doorway. The girl was short and slim, with dark eyes and wet, long black hair twisted in ringlets down her shoulders. I noted that she was wearing a simple brown cloak, though the quality was better than most.

Lillia saw my appraising eyes on her companion. "This is Kather Merklar, my lord."

The girl curtsied awkwardly, and I realized that she was nervous—very nervous. "It's an honor to meet you, lord."

I didn't reply, fixating my gaze back on Lillia. "What's all this about, child?"

My granddaughter indicated the long table in the center of the room. "May we sit, my lord? It's been a long journey."

I nodded, not saying anything while the women took off their cloaks, handing them to Walice before taking a bench by the table.

"Shall I have refreshments brought up, my lord?" Walice asked.

"Yes," I grunted. "But no food for me, just Cordovian wine."

"Very good, my lord," Walice said with a slight bow.

"Oh, and Walice?" Lillia said, her eyes alight with anticipation. "I'd love some of Old Adwig's almond pudding if any is lying about. I haven't had any since I left the castle."

"Old Adwig died a month ago, my lady," Walice replied regretfully.

"Oh, what a shame," Lillia said, looking crestfallen at the news. She shook her head sadly. "He was such a nice old man. Always so kind to me when I was a little girl."

"I'll see what the new Master Cook can do, my lady," the steward promised before he left.

The two women had sat down side by side, thighs touching, and I shuffled my way opposite them, moving aside papers before, with a groan, I lowered myself onto the polished bench. I placed my clasped hands on the worn tabletop, thinking sadly about how many times I'd sat in the same spot over the years, surrounded by friends and council. I could almost feel their ghostly eyes fixated on me and I shrugged away the feeling of depression coming over me. Now was not the time to get misty-eyed in front of these women.

"So, what's all this nonsense about?" I said gruffly. "Why did you come all this way in your condition, child?" I glanced at Kather Merklar. "Surely not just to show me another one of Baine's many offspring?"

My granddaughter's companion blinked in surprise, but she said nothing as I studied her closer. The girl was very pretty, and I could see something of my long-time friend in her, especially around the eyes and the way she held her slim body. Whatever Kather Merklar's reason for being here was, there was little doubt in my mind now that she was blood kin in some way to Baine. Yet, even so, I was determined not to let that influence me. She would get nothing from me this day but a warm meal and a bed to sleep in. I waited as Lillia put a hand on Kather's shoulder, giving her a reassuring squeeze while indicating with her eyes that she should speak.

The slim girl cleared her throat nervously. "My grandmother was Sunna Merklar, lord."

I frowned, for the name meant nothing at all to me. "Am I supposed to know who that is?"

Kather glanced at Lillia for encouragement, then turned back to me. "I think so, yes, lord. At least, I hope so. My grandfather, the man you knew as Baine of Corwick, was rescued by my grandmother and her father after he'd been swept off a ship when he was a young man."

I felt my eyes widen, remembering now. It had been so long ago that my friend had told Jebido and me about his harrowing ordeal that I'd forgotten the names of his rescuers. I felt my demeanor toward the girl softening somewhat. Baine would have died if not for Sunna Merklar and her father. I nodded. "Your grandmother's father was named Nelsun if I'm not mistaken?"

Kather's expression changed to one of relief. "Yes, lord, that is correct." She'd been holding her body tensely all this time, and now she started to slowly relax. "I only recently learned my grandfather's name was Baine of Corwick, lord. Our family only knew him as Drago."

I frowned, searching my memory. Something about that name rang a bell, but I couldn't quite put my finger on it.

"Kather was working in the kitchens at Darkcliff, my lord," Lillia said. She glanced at the other girl and smiled. "We quickly became friends when I arrived, and I made her my lady-in-waiting."

"How wonderful for you both," I said, trying not to show my impatience. *Drago, Drago, Drago, what was it about that name*?

"Anyway," Lillia said. "We got to talking, and Kather told me about how her grandparents met. Her story sounded strikingly similar to what I knew had happened to Baine, so we did a little investigating and quickly realized that he and Drago were the same person."

I held up a hand. "Hold on a moment," I said. I focused on Kather. "I remember Baine telling me distinctly that your grandmother was only a child back then, a girl of ten or so. And he was married at the time, too." I frowned uneasily as I thought of Flora's and Baine's baby son, both of whom had been murdered by a man posing as the Outlaw of Corwick. I felt my anger return. "If you're here to try and smear my friend's good name, young lady, by claiming that he committed adultery with a child, then I promise you—"

"Please, lord," Kather said, looking distressed at my growing rage. "I would never even contemplate such a thing." She shook her head vehemently, sending her many curls flying in all directions. "No, my grandmother and Drago—I mean, Baine, met again years later. I believe when she was around twenty. That is when the liaison happened, lord. As far as I know, it only occurred the one time and they never saw each other again."

"Oh, I see," I said, mollified now. I sat back in relief. "So, what do you want if you're not here for accusations or money?"

"To know more about my grandfather, lord," Kather said. "My grandmother died when I was six, and my mother was always tight-lipped about her father with me, despite my many questions."

"That's it?" I asked, surprised. "That's all you want?"

"Yes, lord."

I glanced at Lillia. "You rode all this way for this, child?"

My granddaughter smiled. "Well, it seemed like a good idea at the time, my lord. Besides, I was restless, and you never actually told me all of Baine's story after he fell off that ship. You always promised me you would, but you never did. Coming here now seemed like a good opportunity to take care of both Kather's needs and mine in one fell swoop."

"You should have waited until spring when the trails were safer," I said sternly.

Lillia grimaced. "Yes, my lord, in hindsight, I should have. I admit I may have let my enthusiasm over Kather's story get the best of me, and for that, I am sorry." She looked down at her hands before meeting my eyes again. I was surprised to see a hint of tears there. "But the truth is, my lord, I dismissed the danger because I miss you and everybody else here in Corwick. The baby will be here soon, and once that happens, I'll have little time to see you. Who knows how much longer—"

The girl trailed off then, biting her lip, and I nodded, feeling a lump of emotion rising in my chest. Now I understood. She was afraid I was going to die soon. It was a valid fear, of course, at least from her perspective. But my granddaughter didn't know about Waldin's codex, nor that I was determined to get it back, even if it meant cheating death a little while longer to do it. I reached across the table, taking Lillia's hand in mine. "And we all miss you too, child, believe me. The castle hasn't been the same without you here." I smiled, letting Lillia see I was no longer angry with her. "And, despite the terrible chance you took, I'm glad you've come."

My granddaughter's face lit up with joy. "So, you'll tell us Baine's story then, my lord?"

"I will," I confirmed as I sat back. I held my hands up at the look of delight on the faces of the women opposite me. "But not right now. You two look worn out after your trip. Besides, I'm a little tired." I stood after my lie, indicating the women should do likewise. I wasn't the least bit tired, in fact, for I'd suddenly felt a rush of energy flowing through my veins that I was trying my best to hide. I glanced toward the open door, but there was still no sign of Walice. "I don't know where that steward of mine went off to, but why don't you both go down to the kitchens and get something to eat? I'll be along later." I indicated the papers on the table. "I still have some things that I need to take care of. We can talk about Baine all you want tomorrow."

"Thank you, my lord," Lillia said, entwining her arm in Kather's as she led the girl away. "We look forward to it."

I waited until the women had left and I could no longer hear their footsteps in the hallway, then I limped to the door and closed it firmly. I headed back to the table and sat, sweeping aside what I'd been writing before I set a fresh page in front of me. I smiled with excitement, feeling alive and vibrant again, a far cry from only minutes earlier. Lillia and Kather Merklar had just given me a precious gift, one which I couldn't wait to get started on. I dipped a quill tip in ink, staring down at the blank page as my mind headed back in time.

It was finally time to tell Baine of Corwick's story.

PART ONE

DRAGO

Chapter 1: Alone

Baine was a dead man. He knew it. The sea knew it. And the storm that howled in victory all around him knew it as well. It was only a matter of time before the helpless man would weaken beneath the combined might of storm and sea and let go of the splinter of wood he clung so desperately to—then he would be theirs. Patience, the storm and sea knew from many centuries of experience, was all that was required now. Surprisingly, Baine didn't feel any fear at the prospect of his imminent death—at least, not for himself, at any rate. No, all he could think about was *Sea-Dragon* and the safety of all those on board her as he watched the mighty ship heading away from him, running with the storm. Her great sail was nothing but tattered shreds of canvas now, streaming out behind her, and Baine felt overwhelming despair well up inside him. He sobbed, for he knew better than any just how devastated both Hadrack and Jebido would be when they learned of his death. The thought of it was almost too much for him to bear.

Uncontrollable anger arose in Baine then, and he thrust aside his despair and lifted his head to the maddened skies, howling his defiance at the indifferent gods. "I will not die here!" he shouted to the heavens as sea spray and rain worked in tandem to lash at his unprotected face. "Do you hear me, you bastards? I refuse to die in this place, so you can do your worst!"

As if in answer to Baine's challenge, jagged streaks of lightning sizzled overhead, cutting through the dark clouds and illuminating the sky, followed immediately by a thunderous boom that set Baine's teeth on edge and his ears ringing. He clamped his mouth shut in awe, deciding it was best not to tempt the gods any further, for it was clear that he was in enough trouble as it was. Instead, Baine glanced again toward the receding vessel, feeling despair and heartache beginning to form in him once again. He lifted a trembling hand to the ship in a gesture that he knew would be futile. No one could see him among the giant waves, and even if they had, there was little they could do about it, for *Sea-Dragon* had no rudder or sail.

"Farewell," Baine whispered as the giant cog finally disappeared from his sight for good, her great bulk swallowed up by the swirling storm. "Stay safe, my friends. I will miss you all."

Baine slowly lowered his hand after the ship was gone, left alone now to the gods and the fates. He'd never felt so lonely in his life, not even as an orphan barely eking out a living as a pickpocket in Gandertown. Huge, dark waves rolled and twisted around him like the backs of gigantic sea monsters, competing, it seemed, to see which one could toss his frail body the highest. He cried out in surprise when one took hold of him without warning, raising the board he clung to ten feet in the air effortlessly in the blink of an eye.

Baine pressed his face to the shattered remnants of the rudder, his eyes mere slits against the sheeting rain and lungs already half-filled with seawater as he hurried to draw in air. He knew what was coming next. A moment later, Baine unconsciously wailed as he plunged downward into a waiting trough churning and seething with angry white froth. His head went under the water first, then the rest of his body, the powerful undercurrents seeking to draw him down further and tear his rigid fingers off the wood once and for all. But Baine held on, for he knew to let go of the rudder meant certain death.

Everything seemed calmer beneath the waves, almost supine compared to the nightmare world above. The storm still raged just as strong as before, of course, but now its power seemed muted below the water. Baine was sorely tempted to remain where he was, reluctant to brave the cold winds and rain again. *Come and join us*, the sea seemed to whisper soothingly all around him. *Come to us. Why fight that which has only one ending*? But Baine refused to heed the sea's call, stubbornly using the last of his waning strength to kick upward in desperation, with the buoyancy of the wood the only thing standing between him and a watery grave—at least for now.

Baine broke through to the surface, shooting out of the sea like an arrow and almost losing his grip as he landed awkwardly. He began to bob up and down precariously on the churning water before another wave grabbed him, lifting him high and spinning him dizzyingly around before it sent him back down into the waiting maelstrom. Over and over, the exultant waves toyed with the foolish man who'd dared to fall among them, pounding away at his resolve with relentless ferocity like a well-fed barn cat torturing a mouse just for fun. Baine lost track of how many times he rose and fell, with each new cycle sapping a little more of his diminishing strength. How long had he been in the water now? he wondered at one point. An hour? Five hours? A day? Baine had no idea. The skies above had remained the same throughout—dark and forbidding except for the odd flash of lightning—so he had no way of knowing whether it was day or night.

Baine groaned in exhaustion when another swell took firm hold of him, tossing him around like a cork. He dragged himself further onto the wood until he was centered, ignoring the aching muscles in his back that screamed at him as he clung to the sides of the rudder. He began to rise, and rise, and rise, higher than anything he'd seen yet. "Please, Mother," Baine whispered as the wind howled and tore at his drenched hair and clothing. *Give up! Give up!* the storm insisted in a high-pitched whistle. *There is no point to this, puny human!* Baine felt the swell of the wave building even more beneath him, gaining ever more strength, and he pressed his face to the wood. He could feel his resolve to live weakening as the storm raked driving rain like tiny nails across his helpless body. He realized there was no hope, for his strength was completely gone now. No hope at all.

"Please, Mother and Father," Baine gasped through chattering teeth, making one last desperate plea as he hovered on the precipice of the wave twenty feet above the churning water. "Please don't take me this way. I'm not ready."

But the gods weren't listening, and as the tiny, ant-like speck that was Baine plunged downward into the gleeful sea, the beleaguered wood beneath him finally cracked from the strain, snapping into pieces. Baine desperately twisted, trying to hold on to anything he could, just as he felt unbearable pain in his left arm, followed a moment later by a sharp blow to the side of the head.

Everything went black after that.

Baine awoke to raging thirst and the harsh sounds of birds screeching. He lifted his head, groaning at the pain that shot through his skull, then opened his eyes, blinking in the intense sunlight as the smell of the sea filled his nostrils. He realized he was lying on a half-submerged piece of wood, with his left arm wedged solidly into a large crack. Blood was oozing slowly into the water from a deep gash on his forearm. He winced, then cautiously tried to extricate his arm, but the pain was excruciating and he was forced to stop. Was the arm broken? He waited, letting the waves of pain wash over him as he fought to catch his breath. Flickering shadows from overhead caused him to look up as a flock of white birds with long beaks and angular wings flew over him, their wings whistling.

Gannets, Baine automatically thought, though he had no idea how he knew that. Some of the birds turned aside, beating their wings toward an outcrop of rock that he could see rising from the waves in the distance. The stone was shaped like the head and shoulders of a man, with the lower sections only inches above the waterline. Baine felt sudden hope and began using his good arm to propel himself through the water toward the rock, hissing in pain with every agonizing sweep. It seemed like an eternity before he reached the outcrop, and when he arrived, he dragged himself onto one of the slick, moss-covered lower sections, crying out each time his injured arm, still encased in the wood, came into contact with the ground. Above him, thirty or so gannets watched his struggles warily from atop the crown of the head, each identical to the next.

Baine finally collapsed five feet from the waterline, exhausted and lying facedown on the wet stone as sea-spray washed over him. Moments later, he fell asleep. He didn't notice hours later when a small fishing boat glided silently toward the rock, nor was he aware when a tall man stepped off the craft onto the shore, then knelt beside him.

"Is he alive, Father?"

The tall man turned to glance back at the boat, where a young girl sat on a bench, using a set of oars to keep the small craft in place. "He is, Sunna," the man grunted. "Though he might be only a step or two away from Judgement Day by the looks of him." The tall man frowned when he saw the stranger's mangled arm hooked up in the broken wood, and he carefully worked it free, hesitating whenever the man moaned in his sleep.

"Who is he, Father?" the girl asked breathlessly, clearly excited.

"Now, how should I know that, child?" the man growled, though he tempered it with a grin. His daughter loved mysteries, and he could tell this poor bastard had already captured her imagination.

Baine stirred, moaning at the pain in his arm. He opened his eyes, barely registering the figure bent over him busily wrapping cloth around his bleeding wound. The man was thin, with a lean face worn by the sun, a battered hat tilted sideways on his head, and a thick silver beard.

"Well now," the tall man said, sitting back on his haunches when he was finished with the bandaging. "Hello, friend. My name is Nelsun. What's yours?"

Baine opened his mouth to answer, but no words came out. He realized with a start that he didn't know his name. Baine felt panic rise in him, and he started to sit up, only to have Nelsun gently push him back down.

"Easy there, friend," Nelsun said. "Looks like you've taken quite a whack to the head, there. Best we take things nice and slow for the time being."

Baine blinked up at the man, a single word filling his mind. He rolled his tongue, trying to make that word come out, though he had no idea what it meant. "Seeeeee," he finally managed to croak around his swollen tongue.

"Yes," Nelsun agreed with a nod. He motioned to the water behind him. "This is the Western Sea."

Baine shook his head in frustration, regretting it moments later as fire arced across his brain. He tapped his chest for emphasis, desperate to make himself understood. "No. Seeeeee. Dragoooo."

Nelsun frowned, sending his bushy eyebrows into contortions. Then his face lit up in understanding, and he laughed. "Your name is Drago, and you were lost at sea. Is that right?"

But before Baine could answer, darkness came for him once again, and he knew nothing more.

Chapter 2: Sunna

Baine awoke to the intoxicating smells of stewing pottage. He stared up at the unfamiliar thatch roof above him, then twisted his head when he felt eyes on him. A girl was sitting on a stool beside the narrow bed he lay upon, staring at him with rapt fascination. "Hello," he rasped, his tongue feeling clunky and unresponsive. He cleared his throat and shifted on the thin straw mattress, wincing as pain shot up his left arm. Baine glanced down at it, not surprised to see bandages wrapped around the forearm from his wrist to his elbow. A thin trail of blood had seeped through the material in a jagged line on the inside portion of his arm. He could feel his head throbbing, and he gingerly examined the back of his skull until he found a welt the size of a crab apple near his right ear. Baine fingered it experimentally, suppressing a gasp as he focused back on the girl. "Where am I?"

The girl smiled, revealing small, perfect teeth. Her hair was long and light brown with a tinge of red, twisted into braids down either side of her head. Her nose was upturned and pert, with a smattering of orange freckles across the bridge and on her cheeks. Baine could tell she was destined to become a beautiful woman one day. "You're in my home," the girl said. "In the village of Weymouth."

Baine nodded, letting his eyes roam around the small dwelling. He'd never heard of Weymouth. A square central hearth—which was really nothing more than a hole in the ground lined with stones—stood in the center of the room, with an iron pot hanging over the weak flames. Wisps of smoke drifted around the pot to an opening in the ceiling. A long bench stood against the far wall with a weathered plank for a table in front of it, balanced on aged wooden buckets. Two knives with black leather grips sat on the tabletop side by side and, for some reason, Baine found them familiar. Shelves holding several tin pots, some wooden bowls, and three mugs were recessed into the wall to the right of the bench and table, with more shelves on the left of it filled to overflowing with netting, hooks, and other fishing gear. An unstrung bow and full arrow bag leaned against the wall in one corner, and Baine found his eyes locking on them in fascination. He didn't know why.

"How come your beard grows all scruffy in patches on your cheeks like that?" the girl asked curiously.

Baine just stared at her, not sure how he should reply. He unconsciously used his right hand to feel the hair on his face, realizing she was right. "I don't know," he admitted.

"How old are you?"

Baine thought about that, and when his mind couldn't come up with the answer, he finally shook his head. "I'm not sure."

"Where are you from?"

"I don't know."

"Why don't you know?"

Baine grimaced. "I...I can't remember."

"Why were you in the water? Was your ship wrecked? Were you in a battle?"

Baine closed his eyes, trying to focus. There was something, something just on the cusp of his memory that he knew was important, but each time he got near it, it wiggled away from him. Finally, he sighed in frustration. "I really don't know."

"Well, that's odd," the girl said with a frown. "It doesn't seem like you know *anything*." She shrugged. "My name is Sunna. I'm almost ten, and I already know a lot more than you do."

Baine couldn't help but smile. "And my name is—" He hesitated, once again stymied for an answer.

"Drago, yes, I know that," the girl said proudly. "You already told us your name."

"I did?" Baine said. The name Drago meant nothing to him. Baine suddenly realized what the girl had said, and he added, "Who is *us*?"

"My father," Sunna replied. "We're the ones who found you out on the Dung Head." She giggled at Baine's questioning look. "All the birds ever do is land there and leave droppings behind, so I call it the Dung Head. That's all it's good for. Most of the villagers call it The Sentinel, but I find that hugely boring."

"Oh, I see," Baine said. He suddenly remembered the tall man who had bandaged his arm. "Your father's name is Nemund, right?"

"Nelsun," a deep male voice corrected with a chuckle from across the room. "Nelsun Merklar."

Baine glanced to the open doorway, where a man stood in the entrance. He recognized him immediately. "My apologies," Baine said. "I meant no offense."

"Bah," Nelsun grunted, waving it off. "Think nothing of it, Drago. You had bigger things to worry about when we first met than remembering an old man's name." Nelsun entered, limping noticeably as he lowered a string of gleaming fish onto the improvised table. He put his hands on his hips afterward. "How are you feeling?"

Baine shrugged, wincing at the ache in his head. "Not too bad, I guess." He hesitated, his tongue feeling even more swollen now and his throat incredibly dry. "Would it be too much to ask for some water or ale if you have it? I'm very thirsty."

"Well, curse me for a fool," Nelsun grunted. "All we have is water, though." He picked up a jug off the table, then fetched a wooden mug, filling it before offering it to Baine. "You don't have to worry, the water is good. We have a spring nearby."

Baine drank gratefully while Nelsun stood beside Sunna, resting a hand on her shoulder affectionately. "I hope my daughter hasn't been talking your ear off." He grinned. "She has a tendency to do that, especially with anyone new in the village."

Baine shook his head as he drank greedily while the girl looked up at her father. "Drago can't remember much of anything,

Father. I thought maybe he was a halfwit like Handy Jamer's son at first, but now I'm not so sure."

"Oh?" Nelsun said, his bushy eyebrows rising as he focused on Baine. "Is that a fact?"

"I'm sorry," Baine said, having drained the cup in two long gulps. He pointed to his temple. "Everything in here seems kind of jumbled up at the moment." He nodded gratefully when the fisherman refilled his cup.

"It was probably that knock on the head," Nelsun grunted as Baine drank again. "I'm sure your memory will come back once you've gotten some rest." The tall man glanced down at his daughter, giving her a pointed look. "Those cod won't clean themselves, child. And I see you haven't finished your other chores yet, either."

"But Father, I want to talk with—"

"Now," Nelsun said in a tone that brooked no argument.

Sunna stood, looking like she wanted to say something more, but common sense prevailed. She plodded over to the fish, scuffing her feet across the floor in an exaggerated way before picking them up and heading outside. Nelsun took his daughter's place on the stool, sighing wearily as he sat. He hooked a thumb over his shoulder toward the door that Sunna had made sure to slam closed with a bang behind her. "Just like her mother, that one, the gods help me. Too smart for her own good, or mine, for that matter."

"Is it just you and her?" Baine asked curiously.

"Sadly, yes," Nelsun replied. "My wife died when Sunna was only two." He hesitated, looking down at his hands. "And my youngest son a year later. He was four at the time. Damn little fool got caught up in some netting in the Blackfill Lagoon and drowned while I was out to sea." Nelsun took a deep breath, blowing air out of his nostrils. Baine could see the hurt of loss hovering in the man's eyes, and he guessed that Nelsun blamed himself for the boy's death. "My eldest son, Tomund, is off fighting in the war," the fisherman added. "He could be dead too, for all I know. I haven't heard from him in several months."

Baine frowned. "War?"

Nelsun studied him thoughtfully. "You really are addled pretty good, now aren't you, lad? I mean the Pair War, of course." The tall man sighed. "It's been a year of fighting already, with no end in sight." He glanced at Baine, suddenly turning cautious. "Are you for Tyden or Tyrale, Drago?"

"I have no idea who they are," Baine answered truthfully.

"No, I expect you don't," Nelsun said after studying him for some time, finally looking satisfied. "But you can't be too careful these days. Say the wrong thing to the wrong person and—" Nelsun made a cutting motion with his finger across his neck. "Anyway, Prince Tyrale and Prince Tyden are brothers—twins, actually. Their father, King Jorquin, died last year, and since then, both brothers have claimed the throne. Ganderland has been split in two because of it, with Tyrale in the north and Tyden in the south." Nelsun sighed. "Even the Houses have fractured, with the Sons backing Prince Tyrale's claim and the Daughters, Prince Tyden's. Only the gods know how this will end." He glanced at Baine appraisingly. "Is any of this making sense to you at all?"

Baine shrugged, feeling frustration welling up inside him. He knew he should know all this, but there was nothing but an empty space inside his head where his memories belonged. It was like they were locked up behind an iron door, and he kept fumbling with the key. "Sorry, Nelsun, no. This is all news to me."

"Ah," the fisherman grunted, nodding his head. "Perhaps you're the lucky one then, Drago. Not remembering any of this means you don't have to worry every day like the rest of us do."

"You're worried?" Baine asked. "About what?"

"Why, the war, of course," Nelsun said. He motioned again toward the door. "I worry for my precious girl, and I worry for my son, Tomund. War rarely works out for poor people like us, Drago.

Only kings and lords benefit in the end—them that don't lose their heads, of course."

"So, which of these princes do you support?" Baine asked, trying to break through the fog in his mind and try to understand.

Nelsun's expression turned fierce. "My liege lord, Lord Porten Welis, supports the South, which naturally means so do I." The fisherman leaned forward and winked. "But even if he didn't, I'd secretly support the South anyway. Prince Tyden is the true heir, everyone from the gods on down knows this. Yet Tyrale refuses to accept the truth, and because of his stubbornness, we now have nothing but death and misery hanging over all of our heads. It's a damn shame."

Baine nodded, losing interest. "Well, Nelsun, I know nothing about this war," he said, suddenly feeling exhausted. "Nor, by the sounds of it, do I want to. All I know is you and your daughter saved my life, and for that, I will always be grateful."

"It's the least we could do, lad," Nelsun said. "The Mother would never have forgiven us if we'd left you out on that rock." He stood, favoring his right leg. "Do you want some more water, Drago?"

Baine shook his head, offering the man back the mug. "No, thank you. I feel much better."

"Food?"

Again, Baine shook his head. "Not right now. My stomach feels a little unsettled. I'd actually just like to sleep for a little while if that's all right?"

"Of course, lad," Nelsun said. "I understand. I'll be outside if you need me, and I'm sure that girl of mine will be close by, too. If she pesters you too much, let me know and I'll take a switch to her behind."

Baine smiled, doubting somehow the fisherman meant it. "Thank you, Nelsun. You're a good man. I appreciate your hospitality."

Baine closed his eyes after Nelsun left, willing his mind to remember. *Who am I? Where am I from? What happened to me?* His questions were met with nothing but frustrating silence.

Baine slept for the remainder of that day and all through the night, only awoken at dawn by the half-hearted crowing of a cock. He opened his eyes, not surprised to see Sunna sitting on the stool again, watching him closely. Nelsun lay on the floor near the table, covered by a threadbare blanket. Baine suddenly felt guilty, realizing he'd taken the family's only bed.

"You don't snore nearly as loud as Father does," Sunna announced by way of greeting.

Baine slowly sat up, pleased to find the ache in his head had diminished substantially. The lump was almost gone as well. "I'm glad to hear that," he said. He moved his left arm and gasped at the jolt of pain searing up to his shoulder. Clearly, that injury still had a way to go before it healed.

Sunna held her hands up about four inches apart. "A sliver of wood this long was embedded in you," she said. "Father had to use his knife and tongs to get it all out. He's pretty sure he got everything, so it shouldn't become infected."

"That's good news," Baine said. He carefully flexed his left hand open and closed, ignoring the pain and feeling relief when his fingers all moved together in unison. At least he wasn't crippled.

"Are you hungry, Drago?" Sunna asked. Nelsun grunted in his sleep and rolled onto his side, then started to snore.

"Shouldn't we wait for your father first?" Baine asked.

Sunna stuck her lower lip out as she thought. "Yes, I suppose we should. He'll be awake soon. Do you need to piss while we wait?"

Baine nodded, realizing that he did—rather urgently. He carefully swung his legs to the floor, then with Sunna's help, stood.

He was pleased to find his head was clear, though he still felt incredibly weak. He glanced down at the single black boot by the bed.

"You lost the other one," Sunna said. She motioned to the table behind her. "Those knives are yours. One was in the boot, the other on your hip."

Baine said nothing as Sunna led him outside, both of them stepping softly around Nelsun. She waited patiently several feet away while he did his business against a bush.

"Still can't remember anything?" the girl asked when he was finished.

"No," Baine answered regretfully. He looked around in the growing light. The farmhouse was built of sod and thatch, with a single crooked door and one narrow window protected by weather-battered shutters. An outbuilding stood off to one side, its thatch roof sagging inward. More thatch houses and outbuildings rose around him, forming concentric circles around a small square of dirt and rock in the center. Nelsun's dwelling was in the inner ring.

The cock crowed again, this time with more enthusiasm. Baine focused on the crown of the sun, which was slowly rising to the east over some forested hills several miles away. He could smell and hear the sea to the west, the tide lapping against the sandy shore two hundred feet away. He turned in that direction after a moment, counting ten small fishing craft pulled up on the beach. He guessed one of them must belong to Nelsun and his daughter, who he was keenly aware was once again studying him with rapt fascination.

"You're very handsome," Sunna said when he flicked his eyes toward her. "Did you know that, Drago?"

"Um, no," Baine said, feeling slightly embarrassed by the girl's obvious infatuation. The truth was, he had no idea what he looked like.

"You're small, though," Sunna added frankly as she looked him up and down. "For a grown man, I mean. You're only a little bit taller than I am."

Baine grinned. "Thank you for pointing that out, Sunna. The little people and I all appreciate your honesty."

The girl giggled. "You are most welcome, Drago." She took his right hand, pulling him toward the water. "Now, let's go down to the beach. I love walking along it at dawn. It's so peaceful there before everyone in the village wakes up."

Baine held the slight girl back easily as he glanced toward the house. He might be small, but there was undeniable strength in his arms and shoulders. "What about your father? Won't he worry when he finds us gone?"

"He'll know where we are, trust me," Sunna said. "I go to the beach every morning before he wakes up."

"All right," Baine said, knowing by the look in the girl's eyes that there would be no dissuading her.

He allowed Sunna to lead him by the hand, grateful that the girl took her time, for the terrain heading down was uneven and he was quickly tiring, not to mention he wasn't used to moving around in bare feet like she was. They reached the beach, the smell of rich loam filling his nostrils as they paused several feet away from the surf, which rolled across the wet sand as if reaching out for them before retracting, only to do it all over again.

"It's beautiful here," Baine said, meaning it. He felt suddenly calm and at ease and breathed in deeply, staring out across the water. Something flickered across his mind, a fleeting image of a dark shape on the water, tattered sails fluttering before it was gone.

"What is it?" Sunna asked, having clearly seen his expression change.

"I'm not sure," Baine said. He fought to bring the image back, but it had already slipped away behind the iron door of his mind. "I think it was a ship."

Sunna looked out to sea. "Are you sure? I don't see anything."

"No," Baine said, realizing she'd misunderstood him. He pointed to his head. "I meant in here. I thought I remembered something about a ship just now, but it went away."

"That's wonderful news, Drago!" Sunna cried. She hugged him. "It's all starting to come back to you." She stepped back after a moment, her eyes gleaming with excitement in the dawn light. "What else did you see?"

"That's all," Baine said with a frown. "A quick glimpse of a huge ship without any sails, then it was gone."

Sunna nodded, her face set in fierce concentration. Baine had to stop himself from laughing. "I bet you're a pirate, probably one of those Shadow Pirates my father told me about. That's why you dress in black."

"What's a Shadow Pirate?" Baine asked.

Sunna pursed her lips, ignoring him. "But your hair isn't gray, nor is your face painted white, so maybe I'm wrong." She pulled Baine along, her excitement palpable as she walked to his right, letting the surf wash across her bare feet. She glanced at him. "Besides, you're too nice to be a Shadow Pirate. They eat children, you know."

"I'm not a pirate," Baine assured her, hoping he was right.

"You're probably a spy, then," Sunna continued as if he hadn't spoken. She shook her head as she thought. "But for which side? The North or the South?" Baine knew better than to bother responding. The girl's imagination was flying high like a hawk at the moment, and he doubted anything he said would matter. She studied him again. "Your clothes are functional but still high quality, and despite your small size, you look well fed. Are you a lord, maybe, out on his ship doing nefarious deeds?"

"I doubt I'm a lord," Baine said with an amused chuckle. The sun to his left had risen fully above the forested hills in the east while they talked, enveloping the land and village in a warm glow of orange and yellow light.

"Sunna?" a deep voice called out suddenly. "Sunna? Where are you?"

Baine and the girl paused, turning to face the village as Nelsun appeared between two houses, though he was looking to the north and hadn't seen them yet.

Sunna waved. "I'm down here with Drago, Father."

The fisherman turned, gesturing for them to return. "Get back here, you two. I need to get out on the water soon, and I have no intention of doing that on an empty stomach. If you want to eat, now is the time."

"We'll be right there, Father," Sunna called. The tall man muttered something Baine couldn't hear, then headed back toward the center of the village. "We'd better go," the girl whispered to Baine. "Father gets grouchy in the morning. It's his leg, you see. It stiffens up from sleeping."

"How did he hurt it?" Baine asked as he and Sunna headed back up to the village.

"I'm not sure," the girl said. "He never talks about it."

Baine nodded, about to reply, when he was interrupted by a sudden scream from the north. He instinctively pulled the girl behind him, watching as a group of roughly dressed men appeared from a stand of trees and began running toward the village—men carrying weapons.

Chapter 3: Raiders

"Come on, Drago!" Sunna cried, sprinting ahead of him toward the village.

Baine followed, doing his best to keep up with the girl, but she was surprisingly fast and nimble and left him behind within moments. He watched her tear across the sand and up the grade, then disappear among the houses just as the attacking force reached the outskirts of the village and began to spread out, kicking in doors. Moments later, Baine heard screams and shouts of alarm coming from inside the buildings. He winced as a screeching woman with a baby in her arms burst out from a house, only to be cut down from behind moments later by a man with a club. Baine felt instant anger and indignation rise in him, and he changed directions, launching himself toward the man with the club, who was laughing as he picked the naked, squalling baby still clutched in his mother's arms up by a hind leg.

"Stop!" Baine shouted in horror as the man drew back his club, clearly intent on smashing in the infant's skull.

The man hesitated, his pig-like eyes narrowing as he saw Baine racing toward him. He finally tossed the shrieking baby to the ground, turning to face Baine with his club held low. Baine darted forward without slowing, watching the man's feet. The moment he was in range, they began to shift position and Baine instantly dropped, feeling the hiss of the club whistling over his head. He focused on his prize—a knife strapped in a leather sheath on his opponent's left side. Baine's right hand moved in a blur, snatching the weapon free even as he somersaulted away, crying out as his wounded arm struck the ground. He came back up on his feet, gritting his teeth against the pain. His opponent seemed unaware that he'd lost his knife, and he cursed at Baine, swinging his club wildly. There was no skill or method to the big man's attack, and Baine retreated beneath it, dodging and darting as he bided his time to strike. He knew if one of those massive blows caught him before he did, he was done.

"You little bastard!" the man hissed in frustration as Baine easily avoided another clumsy blow. The raider was big and strong, but he was incredibly slow. "Stand still."

"All right," Baine said, pausing with a smile on his face. "If that's what you really want, then here's your knife back." He flipped the knife in the air without thinking, the blade slapping firmly into his palm, then he threw it sidearm at his opponent in a blur of motion. The knife sped through the air, catching the startled man in the chest with a meaty thunk. The raider gasped in wide-eyed astonishment and looked down at the blade embedded to the hilt, then, with a strangled cry, he fell face-first and lay still.

"Be careful what you wish for," Blaine grunted as he dropped beside the corpse. He pushed the heavy body on its side to retrieve the knife, then hurried over to the crying baby. It was a boy, Baine saw, relieved to find the infant uninjured. He checked on the mother next, cursing when he saw the back of her head was caved in. Baine looked around in indecision as the baby howled in his arms; then, seeing a small cart filled with hay nearby, he hurried over to it. Baine quickly created a small depression in the hay, then set the baby inside. It was the best he could do for now. "Rest easy, little one," he said, stroking the downy black hair on the baby's head. "All will be well."

The child stopped crying at his gentle caress, staring up at Baine with enormous blue eyes filled with innocence and wonder. Baine smiled down at him, then turned away, the smile fading, replaced by a cold, determined fury. He could hear the terrified pleas of a female coming from the house opposite him, and he stalked toward the building, pausing in the open doorway to let his eyes adjust to the gloom inside. A woman lay on a table in the middle of the room, her dress torn down the front, revealing heavy breasts. The hem of the dress was hitched up, exposing her sex as two laughing men held her feet wide apart. A third man, naked from the waist down with his trousers around his ankles, stood above her, stroking his engorged manhood. All three raiders were young, not yet twenty.

Baine growled in outrage, stepping inside the house, the knife in his hand held low. He had no idea why he was so proficient with the weapon—he was just grateful that he was. The raider to Baine's left was the first to notice him, his gap-toothed grin of anticipation fading, turning to caution. He was tall and thin, with lank brown hair and a long nose covered by red pimples. The man let go of the pleading woman's ankle, dropping a hand to the hilt of a rusty sword thrust in his thick leather belt.

Baine's mind assessed all three of his opponents in the blink of an eye, registering that Pimple Nose was the biggest threat and would need to die first, since only he had a weapon close to hand. The man to Baine's right was unarmed, but a worn cudgel lay on the tabletop near the woman's head. He would have to let go of her and lean over to get it, which would take precious seconds. The raider was short and stocky, with a scraggly beard and sunken eyes filled with animal lust. Baine decided he'd kill him second. The third man, who was moments away from committing rape was also unarmed for obvious reasons, though a sword leaned against the wall several feet away from him.

Baine knew it would take a moment for the half-naked man to pull up his trousers before he could grab the sword, and he was determined not to allow him the opportunity. He rushed forward, flicking the knife toward Pimple Nose, who was desperately fumbling to draw his weapon. The blade caught the man in the throat and he sagged, even as Baine crashed into the half-naked raider, who was only now starting to turn to look behind him. The rapist cried out in surprise, falling heavily on the woman as Baine twisted away, avoiding a wild swing from Sunken Eyes, who'd retrieved his cudgel. Baine whirled, his good hand snaking out to grab the sword leaning against the wall. He flung that sword end over end at Sunken Eyes, who cried out in fear, lifting his arms and ducking beneath the whirling blade. That's what Baine had been hoping for—a distraction to buy more time. Seconds counted in a close-quarters fight like this. He crouched, ripping his knife from the throat of Pimple Nose, then bounced back to his feet.

The rapist was working to extricate himself from the woman, who was screaming hysterically and tearing at his hair with her legs wrapped around him like a lover in the throes of passion. Sunken Eyes waited on the other side of the struggling pair, crouched with his cudgel ready. Baine grinned at him, then without hesitating, dove forward, sliding across the half-naked raider's ass and back before tucking his body in a tight ball as he dropped on the other side. Sunken Eye's swung his cudgel desperately but once again struck nothing but empty air. Baine hit the floor and rolled, springing upward and burying his knife beneath Sunken Eye's ribs until the point punctured the man's heart. Sunken Eyes shuddered, dropping the cudgel from lifeless fingers.

Baine easily caught the weapon and stood, turning quickly at a sound behind him. The rapist had finally managed to stand, his trousers still tangled in his feet and his manhood now shriveled and limp. Baine didn't hesitate, crashing the cudgel against the man's jaw with a crack, spinning him around before he collapsed to the floor.

Baine took a deep breath, then moved to the startled woman, offering her his hand. "Are you all right?" he asked. He could feel a trickle of warm blood running from his bandaged wound down his hand, but he ignored it.

The woman blinked up at Baine in astonishment, then, realizing her vulnerable position, hastily pushed down her dress. "I think so, yes," she managed to say.

"Good," Baine said. He glanced down at the half-naked man, who was groaning, then used the cudgel on him a second and then a third time until his moans finally ceased. Baine tossed the bloody weapon aside and moved to the entrance, pausing to look back at the woman sitting up on the table, still looking dazed. "There's a baby in a wagon near the house opposite yours. The mother is dead. See to him."

"Yes, of course," the woman said, staring at him oddly. "Who are you?"

Baine grinned back. "I'm Drago. I'm a friend of Nelsun and Sunna."

"Who were those men?" Baine asked. He was sitting on the stool by the bed in Nelsun's house, idly flipping the knife he had taken from the first man he'd killed in his right hand. It wasn't nearly as sharp or as finely balanced as the two Nelsun had originally found on Baine's unconscious body, but he liked it, nonetheless. Those other knives were now encased in leather sheaths on his hips, and Baine planned never to let them out of his sight again. Nelsun was sitting on the table with his shirt off while Sunna cleaned a jagged wound on his side. The fisherman's body was thin yet covered with knots of stringy muscle, with long white hairs growing thickly on his chest and shorter, blacker ones on his stomach and arms.

Nelsun had done well, Baine reflected, killing two of the raiders with his bow, though he'd eventually been overpowered by a behemoth of a man with an axe. Nelsun would surely have been killed if Baine hadn't arrived when he had and slit the man's throat. The axe had grazed the fisherman's side during the scuffle, bruising a rib and taking a fair chunk of meat, though luckily, no vital organs had been struck.

"Deserters, I expect," Nelsun sniffed with distaste. He grunted in pain as Sunna probed at his side with a wet cloth, then chuckled a moment later. "By the way we ran the survivors out of here, I'd say running away is something they do a lot."

"Deserters from the war, you mean?" Baine asked.

"Yes," Nelsun said.

"Which side?"

The fisherman shrugged, ignoring the sharp admonishment from his daughter to stay still. "The North or South, who can say for sure? It hardly matters. This isn't the first time some have showed up here, although the miserable bastards usually just beg us for food and then move on."

"Maybe they were outlaws, Father," Sunna said distractedly, her face set with concentration as she worked. She paused to look up at him. "All anyone is talking about these days is the Outlaw of Corwick. Maybe it was him and his Wolf Pack."

A strange feeling came over Baine at the girl's words—an intense tingling. He stopped flipping the knife, listening intently to the exchange between father and daughter.

"I doubt that somehow, child," Nelsun said. "The Outlaw of Corwick is mainly preying on rich merchants in the north. He wouldn't come this far southwest just to raid a poor fishing village like this one. Besides, those men who attacked us were little better than beggars. Most didn't even have proper weapons and couldn't even fight. I expect we'd all be long dead by now if they'd been the Wolf Pack."

"There are some that say the Outlaw of Corwick is working for the South, and the entire *outlaw* act is just that, an act," Sunna stated.

"Nonsense," Nelsun replied with a condescending chuckle. "The House may be divided right now, child, but believe me, there's no way the Daughters would ever endorse such a thing. No, he's just some scum looking to enrich himself during a difficult time for all of us."

"Maybe," Sunna replied, sounding uncertain.

"Who is this man?" Baine asked, all his senses alert. Something told him there was something here—something important that had to do with him.

Nelsun shrugged again, eliciting a second reprimand from Sunna. "Just some peasant who's been damn lucky so far, Drago."

He snorted. "They call him the Wolf of Corwick. I'm sure if it wasn't for the war distracting everyone, the murdering bastard would have been caught by now and strung up for the ravens to feast on."

Baine looked down at the floor and closed his eyes, willing his mind to break through the barrier holding his memories back. But no matter how hard he tried, that door wouldn't open. A moment later, whatever Baine had felt at the mention of the Wolf of Corwick slipped entirely away, leaving him feeling empty and depressed. He sighed in resignation, opening his eyes again.

Sunna glanced at Baine appraisingly. "Are you all right, Drago?"

"Yes," Baine said. He began idly flipping the knife again. "I thought I remembered something just now, but then it just went away."

"It'll come, lad," Nelsun said kindly. "Give it time. Your memory will come back."

"I spoke to Asinda earlier," Sunna added, her eyes glowing with admiration as she stared at Baine. "She had quite the story to tell."

Baine nodded. Asinda was the woman he'd saved from being raped. "How is the baby doing?" he asked.

"Fine," Sunna said. Nelsun suddenly hissed, and she looked at her father guiltily. "Sorry."

"Mind what you're doing, child," Nelsun growled. "This thing hurts something fierce on its own, you know. Sticking your finger inside and poking around doesn't help."

"Yes, Father," Sunna said dutifully. She glanced sideways at Baine. "Asinda told me what you did. She said she'd never seen anyone move so fast."

"I got lucky," Baine muttered.

"How?" Sunna asked pointedly.

Baine hesitated. It was a question he'd been asking himself ever since they'd defeated the raiders several hours ago. How had he done what he had? It was like his body had moved on its own without any help from him.

"You've obviously had training, lad," Nelsun said. He studied Baine frankly. "You're not built to swing a sword in a shield wall, but, by The Mother, I saw what you did to that brute trying to kill me. That was impressive." The fisherman pointed a finger at Baine. "There's more to you than meets the eye, Drago. I was a soldier when I was a much younger man, and I know a quality fighting man when I see one." He motioned to the bow, which was once again leaning in the corner. "I also know a thing or two about using that. Judging by those muscles in your back and arms, and those calluses on your fingers, I'd wager every last Jorq in the kingdom that you're an archer."

Baine glanced at the bow and arrow bag, knowing somehow that the fisherman was right. He wondered if he was as proficient with the weapon as he was with knives.

"There," Sunna said proudly after she'd wrapped her father's wound in cloth torn from an old dress that had belonged to her mother. "You're all done, Father."

Nelsun glanced down, nodding his head with approval. He jumped from the table, wincing before pulling his worn tunic over his head. He motioned to Baine. "Come along, Drago. Unfortunately, we've got some graves to dig."

Baine spent the next few days helping Nelsun, Sunna, and the rest of the villagers collect and prepare the quota of fish that their oath lord had mandated they catch to help feed his army. The work was hard and monotonous, usually lasting from sunup to sundown, with Lord Porten Welis' soldiers expected to arrive soon to collect the cured fish. Baine's ability with a knife had come in handy and, as his wound healed, he quickly became proficient at cutting the fish into thin, lean strips. The strips were then immersed briefly in salt brine before being hung over fires to dry. Sunna spent half her time with Baine, and the other half on the water, assisting her father with the catch.

"Do you think your memory will ever come back?" Sunna asked Baine the morning of his fifth day in Weymouth. He was sitting at a long table filleting fish with three women from the village and an old fellow named Weeger, who rarely spoke.

Baine shrugged as he worked on a particularly fine cod. He sawed with his knife behind the gills until he reached the spine, then expertly sliced toward the tail, cutting just above the backbone. "I certainly hope so," he said, not looking at the girl as she lay strips of fish on wooden racks overhanging a fire. Six other young girls and boys were helping her. Baine cut off the sides of the fish, then sliced out the row of bones down the center line of each before shaving off pieces of the cod about a quarter of an inch thick. He paused to look at the girl, a smile on his face. "Why? Are you trying to get rid of me?"

"Never!" Sunna exclaimed. She hadn't noticed Baine's smile, thinking he'd been serious. "These past few days since you arrived have been the best of my life, Drago."

"Well, I think you might be exaggerating a bit there," Baine said, returning to his work.

"But I'm not," Sunna insisted. She hesitated, looking suddenly shy, which was a rare occurrence for her. "Our liege lord married a girl from Halhaven several years ago, Lady Kalaka."

"Is that a fact?" Baine said, knowing with Sunna, there was more. There was always more. He glanced at the girl affectionately. "And you're telling me this because?"

"Because Lady Kalaka was only eleven at the time," Sunna said, watching Baine closely.

Baine frowned. "Well, that seems a little young to me."

"Father told me Lady Kalaka had already bled by the time they married, so by the Laws of the First Pair, the union was legal."

"That's a fact," one of the women at the table agreed.

"And?" Baine said to Sunna, raising an eyebrow.

"And I'll be ten soon," Sunna replied, staring at Baine with an odd expression. "That's only one year away from being eleven."

"Yes, I can count," Baine said with a chuckle. "My memory might be gone, but at least I can still do that. Is there a point to this story?"

Baine was shocked to see tears threatening in the girl's eyes. "Never mind!" Sunna abruptly shouted. She threw several strips of fish into the fire, then raced away across the sand, sobbing.

Baine stared after her in astonishment until she disappeared from sight. "Now, what in the name of The Mother was that all about?" he wondered out loud.

The three women at the table all chuckled knowingly, while Weeger just shook his head as he worked across from Baine.

"What?" Baine finally demanded, looking from one smiling face to the next. "What am I missing?"

Weeger paused, pointing his knife at Baine. "Just because you have eyes in your head, boy, doesn't mean you can see." He hooked a thumb over his shoulder in the direction Sunna had taken. "That little lass has fallen head-over-heels in love with you, but you're too blind to see it."

"But she's just a child," Baine protested.

"When has that ever mattered?" one of the women asked. "That poor child is terrified of losing you, Drago. Can't you see that? Why do you think she's constantly asking you if you remember anything? Do you really think it's because she wants you to?" The woman shook her head. "No, that little girl is terrified that someday you will."

"Why?" Baine asked.

"Because," Weeger said. "The moment you remember who you were, Drago, you'll go back to that life and forget all about her." He once again pointed his knife at Baine. "Mark my words, boy. Mark my words."

Chapter 4: Time To Leave

The arrow slapped with force into the straw target fifty yards away, precisely where Baine had aimed. He grinned sheepishly, accepting the cheers, whistles, and handclapping from the onlookers. He'd already put five arrows just like it in the same target, all less than a handsbreadth apart. The truth was, Baine had found it ridiculously easy.

"I was positive you were an archer, Drago," Nelsun said, shaking his head in wonder as he came to stand beside the smaller man. "But by the gods, I didn't think you'd be *this* good."

"It just feels natural," Baine said with a shrug. "As if I've been doing it all my life."

Nelsun put his hand on Baine's shoulder and squeezed. "Maybe you have, Drago. Maybe you have at that. Hopefully, one day we'll get to find out."

Baine let his eyes roam over the forty or so villagers who'd taken time from their labors to watch him practice. The catch had been good in the last few days, and they'd made their quota easily because of it. Nelsun—who was viewed as the unofficial leader of the village with most of the men gone to war—had decreed a few hours off, which had come as a welcome relief to everyone. Baine had used the time to experiment with Nelsun's bow, and as word of his prowess spread, it had quickly become something of a spectacle with a festival-like atmosphere.

Baine frowned as he studied the faces of the crowd, noticing one was missing. "Have you seen Sunna? I haven't seen her all day."

Nelsun shrugged. "She and Alper Kant decided to take the boat back out to go diving for cockles. I told her you were going to try my bow, but she didn't seem all that interested."

Baine nodded, disappointed. He'd been looking forward to having the girl's supportive voice behind him while he shot. He thought about Alper Kant, a boy roughly the same age as Sunna. Alper's father and two older brothers were off fighting in the war, leaving just the lad and his mother in Weymouth. Despite his young age, Alper was easily the best fisherman and diver in the village after Nelsun, though Sunna was quickly closing in on his abilities. "I wish she'd told me," Baine muttered. He paused, thinking about how things hadn't been the same between them since the girl had run off crying. Sunna had been aloof and curt with him ever since, rarely showing a smile or that wit that he'd come to cherish. "Did Sunna say anything about me to you? Is she mad at me? I'm starting to think she's avoiding me."

Nelsun eyed Baine thoughtfully. "That girl has always been a little odd, Drago—just like her mother—the gods rest her soul. Two years ago, Sunna found a little chickadee with a broken wing over in Badger Grove and brought it home. She spent day after day digging up grubs, worms, or whatever else she could find, feeding it and determined to heal it. Keeping that damn bird alive became a fixation for Sunna, and I had to keep reminding her to eat and do her chores. Then, one morning about a week later, she got up and found the bird had died overnight in this special basket she'd woven for it. The poor child was devastated and couldn't stop crying for days. She still talks about that damn bird from time to time."

Baine leaned on the bow as the rest of the villagers began to disperse, sensing the show was over. He could feel the sweat rolling down the back of his neck into the collar of his tunic, for the early afternoon sun was unbearably hot despite the cooling breeze coming off the ocean. "What are you trying to say, Nelsun?"

The fisherman squeezed Baine's shoulder again. "What I'm saying, my dear Drago, is that my daughter is just as fixated on you as she was on that chickadee. Maybe more so, if that's possible. Sunna knows, just like I do, that you're going to be leaving soon, and that knowledge has left her crushed just like that bird did. I think she's avoiding you because she knows what's in your heart and can't bear to lose you."

"But—" Baine began.

Nelsun held up a calloused hand. "There's no need to deny it, Drago. I've seen that look in your eyes. I can tell you're getting restless and that you feel like this place is holding you back."

Baine sighed. He'd actually thought he'd been hiding his intentions better from the fisherman and his daughter. The truth was, now that his wound was mostly healed, the need to know who he really was had become an almost unbearable burden for him. Except for a few brief, frustrating flashes, Baine's memory had not returned, and he was beginning to fear it might never come back if he stayed in Weymouth. Baine had reluctantly concluded that he'd have to force the issue by leaving the village. That decision had not been an easy one, though, constantly weighing on his mind, just as Nelsun had quite rightly surmised.

Baine braced one end of the bow on the ground, then put his left leg through the string while keeping the stock pressed tightly against his hip. He used the side of his right foot to hold the lower limb in place, then bent the bow against his body, sliding the bowstring down the upper limb until the string was loose and he could release the tension on the shaft and remove it. Baine had done the maneuver effortlessly and without thinking, which Nelsun clearly had noticed by his expression.

"Don't worry too much about it, lad," Nelsun said kindly after a moment. "It's obvious to all of us that you are on a path toward something and that we were always just your first stop. I don't know where that path will eventually lead you, but I do know Weymouth is not where you belong anymore, much as I've enjoyed your company and will miss you." The fisherman shook his head. "No, there's something special about you, Drago. The gods have marked you for a purpose, and that purpose is waiting for you somewhere else."

"I don't want to hurt your daughter by leaving," Baine whispered, feeling mixed emotions now that his intent was out in the open. "She's come to mean a great deal to me. You both have."

Nelsun smiled. "I thank you for that, Drago. You're a good man, and I know you'd do anything you could to protect my little girl. But sometimes a man has to do what's right, not just for himself, but for everyone else involved, too. We both know staying here isn't going to help any of us in the long run." Nelsun shrugged. "Sunna is young yet and will get over this in time. But the longer you stay here, the harder it will be for her to let go of you. One good thing about being her age is unhappy memories like she's about to experience fade quickly."

Baine sighed, realizing the both of them had just come to an unspoken agreement. "You think I should leave right now?" he asked, just to be certain he understood.

"I do," Nelsun agreed in a solemn voice. His weathered face was covered by a network of craggy lines earned from a lifetime out on the water. "But not with any joy, Drago, believe me. Sunna and Alper won't be back for hours yet. If you've got a thorn in your thumb, you don't let it fester. You pluck it immediately and accept the pain. You understand?"

"I do," Baine said. He could feel a sinking feeling settling into the pit of his stomach at the prospect of leaving, but he knew this was the way things had to be. Baine hesitated, unsure what to say to this kind, gentle man who had saved his life and taken him in without a second thought.

Lost for words, Baine finally offered Nelsun the bow, but the fisherman held up his hands. "No, Drago, you keep it. Weeger has one I can use that's almost as good. Besides, I think you'll need it more than I will before your story is through."

Baine hesitated, knowing by the look in the older man's eyes that there was no point in arguing. He held out his hand, his voice thick with emotion. "I won't forget you, Nelsun. You or your daughter. Thank you for everything you did for me. Please tell Sunna I'm sorry."

Two hours later, Baine stood on a knoll overlooking Weymouth as the sun continued its slow, methodical progression toward the west. He carried three knives on him along with Nelsun's bow that he'd slung over his shoulders. An arrow bag containing eight arrows hung by a leather strap from his belt close to his right hand, with a waterskin looped around his neck. He also carried a leather sack flipped over his left shoulder with some vegetables, several apples and biscuits, and a few dates inside. Baine had expected to be offered some of the village's plentiful cured fish as well, but Nelsun had told him it was essentially inedible without being washed and cooked first due to the salt. Since Baine was reluctant to chance a fire and doubted he'd have access to clean water anyway, there was little choice but to make do with what he'd been given. The village had also provided Baine with a worn cloak and a pair of ragged leather boots, which Baine was eternally grateful for, as his feet still hadn't toughened up enough for trekking over rough terrain.

Baine studied the village with a heavy heart. He had a sudden vision of Sunna's weeping face when she finally learned that he'd left, and he felt his resolve wavering, part of him thinking that life as a fisherman probably wasn't so bad. Would it really matter one way or another if his memory came back? What if he got it back only to learn that he was, in reality, a horrible person? Sunna had joked more than once that she thought he was probably a pirate or an outlaw, but what if those jokes turned out to be real? Could he live with that? Baine shuddered, horrified at the prospect. Maybe poking around inside his brain would only bring him sorrow and regret in the end. Was knowing who he really was truly worth it?

Baine stared down at the village in indecision. Long trails of smoke rose from the roofs of the sod houses, giving the entire scene a peaceful, tranquil look. Beyond Weymouth to the west stretched the ocean, impossibly large on the horizon. He shielded his eyes from the sun, certain that he could see a tiny shadow on the water along the shore to the south. Sunna and Alper diving for cockles? Baine gazed that way for a long time until he finally whispered a curse and regretfully turned away. His love for Sunna and Nelsun was strong, but the need to know who he was, was stronger.

Baine straightened his shoulders and headed north, pausing after a few steps to glance back at the village and the sparkling waters behind it. "I'll return soon," he whispered. "I promise."

Baine had no idea that his vow was about to come true much sooner than he could possibly guess—and in a most horrible and tragic way.

The trail Baine followed was well-worn and perhaps six feet across, with a set of narrow wagon tracks leading off to the northeast through a thick forest known as Badger Grove. That trail, he'd been told, would eventually take him to Nartley Keep, where Nelsun's liege lord, Lord Porten Welis, and his young bride, Lady Kalaka, dwelled. The keep was many miles from the village, but Baine figured it was as good a place as any to start asking questions about himself. It was well into the afternoon now, with the shadows from the tall pines to the west stretching across the trail into the trees and bushes lining the opposite side. Baine knew he would have to start thinking about making camp in another hour or so, though he still had plenty of energy left despite the distance he'd already traveled.

Baine paused in the middle of the trail, uncorking the waterskin to take a small sip of the contents. He didn't know when or if he'd find a stream to refill the waterskin, so it was best to be cautious with his supply. A squirrel began to chatter from the trees somewhere ahead, scolding in a high-pitched series of squeaks before it abruptly fell silent. A moment later, a wood thrush that had been singing musically to Baine's left suddenly stopped in mid-song. Baine frowned, feeling a prickle of uneasiness rising along his skin. He cocked his head, listening, but the forest around him was completely silent now—eerily so. Even the crickets had ceased their incessant chirping.

Baine corked the waterskin and hurried off the trail into the trees just as a faint shout sounded from ahead, followed by the creaking of axles and the plodding gait of horses' hooves against the hard ground. He crouched behind a boxwood shrub, peering through the leaves intently. He thought he could see the vague outlines of horses in the distance, but with the shadows from the trees, it was hard to be certain. Baine wondered who the travelers were, though he wasn't curious enough to show himself. Nelsun had warned him repeatedly that these were dangerous times and that it would be wise to treat all men with suspicion until proven otherwise. He waited, watching in silence as a group of six mounted men eventually appeared, leading a train of seven wagons in and out of the shadows toward him. Six more riders followed the wagons as a rearguard. All the men were heavily armed, flying a yellow banner depicting a red charging boar.

Baine guessed the men must belong to Lord Porten Welis, on their way to Weymouth to pick up the village's cured fish. He waited until the last of the riders were well out of sight, counting to a hundred afterward before cautiously stepping back onto the trail. He continued on, walking for only a few minutes before hearing the sounds of hooves and clinking of metal coming once again from ahead. Baine could tell by the din that whoever was coming down the trail this time was moving a lot faster than Lord Porten Welis' men had been and that there were a lot of them. He cursed his luck, ducking into the trees for the second time just as the first horsemen appeared on the trail. He prayed none had seen him.

Baine knelt behind a thick honeysuckle bush filled with bright green leaves, making himself small as the horsemen swept past him at a canter in a long line, two abreast. He estimated there had to be at least forty of them all told. The lead riders were flying a red banner from their spears depicting the sigil of a swooping hawk. Baine had no idea who these men were, nor did he much care. He let out a sigh of relief when they finally disappeared down the trail and stood, brushing off his cloak and muttering to himself as he once again resumed his march. Baine walked along the path for almost ten more minutes, alert for any more sounds from behind or ahead of him. He'd briefly considered leaving the trail for the relative safety of the trees after the hawk riders had gone, but the forest was thick and would be difficult to traverse, not to mention he might lose his bearings, so he stayed on the path.

Something had been nagging at Baine ever since the second group of riders had disappeared, but no matter how much he dwelled on it, he couldn't figure out what it was. Baine finally gave up trying to figure it out and, instead, opened his sack and drew out a date. He popped the fruit in his mouth and started to chew, then stopped dead in his tracks as he realized what had been bothering him. This was Lord Porten Welis' land, so what were the men with the red banners doing out here? Baine felt a lurch in his gut as the answer struck him like a blow to the stomach. Lord Porten Welis' men were being hunted, he realized. And after they were caught, then logically, where would the hawk riders go next?

"Weymouth!" Baine whispered in horror. He spat the half-eaten date out and turned around, his heart hammering in his chest—then he started to run.

Chapter 5: Tragedy

Baine came across a dead man lying twisted in the middle of the trail after running for what he guessed must have been several miles. Dusk had quickly fallen over the forest during his run, turning every gnarled tree or bush along the path into fearsome, distorted caricatures of themselves. He paused ten feet from the crumpled body, cautiously studying the area around him. He could hear nothing but the faint rustling of the wind through the trees and his own ragged breathing. Finally satisfied he was alone, Baine leaned forward with his hands on his knees, sucking in much-needed air. Once his heart had slowed somewhat, he moved to the body and knelt, rolling the corpse onto its back. He grimaced. The soldier's face was a nightmare of gristle and bone, crushed in by a powerful blow. Was the dead man one of Lord Porten Welis' men or one of the hawk riders? Baine couldn't be sure.

A rustling suddenly sounded from the trees to the north, and Baine rose in a crouch with a knife appearing in either hand. He waited, listening, but when the sound wasn't repeated after several long minutes, he slowly relaxed. Baine slipped one of the knives back into its sheath but kept the other one out as he started to run again. Less than a minute later, he reached a bend in the trail, where he found more bodies lying on the ground on the other side. He approached them warily, counting at least fifteen men scattered around the area. All were dead. A horse lay unmoving fifty feet further up the trail beneath a sycamore tree, still trussed to an overturned wagon. Baine thought he could see the lower half of a man's body pinned beneath the wagon. He hesitated, then said a curse under his breath, knowing he couldn't leave him. Baine hurried around the twisted bodies to the wagon, dropping to his knees by the man's feet.

"Are you alive under there?" Baine whispered, peering beneath the heavy wooden frame. He waited and, when no reply came, shook the man's right boot. There was no reaction.

Baine sighed and stood, glancing up and down the trail before he once again heard movement coming from the forest to the north, followed by a twig snapping loudly. Somebody was watching him. Baine darted into the gloom of the trees, all his senses alert as he headed toward the rustling sound, which was moving slowly away from him at a steady pace. *Careful*, he told himself. *This could be a trap*. Baine paused at that thought, then, coming to a decision, he began to angle away from the noise toward the northwest. He constantly looked down as he progressed, careful where he put his feet, planning to go around and cut off whoever was ahead of him and, in the process, perhaps break up the ambush if there was one. Baine frowned as he listened to his quarry moving slowly, almost aimlessly to his right. Whoever was out there was making no effort to hide their passage now, he noted, clumsily breaking branches and twigs as if they wanted to be heard.

Still wary of an ambush, Baine eventually made his way around his quarry until he'd found a small clearing. The noisy traveler was heading almost directly toward his position now, and by the sounds he was making, Baine guessed that whoever it was would be in view at any moment. There was no one else around that Baine could detect, and he was beginning to wonder if maybe he was, in fact, tracking a wounded soldier who'd lost his way. Baine waited among the trees, crouching down, his knife poised to throw. Moments later, a dark form appeared from the gloom, stepping uncertainly into the clearing lit by faint moonlight. Baine blinked in surprise, then slowly chuckled as he felt the tension in his body slip away. The quarry he'd been stalking all this time was a riderless white horse.

Baine slowly stepped out from the trees, lifting a hand to the horse, which he saw was a saddled mare. The horse hesitated at his appearance, though she didn't look startled to see him. Baine guessed the mare had long ago smelled him. "Easy there," he said soothingly, afraid the animal might bolt if he was too aggressive. "It's all right, pretty girl. I'm not going to hurt you." Baine took a step forward, and the mare hesitated, watching him warily. The horse's reins trailed on the ground, ten feet from Baine's reach. He thought he could see a streak of blood on the mare's chest, though whether it belonged to her or the horse's previous rider, he didn't know.

"My name is Drago," Baine said in a soft, unthreatening voice. He took another cautious step forward. "And I could really use your help right about now." The mare snorted and shook her head. Baine wasn't sure whether that was a good thing or not. He took another half step. "You see," he said, talking in a calm voice. "Some friends of mine are in danger." Baine put his hands to his chest. "They are far away, and I need to get to them as soon as possible, but I'm small and I can't run very fast." Baine took another half step, holding out his left hand. "But you, pretty girl, why, you're magnificent. I bet you can run like the wind. Am I right?" The mare rolled her eyes at Baine, but he could tell she was listening to him just the same. He took it as a good sign that she hadn't run off yet. "Will you help me?" Baine whispered. "For the sake of all those people? Please?"

Baine's outstretched hand was less than three feet away from the horse now, and he wiggled his fingers at her in a reassuring way. The mare's ears swiveled forward with interest at his gesture, and after a moment, she slowly extended her elegant neck until her dark velvet muzzle kissed his hand. Baine could feel the mare's hot breath on his fingers, and he smiled, stroking her nose as he stepped closer. He cautiously reached down until he could grasp the white horse's reins, then with a firm grip on them, let out a sigh of relief.

"Thank you, pretty girl," Baine whispered as he pressed his forehead against the mare in gratitude and closed his eyes. "Now my friends have a chance."

Baine had smelled smoke on the wind long before he'd broken out from the trees of Badger Grove into the open fields. But now, as he rode the mare at breakneck speed toward the west, he could see a distinct orange glow lighting up the night sky where Weymouth lay. Baine knew what that meant, and he felt his heart sink. He put his head down, urging the gallant white horse to go faster, though he was aware she was already giving him everything she had. Baine finally crested the knoll where he'd stood in indecision earlier that day, and he brought the white mare to a shuddering halt, his heart in his mouth at the sight that awaited him below. He had been expecting the worst ever since he'd smelled the smoke, though a part of him had been holding on to the faint hope that Nelsun and the villagers had managed to defend themselves against the invaders. That hope was now clearly put to rest, though, for Baine saw that the entire village of Weymouth was ablaze. Not a single house or outbuilding had been left untouched by the flames, and he could see many twisted bodies lying amongst the burning buildings.

Baine growled low in his chest in anger, kicking his feet against the mare's sides, urging her down the hill. He thundered toward the village, his bow now in his hands. Fifty feet from the outer ring of burning houses, Baine saw two riders, both of whom noticed him at the same time. One of the men shouted, pointing at Baine with a sword before they spurred their horses toward him. Baine expertly used his knees to guide the mare, pulling an arrow in one swift, sure motion from the bag on his hip. He nocked, drew, and shot all in the blink of an eye, already reaching for a second arrow as one of the charging riders screamed and clutched at his chest before sliding off his horse. Baine nocked again, drawing a bead on the second man, who had wisely leaned low over his horse with his shield protecting his head, presenting a smaller target.

Baine grunted in annoyance and immediately altered his aim, then let fly, striking the charging horse in the center of its chest. The animal screamed as the iron broadhead slammed into it, the horse's front legs instantly collapsing, sending the rider tumbling forward with a cry. Baine grabbed the mare's reins with his right hand, aiming her directly at the fallen man. The mare snorted in anticipation as she bore down on the stunned rider, aware now of what Baine wanted from her. She lowered her head in a charge as she increased her gait, then smashed head-on into the man just as he managed to stagger to his feet, weaving like a drunkard. The mare's right shoulder struck the soldier squarely in the chest, spinning him around like a rag doll as horse and rider swept past. Baine glanced back at the broken, crumpled body lying on the ground in satisfaction, then focused on the burning buildings.

Several older women lay on the ground in front of Baine as he approached the inferno, with a decapitated dog lying between them. He glanced around, slowing the mare as he searched for signs of anyone alive. There were none. "Nelsun!" he finally cried out, lifting a hand to protect his face from the intense heat. "Sunna! Are you here?"

"Help!" came a faint cry off to Baine's right.

Baine instantly flung a leg over the mare and dropped to the ground, turning the horse away from the flames before slapping her on the rump with his bow, sending her to safety. He nocked an arrow, then made his way forward cautiously, fighting to see anything through the heavy smoke enveloping him. "Where are you?" he called out

"Over here!" came back the weak reply directly ahead.

Baine took a wide berth around a burning outbuilding, coughing now as the heavy, acrid smoke filled his lungs. He paused, trying to get his bearings. "Call out again. I can't see anything."

"Here, in the pen!" a man's muffled voice arose. "Help me, please! I'm trapped!"

Baine inched his way forward, coming to a chicken coop engulfed in flames. A small corral that housed the village's five milking goats stood twenty feet away from the coop to his right, he remembered. The villagers all referred to it as *the pen*. Baine hurried that way, coming into contact with one of the thin, weathered railings of the enclosure moments later. Baine put his hands on the wooden pole and looked over, grimacing, for the pen contained the bodies of dead goats and people, all of them viciously slaughtered and dumped in a pile. He could see no signs of movement.

"I'm here," Baine finally shouted in exasperation. "Where are you?"

A shaking, bloody hand suddenly arose from the pile of bodies. Baine cursed under his breath. He hooked his bow over his shoulders, then stooped and slipped between the railings. Baine hurried forward, grunting with effort as he fought to remove the corpses of animals and people pinning the man down. Finally, he'd cleared enough away to grasp the outstretched hand, and with great effort, he pulled the man free. It was Weeger, Baine saw, covered in blood and muck. He dragged the old man away from the bodies, leaning him against the fence where the heat and smoke from the chicken coop were only marginally better.

"Drago," Weeger gasped, tapping Baine's arm in gratitude. "Thank the gods you came when you did. I couldn't breathe under there."

Baine knelt. "Where are Nelsun and Sunna?" he demanded.

The old man sucked in air through his teeth. "I don't know about the girl, but Nelsun is dead."

Baine looked down at the ground in dismay. "You're certain?" he finally asked.

Weeger nodded, his eyes half closed as his thin chest rose and fell. "I saw him get cut down, Drago. I'm sorry, but I'm sure."

Baine nodded, feeling nothing but anger and the need for revenge filling him. "Who did this? Who are these men?"

"Sellswords," Weeger spat with disgust. He shifted position, wincing as he put a hand to his ribs. "They're led by a man named Pembry Drake. Bastard claims he used to be a bailiff in Hillsfort, but no one ever believed him. Truth is, he's nothing but an opportunistic cutthroat who will take money from the highest bidder."

"He's working for the North?" Baine asked.

"Sure looks like it, Drago," Weeger said with a nod.

Baine glanced around, but he could see little with the drifting smoke. "Where did they all go?"

"Most of them rode away," Weeger said bitterly. He let his eyes drift over the bodies. "After they were done with us, of course. I heard Pembry order two of his men to stay behind and watch for survivors, so you'd best be careful."

Baine grinned without humor. "I've already dealt with those bastards. They won't be bothering anyone ever again."

"Good," Weeger grunted. "I hope they suffered." He stared at Baine with hard eyes. "So, if they're dead, why are you wasting time talking to an old man? Go find that girl."

"But you're—"

"Go, Drago," Weeger insisted. He tapped his chest. "Got a couple of broken ribs in here, is all. I'll live." He shrugged, wincing in pain. "Besides, my life is all used up, anyway. That girl's has only just begun. You need to find her and keep her safe."

Baine put a hand on the old man's shoulder and gently squeezed. "Do you want me to help you get out of the pen before I go?"

Weeger shook his head. "No, I'll manage."

Baine stood, looking down at the shattered old man. He hadn't failed to notice blood on Weeger's lips, certain he was lying and there was more wrong with him than just a few broken ribs. "I'll come back when I can."

"Just get the girl away from here," Weeger grunted, his eyes closed now. "That's all that matters, Drago. I believe it's what you were always meant to do."

Baine spent the next half an hour scouring the village, going from one body to the next, but there were no signs of Sunna anywhere. The houses and outbuildings had almost burned themselves out during that time, leaving nothing behind but a few sagging sod walls here and there and charred, smoking rubble. Baine eventually made his way to the beach, where he found the burned-out husks of nine fishing boats. He felt sudden hope, thinking that maybe Sunna and Alper had still been out on the water when the attack came. But that hope was soon dashed when he came upon a body lying face-down in the wet sand five hundred yards to the south. The tide was rolling in and out, stubbornly trying to drag the corpse back into the sea as weak moonlight caressed the foaming white water. It was the boy, Alper, although there was no sign of a vessel anywhere. Baine stared out across the enormous expanse of dark water, feeling nothing but heartache and loss. Had Sunna managed to escape in the boat, or had the attackers killed her and sunk it?

"Sunna!" he cried, his voice made small by the pounding of the surf. He cupped his hands around his mouth. "Sunna, where are you?"

But there was no sign of the girl anywhere, and after another hour of fruitless searching along the coastline, Baine eventually was forced to admit defeat. He headed back toward Weymouth and made his way through the carnage toward the pen, feeling despondent and emotionally exhausted, only to find that Weeger had died during his absence. Baine stared down at the body looking so small and frail in the muck and filth. He took a deep breath in acceptance, then went searching for the white mare, finding her cropping grass contentedly a hundred yards away from what remained of the village. Baine felt tears start to roll down his cheeks when the mare trotted over to him, nuzzling her head against him in welcome. He closed his eyes and put his forehead to hers, taking comfort in the horse's presence and strength.

"Well, isn't this an interesting sight for the eyes?"

Baine glanced behind him, startled, already reaching for an arrow as men appeared from the gloom—men with swords and bows ready.

"I wouldn't do that if I were you," a big man said as he strode forward with a sword glinting in his hand. The moonlight caught his face, and Baine involuntarily gasped, for the man's features were a nightmare of hideously burned flesh. Baine gaped, realizing with a start that he knew him. "Odiman?" he said in disbelief, whispering the name that had suddenly appeared in his head. A rush of memories started flooding into his brain a moment later, overwhelming him. *Hadrack! Jebido! Sea-Dragon! Calban! Flora and the baby!*

"By The Mother," the burned man replied, his eyes widening in surprise as Baine moaned and sagged to his knees. "Baine? Is that really you?"

Chapter 6: Odiman

Odiman was a House Agent, Baine remembered—and a real bastard as well. That unpleasant memory was unfortunately all too clear in his mind. It had been Odiman who had thrown hundreds of men against the walls of Springfield with little care for their welfare, determined to capture the scholar, Rorian, who was hiding inside, at any cost. The city was eventually taken after Hadrack had located a secret tunnel leading to a granary inside the walls. But despite that success, the scholar had managed to elude them anyway, cleverly posing as one of Odiman's wounded soldiers to make his escape.

Hadrack and Malo—another House Agent—had enlisted the help of a girl named Sabina, whose particular skills had allowed them to track Rorian and his men to the coast, where they'd managed to capture *Sea-Dragon* after a vicious battle with Cardians. From there, Hadrack and his Wolf Pack, including Baine, had set off after Rorian, who'd sailed away in another ship, only to have *Sea-Dragon* get hit by the storm that had swept Baine overboard. The story seemed hard to imagine from Drago's limited perspective, but now with his memories fully restored, Baine knew the truth, though it had left him feeling strangely relieved and disappointed at the same time. He wasn't entirely sure why. The good news was he'd learned from Odiman that Hadrack and the others had made landfall safely, though that's all he had been told so far. He was eager to learn more now that they'd made camp.

"Here," Odiman grunted, coming to stand over him.

Baine looked up at the gruesome face of the House Agent, accepting the wineskin being offered without comment. He uncorked it and took a long pull, relishing the wine wetting his parched throat and the warmth already starting in his belly.

Baine moved to hand the wineskin back once he'd drunk his fill, but Odiman just waved him off. "Keep it," the House Agent said. "You look like you need it more than I do." The big man shifted several feet away, then, with a groan, sat down cross-legged, facing a roaring campfire. Half a dozen fires just like it burned around the clearing where they'd pitched their camp, with Odiman's men huddled around them, drinking and eating quietly. The shadowy forms of sentries walked the perimeter of the clearing, alert for any signs of threats, with a second set posted further out within the trees. Baine could see no fault in the House Agent's defensive planning. The man might be an ass, but at least he wasn't a stupid or careless one.

The night had turned cool with occasional drizzle falling, and Baine was glad for the fire's warmth as he pulled his tattered cloak tighter around himself and took another sip of wine. He was still trying to process the multitude of memories that had come storming back to him, which was no easy task. It seemed Baine's life had been one rollicking adventure after another from the moment he'd met Hadrack and Jebido in that cursed wagon owned by that weaselly little bastard, Carspen Tuft.

At least I'm not a pirate or an outlaw as I'd feared, Baine thought. *Well, not a real outlaw, anyway,* he amended, thinking of the role Hadrack was playing as the Outlaw of Corwick. Sunna had been right all along, for Baine's friend was working for the South, doing whatever he could to weaken the North, just as she'd insisted. Baine was proud to think that he'd been involved in that almost from the beginning, knowing both Nelsun and the girl would have heartily approved. He felt sudden sadness as he thought of Nelson's loss, wishing the fisherman's daughter was there with him now so he could share with her who he really was. A part of him was still holding out hope that Sunna had somehow managed to escape the bloodbath in the village, though that hope was admittedly dwindling.

"Must have been tough," Odiman commented, cutting into Baine's thoughts. "All alone in the water like that." The House Agent actually shuddered noticeably, surprising Baine before he tossed several twigs into the flames. "Never much liked water, myself. Won't go near the damn stuff." He nodded to Baine. "Something like what happened to you usually means Judgement Day is next. You're lucky to be alive."

"I know," Baine agreed. "I was lucky. I guess the gods weren't ready for me yet."

Odiman studied Baine thoughtfully. "You're a tough little bastard," he eventually said grudgingly. "I'll give you that. I noticed that right off when we were fighting to get out of that damn granary. Most of the men in there panicked when the walls went up, but you were calm and thinking clearly the entire time. You remind me a lot of Hadrack in that way. You might be less than half his size, but you've got that same stubborn look about you that he has. Malo told me Hadrack's a hard man to kill. It looks to me like you share that quality, too."

"Where is Hadrack?" Baine asked, brushing off Odiman's praise. He hardly needed it coming from a man like him. "Is he close? Did he catch up to Rorian?"

"He did," Odiman confirmed. "Last I heard, he's on his way to Mount Halas."

Baine blinked in confusion. "Mount Halas? Why would Hadrack go there?"

"Word in Halhaven is he joined The Walk," Odiman said. "Him and that red-haired girl, Sabina."

Baine gaped at the House Agent in astonishment. "Hadrack did what? Why in the name of The Mother would he do something like that?"

"Who can say for sure?" Odiman answered with a shrug. "That was a while ago. I haven't heard anything more about him since."

Baine had seen something in the other man's eyes as he'd spoken—a hint of caution, perhaps? "That's all you know, or that's all you're going to tell me?" he asked suspiciously.

Odiman stared at Baine, the light from the flames reflecting off his ravaged skin making the wounds look fresh, red, and raw. Baine knew that wasn't actually the case, of course, since Odiman had been disfigured many weeks previously during their escape from the burning granary in Springlight. But in the harsh light, the wounds looked convincingly new—that and very painful. "Does it matter either way?" the House Agent finally asked, looking away.

"No, I suppose it doesn't," Baine muttered, knowing by the man's blank expression that he would get nothing further from him.

Odiman was indeed a disagreeable, arrogant bastard, and Baine definitely remembered the intense dislike he'd felt for him the last time they had seen each other. No one actually liked Odiman during the siege of Springlight, he recalled—except for Malo, maybe—which seemed fitting since he was just as bad as Odiman, if not worse. Hadrack had always insisted that being mean and unpleasant was the main requirement for becoming a House Agent. Odiman and Malo were living proof of his theory.

"Why were you and your men in Weymouth?" Baine asked. "Was it just a coincidence you happened by?"

"No," Odiman said with a quick shake of his head. He gestured over his shoulder to the west where the village had once stood. "We've been tracking these shit-eaters for weeks now. They have been working behind our lines, trying to disrupt our food supplies. That village is just one of many they've razed recently. Bastards hit hard and fast, and then they disappear again."

Baine nodded glumly, not surprised. What had Nelsun said? *War rarely works out for poor people like us.* Sadly, the fisherman's words had ultimately been proven to be prophetic.

Baine and Odiman looked up at a sharp challenge from the sentry posted in the trees to the north. The House Agent stood quickly, one hand resting on the hilt of his sword before moments later, the all clear sounded and he relaxed. A horseman appeared shortly afterward, making his way toward the campsite on a sleek bay mare. He dismounted, then hurried toward Odiman. Baine stood, guessing by the man's demeanor that something of interest had happened.

"Well?" Odiman growled, not waiting for the new arrival to speak.

"We found 'em. 'Bout four miles to the northwest. They're camped in an arroyo near a stream."

"Finally," Odiman grunted in satisfaction. "How many are there?"

"Near 'bout thirty, I'd say."

Odiman pursed his lips. He glanced up at the dark sky while intermittent raindrops fell, then motioned to the ground. "Show me the layout of their camp."

The scout squatted near the fire, using a knife to scratch away at the sparse, heat-shriveled grass before sketching out a rough map in the fresh dirt underneath. "There's a bend in the stream, here," the man said as Odiman crouched opposite him. Baine moved closer to see. "That's where they set up." He shifted the point of his knife, drawing a crude circle. "There's a good-sized hill right here to the east, overlooking their position."

"Cover?" Odiman asked.

The scout nodded. "Yep. Lots of trees, but not a lot of scrub. That's where I snuck up on 'em."

"They didn't have sentries posted?" Baine asked in amazement, the warrior in him already picturing various scenarios for attack.

The scout looked up with scorn in his eyes. "Course they did. They ain't complete fools. But they haven't had to deal with the likes of me before. They never set eyes on me." The man focused back on his drawing. "This here bend has some nice, soft grass on the right bank. That's where they pitched."

"What's on the opposite side?" Odiman asked.

"A rocky overhang with forest beyond, mostly scraggly pine and spruce from what I could see," the scout answered. He looked up at the House Agent. "The ground there is rife with hawthorn bushes, though. I thought I noticed a trail through them, but even so, it's going to be difficult to move men through all that if you decide to attack from there."

"And downstream?" Odiman grunted.

"Pretty much the same for a quarter mile or so," the scout replied. "Terrain gets even rockier after that, with a few gullies leading to only the gods know where, but that's about it." He tapped the hill to the east overlooking the camp with his knife. "This is your best bet. As long as we eliminate those sentries first, we can be on top of them before they even know we're there."

Odiman stood, nodding his head. "I agree. Tell the men to get ready. I want to move out in fifteen minutes."

The scout rose and turned to go, then hesitated. "Oh, I forgot to mention something. Those bastards have some captives from the village with them." Baine instantly stiffened at that news. "Looks to be about three or four women." The man grimaced. "They was passing 'em around pretty good, too. Poor things."

"They aren't my concern," Odiman responded gruffly. "Wiping those traitorous bastards out is."

"Was one of them a girl?" Baine demanded anxiously.

"They was all girls," the scout grunted. "I just said that."

"No, I mean a child. A girl of about nine or ten years old?"

"Oh." The scout scratched his chin as he thought. "Maybe one of 'em could have been a child," he said doubtfully. "I wasn't there long enough to get a good look. I seen them females on their backs being used, but that's about all. Hard to tell their age from that angle with a man humping away on top."

Baine nodded, turning to Odiman as the scout left. "Listen, there's a young girl I befriended from the village, Sunna. I tried to find her after the attack, but I couldn't. I think there's a good chance she's with these men."

"So?" the House Agent said.

"So," Baine replied hotly, angered by the look of disinterest on the man's face. "We need to ensure the safety of those captives."

"They're just peasants, Baine. Meaningless. Besides, I doubt there'll be much left of them by the time we get there." The House Agent turned to go.

"That's it?" Baine demanded.

Odiman sighed, pausing to look up at the sky. He slowly faced Baine again. "What do you expect me to say? You know how this works as well as I do. We'll do what we can to protect those women from harm. But if it comes down to them or the lives of my men, I pick my men. You get me?"

"I get you," Baine growled, shaking with anger. He took several steps forward until they were less than a foot apart. Baine looked up into the man's ravaged face, holding the House Agent's eyes. "That girl saved my life, Odiman. I owe her. So if something happens to her because of your actions, then you and I will have a big problem." Baine poked a finger against the other man's chest. "You get me?" Then he stalked away to find his horse.

Two hours later, Odiman and Baine, along with sixty men, slipped as silently as they could through the trees in single file half a mile from where Pembry Drake's forces were reportedly encamped. The scout, whose name was Ancin Bori, was in the lead, with ten men left behind to guard the horses. The intermittent rain had persisted during their ride but now was coming down with more enthusiasm, quickly soaking the trees and turning the ground covered in pine needles into slippery muck. Little could be seen in the darkness other than vague outlines. A soldier behind Baine suddenly slipped and fell, cursing softly afterward as he forced himself to his feet. Moments later, Baine heard Ancin whisper a halt from ahead, and he turned and passed the command on to those behind him.

"Baine," Odiman hissed under his breath from the darkness. "Get up here."

Baine made his way forward, pausing beside Odiman and Ancin, who were conferring in low whispers.

Odiman put his hand on Baine's shoulder, leaning close to his ear. "Ancin says we can't go any further until the sentries are eliminated. We're making too much noise."

"All right," Baine agreed with a nod. "How many are we dealing with?"

"Three on this side of the stream," the scout replied. "They're spread out across the hill. The ones on the other side won't matter."

"Ancin can't handle all three of them on his own," Odiman continued. "I've seen what you can do with those knives, Baine, so I want you to go with him. Kill those scouts, then come back for the rest of us."

Baine and Ancin slipped away silently, the scout with a sword in his hand and Baine with a knife. They progressed another hundred yards before Ancin paused once again. He pressed his lips to Baine's ear, filling his nose with the scout's stench. "There should be one in front of us, maybe fifty feet or so. Another to the right, and one to the left. You take the man to the left. I'll deal with the other two."

Baine nodded but said nothing, and a moment later, Ancin was gone, swallowed up by the trees and darkness. Baine listened, impressed, for he couldn't hear even the slightest sounds of movement coming from the direction the man had taken. The scout was clearly as good as he had boasted. Baine headed off to his left, moving slowly and carefully up a steady grade, alert for any signs of his quarry. He paused every few feet like a hunter following a wounded boar, head cocked sideways, listening for anything out of the ordinary. But all was silent except for the steady patter of the rain. Baine continued onward for several more steps, then hesitated when he thought he heard something from behind him—a soft thump—but it wasn't repeated. Had it been Ancin eliminating the first sentry? Baine couldn't be certain, knowing that he would have to put his faith in the man's abilities and assume that's what he'd heard.

Baine started moving forward again, progressing another few yards before stopping to listen. He almost jumped out of his skin moments later when a subdued cough sounded less than ten feet in front of him. Baine froze, but the noise didn't come again. He remained where he was, standing like a statue as thin rivulets of rain slid off the branches above him, pattering against his head and working their way beneath his cloak. Baine ignored the cold discomfort wiggling down his sides and back, barely breathing until finally, his patience was rewarded when a shadow detached itself from the surrounding darkness ahead.

A heartbeat later, Baine heard the rustle of clothing, followed by the unmistakable sound of someone urinating against a tree. The man sighed softly in relief while he emptied his bladder, and Baine smiled. He glided forward in a crouch, silent and deadly, all senses focused on the splashing sounds. He could smell the acrid stench of piss on the air, mixing with the heady scent of spruce. The man finally finished relieving himself, fumbling with his clothing just as Baine reached him.

He rose out of the darkness like a wraith, clamping one strong hand over the startled scout's mouth while simultaneously pulling his head back, exposing his throat. Baine had spent hours sharpening his knives in the village after each day's work had been completed, and that time proved well spent, for the blade sliced through vulnerable flesh and muscle with ease. Hot blood instantly gushed out from the gaping wound, spraying the branches and tree trunks while Baine waited with the man's lifeless body slumping in his arms. He slowly lowered the scout to the ground once the blood flow had slowed, careful not to make any noise, then straightened just as an urgent shout arose from the north.

"Pembry! Enemy in the trees! To arms! To ar—!"

The cry was suddenly cut off, replaced by a scream of mortal pain. Baine hesitated in indecision as shouts of confusion and alarm arose from the campsite to the west, followed moments later by breaking branches and men cursing to the east as they fought their way through the undergrowth. The element of surprise was clearly gone, and Odiman and his men were making a desperate rush to get to the encampment before their quarry could flee or set up a proper defense. Baine knew they would be too late to stop either. He started to hurry toward the noises coming from the campsite with his only thought finding and protecting Sunna.

Baine pushed his way through the trees until he reached the crest of the hill Ancin had described overlooking the enemy encampment. Below, the sellswords were moving about in confusion, their bodies backlit by campfires, weapons glinting in the firelight. There were no signs of the women anywhere that he could see. He quickly sheathed his knife, then took his bowstring from his pocket where he'd placed it to keep it dry and hurriedly strung his bow. He dropped to one knee and nocked an arrow, searching for a clear target. A man appeared from the trees across the stream, shouting and waving his arms while running down the rock-strewn hill toward the camp, sending small and larger stones tumbling in all directions.

Good enough, Baine thought. He drew, aimed, then let fly, the arrow hissing through the night air over the heads of the confused men below before smacking into the chest of the mercenary just as he reached the stream. The man cried out, then fell face-first into the shallow water. Baine drew another arrow, pausing as a form appeared from the trees to his right. He hurriedly shifted aim, then relaxed. It was Ancin.

"What happened?" Baine hissed as the scout dropped down beside him.

"There was a fourth man," Ancin grunted. "Bastard wasn't there the first time. He ran when he saw me, yelling his head off.

Shit-eater screamed like a woman when I caught him, but the damage was already done."

"Are you hurt?"

The scout shook his head. "Just annoyed is all," he growled. "I shouldn't have missed him."

Baine glanced below. Pembry's men had gotten over their confusion quickly and were forming a shield wall facing the hill. The sellswords hadn't noticed the dead man in the water yet, but Baine knew they would soon enough. But where were the women? He could see crumpled bedding lying around the campfires, but from his vantage point, they all looked empty. He glanced again at the dead mercenary in the stream. What had he been trying to tell his companions? Did it have to do with the sentry who'd cried out, or was it about something else—something to do with the missing women perhaps? Baine stood, coming to a decision.

"Where do you think you're going?" Ancin demanded, resting a hand on Baine's arm. "We wait here for Odiman." Baine glanced down at the man's hand, then his face, letting the scout see his determination and what trying to stop him would cost. Ancin hesitated, looking suddenly uncertain, then slowly drew his hand back. "Fine," the man said with a shrug. "Do what you want. It's your life."

Baine darted away to the south, while behind him, he heard a roar as Odiman's men reached the crest of the hill and streamed out from the trees, charging down the grade toward Pembry Drake's hastily forming shield wall. As the two forces met, Baine continued onward, ignoring the screech of metal, curses, and screams of pain. He'd never been much use with shield and sword and knew his presence would hardly be missed. Baine slipped through the trees for a good fifty yards, following a downward slope until he reached level ground. He turned west then, making his way through a stand of young poplars until he stood along the bank of the winding stream. He looked north to where the water curled around the campsite, the clanging of iron against iron and shouts much louder now that he was in the open. Odiman's men had a two-to-one advantage, and they were making good use of it, forcing Drake's beleaguered force back toward the stream, though the defenders were putting up a strong, determined front.

Baine watched the battle for a moment, then splashed through the ankle-deep water to the opposite bank, which was covered with small stones and pebbles. He shifted directions, heading northwest, hooking his bow over his shoulders before using his hands to help pull himself up the rocky, shifting grade. Baine finally reached the top, and he cut across the crest of the ridge along the treeline toward the spot where the mercenary he'd killed had first emerged. He paused there to peer eastward, now directly above and behind Pembry Drake's men. Odiman's forces were pressing the defenders to the front and the sides, but so far, the sellswords had maintained their discipline and were holding their own.

Baine decided it was time to change that. He unhooked his bow and nocked an arrow, focusing on a big man in the center of the enemy shield wall. Could it be Pembry Drake? Baine had no way of knowing. He aimed at the man's broad back and released, already nocking a second arrow and sending it on its way just as the first one smacked into the big man's hip. Baine's target bellowed like a bull and staggered, dropping to one knee while Baine's second arrow struck the shoulder of the man standing next to him, spinning the mercenary around. Baine grinned in satisfaction as a breach appeared in the shield wall—a breach Odiman's men were quick to recognize and take advantage of. The attackers immediately rushed into the gap, screaming in victory while the sellswords' shield wall wavered and gave ground under the onslaught. A moment later, the besieged enemy's defenses collapsed entirely as two men on the left flank flung aside their shields and weapons and started to run north through the shallow stream. Five of Odiman's men raced after them, hooting and laughing while sheets of water sprayed upward around their feet.

The battle had now become a free-for-all, with the House Agent's superior numbers already dictating the outcome.

His job done, Baine hooked his bow over his shoulders again, then turned his back on the fight, heading deeper into the trees along a faint trail. The hawthorn bushes Ancin had warned Odiman about were growing everywhere, pushing their way onto the path that clearly had been rarely used. Baine grit his teeth against the pain as sharp barbs punctured his cloak and skin repeatedly while he fought his way through the bushes. The undergrowth was dry and brittle in places, crunching, snapping, and rustling with every step he took. Baine knew if anyone were around, they'd hear him coming from a mile away. There was little he could do about it, though, so he pressed onward determinedly, a knife in each hand now. If someone was lying in wait among the hawthorn, Baine knew he'd have a better chance with the blades than the bow in the tight confines.

Baine progressed along the trail for several more minutes, heading westward. Behind him, he heard sudden cheering and swords clanging against shields, guessing that Odiman's men had finally claimed victory. He broke out from the bushes not long afterward, finding himself in a wooded area dominated by tall, pole-like pine trees that towered over his head. Baine hadn't noticed the rain had stopped at some point during his journey, with the clouds moving on, revealing a bright, three-quarter moon. Thin beams of moonlight cut through the canopy of branches above his head, throwing shadows across the ground strewn with a thick blanket of brown pine needles. Most of the lower branches of the trees were long dead and bare of needles, covered in moss. He thought in the weak light that they looked remarkably like skeletal limbs reaching out for him.

Baine glanced down, noticing the pine needles had been disturbed in places, leaving partial footprints and scuff marks where people had clearly passed recently. They'd headed off toward the north, he saw, though he couldn't be sure how many of them there were. Baine cautiously followed the vague trail of marks and prints around the trees for fifty yards until he came to a small clearing dominated by a gigantic white fir. Three bodies lay sprawled beneath the tree in various poses of death.

Baine groaned, for he could tell by their clothing that they were women. He rushed forward, dropping to his knees beside the closest body before gently rolling the woman over, grimacing when he recognized her. It was Asinda, the woman he'd saved from being raped almost a week ago. Someone had cut her throat. Baine touched the blood on the corpse's neck, registering that it was still warm. He cursed under his breath and moved to check the other bodies. Both were younger women that he recognized from Weymouth, and both had been murdered in a similar fashion.

Baine stood, seething with anger as he looked around, but he could see no obvious trail leading away. He wished Ancin was with him to help track whoever had killed the women, or better yet, the red-haired girl, Sabina from Springlight. Something small and white caught Baine's eye, hooked at the base of a line of low bushes twenty feet to his right. It appeared to be a small strip of torn cloth. Baine cautiously approached the area, certain that he could feel eyes on him.

"Stop!" a trembling male voice cried out when he was less than ten feet away from the bushes. "Not another step! I'm warning you!"

Baine hesitated. He could see no threats to the sides or behind him, guessing that if there were more men about than this one, he'd already be dead. "What do you want?" Baine finally asked calmly.

"For you to go away and leave me be!"

The voice sounded young to Baine, alternating between low and high like a boy on the cusp of manhood. "Why should I?" Baine responded, knowing he had the upper hand. Whoever was behind that bush did not sound like much of a threat. "You're obviously all alone out here. Drake's men are dead, so you might as well just surrender."

"You're lying! Now go away, or I'll kill this little bitch I've got with me! I swear it!"

Baine felt his heart skip a beat. Sunna? He slipped his knives into their sheaths, then lifted his hands high. "I'm not lying. Your friends are all dead. Promise me you won't hurt her, and I promise we'll let you live."

"You swear?" the voice responded shakily. "By The Mother?"

"I do swear," Baine said solemnly. "By The Mother. Now show yourself."

Baine waited, tense and ready to pounce as the bushes moved before two forms finally appeared, hidden in the shadows beneath the canopy of the great tree. One was clearly the boy by his size, but the second was much smaller and looked to be wearing a dress. "Sunna," Baine breathed in relief. The girl tried to say something then, but her voice was muffled and incomprehensible.

Baine realized Sunna's captor had his hand clamped over her mouth. "Let her go," he growled. "Do that, and I promise you can leave. No one will come after you." Silence filled the forest, with neither the boy nor the girl moving. "What's your name?" Baine asked after a moment. "What do I call you?"

"Kraven," the answer came back grudgingly. "Kraven of Woodwind."

"Ah," Baine said agreeably. "A splendid little village, Woodwind. A lovely place."

"It's a cesspool," Kraven spat back bitterly. "Nobody lives there now but thieves and whores."

"Yes, well," Baine said with a shrug. "One man's cesspool is another man's haven, I suppose." Baine shifted his feet and Kraven took a step back, his hand still pressed firmly over the girl's mouth. "It's all right," Baine said soothingly. "You have my word that no harm will come to you if you don't hurt the girl."

"How do I know I can trust you?" Kraven asked uncertainly.

"I gave you my word," Baine said, trying to control his temper. He smiled, though he doubted the boy could see it. "And my word means everything to me."

Kraven paused, then shook his head. "No, the girl comes with me," he said. "Until I'm safely away. Then I'll let her go."

"That's not going to work for me," Baine replied. He lowered his right hand a fraction of an inch while moving his left back toward his head.

"Too bad!" Kraven shouted, clearly trying to bluster now. "I've got a knife at this bitch's throat. You understand?"

"I do understand," Baine said softly. He glanced toward the giant fir and the three murdered women beneath it. "Is that what you used on them?"

Kraven snorted. "I didn't do that. Pepan did. Those whores tried to run away. Pepan warned them what would happen if they tried that."

"Uh-huh," Baine grunted, guessing that Pepan was the man he'd killed with his bow. Baine lowered his right hand another inch. "Last chance. Let the girl go."

"No. We're going now. I swear I'll cut her throat if you try to follow me."

Baine had a sudden vision of Ania, the Pith girl Hadrack had taken for a lover after they'd been rescued from Father's Arse by Einhard. He almost smiled then, thinking it had actually been Ania who had taken Hadrack for a lover, showing him things his friend had never even dreamed were possible. Ania had been a master with the bow, and Baine had been fascinated by how quickly she could get off an arrow, even with her bow across her shoulders. Baine had spent hours under Ania's tutelage—hours that had given back great dividends over the years.

"Don't say I didn't warn you," Baine said softly.

He moved in a blur—left hand snatching the bow off his back, right hand whipping an arrow from the bag at his hip. *Be smooth and quick, and don't think*, Ania had instilled in him. Baine did just that, nocking, drawing, and letting fly all in one effortless, lightning-like motion. The arrow hissed across the short distance, catching Kraven in the left eye with a solid thunk. The boy screamed, losing his grip on the girl as he fell, disappearing behind the bushes. Baine didn't bother to check on him. He knew Kraven was dead before he'd hit the ground.

"Drago!" the girl cried, sobbing as she ran around the bushes into his arms.

Baine hugged the slight form to him, stroking her hair and whispering that she was all right now as she trembled in his arms. Finally, he gently pushed the girl away, brushing back the long hair that had fallen into her eyes. He felt a thud in his gut at the tear-streaked face looking up at him. It wasn't Sunna, he realized in dismay, but instead, a friend of hers from the village named Eryn.

"Thank you, Drago," Eryn whispered. She shuddered and pressed herself to Baine's chest again. "Thank you for what you did for me!"

Baine held the girl against him, patting her back while clamping his jaws tightly shut to keep himself from cursing out loud. Any last hope that Sunna was still alive had just been dashed, and he felt nothing but sorrow and heartache, knowing he'd done what he could and it was time for him to leave. Baine's wife, Flora, and hopefully a newborn, were anxiously waiting for him at Witbridge Manor after many months away. It was time to focus on his family now.

Baine had no idea that he was wrong about Sunna's fate, and that they were destined to meet again many years later.

Chapter 7: Heading North

"So, where to now?" Odiman asked as Baine tied a leather sack filled with supplies along with several skins of wine to the saddle perched on the white mare's back.

Baine glanced over his shoulder at the big House Agent standing behind him. Dawn had arrived some time ago, and the great orange ball of the sun was now halfway above the trees to the east. Blackflies had begun to swarm over the stream a hundred feet away from where the two men stood the moment the air had warmed, which Baine knew was not a good sign. Odiman's men were busily striking camp near the water, many slapping at and cursing the biting flies. Baine wondered if a storm was coming by the insects' frenzied activity, already feeling the sweat beading on his forehead from the hot, humid air. He thought he could detect a faint hint of decay on that air from Pembry Drake's men left to rot by the stream half a mile downwind, but guessed it was probably just his imagination.

"I'm heading to Witbridge Manor to see my wife," Baine finally answered the House Agent, turning back to the mare. He didn't bother mentioning the baby, which Baine was certain must have been born by now. A bastard like Odiman didn't need to know all his business. The horse stamped her front hoof and swished her tail, annoyed by the flies that had recently found her. She took a playful nip at Baine's arm with her yellow teeth, and he fondly stroked the long white strands of the mare's forelock that grew thick and unruly between her ears to hang down just above her gentle black eyes. "Hopefully, Hadrack will already be there," Baine added. "If not, maybe someone at Witbridge will know where I can find him."

"And if he's not there and they don't know?"

Baine shrugged. "Then I guess I'll ride to Mount Halas and find out on my own."

"That's a long and dangerous ride to take by yourself," Odiman warned. "Even getting to Witbridge will be difficult. The North's forces have sealed off all the roads."

"I'll find a way," Baine said determinedly. "It's nothing I haven't dealt with before."

"Uh-huh," Odiman grunted, his voice heavy with doubt. "Are you sure you won't change your mind and stay until we hear from Hadrack? I could certainly use a man like you."

"I'm sure," Baine replied firmly. The truth was, he needed to be gone from this place now that Sunna and Nelsun were dead. Besides, a part of him knew that wherever Odiman went, trouble and heartache were sure to follow. He was better off on his own. Baine glanced again at the House Agent. "So, what's next for you?"

Odiman shrugged. "Off to find that bastard, Pembry Drake. Lord Porten has offered twenty Jorqs for his head, and I'll be damned if I return to Norhall without it—even if I have to spend a month out here looking for him."

Baine nodded. Norhall was Lord Porten's castle. Several of Odiman's men had known Pembry Drake before the war, and they'd confirmed that the man was not among the dead. From the description he'd heard, Baine was fairly certain Drake was the big man he had wounded with an arrow to the hip. He swung up into the saddle. "Well, I wish you luck in finding him, Odiman."

"Luck to you as well, Baine," the House Agent said. "And stay off the roads," he called moments later, cupping his hands around his mouth as Baine kicked the white mare into a trot.

Baine raised a hand in acknowledgment, not looking behind him, focusing on nothing now but what lay ahead. Had he known the misery and pain waiting for him in the north, though, he might have thought twice about dismissing Odiman's offer to stay.

The storm Baine had feared might hit arrived around midday, and it did so with relish and gusto. Blackflies never lie, Jebido had once told him. Ominous dark clouds had rolled in not long after Baine had left Odiman and his men behind, but the rain had mercifully held off, giving him several hours of unencumbered travel time. Now, however, that brief interlude had ended, and the rain was coming down hard and fast, pounding against the swaying canopy above his head with determination. The deluge had quickly overwhelmed the meager protection the branches had provided, leaving both Baine and the mare thoroughly drenched within minutes.

Baine could do little about the rain but pull the drawstring of his cloak tighter around himself. He bowed his head as the wind howled above and through the trees, peering out from beneath the dripping cowl of his hood while his mount moved slowly along a dirt trail. That trail was heading north and would eventually lead him to Lord Porten's castle, where Baine hoped the lord might know more about what had become of Hadrack.

A bolt of lightning sizzled overhead, and the mare paused, rolling her eyes as the gloom hanging over the forest was suddenly lit up in stark relief for several heartbeats. Thunder answered the lightning's call moments later, the boom so loud that it rattled Baine's teeth and seemed to shake the very trees themselves. He detected a strange odor in the air soon after the lightning had fizzled out, one he'd smelled many times before during storms. Baine couldn't help but be reminded of the storm that had plucked him off *Sea-Dragon*, though this one was actually quite mild in comparison.

"It's all right, pretty girl," Baine said soothingly, leaning over to stroke the horse's slick neck. "There's nothing to be frightened of." He glanced upward, blinking away the falling rain. "It's just the gods having a disagreement, is all. They care nothing for either of us. Trust me."

The mare shook her head like a dog, sending droplets of water flying in all directions, then, at his urging, continued plodding onward. The trail had become a gully filled with water and muck, the oozing mire reaching well past the mare's stained fetlocks with every slurping, sucking step. Baine eventually sat back in the saddle, the tail of his cloak spread out over the mare's rump to either side. He decided to make the best of the situation, so he began to sing. Baine's singing voice was surprisingly good—a talent that had done wonders for him in pursuit of many a comely barmaid—until Flora had taken his heart, of course.

The mare's ears swiveled back and forth in appreciation at the sound of Baine's voice, and he laughed, feeling his spirits soar despite the gloom of his surroundings. "See," he said, pausing in his singing. "Even you can't resist me, pretty girl. Just be glad I don't hump horses like Cardians are said to do. Then you'd really be in trouble."

Baine started singing cheerfully again. He was finally on his way to see his beloved wife, a woman who had once been a whore in Hillsfort, but had since been lifted from that life of squalor and desperation by his dear friend, Hadrack. Flora and Baine had been a natural fit almost from the moment they'd met, despite the disparity in their sizes. Flora's forthright manner and unabashed ability to tell people exactly what she thought had captivated his imagination—not to mention her obvious womanly charms. Baine thought about how close Flora had come to dying in the bowels of Calban Castle, wounded grievously by Lady Shana's then-husband, Lord Demay. Baine had spent weeks by Flora's side, praying and tending to her every whim as she'd slowly recovered. It was during that time they'd both realized how much they meant to each other—over and above the mere physical attraction, that is.

Baine and Flora had married the moment she'd been allowed out of bed by Haverty the apothecary. Not long after that, Flora told him she was pregnant, insisting it would be a boy. Baine had feigned indifference about the sex, just happy to be a father, but the truth was, he was desperately hoping for a son. Baine had never known his father, and he had only vague memories of his mother—long black hair and a soothing voice—that was it. She'd left him on The Waste when he was six years old to go off with a man but never returned. It had been the worst time of Baine's life, worse even than when he'd been beaten by Cardians and shoved in a cage along with Jebido and Hadrack. Baine's song faltered as he reflected on his childhood until, finally, he shook off his growing black mood. That had been a different time and was long in the past—a time that, by rights, should never be revisited.

Baine had vowed to do everything in his power to ensure what he'd endured as a boy would never be experienced by any of his children, no matter how many he fathered. Besides, he knew those children would never be orphaned like he'd been, for they would not only have him and Flora to dote upon them but an army of eager uncles like Hadrack, Jebido, Putt, and Tyris just waiting to spoil them. Baine smiled, thinking of his friends as he belted out the words to the Old Man and the Hare, a comical tale about the death of King Jorquin's father, Lord Arforth Raybold.

> And there be old Arrie sittin' astride his horse
> Both man and beast drunk and a losin' their course
> Along comes a jack hare with a bone to pick
> For he'd just lost his fair mate to a farmer's stick
>
> The horse be a ploddin' and a noddin', sicker than sin
> The man above barely hangin' on, pale and thin
> And upon the vengeful jack hare, came the two
> Both bleary-eyed and dumb, not knowin' what to do
>
> The jack hare rose up with a mighty roar
> Poor old Arrie, in his derangement, thinkin' it be a savage boar
> With a squeak and a whiny, the horse did buck

Sending poor old Arrie wet-arsed to the ground like a duck

The noble steed up and galloped away
Leavin' poor old Arrie behind with a price to pay
The jack hare came on, all fangs and claws
But too late he was, for poor old Arrie's heart had flaws

Twas nothin' but a—

Baine paused in his song, some inner instinct causing him to look over his shoulder. The trail behind was empty, but he could swear there were eyes on him. Baine had learned to trust his instincts, and he halted the mare, turning her sideways. He lifted a hand to the cowl of his hood, blocking the dripping rain as he studied his backtrail and the trees. There was nothing there. Baine glanced down at the mare, but she stood waiting patiently, not reacting. Had he imagined it? Baine frowned. He never imagined things. Someone was out here with him; he was convinced of it. But what to do? Baine fumbled inside his cloak, drawing a knife, though he kept it hidden within the folds of the cloth. He pulled back his hood, letting the rain drench his hair so he could see along his periphery, then turned the mare back onto the trail. He clucked at her to move, bending forward in the saddle to present a smaller target.

Baine let his eyes roam the trees to the front and sides, keeping the mare moving at a steady pace. The feeling of being watched had grown stronger, yet he could see nothing out of the ordinary. Baine could hear Jebido's scornful voice preaching in his head. *"If everything looks normal, lad, then that's the time to be worried."* Lightning cascaded across the sky again, followed by the rumble of thunder, though it seemed further away now. The light hadn't lasted long, but it had been enough to reveal rain-filled, muddy footprints coming down one side of the path ahead.

Baine halted the mare again. The prints had stopped fifty feet from where he waited, heading west into the trees. Baine studied the area carefully, but he could see no indication that anyone was there. Had it just been a simple traveler who'd heard his singing and had hidden from the unknown? Or was this something else? Baine thought about the deserters who'd attacked Weymouth, knowing a vast forest like this would be a good place for scum like that to hide.

Perhaps upon reflection, I shouldn't have been so passionate in my singing, Baine thought. *Too late now.* "Well, what do you think we should do?" he whispered to the mare. The horse lifted a front hoof and pawed at the trail, the squelch of mud the only sound other than the steady drumbeat of the rain.

Baine briefly considered unhooking the bow stave from his saddle, but with the amount of rain falling, he knew the hemp string would get wet in seconds. That string was inside his leather sack, where it remained nice and dry. Baine had always been meticulous about his bow and strings, keeping them clean, dry, oiled, and waxed, for doing so might mean the difference between life and death. But though Nelsun's bow was a perfectly fine weapon, it had not been as well maintained as Baine would have liked. The stave had been oiled occasionally, but the string was old, frayed in places, and hadn't been waxed in a long time, leaving it vulnerable. Baine had repaired it the best he could but knew he couldn't take a chance the string would fail in this weather, so his knives would have to suffice. Besides, it would take time to string the bow—time Baine didn't think he had.

He debated what to do next. If someone were truly lying in wait for him, they'd logically attack the moment he drew even with them. Should he just gallop the mare past the spot where the watcher was hiding? Maybe that's exactly what the man expected him to do and had planned for it. Running certainly seemed the prudent choice, but the trail ahead was riddled with water-filled ruts and holes that a horse moving at speed could easily break a leg in. Baine was reluctant to risk the mare's welfare for a threat that might not even exist, but neither did he want to constantly be watching his backtrail afterward if it did, which left him only one option—deal with the problem head-on.

Baine kicked the mare into motion, using his knees to guide her while drawing a second knife. If there was a hunter out there in the trees waiting to pounce, then the bastard was about to find out that this prey had teeth.

Baine stopped the horse where the tracks turned off the trail. "I know you're in there, whoever you are. So come out now. I mean you no harm." Baine waited, but there was no reply or movement. "Last chance," he called, peering into the trees. Again, nothing. Now what?

The mare's ears suddenly shot up straight and she snorted, her head turning to the east even as Baine heard a sharp snapping sound coming from behind him. The footprints had been a ruse! He turned in alarm, aware of a dark form holding a sword rushing toward him from the opposite side of the trail. Baine automatically snapped his right wrist outward, sending the knife he held whisking through the air. He heard a sharp clang a moment later and he cursed, realizing that despite all the odds, the knife had struck the flat blade of the attacker's sword.

Perhaps the gods are watching, after all, Baine thought. *Though if they are, the bastards clearly aren't on my side.*

A flash of forged steel whistled for Baine's head a moment later, and he ducked just in time, then cried out as the man latched onto his right arm with a strong grip and dragged him from the saddle. Baine landed hard in the muck with the wind knocked from him. He sucked in air, getting a mouthful of muddy water to go along with it even as he desperately rolled aside, knowing what was coming next. The mare whinnied, rearing back in fear, her front hooves landing perilously close to Baine's head when she came down.

Baine managed to stumble to his feet, and he spun away as his attacker took several savage hacks at him. He retreated, gagging and spitting out foul-tasting muck, followed by a curse when he realized he'd lost his grip on the second knife when he fell. The blade was now lying half submerged in a puddle six feet away. Thankfully, Baine still had the deserter's knife, which he'd strapped to his right ankle beneath his trousers.

"Ha," Baine's attacker grunted in satisfaction, pausing with his sword in front of him as he studied Baine critically. "You're just a boy. I thought this would be harder." He gestured to the mare with his weapon. "I'll be needing that horse of yours right now, friend. Mine went lame on me."

Baine recognized the man he'd struck in the hip with an arrow the day before. Was this Pembry Drake? If it was him, the man was limping noticeably, which was a good sign. "And if I say no?" Baine said, buying time to catch his breath.

"I recommend that you don't," the big man replied. He straightened his shoulders proudly. "I'm Pembry Drake. I imagine you've heard of me, which means you know I've killed men for much less. Count yourself lucky I'm feeling generous today, boy. There are men out here hunting me, and I just want the horse. Nothing else. You don't need to die."

"Odiman told me just this morning that Lord Porten is offering twenty Jorqs to the man who brings him your head," Baine said calmly. He grinned mockingly. "I can't imagine why the lord would want it, though, seeing as how ugly you are."

Drake scowled. "You ride with that bastard House Agent?"

"I do," Baine confirmed. "Or at least, I did." He motioned to Drake's hip. "I'm the one who did that to you." He smiled. "Damn shame I missed. I was aiming higher, but you moved."

Drake blinked at him, his expression darkening. "I was going to let you to live if you gave me the horse without a fight, but now I've changed my mind. I'm going to cut out your heart and eat it first no matter what you choose. Then I'm taking the horse."

Baine snorted, knowing the man had never had any intentions of letting him live anyway. The ambush he'd conceived was proof of that. Baine undid the drawstring of his cloak, then shrugged it off his shoulders. He wanted to be able to move unencumbered. He motioned to Drake as the rain continued to fall around them unabated, soaking their clothing, hair, and beards. "Then come on, you ugly bastard. Do your worst. I don't have all day."

Drake growled, moving awkwardly forward, clearly favoring his right hip. Baine smiled. The man was big and obviously strong, but he appeared slow, made worse by his wound. Drake's sword was what was known as an Oakeshott, with a long, narrow blade and straight crossguard. Many of Baine's friends, such as Putt, Niko, and Jebido, used similar weapons. Baine was intimately familiar with the longsword's strengths and weaknesses, having sparred against his friends many times using just his knives. Not one of them had been able to defeat Baine's lethal combination of speed and skill except for Hadrack, who lived in a separate, higher realm from everybody else when it came to combat.

"What are you grinning at, you little worm?" Drake growled. He motioned to his bad hip. "If you think this will slow me down, you've got another thing coming. Because I—"

Drake moved then without warning, launching himself forward with surprising speed while thrusting the point of his sword toward Baine's midriff in a lunge. Baine realized the man had been playing possum all along, deliberately feigning he was slower and hurting worse than he actually was. Baine instinctively twirled away, though not quite fast enough, as he felt a searing burn tear across his left shoulder. He cried out, reaching desperately for the knife at his ankle while Drake came on, grunting in determination like a bull as he hacked and slashed, not giving him any breathing room.

Baine was forced to scramble away, slipping and sliding in the mud as he used all of his skills just to stay out of reach of the sword or the big man's clutching grip. He had no illusions about what would happen to him if Drake managed to get his hands on him. Baine finally put enough distance between himself and Pembry Drake to allow him time to wrench his knife free from its sheath. He paused along the tree line away from the mud, crouched and ready while the big man hesitated in surprise. It was clear by Drake's expression that he'd thought Baine unarmed, nor that he'd forgotten how lucky he'd been the last time a knife had appeared in his opponent's hand.

"You're faster than I expected, boy," Drake said grudgingly. The big man kept his sword in front of him, swishing it back and forth as if hoping to ward off another thrown knife. He made a tempting target, though, one Baine had hit a thousand times before with ease. Baine felt sudden doubt well up inside him, a part of his mind wondering if the gods were still against him. If he threw his last knife and somehow missed, then the fight was as good as over. "I have to admit I thought you'd be dead by now," Drake added, watching Baine carefully.

"That's interesting," Baine replied. "Because I was thinking the same about you, ugly man."

Pembry Drake chuckled. "You've got one shot with that little toad sticker of yours, boy," he sneered. "Then you're mine. So you'd better not miss." The big man suddenly feinted an attack, then deliberately spun away to his right, sending a sheet of water and mud splashing in all directions.

It was masterfully planned and executed, but Baine didn't bite, biding his time until the right moment to throw the knife. He grinned mockingly at the obvious disappointment on Drake's bearded face. Baine thought he could see a hint of pain there, too, hidden beneath the streaks of dirt and muck. He guessed the man's wound hurt more than he was letting on, which was a positive sign. Baine glanced past Drake to where the mare waited for him down the trail, looking confused, wet, and miserable. He couldn't help but feel sorry for her. This needed to end.

Baine planted his feet firmly in the slick grass, positioning his left foot slightly in front of the right with the toe of his boot pointed toward his adversary. He held the butt of the knife handle lightly cupped in his right palm, his thumb pressed against the side of the leather handle and his index finger extended down the spine of the blade. The knife he'd taken from the deserter was blade-heavy, meaning the blade was heavier than the handle. That meant Baine didn't need to reverse the weapon before throwing it. He knew he had an advantage because of that, though not much of one.

Pembry Drake was in what Baine considered close range—ten feet or less—which meant all he needed was a quick snap of his wrist back toward his forearm without moving the rest of his body, then throw, not allowing the knife to spin before hitting the target. But if his wet grip slipped, or something went wrong like the last time—

Baine shook his head to clear his eyes, shedding water from his wet beard and hair. He watched Drake warily as the big man took a shuffling step closer through the mud, his grip tightening and untightening on the hilt of his sword as he prepared to charge. Baine gauged the shortening distance between them, knowing it was now or never. He glanced up through the branches at the storm-filled sky as lightning flashed. Had that just been a sign from Mother Above? And if so, for who? Baine thrust aside all his doubts, his wrist already moving backward as Pembry Drake screamed and attacked, sword held over his head for the killing blow.

Then Baine threw the knife.

Chapter 8: Pembry Drake's Head

Baine finally set eyes on Lord Porten's castle the next day around mid-morning. Norhall had originally been built in the motte and bailey style, with wood and mud buildings and a wooden palisade surrounding the upper and lower sections. The Lord had spent a fortune upgrading the castle ten years before the Pair War began, almost impoverishing himself in the process to accomplish it. He'd replaced the sagging palisade walls with much higher and thicker ones of stone and upgraded many of the buildings to stone as well, including the new square keep, which Baine could see rising on a high hill in the center of the inner bailey. Sunlight reflected back to him off the gray limestone like a million tiny jewels, easily seen for miles and impossible to ignore.

A moat completely encircled the outer and inner baileys of Norhall, with a narrow channel running between the two, connected by an imposing drawbridge and gatehouse. A second, smaller gatehouse and bridge protected the entrance to the outer bailey, with a sloping, grassy berm rising on the outer side of the moat. Light blue banners depicting a white dove flying over an orange sun flew from the keep, battlements, and turrets, snapping in the steady breeze coming in from the south.

Baine paused the mare on a knoll half a mile away while he studied the castle with an experienced eye. The defenses were formidable, and even with siege engines, he knew Norhall would be difficult and costly in both men and resources to take. Luckily, according to Odiman, Lord Porten was a staunch supporter of Prince Tyden's claim to the throne. Now that Baine had seen the strength of Norhall for himself, he was doubly glad of that fact, for the fortress would be a clear strategic prize if it ever fell into the North's hands.

Many of the lords near the unofficial border separating the two warring sides had switched allegiances back and forth in the past year, depending on which way the winds of war were blowing. Lord Porten had never wavered in his support for Tyden, however, nor would he, according to Odiman, who had uncharacteristically sung the man's praises. The House Agent had described the lord as intelligent, forthright, and fiercely loyal to his friends and allies—all rare compliments considering the source. Odiman had also informed Baine that Lord Porten knew the truth about what Hadrack and his Wolf Pack were actually doing in the North. Baine hoped because of that fact, the man might be more informative than Odiman had been about why Hadrack had gone to Mount Halas to join The Walk. Lord Porten might even know what had become of him since then as well.

Baine finally urged his mount down the dusty road leading to the castle. A small village rose to the west about a quarter of a mile to his left, partially obscured by a copse of black ash trees. A man leading a donkey and a cart covered with canvas cloth shuffled toward Baine, watching him warily. Baine nodded a greeting as they passed each other but was met with nothing but an unfriendly glare. No one else was on the road, although Baine could see a large group of men, women, and children in the field to his right harvesting and loading hay onto wagons. They all stopped in their labors to stare at him suspiciously. After a year of civil war, their attitude was hardly surprising.

Baine leaned forward and stroked the mare's neck. "There'll be grain and a rubdown coming for you very soon, pretty girl," he assured her. "I promise. And maybe after that, some venison and an ale or two for me, eh?" He sat back in the saddle, then glanced down at the crude sack hanging by his right leg that he'd fashioned from Pembry Drake's tunic. Baine grinned, for inside was the dead man's severed head—twenty Jorqs was twenty Jorqs, after all. "And you'll have a place of honor soon where you can finally rest, my ugly friend," he added with a chuckle as the improvised sack bumped and twisted against the mare's side with every stride. "I'm sure Lord Porten has a nice spot on the battlements reserved just for you." Baine winked down at the bloodstained sack. "On the pointy end of a pike, of course."

A familiar rattle and screech of hinges sounded from ahead, and Baine looked up, watching as the castle gates swung slowly inward. A small knot of riders burst through the gap before the gates were fully opened, galloping toward him down the road. One held a pike with a fluttering dove banner tied around the gleaming point.

Baine could see the glint of helmets on the battlements as the defenders stared out at him, with shouts echoing along the walls. "Ah," he grunted to the mare. "It would seem the locals have finally taken an interest in us."

The riders sprinted down the road, leaving a trail of dust billowing in their wake. All held swords or pikes in their hands, Baine noted uncomfortably. He halted the white mare and waited calmly with his hands easily seen on the saddle's pommel. There was a war on, after all, and no doubt everyone around these parts was jumpy these days. Baine saw no reason to give Lord Porten's men an excuse to put his head on the wall alongside Pembry Drake's.

The riders reined in their blowing horses fifteen feet away, all of them deferring to a handsome man dressed in a fine black cloak lined with silver wolf's fur. Baine guessed the man to be around his age or slightly older. He could see the gleam of mail hidden beneath the handsome man's rich cloak as he nodded to the small group in a friendly fashion. "Greetings. I've come to speak with Lord Porten."

The leader of the mounted men studied Baine critically, taking in his tattered clothing and mud-splattered boots with obvious disdain. "My father is a busy man. Who are you, and what is this concerning?"

"My name is Baine," Baine said pleasantly. "And you would be?"

"Daholf Welis," the man declared with a barely concealed sneer. "Lord Porten's eldest son and heir to Norhall."

Baine thought that the last part had seemed an obvious and unnecessary announcement to make, wondering why Daholf had chosen to voice it. Was the man insecure in his inheritance, perhaps, or was he just an ass and a braggart? Having just met the fellow, Baine was already leaning toward the latter. He indicated the sack by his leg and gave Daholf his most charming smile. "Then I believe your father owes me twenty Jorqs, my good man."

Daholf's eyes widened before he flicked them down to the stained sack. "Are you saying Pembry Drake's head is in there?"

"I am," Baine confirmed.

Daholf smiled wolfishly in triumph as he urged his horse forward, holding out a gloved hand. "You can give that bastard to me. I'll make sure you're rewarded for your trouble."

Baine clucked his tongue regretfully. "If it's all the same to you, I'll just give it to the *Lord* of Norhall myself." Baine had stressed the word lord, trying his best not to smile when Daholf flushed crimson. Yes, there were indeed issues there.

"You think I would try to cheat you out of my father's reward?" Daholf finally demanded with a look of contempt on his face. "I am the son of a lord, not some sniveling thief who takes credit for the accomplishment of others."

"Of course, you're not," Baine said agreeably while thinking the exact opposite. "But I risked my life to get this ugly bastard's head, and I think it's only fitting that I be the one to present it to the man who requested it." He raised an eyebrow. "Don't you?"

Baine and Daholf held eyes for a moment, then with a snort, the handsome man jerked savagely on his horse's reins, turning the beast around. "Come along then. I'm sure my father will be overjoyed to meet with you."

Baine hadn't failed to notice Daholf had said that last bit sarcastically. He followed after the group of riders, not missing the looks of contempt and dislike the man's companions shot towards him. He sighed. Why couldn't things ever be easy?

Once inside the walls, Baine left the mare in the care of a bent old fellow in the outer bailey who promised he'd rub her down thoroughly and feed her well. Baine believed him, knowing instantly that his horse was in good hands by the honest and trustworthy look on the old man's face. Baine left his bow, arrow bag, and the sword he'd taken from Pembry Drake with the mare, slinging the sack containing the decomposing head over his shoulder as he followed after Daholf. He'd briefly considered wearing Drake's heavy sword while in Norhall, but in truth, he wasn't very good at wielding one like Hadrack or Jebido were. Baine's advantage in combat had always been his speed and all a sword did was slow him down.

The lord's son kept looking at the stained sack slung over Baine's shoulder enviously as they walked. "How did Pembry die?" Daholf finally asked.

"Uncomfortably," Baine replied with a straight face.

The other man frowned, absently waving a hand in annoyance at two curtsying scullery maids who'd just stepped out from an alley. "That's not what I asked," Daholf grunted as they brushed past the women. "Are you deaf or just stupid?" The lord's son looked Baine up and down, not hiding his scorn. "I once saw Pembry Drake disarm three men with his sword without breaking a sweat. So, you understand why I'm having trouble imagining a runt like you getting the better of him."

Baine just smiled, not allowing Daholf's needling to get to him. "Oh, I'm just full of surprises." He held the other man's eyes. "Maybe one day you'll find that out."

"Uh-huh," Daholf grunted doubtfully, though Baine could tell the man was surprised and a little bit confused by his lack of deference and fear. He guessed the bastard was used to intimidating people who couldn't fight back. "The last we heard, that House Agent, Odiman, was hot on Drake's trail," the lord's son added. He glanced at Baine suspiciously. "You sure you didn't just snatch the head from them when their backs were turned? You look more like a thief to me than a fighter."

Baine shrugged but held his tongue, for he knew killing the son of a lord—whether an obnoxious bore or not—wouldn't be prudent at the moment. Hopefully, Odiman was right about Lord Porten and he'd be less of an ass than his son had turned out to be. Baine was also hoping the lord was currently in good health and would live a long time, guessing that once Norhall fell into this fool's hands, there would be nowhere for the place to go but down. Besides, there was always the chance that he and Daholf would meet again in the future, somewhere less formal where they could continue the current conversation.

Daholf led Baine into the inner bailey and up to the third floor of the keep, where Lord Porten was at prayers in a large room that had been converted into a Holy House. A Daughter was giving the morning sermon, and Baine and Daholf knelt quietly in the pew behind Lord Porten, who was the only one in attendance. The priestess eyed the new arrivals with a hint of disapproval on her weathered face but did not pause in her sermon, with most of it spent railing against the North and the Sons who'd dared to support the wrong prince.

When the Daughter was finally finished, looking worn from her impassioned tirade, Lord Porten rose. He paused to say a few words to the exhausted priestess before, with a kiss to the back of her hand, he turned, finally noticing Baine and Daholf. Lord Porten Welis was surprisingly tall—almost rivaling Hadrack in height, though he was not nearly as thick-bodied. The lord's hair was grey and closely cropped to his scalp. His beard was also grey and thick, with a pair of startling bushy black eyebrows growing above his brown eyes that contrasted starkly with the rest of him. The lord's impressive eyebrows gave him something of a cross look, Baine thought, and he wondered as the man approached if Odiman had been wrong in his assessment of him.

"Ah, Daholf," Lord Porten said in a pleasant voice as the two men rose to their feet. Baine's doubts instantly fizzled away at the look of welcome and kindness crossing the man's face despite the ominous eyebrows. "It warms my heart to see you here. It's been a while since you joined me at prayers." He glanced behind his son toward the entrance. "But where is Fitzery? Why isn't that wonderful boy with you?"

Daholf couldn't hide the look of annoyance on his face. "My precious brother has gone to Bentwood, Father, if you recall? He'll be back by sundown, I expect."

A brother, Baine thought, understanding now. Clearly, there was some form of sibling rivalry going on between Daholf and this Fitzery person.

"That's right, that's right," Lord Porten agreed, nodding. "I'd forgotten all about that." He grinned good-naturedly. "Who better than Fitz to take care of that little problem in Bentwood, eh? When the gods handed out brains, they gave your brother twice as much as the rest of us." Lord Porten chuckled as he glanced at Baine, unaware that his son had flushed with anger. "And who might this handsome young lad be?"

"My name is Baine, lord," Baine said before Daholf could respond. He lifted the sack off his shoulder and placed it on the floor by Lord Porten's feet. "And I bring you a gift." On inspiration, he added, "Consider it courtesy of the Wolf of Corwick." Lord Porten's bushy eyebrows shot up in surprise before he gave his son a cautious look. Daholf was staring at Baine in confusion, but Baine ignored him. He indicated the sack. "Your problem concerning Pembry Drake has been taken care of, lord."

"I see," Lord Porten said, not looking at the sack. He was instead studying Baine with a great deal of interest. "And you say this is a gift from the Wolf? The outlaw, Hadrack?"

"Yes, lord." Baine glanced sideways at Daholf. "I wonder, lord, if I might have a moment to speak with you in private?"

"Just who do you—" Daholf began hotly.

"That will be enough, my son," Lord Porten grunted, his tone all business now. He indicated Baine. "I will speak with this man alone."

Daholf's features twisted in outrage, and Baine could tell it was taking all of the man's will not to protest further. Finally, Daholf nodded in acceptance, bowing his head. "As you wish, Father. I will be in the stables if you need me."

Baine and Lord Porten waited in silence until his son had left, sharing a knowing look. The lord finally sighed, appearing suddenly weary. "Do you have any children, Baine?" he asked.

"I believe so, lord," Baine replied. "At least, I hope I do." One of Lord Porten's unkempt eyebrows rose in an obvious question. "My wife was heavy with our first child when I saw her last, lord," Baine explained. "I expect the baby will have been born by now."

"Ah," Lord Porten said in understanding. "I only have two sons that managed to live to manhood." The tall man sighed a second time. "Unfortunately, those sons are as different as night is to day. One has nothing but blackness and distrust in his heart, and the other nothing but goodwill and sunshine." The lord shook his head. "Sadly, the man most suited for the job of ruling Norhall is not the same man who walked out of here moments ago, although the task will fall to him by default anyway."

"An unfortunate twist of fate, lord," Baine said regretfully.

"Without question," the lord responded. He shrugged. "But that is the will of the gods, my young friend, so who am I to question them?" He put a hand on Baine's shoulder, guiding him around the blood-stained sack on the floor. They sat together on a bench in the pew. "So tell me, Baine. You deliberately mentioned the Wolf just now, giving him credit for killing Pembry Drake when I know that can't possibly be true. I'd like to know why."

"I wanted to get your attention, lord," Baine answered. "Odiman told me you know the truth about Hadrack and his outlaw mission against the North."

"I do," Lord Porten said, looking thoughtful. "But I don't see why any of that matters now."

Baine blinked in confusion. "Why would it not matter, lord?"

Lord Porten looked down at his hands. "Because I just received word from Halhaven not two days ago that Hadrack of Corwick died during The Walk."

Chapter 9: The Boar That Starts It All

Two weeks later, Baine finally reached the village of Laskerly, which sat nestled in a small valley about thirty miles southwest of Witbridge Manor. The town was small—one of many in the area with a population of fewer than fifty residents—though it was well known for its four mills that lined the river nearby. The father of one of Hadrack's men—Hanley—operated one of those mills, though father and son were no longer on speaking terms. Laskerly's liege lord was named Lord Falmir, who was a despicable old bastard that was notorious for bedding any female—related to him or not—with a comely face, long hair, and anything remotely resembling tits. Luckily, Laskerly was so far off the beaten path that the lord rarely visited or paid it much mind, which was a good thing since he strongly supported The Father and Prince Tyrale. Baine knew most of the townspeople secretly favored The Mother, though they were careful not to advertise that fact to strangers or the lord's tax collector and his men when they arrived every three months to collect the levy.

Baine guided the mare down the muddy street, careful to keep his hood up and head down just in case someone recognized him. He passed The Jolly Cock—the town's only tavern—keeping his face averted away from two old men leaning against the building's exterior wall near the entrance. Baine and most of Hadrack's men had been regular customers in the Jolly Cock over the past year up until Putt had been caught cheating at dice there and almost hung by the locals. After that, Hadrack had banned any of his men from going to Laskerly, sending only his steward, Finol, for supplies when needed since he rarely drank, gambled, or showed much interest in whores.

The sun had long since slipped behind the many peaks of the Father's Spine Mountains that rose in a long line to the northwest, casting the valley and town in an eerie, premature semi-darkness. But despite full dusk arriving in what he guessed might be less than an hour, Baine pressed onward through Laskerly, choosing not to stop for the night. He knew the bulk of his remaining journey involved traveling through thick forests where any number of brigands, cutthroats, and deserters could be hiding, yet even so, he was willing to take the risk if it meant getting home quicker. Baine could feel an almost overwhelming need to hold his wife and new babe in his arms after being gone for so long, and he had no intention of letting something like a little darkness or possible threats along the trail stop him.

    He looked behind him toward the mountains, where the sky above the towering peaks was streaked with bright oranges, reds, and pinks. "I will see my wife and child before you rise again in the morning," he vowed to the retreating sun. "And woe to any fool who dares to try and stop me!"

    Baine had traveled back and forth from Laskerly to Witbridge Manor so many times in the last year that he knew it like the back of his hand—daylight or not—and because of that, he had complete confidence in his ability not to lose his way. He'd also developed an almost sixth sense when Northern patrols were nearby during the long journey from Norhall, which he would be relying on to continue to keep him safe. That talent, coupled with his intimate knowledge of the forest, gave Baine plenty of confidence that he would be home well before Flora and the baby retired for the evening.

    Once the village of Laskerly was left behind, Baine guided the mare along a well-used trail, finally reaching Barnwin's Channel—a wide, fast-flowing tributary of the mighty White Rock River. He splashed his way across the only ford around for miles, then urged the mare up a short incline on the other side, following the trail that cut through an overgrown meadow dominated by purple lavender. The rapidly weakening sun briefly slipped out from behind Mount Halas's snow-capped summit, igniting the tips of the flowers in an explosion of purple tinged with orange and gold. The sweet smell of the lavender had always lifted Baine's spirits whenever he'd passed this way in the past, and this time was no different, for it greatly reminded him of Flora.

A dark, impenetrable wall of trees rose several miles away on the horizon—the forest known as Thurston's Gulch. It was there, Baine knew, that trouble—if any—would find him. It had been within those very trees that Hadrack and Sim had come up against the outlaw Black Tomlin over a year ago. Hadrack had killed the bastard, then, being the great leader of men and the opportunist that he was, he'd somehow managed to convince Black Tomlin's little band to join him. Those men had turned out to be Putt, Tyris, Hanley, and Niko, all of whom were now valuable and indispensable members of Hadrack's Wolf Pack. The giant bald man, Anson, and the stonemason's apprentice, Cain, had also been among the outlaws, but sadly they had both been killed during Lady Shana's daring rescue from Calban Castle.

Baine thought suddenly about Hadrack's supposed death, unable to stop himself from chuckling. Lord Porten had been adamant that Hadrack had died during The Walk, but he knew better. Hadrack was like a brother to him, and if he were truly gone from this world, Baine would feel it in his very soul. He felt no such thing, which meant, as far as Baine was concerned, that Hadrack was still very much alive and no doubt shedding Northern blood somewhere.

The Overseer of Mount Halas—a man named Son Lawer—had insisted that Hadrack had slipped and fallen off The Black Way, which was an ice-covered chasm leading to the Complex. Baine had developed a healthy distrust of the Sons over the years, regardless of their station, and he knew the man had lied about Hadrack's death. The only question was, why? Lord Porten had informed him that Malo had returned to Halhaven while Jebido and the others had gone home to Witbridge Manor—which was another reason why Baine was so eager to arrive there. Hopefully, Jebido would have more information about what had happened to Hadrack and where he was now.

The biggest surprise came when Lord Porten revealed why Hadrack had gone to Mount Halas in the first place. It seemed the scholar, Rorian, who'd caused them so much trouble lately, had discovered that a second copy of the Halas Codex was hidden somewhere in the vast mountain complex. Mount Halas was protected by the North's forces, so the only feasible way to get past them had been for Hadrack and Sabina to join The Walk as pilgrims, taking the place of Rorian and his wife. Now Baine fully understood why Malo and Odiman had been so adamant that the scholar be captured at all costs. The codex was an incredibly powerful weapon, giving immense leverage to anyone who held it. As for Sabina, Baine wasn't surprised that she'd agreed to help Hadrack pose as pilgrims. After all, he'd seen how the girl had looked at his friend during the journey from Springlight to the western coast, knowing a smitten female when he saw one.

Baine looked up. He was less than fifty yards from the forest line now, and he thrust all thoughts of Hadrack and the codex aside, needing to stay alert. He unhooked his bow, keeping the arrow bag close to hand while he guided the white mare into the trees. Both man and horse were swallowed up moments later by the darkness. Baine picked his way carefully along the barely seen trail for another half an hour, all senses tuned to the forest around him. Finally, a weak moon appeared from behind a vast swathe of clouds, with the faint glow filtering through the branches overhead, allowing him to increase the mare's pace.

The incessant drone of insects filled Baine's ears, but they weren't the only sounds he could hear, for the night was filled with nocturnal activity. Snakes and small rodents slithered and scurried through the leaves around him, while an owl out hunting them occasionally hooted from the trees. Bigger animals such as hares, foxes, raccoons, and possums darted here and there through the undergrowth, with Baine catching the odd glimpse of shining eyes or furry bodies. A lonesome frog croaked somewhere off to his left, answered a moment later by the faint cry of a coyote lamenting far to the east.

Baine heard the trickling of a stream ahead long before he reached it, knowing as the mare splashed through the water that he was now a third of the way to Witbridge Manor. The thought warmed his heart. He pictured the look of joy on Flora's face when she saw him, then frowned. He hadn't given much thought to it, but it suddenly dawned on him that Jebido would have informed everyone at the manor that he was dead. Baine felt a moment of discomfort, feeling a niggling doubt come over him that he desperately tried to squash. Flora was forthright and honest when dealing with people, but she was also a hugely practical woman. Had she, on learning of his death, returned to her previous ways to help alleviate the stress of the men? Baine instantly shook his head, angry at himself for even contemplating such a thing. All Flora would be doing now is grieving and concentrating on the babe. To think anything else of her was unforgivable and wrong of him.

Baine felt ashamed of himself, thrusting any thoughts of his wife's possible infidelity away while, in a part of his mind, a faint whisper sounded—*But in her eyes, you are long dead, lad, so where's the betrayal?* He snorted in annoyance, focusing on the trail. He'd come to an area of the forest thick with oak, alder, and twisted beech trees. A large, rotten stump stood along the trail to Baine's right, one he knew well. This was the place where Hadrack's infamous run-in with Black Tomlin had occurred. Baine decided this was a good time to stop and stretch his legs, for he'd been riding for many hours without a break. Besides, he needed to walk off his doubts and get his mind straight.

Baine halted the mare and dismounted, leaving her reins trailing on the ground while she happily cropped at the grass growing along the trail. He kept his bow, eyeing the trees suspiciously as he walked back and forth, getting the kinks out of his legs and back. Finally satisfied that he was alone and there were no threats, Baine leaned his bow against a tree and began going through a series of exercises that loosened his muscles and got his blood flowing. It was a trick he'd learned from Haverty the apothecary during his recovery from a broken leg, and he had to admit the strange movements had helped keep him limber, fast, and strong.

When he was finished, Baine retrieved his bow, breathing evenly with a fine sheen of sweat covering his skin. He felt much better, replenished in both body and mind, as he headed back for the mare, who had wandered off down the trail during her grazing. A branch snapped in the trees to Baine's left, and he hesitated, already reaching for an arrow just as the largest wild boar he'd ever seen stepped out onto the trail. The mare's head shot up in alarm, and before Baine could do anything, she bolted away, disappearing down the trail.

Baine cursed under his breath as the boar sniffed the air, staring at him suspiciously while effectively blocking his path. He moved very slowly and drew an arrow from his bag, then carefully nocked it, praying to The Mother that he wouldn't be forced to use it. Baine wondered nervously if an arrow could even bring down the monstrous creature. He knew if the beast did charge, he'd only have one shot to find out. The boar snorted, turning its head back and forth as it tried to decide what Baine was. Baine knew boars had notoriously bad eyesight, and he waited, holding his breath. Most wild boars will avoid conflict if given a chance, usually only becoming aggressive if they feel threatened or cornered. This boar was a male, Baine guessed, judging by its immense size and formidable tusks growing from its lower jaw. He estimated the beast to be six feet long and weigh at least five hundred pounds.

Baine glanced at the nearest tree, a hundred-foot-tall black alder. Could he scurry up it in time before the animal reached him? Pounding hooves suddenly sounded from down the trail, and the boar snorted in alarm, turning its head to look that way with one eye while keeping the other fixed warily on Baine. The mare was returning. A moment later, the boar headed west into the trees with a swish of its tail, disappearing into the foliage while Baine sighed with relief. He lowered his bow just as the mare hove into sight at a run, then cursed again, for he could hear many more hooves than just hers approaching. Baine ducked into the trees to the east, watching as a large group of riders burst into a patch of moonlight, the lead one leaning over to snag the white mare's bridle. Baine groaned for he'd become quite attached to that horse, which he'd decided to name Pretty Girl.

The lead rider managed to grab the mare's reins and yanked on them savagely, bringing her to a halt less than fifty feet from where Baine crouched. "Anyone see him?" the man grunted as the rest of the mounted men slowed their horses.

Most of the riders' faces were hidden by the shadows, though Baine could clearly see the leader's features. That man was big—almost as big as Hadrack—with a long beard hanging down to his saddle that gleamed like gold in the moonlight. Baine thought there was something odd about the man's beard, but he couldn't determine what it was.

"No sign of him, Jark," a second man growled. "You want us to search the trees? The bastard probably stopped to take a piss and his horse got spooked. He's bound to be around here somewhere."

The big man named Jark hesitated, then finally shrugged. "No, there's not much point in looking for him in the dark. I doubt he's worth it anyway, whoever he is." Jark chuckled, the sound deep and guttural. "Besides, I'd say we've made our money and shed enough blood for one night, don't you lads?"

A chorus of cheers rang out before the big man handed the mare's reins to someone else, then kicked his horse into motion. Baine watched bitterly as they trotted away with Pretty Girl in tow. Unfortunately, there wasn't much he could do to stop them. He waited until they were lost from sight, then stepped back onto the trail and continued on his way.

I'm going to miss that mare, Baine thought with sadness. *Maybe someday soon, I'll meet up with that big bastard again and get her back when the odds are more in my favor.*

It was hours later when Baine finally crested the ridge overlooking Witbridge Manor. He paused there as he stared across the valley to where the holding stood, not believing what his eyes were telling him. The village that he remembered was gone, reduced to a smoking ruin, while inside the manor, flames lit up the night sky. Baine could hear the faint echoes of men shouting and cursing within the walls as they fought the fires. Without even being aware, he ran down the slope, tripping and skidding over rocks before reaching the valley floor. He sprinted across the fields and onto the narrow road that led to the devastated village—a small dark figure unnoticed among the tragedy unfolding around him.

Baine grit his teeth as he ran, fighting a stitch in his side as he hobbled past crumpled and burned bodies lying among the houses, thinking only of finding Flora and the babe. He finally reached the smithy and paused there, unable to continue with his chest heaving and his side howling in protest. An enormous form lay spreadeagled in the middle of the road. Baine recognized Ermos, the blacksmith, even though an axe had caved in the right side of his face. Ermos' wife, Samay, crouched on her knees above him, her head pressed against the corpse's barrel chest as she wept. Three of the blacksmith's young children knelt around her, crying and clutching at each other in confusion. There was no sign of the man's oldest son, Ira, and Baine guessed that he was most likely dead, as the boy was as headstrong as he was brave and was unlikely to have run away.

Samay looked up then as if sensing Baine's presence, but her eyes held no recognition of him, only grief and agony. She looked away moments later, collapsing across the blacksmith with her thin shoulders shaking with emotion. Baine started to run again, pressing one hand to his side as he raced up the slope toward the manor. The gate lay askew in the entrance, hanging by one warped hinge. Baine slipped inside, stepping over the body of a man he didn't recognize. Shadowy figures formed a line in front of him, leading from the well to the stable as men and women passed slopping buckets of water from one person to the other. Sim was at the end of the chain, flinging water on the burning roof and walls. Jebido was on the other end of the line, working feverishly to haul up buckets of water from the well and hand them off. Baine could see his friend's silver hair and beard glowing in the firelight, though his face and clothing were covered in soot.

Baine ran over to Jebido, putting a hand on his shoulder and spinning him around. "Where's Flora?" he shouted over the roar of the flames. Jebido just stared at Baine in shock, his eyes going round as he dropped the bucket of water he held. Baine shook his friend. "Where is she, Jebido? Where is Flora?"

"By the gods," Jebido managed to gasp. He reached out a shaking hand, pressing it against Baine's chest as if to see if he was real. "Is that really you, lad? I can't believe it!"

"It's me, Jebido," Baine insisted, grasping Jebido's hand. "I'm alive. Now, where are my wife and child?"

"Oh, my poor boy," Jebido whispered, pulling Baine to him and wrapping his arms around him. "I'm so sorry, lad. I'm so sorry. They're both dead, and it's all my fault."

Chapter 10: Hadrack Will Understand

Baine barely noticed the steady rain falling, the clinging muck he knelt in, nor the wind whipping at his cloak. It was still dark out, though dawn was now only a few hours away. He neither realized nor cared. Baine remained where he was, as still as a statue with his knees pressed into the fresh dirt at the edge of his wife's and newly born son's grave. His hands hung limply by his sides while he stared in despair at the round wooden marker he'd pounded into the ground at the head of the grave hours ago. A lantern sat on a flat stone to his left, sputtering and flickering in the wind, though the faint light wasn't enough for him to clearly make out the words cut into the wood. Baine didn't need to see them anyway, for he'd carved those words himself and each one was forever etched in his mind.

> *Here lies Flora and baby Hadrack*
> *Wife and son of Baine*
> *I will not rest*
> *I will not eat*
> *I will not sleep*
> *Until their killers pay*

Baine bowed his head and closed his eyes. He was so, so tired. *There is nothing left for me now*, he thought bitterly. *My soul is broken. First Nelsun and Sunna, and now this.* He sniffed, wiping the double lines of snot mixed with rain from his upper lip with the back of his hand, though his eyes were dry and burning like twin coals in a roaring fire. There were no more tears left inside him, having all been shed over the many hours he'd knelt in vigil by the grave. Baine had dug that grave himself, refusing any help from his friends, who, to a man, had reluctantly stood by and watched from afar despite the downpour. Baine had felt nothing but sorrow and pity emanating from the silent watchers—though none more so than Jebido. But the pain of loss he felt inside couldn't be blunted by kind words or gestures, no matter how much his friends wished otherwise. There was only one thing left that would help him now, Baine knew, and that was to wreak bloody vengeance upon those who had taken Flora and his son from him.

Until their killers pay

That was the last line Baine had written on the marker with his knife, and each letter burned hot and feverish in his mind. Now, more than ever, he understood Hadrack's unquenching thirst for revenge against those who had murdered his father and sister. Hadrack and Baine had been close almost from the moment they'd met as boys, bonded at first by need and then friendship, followed by mutual respect and unquestioning brotherly love. But now they shared something more, a grief and inner fury that few ever experience and fewer still could possibly understand.

"May I wait with you, lad?" a hesitant voice asked behind him. Baine didn't bother to turn. It was Jebido, of course. The others had all left one by one as the hours passed, returning to the smoldering manor. But not Jebido. Baine didn't bother answering his friend, knowing the older man wouldn't go away even if he refused his request. Jebido was just as stubborn as he was loyal. Baine heard the sound of his friend's boots sloshing through the mud and water a moment later, and he had to force himself not to moan out loud in despair when he felt a gentle hand rest on his shoulder. "I am truly sorry, Baine. No words can properly express how much."

Baine nodded, knowing it was true, though he couldn't bring himself to speak. Not yet, anyway.

"Are you coming in out of the rain soon?" Jebido asked kindly. "You're soaked to the skin, lad."

Baine just shook his head.

"Can I get you anything, then? Something to eat, perhaps? Some ale?"

Baine shook his head a second time, staring at the mound of rain-soaked earth as rivers of muddy water trickled down from the rounded crest.

"Will you at least let me get you some dry clothing?"

Baine shook his head once again.

An awkward silence broken only by the wind and driving rain rose between them then, until finally, Jebido sighed. "I shouldn't have left the manor. I don't know what I was thinking. I just, well—"

Baine finally stirred, moved by the intense heartache and self-recrimination in his friend's voice. He half-turned, glancing up at Jebido as the rain slapped against his unprotected face. "It's not your fault," he managed to say, though, in his heart, he couldn't deny the bitterness he felt toward his friend. By riding away from the manor to go off on a wild goose chase, Jebido had left Witbridge weak and ripe for the taking.

"If only that were true," Jebido replied sadly as he squeezed Baine's shoulder. "But we both know differently. Even so, I thank you for your kind words. The Mother knows I wouldn't blame you for wanting to gut me over this after what you've been through these past weeks."

Baine closed his eyes, then rubbed a hand down his face, slicking away the rain. Finally, he stood wearily, turning to his friend. "You did what you thought was right at the time, Jebido. None of us can foresee the future. You know that just as well as I do. There were too many of the bastards, and even if you and the others had been here, the result would most likely have been the same. The only difference is I'd be mourning more loved ones and digging more graves right now." He put a hand on Jebido's shoulder. "I forgive you, my friend, so stop blaming yourself."

For some reason, Baine felt better the moment he'd voiced his forgiveness, feeling his animosity toward Jebido slipping away. It was easy to attach blame after the fact, he knew, and he hadn't been here; Jebido had. If he'd learned what his friend had, Baine guessed the chances were good he would have done the very same thing too.

Jebido took a deep breath, clearly fighting tears as he shook his head regretfully. "I should have known it wasn't Hadrack out there, Baine. I should have thought things through first. But instead, I rode off like a fool when I heard that someone had seen the Outlaw of Corwick near here. It never occurred to me that it might be an imposter, but I should—"

"You thought Hadrack was dead all this time," Baine finished for him. "And me as well. You'd lost both of us, Jebido, and the thought that one of us might still be alive somewhere was too much for you to ignore. How could you? I understand, believe me, for I would have done the same thing if it were me."

Jebido just stared back, looking at a loss for words for one of the very few times in his life. Finally, the older man reached out, grasping Baine by the crown of his rain-soaked hair. He drew him closer, pressing his forehead to Baine's. "What a man you have become. I am so proud of you, lad. I know Hadrack is too."

The two men stood that way for a long time until Baine finally drew back. He could feel his face hardening as he thought about the men who'd taken his family from him—the same men he now knew who'd stolen Pretty Girl earlier that evening. "Tell me about them again."

Jebido frowned. "I already told you everything I know."

"Tell me again," Baine said softly.

Jebido sighed. "We didn't get back until the attack was over, so like I said before, I didn't see them. But from what I heard from the survivors, they were led by a big man with a blond beard who called himself the Outlaw of Corwick." Baine nodded. That would have been the man who'd grabbed the mare's bridle, Jark. "Those that saw him say he's terrifying to behold," Jebido continued. "With human bones knotted in his beard and crazed eyes."

Baine nodded again, understanding now why the man's beard had looked odd to him. "How did they know about the cache?"

Jebido spread his arms helplessly. "I can't imagine. But somehow, they knew just where to look."

"Probably because somebody told them where it was," Baine said in a gruff voice.

Jebido stroked his wet beard as he thought. "You're talking about a traitor? Here, at Witbridge?"

"Do you have a better explanation for how it could have happened?" Baine asked. "As far as anyone knows, Lord Alwin is nothing but a pathetic cripple with bandages on his face and a bent back, banished here by Daughter Gernet. No sane person would expect a man like that to have a horde of coins hidden under the keep's floorboards, least of all our imposter outlaw. And you know just as well as I do that none of the villagers had any clue their lord was really the Outlaw of Corwick. Hadrack was always careful about that. Which means the only explanation left is we were betrayed by someone close to us—someone from the inside who knew all about the gold."

Jebido shook his head stubbornly. "I can't believe that. They all swore an oath to him, even the women."

Baine snorted. "Gold has a way of overcoming a man's loyalty, Jebido. At least for some people, anyway."

Jebido pursed his lips. "Any idea who it might have been?"

Baine shrugged. "No, though I'd obviously rule out Flora, and of course, Margot."

Jebido's bushy eyebrows rose. "What makes you so sure about her?"

"Flora told me she worships Hadrack after what he did for them," Baine explained. "She'd never betray him. Not for anything."

Jebido started to reply, then hesitated when he saw Niko hurrying toward them. He held a small piece of parchment up in his hand. "A carrier pigeon just arrived, Jebido," Niko said breathlessly. "It carries Daughter Gernet's seal."

Jebido glanced at Baine worriedly, then held out his hand for the tiny scroll. He quickly broke the seal and unrolled it, then frowned as he tried to decipher what was written. Hadrack had insisted both Jebido and Baine learn to read and write, but though Baine had become somewhat proficient in the last year, Jebido's ability was sadly lacking.

Baine knew Jebido was quite sensitive about his struggles, so rather than embarrass him, he held out his hand. "Don't tell me what it says," he said. "I'd like to read it for myself." Jebido couldn't hide his relief as he handed over the message.

Baine studied the tiny, scribbled writing, bending over to protect the parchment from the rain.

Hadrack alive, captured by the North and taken to Gandertown. Escaped. Whereabouts now unknown. Might be on his way back to Witbridge Manor. If so, tell him I MUST SEE HIM! Great things are afoot! Daughter Gernet

Baine hesitated, then reread the message out loud for Jebido, who didn't even bother pretending that he already knew what it said after hearing the first line.

Jebido whistled when Baine had finished reciting the entire message. "Gandertown? Why in the name of The Mother did they take Hadrack there?"

"A damn good question," Baine muttered as he rolled the parchment back up. "And more to the point, why didn't they just kill him?"

Jebido shrugged. "Knowing Hadrack, I'm sure he'll be here soon and we can ask him that together."

Baine pressed the scroll into Jebido's hands. "No, you can ask him because I won't be here."

Jebido blinked in surprise. "What do you mean you won't be here?" His face darkened as he studied Baine. "You're not stupid enough to be thinking about going after those bastards on your own, are you?" Baine said nothing, staring with unblinking resolve at his friend. Jebido finally snorted. "You fool. What good will getting yourself killed do?"

The rain had begun to lessen while they talked, and now it stopped altogether, with the hint of dawn beginning to show in the east. Baine knew it was time to go. He brushed past Jebido. "What choice do I have?" he growled. "They murdered my family."

Jebido reached out and grabbed Baine's arm, stopping him from walking away. "You can wait until Hadrack gets here," he said. "That's the right choice. We'll do this thing together when he gets back."

Baine shook his head. "No, we won't because we have no idea if Hadrack is even on his way here at all. That message from Daughter Gernet just assumes he's coming back to Witbridge. She doesn't know for sure any more than you or I do. But what I do know is every minute I wait around here means those bastards are getting that much further away. I need to go after them while their trail is still warm."

"Then I'm coming with you," Jebido said stubbornly.

Baine sighed, gently removing his friend's hand from his arm. "No, you're not." He gestured toward the destroyed village and smoking manor. "Your place is here, Jebido, helping the survivors and repairing our defenses."

"But—"

"No buts," Baine said firmly. He softened his tone. "I've always looked up to you ever since I was a boy, Jebido. I'm sure you know that. All I've ever wanted was to make you proud of me."

"I am proud of you," Jebido protested. "I told you that very thing not five minutes ago."

"I know you did," Baine said in agreement. "And trust me, hearing it from you means a lot to me. But we both know Hadrack has always been the one everybody looks to for answers, including you. He's the one constantly pulling our asses out of the fire, and believe me, I appreciate who and what he is. But this time, it's different." Baine gestured to the grave, his voice catching. "That's my wife and son under that dirt, Jebido. And I'll be damned if I let you or Hadrack avenge them in my stead. That's my job, and I intend to see it through to the bitter end—alone." Baine put his hand on Jebido's shoulder. "Do you understand?"

"I do, lad," Jebido said regretfully. Baine could see the fire of protest dying in his friend's eyes. "But I just got you back from the dead—both of you. So you need to understand how hard it is for me to let you go. I'm afraid that this time I'll never see you again."

Baine smiled as he patted Jebido's shoulder fondly. "I have no intentions of dying anytime soon, my friend. Trust me. There's still too much for the three of us to do in this world."

Baine turned then, striding away. "What about your theory that we have a traitor at Witbridge?" Jebido called out to his back. "I could really use your help talking to the men. They're more open with you than they are with me."

Baine paused and looked over his shoulder. "I don't have time for that right now, so you'll have to handle it yourself. I'm sure you'll figure out who it was eventually." He grimaced as a thought struck him. "But don't kill the bastard whatever you do. I'll deal with whoever it is when I get back."

"And what about Hadrack?" Jebido asked doubtfully. "What am I supposed to tell him when he gets here? You know he's going to be furious with me for letting you go."

"No, he won't be," Baine said with confidence. He grinned sadly. "Because Hadrack knows better than anyone alive why I have to do this alone."

PART TWO

VENGEANCE

Chapter 11: The Hunt Begins

It was almost midday by the time Baine made his way back to Laskerly. He was hoping since the outlaws had originally been heading west toward the town when he'd run into them that it had been their destination all along. Baine knew the kind of men he was after—nothing but unintelligent, dishonorable, merciless beasts dredged up from the cesspools of humanity. Yet, even so, creatures like that were almost always predictable in the end, which was what he was counting on. With blood on their hands and ill-gotten gold in their pockets, Baine was betting the outlaws would be itching to spend some of that coin on ale, venison, and whores at the first opportunity. The Jolly Cock was close and could provide all three, although the ale was watered down, the food horrible, and the few pitiful creatures selling their bodies inside were mostly pox-ridden and well past their prime. Putt had once joked that the ale in The Jolly Cock tasted like the sweat pooling between the king's hairy arse cheeks, though the red-bearded outlaw never could explain how he knew that.

Baine doubted the imposter's men would care all that much about the tavern's poor offerings, giddy as they probably were from the sudden riches they had just stolen. But, even if he was wrong and they'd just ridden through or around Laskerly without stopping to enjoy themselves, he was hoping somebody would have seen which way they went. That many men on horseback were hard to miss. Baine knew it might be a long shot, but he had to start somewhere. He paused the feisty three-year-old brown mare he rode beneath the welcoming spread of a giant oak tree just outside the town's limits, grateful for the shade. The day had turned hot and sticky after the long night of rain.

Baine studied the almost deserted street, frowning with disappointment, for as he'd feared, no horses were tethered outside The Jolly Cock. "What do you think, eh girl?" he said to the mare. "Shall we go ask some questions of these fine folks?"

The horse's name was Piper, named that because she tended to breathe with a musical, high-pitched whistling sound when galloping. Baine had ridden her from Springlight to the western coast while they chased after Rorian, and he had found her eager to please and tireless. He'd been forced to leave the mare behind in the capable hands of Sim, who'd returned to Witbridge Manor with the entire company's horses while Hadrack and the rest of his men had sailed away on *Sea-Dragon*. Baine was glad to be reacquainted with Piper, although a part of him still pined for the white mare. Hopefully, he'd get her back soon.

Baine clucked his tongue, sending Piper out from the shade and back into the scorching sunlight. His cloak lay rolled up behind his saddle, and he was dressed in loose-fitting black trousers, a black tunic, and black, sleeveless leather armor. He also wore black leather bracers that covered his wrists to his elbows and a pair of matching leather greaves that protected his shins. Baine's bow was strapped over his shoulder, with his stuffed arrow bag hanging off his saddle close to his right hand. He'd replenished all his knives from his stock at Witbridge, carrying one openly in a sheath at his waist, two hidden in slits beneath his bracers, and two more fitted into special compartments in his boots. He hadn't bothered to bring Pembry Drake's sword along, having given it to Jebido instead. The damn thing would only get in the way, anyway. Baine was ready for war.

He guided the mare into town, stopping her on the street outside The Jolly Cock. The tavern was a rundown, wattle and daube three-story structure with peeling paint and a wooden shingle roof that was badly in need of repairs. Smoke rose lazily from a single stone chimney on the building's western side, with the weathered shingles surrounding it slowly caving inwards on sagging rafters. The muddy street had mostly dried up in the intense heat despite the previous night's rain, leaving only a few shrinking puddles and hardened, uneven ruts crisscrossing the cracked ground. An ox-pulled cart filled with straw bumped and rolled past the tavern, with the man leading the ox by a frayed rope giving Baine a disinterested look. Several young boys and a girl of no more than four years old sat perched on top of the pile of straw. The little girl stuck her tongue out at Baine when he glanced at her, then giggled, hiding her face in the chest of the nearest boy.

Baine turned his attention back to the tavern, not surprised to see the same two old men he'd noticed the day before leaning against the wall, one to either side of the entrance. They watched him expressionlessly from the shadows cast by the tavern's rickety veranda roof. Baine dismounted, tying his horse to a pitted brass ring attached by rope to one of the posts supporting the roof. He unhooked his arrow bag and clipped it to his belt—a move that the two old men clearly hadn't failed to notice. The silent watchers shared a look.

"Hot day," the man to the left of the doorway finally stated as Baine climbed the stairs, though he wasn't entirely certain whether the words were directed toward him or not.

"Damn hot," the other agreed. He flicked his eyes to Baine. "Haven't seen you around for a while, lad. You or the rest of your crew, for that matter, except for that uppity fellow, Finol. I thought maybe Lord Cripple had sent you all off to fight. Not too many young men left around here these days since the war started."

Baine nodded but said nothing. The locals contemptuously referred to Hadrack as *Lord Cripple*, though if anyone ever learned the truth about him, Baine was certain their attitudes would change in a hurry. He studied the two men—brothers who looked almost identical— though he knew one was several years younger than the other. Both men were dirty and disheveled, dressed in rags with long unkempt silver hair and beards. The brother who had just spoken was named Tholex Waffen, Baine remembered, and the other one was called Fosco. The Waffen brothers claimed to be hunters, but in the time Baine had spent in the area, he'd rarely seen them do anything except stand by The Jolly Cock's door begging for coins so they could buy ale.

Baine stepped up onto the veranda, relieved to be in the shade. "I'm looking for some men," he stated bluntly.

The brothers chuckled knowingly before Fosco said in a sarcastic tone, "You don't say?" He motioned to Baine's bow and arrow bag. "Looks to me like you're getting ready to take on the entire Southern army all by yourself, lad."

"A large group," Baine continued softly. "Led by a big fellow with a blond beard. He might have had some bones or something tied in it. Goes by the name of the Outlaw of Corwick."

Fosco and Tholex shared a look. "They was here," Tholex admitted. "Didn't know that's who it was, though. They drank their fill, humped some whores, then rode off about four or five hours ago."

"Rode off where?" Baine demanded.

The brothers shrugged at the same time. "Don't know," Fosco replied, though he'd said it with his open palm held out. "My memory ain't what it used to be, you see. My brother's neither, for that matter."

"Kinda comes and goes," Tholex added with a grin, his eyes alight with greed.

Baine took two determined strides forward until he was face to face with Tholex. The smell coming off him was overwhelming. Baine put his hand to the hilt of his knife and drew it slowly. He twirled it expertly in the palm of his hand several times. "So, which is it right now?" he asked. "Is it coming, or is it going?" Tholex opened his mouth, and Baine added, "Bear in mind that it's been a long night and I'm in no mood for games, so answer carefully."

Tholex hesitated at the look of deadly promise on Baine's face, the weathered skin above his beard turning white. He held up his hands defensively. "Now, we want no trouble, lad. We was just hoping for a little charity, is all."

"Consider the fact that you're both still breathing charity enough," Baine growled. "Now, which way did they go?" Tholex hesitated, then reluctantly pointed a shaking hand southward while his brother bobbed his head repeatedly in agreement, looking thoroughly frightened. "Did they say exactly where they were heading?" Baine asked.

"No," Tholex admitted. He wiggled a grimy thumb back and forth between himself and his brother. "But then again, they didn't bother talking to us much."

"Wouldn't give us nothing, neither," Fosco said bitterly. "And them flush with gold. It just ain't fair."

"No, it isn't," Baine grunted dismissively before he sheathed his knife, opened the door, and brushed past the two men. "For a lot of people."

The Jolly Cock looked just as rundown on the inside as it did on the outside. Baine paused in the entrance, waiting for his eyes to adjust to the gloom. He wasn't expecting any trouble, but he dropped a hand to his arrow bag regardless as he surveyed the room. The place was almost empty except for three grey-haired men playing dice at one of the round, battered tables. Another man stood leaning into the huge open fireplace at the back of the room, stirring something in an iron pot that hung over glowing coals. Baine recognized the owner, Rooni Suha. He wiped the sweat from his forehead, relaxing somewhat. He'd found it almost unbearably hot outside, but with the fire, the interior of the building seemed even worse, though no one else in the room seemed to be all that affected by it.

Baine strode toward the dice players, glancing at the stairs that led to rooms on the second floor. A whore was leaning on the railing overlooking the main floor, staring down at him with eyes filled with resigned disinterest. Baine didn't recognize her, guessing she was new since the last time he'd been here. He hesitated halfway across the room, then switched directions, heading for the stairs. The worn plank steps creaked beneath his weight with every step, and when he reached the landing, he nodded to the woman. The whore turned to face him, her features blank and hard. Baine guessed she was probably in her early thirties, though with the hard life she'd clearly lived, it was difficult to be certain.

"At least your handsome and look reasonably clean," the woman grunted, looking Baine up and down. She indicated a doorway to her right. "That one. But you have to pay first."

Baine studied the whore, noting her sunken eyes, lank hair, and yellow teeth. Her dress had once been white, he guessed, but was now a dirty grey and splattered with stains that he preferred not to think about. Baine held up a hand as the whore turned toward the closed door. "That's not what I'm here for," he said. "I just want to talk."

The woman turned back, confusion in her eyes now. "Talk? You don't want to hump me?"

"No," Baine said. He fished in his pocket, withdrawing a Jorq that had been cut in two. He flicked the half piece of gold to the whore. "All I want from you is information, nothing else."

The whore caught the gold deftly, glancing slyly down to the lower floor, where the tavern owner continued to stir the iron pot over the coals. She looked relieved that he seemed oblivious to them. She turned back to Baine. "What kind of information?"

"The Outlaw of Corwick kind," Baine answered. "I understand he and his men were here earlier."

"There were a bunch of men here," the whore agreed cautiously. "Though I don't know nothing about no Outlaw of Corwick."

"Did you speak with any of them?" Baine asked.

The whore nodded. "Of course. That's what Rooni pays me for, after all. That and humping." She shuddered. "Nasty, filthy bastards, the lot of them. Got no manners. Stick it in, grunt and groan till it's over without a second thought about me. Why, I remember a time not that long ago when a lady of my persuasion was looked upon with respect. But ever since the war began, things have—

"So, at least some of them used your services, yes?" Baine cut in impatiently.

The whore smiled, which surprisingly lit up her face. Baine realized she could be quite attractive despite her teeth, depending on the circumstances and the lighting. A moment later, the woman's smile faded and her dull, listless features returned. "Of course they did. I just told you that." She lifted her head proudly. "I made Rooni a good handful of Jorqs. Lost track of how many of those bastards climbed on top of me. They just kept coming in my room one after the other, all giggly and making jokes about who was bigger down there." The whore cupped a hand around her mouth as if telling him a secret. "Truth is, none of them were much to write home about except for one young lad. Now that one, he was special. Had himself a fine, handsome face and a hard willy that nearly broke me in half."

"Did any of these men say where they were heading from here?" Baine asked hopefully.

The whore pursed her lips, looking up at the ceiling as she thought. "No, not that I recall." She hesitated. "Though the handsome one did call out a name when he spilled his seed." The woman smiled wearily. "You wouldn't believe how many times that happens."

Baine frowned. "That's all?"

The whore shrugged. "I'm afraid so." She suddenly looked cautious, closing her fist protectively around the half Jorq. "You're not going to take this back or tell Rooni about it, are you? I earned it fair and square."

Baine sighed, disappointed as he shook his head. "No, it's all yours. And I won't say anything to Rooni." He turned to go, then hesitated as he looked back at the whore. "What name did that handsome lad call out?"

The whore chuckled. "Elyn Arror of all people. Can you believe it? Talk about having unrealistic expectations."

"And who might that be?" Baine asked, perplexed. He'd never heard the name before.

"Why, Lady Elyn of Caray Castle, of course, silly. Lord Falmir's new bride."

Baine mulled that over for a moment. "Did their leader, the big man with the blond beard, use your services?"

The whore shook her head. "No, he didn't seem interested in me or the other girl working, Samma. All he wanted was some food and beer. Nothing else."

"Is Samma still here?"

"No, she left about an hour ago. Got a young babe at home."

Baine thanked the whore, then returned to the main floor. The owner, Rooni, was gone, presumably into a back room, leaving the three men drinking and playing dice as the only occupants. Baine decided he'd question them next, then speak with the owner. As he drew closer to the gamblers, he realized he knew one of them; it was Hanley's father, Nute Wyne. Baine and the miller had spoken on occasion in the past, exchanging a few words here and there but that was all. Baine had found him to be a little curt and impatient at times, but he seemed a decent man overall, despite what Hanley claimed to the contrary.

Baine approached, waiting for Nute to cast the dice he was shaking vigorously in his right hand. The men were playing a game Baine knew well—Passes Ten—a favorite of his. Nute rolled, with the three dice adding up to a total of twelve. Both the miller and the man sitting to his right cheered, while a balding, grey-haired fellow with brown age spots on his scalp sitting opposite them groaned. The bald man grumbled something under his breath, then pushed a small stack of chipped fragments of coins toward the other two men. Baine waited, knowing better than to interrupt as the three men put in their stakes for the next round. The game was relatively simple, and though there were only three players at the moment, any amount could join in.

Baine had personally been involved in games of Passes Ten with twenty or more players, and despite his purpose, he felt drawn to what was happening. One man was always the banker in the game, alternating between rolls. If whoever controlled the dice rolled for a score under ten, everyone in the game was required to give their stake to the banker. If the dice came up more than ten, then the banker was obligated to hand back double the original stake to each player. Baine had played the game numerous times with Jebido and Hadrack. And though he liked to pretend he was far ahead of the other two in winnings, he knew in reality that it was Jebido. The old bastard had an uncanny knack for Passes Ten, always knowing when to bet big or small, depending on the roller. Baine had always found it exceptionally frustrating.

Nute looked up after he'd placed his wager, frowning when he noticed Baine standing there. "Well, what do you know? Baine, is it?"

"Yes, sir," Baine said.

"Been a while since I've seen you around, lad. Care to join us? The ale isn't half bad today."

"It tastes like horse piss," the bald man said moodily. "As usual."

"Thank you, no," Baine said. "Do you know where those men who rode into town earlier were heading?"

Nute paused, taking a long drink from his mug. He smacked his lips afterward, ignoring the dark look the bald man gave him. The miller shrugged. "No, lad, can't say that I do. I heard about them, but they were gone before I arrived." He glanced at his companions. "Either of you talk to them?"

The bald man just shook his head, with his eyes fixated on the coin chips in the center of the table. The second man took up the dice, shaking them as he looked at Baine. "South, I heard."

"I heard that too," Baine said. "But south covers a lot of land."

"You looking for the Outlaw?"

Baine glanced to his right, where The Jolly Cock's owner had appeared through an open doorway with a small cask under one beefy arm.

"Yes," Baine said. "The bastards raided Lord Alwin's manor last night. Killed a bunch of women and children." Nute Wyne cursed, a sudden look of concern crossing his features. "Your son is fine," Baine added, reassuring the miller. "A couple of scratches, that's all."

Nute looked away, smoothing his features and feigning indifference. "That deserter isn't my son. Not anymore. He's just lucky Lord Cripple has vouched for him, or some of Lord Falmir's soldiers would have hung him by now."

Baine focused back on the owner of the tavern. "Do you know where these men were heading?"

"Word I heard from Samma is the band was breaking up and going their separate ways," Rooni said. Baine groaned, knowing the bastards could be scattered in every direction by now. The tavern owner moved to the weathered bar, grunting as he set the cask on the scarred surface. He paused there, leaning on the wood. "I'm sorry to hear about Witbridge, Baine, but it's a war out there, after all. These things happen."

"They killed my wife and baby son," Baine growled, annoyed by the man's lack of empathy.

The tavern owner sighed. "Damn, lad. I didn't know that. Listen, you might want to check with Widow Byrne. She's got a fellow over there who was in a bad way, last I heard. He came in with the outlaws—got some cold steel through the guts, it seems." Rooni shrugged. "He might already be dead for all I know, but it's worth checking out."

Baine felt sudden hope. "Where can I find this woman?"

"Lives on the outside of town," Nute answered, sounding distracted now as the bald man shook the dice. "Just go west until you see a copse of birch trees. Got herself a little house in the middle." He hesitated, glancing sideways at Baine. "You're sure the boy is all right?"

"I swear it," Baine said. "Hanley is well thought of in Witbridge. He's the lord's apprentice steward now."

"Apprentice steward, huh?" Nute grunted doubtfully, though Baine could tell he was secretly pleased. "Will wonders never cease?"

Baine found the copse Nute had described easily. He left Piper tied to one of the many tall birches growing along the treeline, then followed a narrow pathway of chipped stone until he came to a small clearing. A low sod house with a thatch roof stood in the center of the clearing, with a woman sitting on a stool outside the building busy plucking feathers from a goose. She looked up as Baine approached, showing no signs of fear. The widow's grey hair was piled on top of her head, and her eyes were light blue and intelligent. Baine guessed her to be around forty years old.

"You'll be here about the wounded boy, I imagine," the widow said, not stopping in her task. A yellow mongrel lay at her feet, staring longingly at the dead goose with intense concentration.

"I am," Baine confirmed. He glanced at the house. "Is he still alive?"

"He is," the widow said. She paused to study Baine with knowing eyes. "But I'm guessing not for much longer, eh?"

Baine leaned on his bow. "Is that going to be a problem?"

The widow chuckled, resuming her defeathering. "He paid me gold to tend to his wound, which I did." She glanced at Baine again. "But there ain't enough gold in the world to make me try and stop a man with a look on his face like you're wearing right now."

"I appreciate the courtesy," Baine said. He nodded to the woman, then headed for the house.

"Mind telling me what that fool child in there did?" the widow asked, not looking up.

Baine leaned his bow and arrow bag against the wall of the house, then paused in the open doorway to look back at her. "He and his friends murdered my wife and son last night."

The widow pursed her lips, nodding her head sadly. "Can't say as I'm surprised." She looked up then, meeting Baine's eyes. "Try not to get blood everywhere if you can. I just changed the rushes on the floor."

"I'll do my best," Baine said softly before stepping inside the house.

And he did.

Chapter 12: Cairn

The widow had finished plucking the feathers from the goose by the time Baine exited the sod house almost an hour later. She'd now moved on to the tiresome task of scraping the puckered skin gently with a knife to remove the down. The older woman paused in her work, her tanned features covered in a thin sheen of sweat as she watched Baine pick up his bow and arrow bag.

"I haven't heard screams like that in a long time," the widow commented as Baine hooked his bow over his shoulders. She pushed a wet, errant strand of hair from her eyes and shuddered. "I hope I never have to again."

"So do I," Baine agreed softly. "I am sorry for that." He wiped his cheek, not surprised to see redness on his palm and fingers afterward. He'd done his best to control the spray, but no matter how many times he'd been forced to kill a man, he was always amazed at how much blood a person's body contained.

The widow regarded Baine steadily. "Did this boy tell you what you wanted to know before you sent him on his way to Judgement Day?"

"He did," Baine answered in a tight voice. "He didn't know much in the end, but it's enough to get me started." Baine crossed the distance between them while pulling a canvas sack from his pocket. He hefted it in his palm, then offered it to the seated woman.

"What's this?" the widow asked, looking surprised. She didn't reach for the sack.

Baine motioned behind him with his head. "That bastard and his friends robbed Lord Alwin last night. This is his share of the plunder they took. I want you to have it."

The widow looked up at Baine in shock, then dropped her eyes back to the sack of coins. She licked her lips, clearly tempted. "Didn't you tell me these men also killed your wife and child?"

"Yes," Baine agreed. "They murdered many others too."

The widow sighed before she shook her head regretfully. "Then, if that's true, that's blood money you're holding right there, young man. Thank you, but I don't want any part of it."

Baine frowned. He hefted the bag again, which was more than half full. "You realize what's in here could change your life, don't you?"

The widow snorted. "Yes, but not in a good way. Once word gets out that I have money like that lying around, every scoundrel and half-starved wretch for miles will come sniffing around here looking for it. I'd be dead faster than you can say, Prince Tyrale."

"You could leave," Baine suggested. "Go to one of the bigger towns and buy yourself a nice house with a servant."

The woman smiled sadly. "This is my home. There is nowhere else I want to be than here." She looked down at the mongrel still lying at her feet and patted its head fondly. "No, I think it best that you keep the coin yourself, young man. Something tells me you're going to need it more than me. Besides, that foolish boy in there already paid me a Jorq to care for his wound. That's more than plenty for my needs."

Baine sighed, knowing there would be no arguing with the woman. "Will you at least take another Jorq for all the trouble I've caused you? Lord Alwin would insist on that at the very least, I assure you."

The widow hesitated, her features softening at the earnest look on Baine's face. "Very well," she relented. "If that is your wish." Baine gladly pulled out a coin from the sack, handing it to her with a flourish before she tucked it away in her dress. The widow bowed her head. "You are a true gentleman, sir."

Baine hesitated, feeling guilty about what he'd left behind in the woman's house. He gestured to the little sod building. "I would normally offer to bury him for you, but—"

The widow waved away his words. "Don't concern yourself about that. I'll get someone from the village to drag the body out of there and dump it in the river. Actually, I know just the two young lads for the job. I'm sure they'll find the task deliciously fascinating. Besides, I think you have more important things to do right now than burying a good-for-nothing murderer like that."

Baine thanked the woman, then headed back down the path, returning to the waiting mare. He mounted and headed out, cutting around the outskirts of Laskerly until he reached the road leading south. Cairn—the dead boy inside the widow's house—had told Baine where he believed some of the imposter's men were heading, though he'd sworn he didn't know where Jark was going. The outlaw leader had apparently been tight-lipped about that. Cairn had just turned sixteen years old last month, though that fact hadn't mattered to Baine in the least when he'd brought out his knives. Flora and baby Hadrack were dead—murdered in cold blood—and Cairn was just as responsible as all the others were for their deaths. The thought of granting the boy mercy due to his age hadn't even crossed Baine's mind. Besides, the wound Cairn had received during the attack on Witbridge—at the hands of Hanley, no less—had ripped through vital organs, meaning his death was a forgone conclusion anyway. Baine had just helped it along a little.

The good news was Baine now had four more names to go along with Jark Cordly, the imposter Outlaw of Corwick. There was a tall, thin man named Pater Dore, Tadly Platt, Bent Holdfer, and the handsome lad the whore had described, Rupert Frake. According to Cairn, he, Frake, and Platt were all friends, having lived in the town of Crestpool near Caray Castle all their lives. The three had joined the outlaw gang together on a whim, hoping to find a better life filled with riches and adventure. Cairn was convinced that his friends would be heading back to Crestpool now that they had gold to spend, and it was a theory Baine tended to agree with.

Jark had reportedly cut the three friends loose after leaving Laskerly, which Cairn had claimed he'd done because the imposter had announced he'd made his riches and was now done with outlawing. But Baine doubted that was the truth somehow, guessing the real reason the boys were sent away was that they were a liability and couldn't be trusted. Baine was actually surprised Jark had let any of them live, not to mention sharing some of the loot with them.

Cairn's friends had promised they'd return once it was safe to move him, which Baine guessed was another lie. One look at the boy's grievous wound was enough to know he was a dead man. Baine doubted even the brilliance of Haverty the apothecary could save him. Platt and Frake were both young and likely stupid, which meant Cairn was right and they would return to their roots where they could brag and flaunt their newfound wealth. Baine was determined to make the youths regret that choice. He let Piper have her head on the trail as he reviewed the rest of the conversation he'd had with the wounded boy.

"How many men attacked Witbridge Manor?" Baine demanded from the stool he sat on. Cairn was lying at Baine's feet on his back on the rush-covered floor. A threadbare blanket had been thrown over him when Baine arrived, but it now lay on the floor nearby. Blood trickled down the boy's face from two gashes on his forehead, courtesy of Baine's knife. Cairn was also missing a thumb on his right hand and several toes on his left foot, the penalty for being evasive in his answers at the beginning of the questioning.

"Twenty," the youth responded. "Twenty men."

Baine nodded, processing that number. It was more than he'd been expecting, though it didn't affect his determination any. "And Jark Cordly?" he finally asked. "The so-called Outlaw of Corwick. Tell me about him."

"He's a mean bastard," Cairn replied meekly. The stubborn resistance he'd initially put up against Baine's questions was now gone, replaced with resignation and the fear of additional pain. "I was terrified of him." The boy looked away bitterly, his left hand pressed against the bloody stump of his missing thumb. There was nothing but hopelessness in his eyes now, for he'd seen Baine's expression and knew how his story would end. "I should never have let Rupert convince me to go with him," the boy added softly. "I just knew nothing good would come of it."

"Yet you went anyway," Baine grunted.

Cairn nodded, wincing at the pain. "Rupert always gets his way. With me, Tadley, and everyone else. That's just the way he is. Nobody can resist him. Every girl in town makes mooneyes at him whenever he's nearby, but he won't even look at them. The only girl Rupert ever talks or thinks about is Lady Elyn. He's been obsessed with her ever since the moment he saw her last year." Cairn glanced at Baine. "That's why when Jark showed up in Crestpool looking for men to join him in *a great adventure*, as he called it, Rupert jumped at the chance. He figured if he had enough gold and became important enough in Lady Elyn's eyes, he'd have a chance at wooing her."

Baine frowned, remembering what the whore had told him in The Jolly Cock. "Isn't Lady Elyn newly married to Lord Falmir?"

Cairn chuckled weakly. "Of course she is. But when Rupert fixes his mind on something, there's no changing it."

"Which is why he'll head back to Crestpool now that he's got all that coin," Baine said thoughtfully. The boy merely nodded wearily and closed his eyes. "Why was Jark recruiting in Crestpool?" Baine asked. "Why would he need inexperienced boys like you to ride with him?"

"The story I heard was most of his original men were wiped out three weeks ago in an ambush," Cairn explained, opening his eyes. "Jark learned one of the lords taking The Walk from Taskerbery Castle had brought a lot of gold with him, so he decided to attack it."

Baine gaped at the boy in surprise. "They attacked The Walk? Is this Jark a raving lunatic?"

"Maybe," Cairn replied seriously. "He'd have to be to do that, wouldn't he? Anyway, they apparently managed to steal some of the gold, but in the process, many Pilgrims were killed."

"Mother Above," Baine whispered in horror, still finding it hard to imagine anyone would be foolish enough to risk their soul by attacking The Walk and killing Pilgrims. He thought suddenly of Hadrack, who'd been on that same Walk, though Baine knew he'd taken the route from Calban Castle, not Taskerbery. He wondered if his friend knew there was another man out there posing as him. Baine motioned to the boy. "Go on. Tell me the rest."

"There was already a bounty on the Outlaw of Corwick's head before the attack," Cairn continued. "Two hundred Jorqs offered by Prince Tyrale, I think. But after what Jark did, that bounty jumped to a thousand, with ten Jorqs added for each of his men."

"Let me guess," Baine said, understanding now. "The temptation was too much and Jark was betrayed by one of his own."

"Yes," Cairn agreed. "Jark fled south after the ambush with just a few men he knew he could trust."

"And he's been recruiting fools like you and your friends ever since," Baine said with disgust. He leaned forward, not hiding his anger as Cairn shrank away from him fearfully. "Was it worth it, you bastard?" Baine demanded. He put the blade of his knife to the boy's tender throat. "Was murdering my wife and son worth this?"

"I'm sorry," Cairn replied weakly. "Had I known what was going to happen—" The boy trailed off helplessly, sniffing as moisture filled his eyes. "We just thought it would be fun."

"Who told Jark about Lord Alwin's cache?" Baine growled, unaffected by the boy's tears.

"That I don't know. Rupert, Tad, and I only joined him the day before the raid. No one told us anything about what we were doing. We just did whatever we were told."

Baine snorted in disbelief, running the point of the blade down the boy's neck to his chest, then lightly across his bandaged abdomen until he stopped at his waist. "Maybe I need to cut something else off you to get to the truth."

"I am telling you the truth!" Cairn insisted. "I swear it upon my soul!"

Baine studied the boy, his gut telling him he was being truthful. "How come you only remember two of the outlaws' names out of that many—Bent Holdfer and Pater Dore?"

"Because I'm really terrible at remembering names," Cairn answered immediately. "I've always been like that. I don't know why." Baine just glared at him as the young outlaw hurried to explain. "Bent Holdfer used to live in Crestpool years ago when I was a boy; that's how come I knew him. And Pater is my uncle's name, so that one was easy to remember. Bent joined the outlaws about a week before me and the others, and he's the one who told me about what had happened to Jark in the North. That's the only reason I knew about it." Cairn lifted his good hand in the air in exasperation when Baine remained quiet. "Why would I lie about this to you now? You're going to kill me anyway. If I knew more of the bastards' names, I promise I'd tell you. I just can't remember."

Baine mulled that over, guessing he'd gotten about as much useful information from Cairn as he ever would. "Then I guess our business is concluded," he finally grunted.

Baine snatched up the blanket from the floor with his left hand without warning, throwing it over Cairn's face even as he stabbed upward with his knife into the boy's vulnerable throat. Cairn made a startled, strangled sound as hot blood shot out from his neck, quickly drenching the blanket. Baine withdrew his knife through the thin cloth after a moment and stood back, watching dispassionately as Cairn continued to thrash wildly on the floor. The boy somehow managed to pull the blood-soaked blanket from his face, clutching at his neck in desperation as blood squirted in streams onto the thrushes around him. Baine cursed under his breath at the mess—he'd promised the widow he'd be careful.

Cairn looked up at Baine with pleading eyes, his mouth working to say something that sounded vaguely like *forgive me*.

"Not likely, you bastard," Baine whispered as the light in Cairn's eyes finally went out and he went still. Baine stood over the body while blood slowly spread around it, seeping into the rushes. He thought sadly of his wife and the son that he'd never met, taken from him by this foolish, greedy boy and others just like him.

Finally, Baine turned and headed for the door. "Nineteen more to go," he whispered. "Nineteen more."

Chapter 13: Tadley Platt

Crestpool was much larger than Baine had been expecting, sprawling for a quarter of a mile along both sides of the northern bank of Barnwin's Channel. He guessed the town could easily house a thousand souls or more, with additional dwellings rising further back from the river among the rich farmland. A veil of black smoke hung over Crestpool, courtesy of the town's many busy forges and smokehouses—there was a war on, after all. Baine could hear the strident ringing of the anvils echoing from within the wooden walls protecting the town, with the sounds overwhelmed moments later when a bell began to toll from the tower of a graceful Holy House. A small castle of weathered limestone with rounded turrets stood on the southern side of the river, connected to the town by an arched stone bridge with a three-story gatehouse at its center. A long procession of people dressed in finery were crossing that bridge, though Baine was too far away to see faces clearly.

Lord Falmir and his retinue, Baine guessed as he studied the fluttering banners and brightly colored clothing. *No doubt on his way to morning prayers*.

He guided Piper down a sandy towpath that hugged the curvature of the river. Long reed grass and cattails danced in the wind along the shoreline to his left, the hearty stems filled with energetic and vocal red-wing blackbirds, yellow finches, and chickadees. A field of almost ripe barley lay to Baine's right, with a road leading to the town cutting through the waving greenish-yellow stalks half a mile away. Baine had avoided the main roads as much as possible during his journey since he'd noticed large groups of Northern soldiers, both on foot and mounted, migrating southwards almost from the moment he'd left Laskerly. Baine guessed the presence of so many troops meant some kind of offensive was being planned closer to the front lines. The last thing he needed right now was a run-in with the North's army, as it wasn't unusual during wartime for strangers like him to be pressed into service without warning. Baine couldn't allow that to happen.

He reached a swooping bend in the river where the channel narrowed dramatically, halting the mare as he watched a team of two men and four powerful draught horses struggling to tow a barge heavily laden with bales of goods through the shallow water. Several more barges were awaiting their turn at the mouth of the bend. Three men holding long poles reclined on the bales of the flat vessel being towed while a fourth man at the back steered. One of the men at rest called out cheerfully to Baine, who didn't bother responding. He swung the mare off the path and guided her around the cursing workers and their straining horses before heading back onto the trail. The towpath started to narrow dramatically a few minutes later, transforming from a dirt road chewed up by horses' hooves into nothing more than an overgrown footpath now that the channel had become deeper and straighter and the draught horses were no longer needed in that area.

Baine heard shouts and the barking of dogs mixing with the bleating of sheep when he was less than two hundred yards from the town walls. He halted Piper on the crest of a knoll, waiting as two enthusiastic black and white dogs herded a frightened group of sheep along the path toward him before, with growls and nips at their haunches, the dogs turned the sheep down a small ravine to his left. A boxed-in sheep wash of stone and brick awaited the terrified animals at the bottom, built along the waterway's shore. More men were waiting below, balanced on top of the wash's walls as the sheep stampeded down the slope and jumped into the water, bleating even louder when they realized there was no way out.

Baine continued toward the town, finally reaching the side gate, which was open but guarded by several bored-looking soldiers. He dismounted, leading Piper forward by the reins.

"Your business in Crestpool?" one of the soldiers demanded, stepping in front of Baine to block his path. The man was tall and thin, perhaps as much as forty years old, with worn leather armor, a pinched face, and a milky-white left eye that never moved.

"I've been sent here by Lord Alwin of Witbridge Manor with a message for Lord Falmir," Baine said, giving his prepared answer.

"Is that a fact?" the soldier grunted, looking Baine up and down. He didn't appear all that impressed with what he saw. "How do we know you're not a spy for the South?"

"How do I know you're not?" Baine shot back. The tall soldier's eyelids fluttered in surprise, and he hesitated as he searched for an answer. Baine grinned. *Not too smart, this one.*

"I'm watching the gate," the soldier finally volunteered weakly as his companion snickered. "So, how can I be a spy?"

"Exactly my point," Baine said, leading Piper around the soldier. "Which means you're as likely to be one as I am."

Baine kept going, feeling the tall soldier's good eye on his back as the man mulled that over, but he didn't try to stop him from entering. The side gate opened onto a narrow alley with a cooper's shop on his left overflowing with wooden barrels and washbasins stacked three high along the front wall. A tinker's shop rose on his right with a man wearing a leather apron standing in the building's shadowed entrance holding a metal pot. The tinker lifted the pot hopefully, but Baine just shook his head and looked away before the man could speak, ignoring his disappointed look. He pressed onward past shops and warehouses of all kinds, including wheelers, farriers, blacksmiths, butchers, tanners, and breweries. Crestpool was an industrious place, it seemed. Baine eventually found a stable, where after some haggling, he paid half a Jorq to a wizened old groom with shaggy hair and no teeth in his head to feed, water, and rub down Piper.

"I'm looking for some friends of mine who live in town," Baine said to the groom once the deal was made. "Maybe you know where I can find them?"

"Maybe," the groom grunted with a shrug of his bony shoulders. "Maybe not. I used to know everyone in Crestpool once upon a time. But things have gone to The Father's pits in the last few years, what with all the cutthroats, thieves, and beggars flooding in recently." The old man shook his head. "There's even a rumor floating around that the Outlaw of Corwick was here just the other day if you can imagine such a thing. If it's true, the bastard must have balls like goose eggs to take a chance like that. Lord Falmir's men would cut his throat without even thinking about it if they caught him. There's a bounty on his head, after all."

"Rupert Frake and Tadley Platt," Baine said, trying to bring the man's focus back to the question. "That's who I'm looking for."

"Oh, them," the old groom said with a nod. "Sure, I know those two lads." He scowled. "A couple of scoundrels they are, too. Always looking for trouble. Them and that friend of theirs, Cairn Bethen. Like three peas in a pod, they are. Not worth the—"

"Do you know where they live?" Baine asked, doing his best to hide his impatience.

The groom shook his head. "No, can't say that I do. But I know Tadley Platt's father, Gembart. He runs a public bathhouse on Woodcutter's Road. Chances are Tad will be there, but if not, I'm sure his father will know where he's at."

"Where is Woodcutter's Road?"

The groom led Baine out from the stables and pointed northeast. "Two streets over that way. The bathhouse is right next to the big tithe barn. You can't miss it."

Baine nodded. A tithe barn was where rent and levies payable to the Holy House and the liege lord from local farmers were stored—with usually one-tenth of the production from the farms going to the House and a further sixty to the lord. The system wasn't fair by any means, Baine knew, at least from the farmers' point of view, but that, unfortunately, was the way of things in most of Ganderland. He headed northeast down an alley that led him to a busy street, which he crossed while ignoring the gaggle of begging one-armed or one-legged castoffs from the war before passing along another narrow street hemmed in by three-story houses. He finally came to Woodcutter's Road, where he saw the tithe barn the groom had described. A modest-sized, two-story warehouse with a vaulted roof that Baine guessed was the bathhouse sat in the shadows beside the massive building. More warehouses lined both sides of the street. Two well-dressed men stood outside the entrance to the bath, talking animatedly as Baine approached.

"Everyone knows she's been humping with Bendigo Bard," the man with his back to Baine said. He was short but with wide shoulders, wearing a dark grey cloak. "The only one that's blind to it is Lord—"

"Shhh!" the second man hissed warily when he looked up and saw Baine. This man was tall and reed thin, with a hooked nose and deep-set eyes.

Baine paused before the two. "I'm looking for Gembart."

"Inside," the tall man said gruffly, indicating the doorway. "But you can't go in."

Baine frowned. "I thought this was a public bathhouse?"

"It is," the tall man agreed. "Normally, anyway. But Gembart is hosting a private celebration for his son this morning." He grinned knowingly and winked. "If you know what I mean."

Baine tried to keep his face expressionless. It was rare for rough farming settlements like Crestpool to have bathhouses, being more common in big cities like Halhaven and Gandertown, where more affluent citizens tended to live. Having attended some of the baths in Halhaven himself before he'd married, Baine knew most were little more than fronts for prostitution rings, which it appeared by the sounds of things was also the case here.

"The bath will reopen sometime after midday," the short man added not unkindly. "So, I suggest you come back then to get your bell rung."

"Yes, of course," Baine said with a slight bow. "I'll do that. Thank you."

He turned and headed back the way he'd come, walking down the first cross street he found. When Baine was out of sight of the bathhouse, he reversed directions, using the bulk of the building on the corner to shield him as he peeked around the corner. He cursed softly. The two men were still standing by the entrance, talking and looking as though they were in no hurry. He waited a good ten minutes, growing more and more impatient, until finally, the men said their goodbyes. The short one began walking toward Baine while the taller man headed off in the opposite direction. Baine shrank back, pressing himself into the wall of the building as the short man headed down the street, whistling and totally oblivious that he was there. He counted to fifty once the man was out of sight, then headed back to the bathhouse.

When Baine reached the building, he paused in front of a wide flight of three stone steps that led up to a pair of rounded, carved mahogany doors guarding the entrance. A wooden sign above the doors announced in flamboyant, bold letters—*Gembart's Fine Bath & Parlor*. Baine looked up and down the street, but there was no one around other than a group of washerwomen in white aprons walking past on the opposite side of the road. None glanced his way. Baine tried the doors once the women were gone, not surprised to find they were barred. Matching iron knockers depicting a snarling bear's head hung from each door, but Baine was reluctant to use them, guessing even if someone came, they'd just shoo him away. Unless Tadley Platt himself came to see who it was, which was highly unlikely, Baine could see no way to gain entry without resorting to violence against a person who had no stake in this game.

He could hear Jebido's voice in his head lecturing Hadrack. *"When you choose to swing a sword with vengeance in your heart, my boy, sometimes the innocent are the ones who pay the ultimate price."*

Baine wasn't certain Hadrack had given much attention to Jebido's words at the time, although he had to admit his friend's quest for vengeance had so far proven the older man's dire warning wrong. But Baine knew he wasn't Hadrack, so for the time being, he'd rather err on the side of caution and find another way. He looked up at the second floor but could see no obvious means of entry from the front except for the locked doors. Baine headed around the building, examining the dark wooden beams and dirty white stucco exterior with interest. The warehouse's corners were buttressed by dark grey stone slabs, and the high, sloping roof was covered in thick shale shakes with at least four huge chimney's that he could see from his vantage point spewing smoke.

Baine found a rear door in an arched alcove in an alley in the back, but it was securely locked. All the windows on the first floor were shuttered and bolted as well, with the rest of the building blocked off by the towering bulk of the tithe barn. Stymied, Baine looked up, fixating on an open window near the back corner of the bathhouse about twenty feet above street level. The window was the only one he'd noticed that was unshuttered, which meant it represented his only chance to get into the building undetected. Baine hurried forward, running his hands over the rough granite along the bathhouse's corner. Satisfied that the stone was secure and would afford decent hand and footholds, he shifted his bow on his back, then began to climb slowly and methodically.

Once he was level with the open window, Baine used his left hand and his feet to support his weight while leaning as far to his right as he could. He stretched, grimacing with effort as he reached for the window sill with straining fingers but found no matter how hard he tried, he was still a foot short. *Oh to be tall like Hadrack.* Baine heard sudden voices below him, and he froze, clinging to the stones with both hands again and not daring to breathe as a man and woman appeared below him, strolling down the street arm in arm. The man glanced up at Baine and their eyes met briefly, but all he did was give a conspiratorial smile and a nod of his head before continuing on with the woman, who seemed unaware that Baine was there. He breathed out in relief when the two were gone, guessing the man might have entered a bathhouse in a similar fashion at one point in his life.

Baine focused back on the window, setting his feet determinedly before he took a deep breath and sprung sideways toward the open sill. His right hand slipped off the edge of the slick stone at the moment of impact, but he managed to hook his left over it, ignoring the sharp pinch in his arm just above the elbow. Baine hung that way precariously for a moment, his feet dangling and his body weight dragging him down before he was able to swing his right arm up and gain a firm hold on the sill. He slowly drew himself upward until his head was level with the window. Then, with the toes of his boots scraping against the plaster wall beneath him and the arrow bag at his hip twisting and turning, he used the strength of his arms gained from years of shooting a bow to drag his upper body up and over the sill.

Baine remained where he was, sucking in air with his body hanging half inside the building and half out as he scanned the interior, relieved to see that he'd found an unoccupied room filled with dusty furniture. Once he'd caught his breath, he wriggled forward, doing his best to stay silent as he slowly and carefully dragged himself along the wooden floor like a snake until his entire body was inside the room. Baine half-stood, then froze as muffled feminine laughter arose from just beyond a closed door across from him, followed a moment later by a male voice joining in the merriment. He waited, listening as several shadows passed beneath the door, followed by receding footsteps before finally, he moved stealthily forward.

Baine pressed his ear to the door and satisfied that whoever it had been was gone, unlatched and swung it inward on creaking hinges. He paused then, listening with his head cocked sideways as a high-pitched squeal of delight followed by the sounds of splashing arose from somewhere below on the lower floor. A man was singing and playing a lute down there as well, Baine noted with a grimace—and doing both badly. The off-key and grating voice was setting his teeth on edge, and he dearly hoped the horrible musician was Tadley Platt, if for no other reason than it would be just one more reason to slit the bastard's throat.

Baine stepped out into a narrow corridor. The floor was red and black tile, and the wood-paneled walls were painted in a wash of garish yellow that hurt his eyes. Another door faced him, which Baine opened just in case Platt was inside. The room was empty, though it was much larger than the one he'd just come from and looked recently used, with a four-poster bed with the bedclothes in disarray, a desk covered in rolls, parchments, and several empty wine flasks, as well as a large fireplace filled with glowing coals.

Baine carefully closed the door, then headed down the corridor until he reached a set of stairs. The singing had gotten louder from below, and if anything, it was even worse now than it had been earlier. He could tell the sounds were coming from somewhere off to his right, but the man responsible for them was hidden from view by a series of ribbed vault arches and rounded columns. He began to descend, able to catch the occasional glimpse of a large, firelit chamber through the arches as he neared the lower floor, where a modest entrance hall with ornate paintings and stenciled motifs on the walls awaited him.

Another squeal of feminine laughter echoed from the chamber as water splashed. The singer abruptly stopped plucking on the lute, thank the gods, and he chuckled. "You ladies look lonely in there all by yourselves," the man said in a slurred voice. "Would you care for some company?"

"But of course, Master Platt," came back a female reply.

"What took you so long?" a second woman asked coyly. "We're starting to get cold."

"Nonsense," the singer responded with a laugh. "My father's servants are feeding the furnaces as we speak. If that water gets any hotter, you two will look like boiled beef."

Baine grinned, knowing he'd found Tadley Platt. He heard a splash a moment later, quickly followed by squeals of delight from the women. Baine reached the entrance hall and drew an arrow from his bag, walking on the balls of his feet across the tiled floor as he followed the noises. A moment later, he passed through one of the arches into the chamber, pausing there unnoticed by the preoccupied occupants as he surveyed the room. Tall bronze braziers with sculpted animal heads and clawed feet burned every ten feet along stone alcoves set in the walls. The floor was covered in etched tiles alternating between war scenes, landscapes, sea life, and religious themes. A raised platform formed in a hexagon pattern stood in the center of the room, surrounded by arched columns with an immense vat of heated water set in the floor inside, giving off long tendrils of steam. Smaller rectangular vats lay outside the platform's base along all five angles, also sending up steam.

Two naked women and a naked man were frolicking at the far end of the central vat, still oblivious to him. That was about to change. Baine strode forward determinedly, climbing the three steps up to the platform as silently as a stalking cat. He could smell the heady scent of oranges and lavender all around him, guessing they'd been placed inside the braziers for added ambiance. Tadley Platt had his back to Baine, and he was fondling the pert breasts of the prostitute to his right with one hand. She was young, perhaps no more than fifteen, with wet, long brown hair and a weak chin. The prostitute's eyes were closed and her head was titled back, exposing her white, swan-like neck.

The second prostitute had her hands braced on the stone steps leading into the vat with her glistening, shapely rear end and back arched to accept Platt's manhood while he tugged with vigor on her long, ash-colored hair with his left hand. This girl was darker skinned than the first, with a jagged scar on her right shoulder and large breasts that flopped and jiggled with each enthusiastic thrust from the boy.

Baine nocked the arrow he held to his bow, then waited as the prostitute moaned and whimpered with each thrust, impressed despite himself by Platt's enthusiasm and stamina. After a full minute of this, Baine finally lost patience and cleared his throat. The boy and darker-skinned whore didn't seem to notice, but the other girl opened her eyes and saw him. Those eyes went round in surprise, mirroring the form of her mouth before she abruptly screamed.

"Damn, Mava!" Tadley Platt gasped, slowing his efforts dramatically. "What's gotten into you?"

The young prostitute just shook her head, pointing a trembling finger at Baine. Platt glanced over his shoulder, his drunken features sobering when he saw Baine and what he held in his hands.

"Tadley Platt?" Baine asked pleasantly.

The boy blinked as if he had to think about it, then he reluctantly nodded, disengaging himself from the bent-over prostitute as his manhood quickly shriveled. "Who are you?"

Baine glanced at the whores, who were hugging each other and trembling as they stared at him in terror. "This doesn't concern either of you," Baine said to them in a firm voice. "So I suggest you leave while you still can."

"They're not going anywhere," Platt said belligerently, showing no fear. He glared at Baine, who had to admit he was impressed. The boy might be a turd-sucking thief and a murderer, but it appeared he was no coward. "Do you know who I am?" Platt demanded. He slapped the water around him with his palms for emphasis. "Do you know who owns this place?"

Baine drew back the bowstring, aiming the arrow's iron tip at Platt's heart. "The better question, you bastard, is do you know who I am?" he growled. Baine glanced again toward the women, who seemed frozen in indecision. "Last chance to get out of here before the blood flows. Choose now or deal with the consequences."

The whores both turned without a word and fled up the stairs, sending water spraying in all directions. Some articles of female clothing lay strewn about on padded benches around the bath, but they ignored them, their bare feet slapping against the tiles as they hurried away, still clutching at each other. Baine focused back on Platt after the women were gone. The boy was tall and thin, with long black hair and sparse growth sprouting on his chin and cheeks. Platt's chestnut-colored eyes were close-set and smoldering with both indignation and impotent rage as he glared up at Baine.

The boy might have been handsome, Baine thought, if not for his piggish nose, hollow cheeks, and pasty white skin covered with purple pockmarks. "Now then," he said, keeping the bowstring pulled taut as the arrow's goose feathers caressed his cheek. "I asked you a question. Do you know who I am, boy?"

Platt snorted in contempt. "A dead man. That's who you are. My father has many friends, and he'll see that—"

Baine released the string, sending the arrow hissing through the air an inch over Platt's head. The boy automatically ducked low in the water, crying out as the arrowhead smacked into the stone wall behind him with a crack. He stared at Baine in shock, the arrogance gone from his face now, replaced by the first stirrings of fear. Baine grinned mockingly as he slowly drew another arrow from his bag and nocked it. "Do you know who I am, boy?" he repeated a third time.

Platt shook his head as he slowly straightened to his full height. "If it's gold you want, I have—"

Baine calmly drew back his bow and shot in one smooth motion. This time the arrow's feathers nicked the boy's right ear as it passed, drawing blood. "I can do this all day long," Baine grunted as he selected a third arrow. "Do you know who I am, boy?"

"No, I don't," Platt said, looking shaken now as he pressed a hand to his bleeding ear. He glanced at his red-stained fingers afterward and cursed before looking back up at Baine. "Have you lost your mind? I've never seen you before."

"That's true," Baine agreed. He shot again, this time the arrow striking the boy in the right shoulder.

Platt screamed in shock, knocked off balance by the impact. He fell backward, plunging beneath the water only to reappear moments later, sputtering and sobbing as he fought to regain his feet. Baine calmly drew another arrow as Platt turned with a terrified cry, desperately trying to propel himself through the water toward the steps and freedom. Baine let him go, waiting until the boy had gotten halfway up the stairs, revealing his hairy white buttocks before he let fly again. Platt screamed even louder this time as the arrow buried itself halfway into his right ass cheek and his leg gave out. He collapsed on the stairs, the arrow shaft in his shoulder snapping off with a sharp click, followed by another cry of pain. Platt glanced back at Baine, weeping hysterically as he fought to drag himself upward while frantically trying to yank the second arrow from his buttock.

Baine walked around the vat, pausing over the wounded youth to stare down at him. He slowly drew his knife from its sheath and then crouched. "Do you know who I am, boy?" he repeated softly.

"No!" Tadley Platt screamed up at him, his eyes filled with tears as spittle flew from his mouth. "No, damn you! I told you I don't know! Why do you keep asking me that?"

Baine leaned forward and smiled. "Because I'm death itself, you bastard," he whispered. "For you and everyone else who murdered my wife and son at Witbridge Manor. I wanted you to fully understand who I am before you burn at The Father's feet."

Platt's eyes went round in horror just as Baine's knife flashed, ripping open his neck from ear to ear. The boy emitted a strangled, almost feminine scream, his left hand flopping uselessly against Baine's chest as if begging him to save him somehow. Baine watched dispassionately as thick blood gushed from the boy's neck, spraying the stairs in a fine mist before it began to roll in small streams into the vat, quickly staining the hot bathwater red. Baine leaned over and cupped some untainted water in his hands as the body twitched and jerked in its death throes, cleaning the blood off himself as best he could. He finally stood when he was finished, looking down at the contorted body.

"Eighteen, my beloved," Baine whispered as he turned away. "Eighteen more of the bastards to go."

Chapter 14: When Is A Juggler Not A Juggler?

Baine knew he'd made a mistake. He cursed himself for being a fool as he unbolted the back door of the bathhouse and slipped out unseen into the alleyway behind. He'd gotten carried away inside, letting his anger and need for revenge overcome his common sense. Baine realized now, after the fact, that he should have taken more time to question Tadley Platt before sending him to Judgement Day, since the chances were good he'd known where Rupert Frake was. Baine had been in a hurry, though, concerned the whores might have reported him to the town wardens or the lord's men, and so he had rushed things. It had been a valid fear. Yet even so, in hindsight, he should have risked taking the time to interrogate Platt.

Baine still knew nothing more about his remaining adversaries than he had before he'd killed the boy, with the opportunity to learn potentially valuable information about them squandered by foolishness and stupidity. Stupidity could get you killed faster than a striking rock snake, as Jebido was fond of saying, and Baine vowed not to make the same mistake again with Frake when he found the bastard. He still had eighteen men yet to feel his justice, with only three names remaining to connect them all together—four if you counted Jark Cordly. Baine needed to start thinking of each of the men he sought as stepping stones from here on in, with one leading to the next and so on and so on, until he'd found and killed them all.

He paused in the shadows of the alley as a clatter of hooves and squeak of axles arose from the cobblestone street out front. A covered wagon appeared in the wide gap between the bathhouse and the warehouse sitting on the opposite side of the alley, escorted by riders in front and behind wearing dark square helmets and bright white surcoats depicting the Rock of Life. House Agents. A middle-aged Son with a neatly trimmed beard that struggled to hide his drooping jowls sat inside the cart, staring out the open window beside him at the scenery with bored disinterest. Baine and the Son's eyes met for the briefest of moments, though the priest seemed as uninterested in him as he was in his surroundings before the wagon bumped and rolled out of sight. Baine hesitated when he heard the double front doors of the bathhouse burst open with a crash.

"Murder! By the gods, someone has butchered my son!"

Baine immediately turned his back and hurried away at a fast walk in the opposite direction just as a man with a bulging belly dressed in a white tunic ran into the street, lifting his hands to the House Agents following the wagon. Gembart Platt, Baine had no doubt.

"In the name of The Father," he heard the bathhouse owner pleading to the mounted men. "Please stop! I need help!"

"Wait, there he is!" a female voice shouted a moment later. Baine took a quick glance over his shoulder and groaned, recognizing the whore with the ash-colored hair. She was wearing a blue robe wrapped tightly around her naked frame and pointing excitedly in his direction. "That's him! That's the man who killed Tadley!"

"After him!" Gembart roared, his face bright red with fury. "Fifty Jorqs to the man who brings me his head!"

That was enough for Baine and he started to run, ducking around a building at the end of the alley even as shouts arose, followed almost immediately by pounding hooves. He heard the unmistakable ring of steel as swords were drawn and redoubled his efforts, for it seemed even House Agents were not above the lure of easy gold. Baine ran, turning down another side street hemmed in by tall buildings on both sides. An arched stone entranceway stood at the far end of the street—his only obvious recourse. Baine sprinted toward it, dodging around passersby while ignoring several curses thrown his way before he passed through the archway, where he came to a shuddering stop on the other side. Baine found himself in a walled courtyard filled with people, though none seemed interested in him.

He hesitated, his heart pounding in his chest. Ten or so tables occupied mostly by men sat in the shade cast by an enormous hazel tree. All the lower branches were trimmed neatly fifteen feet above the ground, giving the impression of curtains as they swayed in the breeze. Three barmaids wearing white and red dresses moved purposefully among the tables, taking orders from the patrons or bringing them wine and ale. There was a festive mood in the air, Baine noted as he turned to glance at a wooden platform that stood in the center of the courtyard in full sunlight. Three garishly dressed, sweating acrobats entertained the appreciative crowd there with an endless array of complicated flips and rolls. A second, smaller platform rose behind the first near a covered well, where a group of enthusiastic musicians played citterns, flutes, crumhorns, or drummed on clay knackers.

An arched exit identical to the one he'd just passed through stood on the other side of the courtyard, but Baine knew his pursuers were bound to see him before he got halfway there, so he discounted it. He needed somewhere to hide right now, having no desire to try matching himself against a troop of House Agents eager to take off his head. Baine wished he'd thought to bring his cloak with him, but the day was hot, so he'd left it at the stable with Piper. The black leather armor he wore and the weapons he carried stood out like a sore thumb among the unarmed and more plainly dressed townspeople, making him easily recognizable.

Baine hesitated in indecision. A woman stood at a tiny stall off to his left in front of an out-of-the-way nook, with the tent-like canvas awning surrounding it fluttering weakly in the light breeze. Several dozen pairs of iron shears, scissors, and snips hung from a rope suspended above a waist-high bench, with a customer examining three pairs of scissors laid out on the benchtop. A squat building rose ten feet behind the stall, wedged into the nook, with the front door wide open and a sign on the overhanging slanted roof above the door that said *Cremwill's Fine Tailoring*. Baine glanced back the way he'd come just as half a dozen mounted House Agents burst through the archway and into the courtyard. His time was up. A woman walking close to the entrance screamed and dropped the basket of apples she'd been carrying, startled by the sudden appearance of so many riders.

Baine scampered around the stall, hidden from his pursuers' view by the awning. He hurried toward the tailor shop, forcing himself not to run while not daring to look behind him, expecting a shout of discovery at any moment. That shout did not come, and he breathed a huge sigh of relief when he entered the shop undetected. A massive table dominated the single room, with six men sitting cross-legged on top of it as they stitched and sewed garments spread out across their knees. A seventh man stood off to one side of the enormous table, bent over a slanted desk with his weathered features etched in serious concentration as he drew lines on a piece of cloth with chalk. His hair and beard were the color of silver with only the odd dark streak left behind to remind of younger days, and he was dressed in a tight-fitting black jerkin and brown hose. The room's walls were lined with shelves from floor to ceiling, all of which were overflowing with spools of thread and bundles of linen, cotton, hemp, wool, and silk.

"Yes?" one of the men sitting on the table asked, looking up. He was perhaps thirty years old, with close-cropped brown hair and a cleft pallet partially hidden by a thick mustache. "Can I help you?"

Baine paused, wondering what to say. He glanced back outside, but the stall and awning blocked most of his view. All he could see clearly was one corner of the platform where the acrobats were performing. Had the House Agents given up, or would they continue the search? Baine had to assume they would keep looking, at least for a little while longer. The promise of that much gold was a strong incentive, after all. He thought about using a back door and possibly slipping away that way, but doing so would undoubtedly raise the suspicions of the tailor and his employees. The fuss they'd make would surely draw the House Agents' unwanted attention, though they might already be on their way here for all Baine knew. Besides, judging by the tailor shop's odd location, there was no guarantee a back door might even exist to escape through.

Baine finally smiled sheepishly at the questioner as an idea began to form in his mind. He would gamble that he had a few minutes grace before the House Agents noticed the shop tucked away where it was. Baine spread his hands wide. "I have something of an embarrassing problem that I hope you can help with." The man waited politely, though none of the other workers seemed interested. Baine forged onward. "I was hired to perform for the—" he hesitated there, pretending to be searching for the words as he looked up at the ceiling.

The man frowned in annoyance, sending his cleft lip into spasms. "You mean the celebration honoring the betrothal between Lord Falmir's third cousin and Lady Anda Shebert?"

"Yes," Baine agreed, relieved the man had taken the bait. "But thieves stole my belongings this morning, and now I have nothing proper to wear." He motioned toward the courtyard and cavorting acrobats outside. "If I don't join the others soon, my employer won't pay me and I will likely be terminated." Baine gestured helplessly to his clothing. "But I can't go out there dressed like this, and I desperately need this job. Can you help me?"

"Bertio?" the man with the cleft lip said inquiringly, glancing toward the man leaning over the desk. "What do you think?"

Bertio looked up with a world-weary expression, examining Baine with suspicious eyes. "You don't look like an acrobat to me, lad. If I had to guess, you appear more like a thief or a killer."

"Oh, I assure you I'm neither killer nor thief," Baine said with a forced laugh. "Nor am I an acrobat." He barely seemed to move and a knife appeared in his hand from beneath one of his bracers.

"I'm a juggler. The best in Ganderland, I'd wager." Baine twisted his wrist effortlessly, and the knife point was suddenly balanced on the tip of his index finger as straight as an arrow. He flipped the knife in the air, with the base of the handle coming down and landing on the back of his palm, suspended there like magic.

The man with the cleft lip whistled loudly at the move, and a part of Baine's mind wondered how he'd managed to make the sound at all with that lip.

"Then why the bow if you're a juggler?" Bertio asked, still looking suspicious.

"It's part of my act," Baine replied. "I do trick shots as well. You know, shooting apples off the top of someone's head, that sort of thing."

Bertio sighed and straightened, automatically stretching his aching back. "Well, whatever you may actually be, my friend, I'm afraid most of our clothing is made on consignment and to specific size requirements. There wouldn't be time to fashion you anything suitable. I'm sorry."

"Oh, just about anything here will likely do," Baine said hurriedly, knowing he was running out of time. "As long as it's colorful, that is. I'm not particular. Even an old cloak or tunic will be fine."

"Bertio?" the man with the cleft lip said. "What about Wengam's order? It's just sitting there gathering dust."

The tailor scowled. "We don't know for certain that he's not coming back for it."

"Katra Lim told my wife he died at the Battle of Whispering Woods," another of the workers volunteered without looking up from his task. "Said she had it on good authority from someone who was there." The man shook his head sadly and shrugged. "He's not coming back, Bertio, so you might as well get something for all that work while you can."

"How much does this man owe you?" Baine asked the silver-haired tailor, starting to feel anxious. This was taking too long.

"Four Jorqs," Bertio replied, looking conflicted. "That's for two sets of hose, mind you, along with two tunics, a vest, and two doublets."

"I'll take it all," Baine said without hesitation, already reaching for his money bag.

Bertio held up a hand regretfully. "As much as I wish I could help you, I'm afraid the garments are much too large for you."

"Nonsense," Baine said dismissively, pressing the coins into the man's hands. "I'll wear them over my clothes. My routine won't take that long anyway." Baine closed the tailor's fingers over the Jorqs, looking into his eyes. "Please, you are all that stands between me and unemployment."

Bertio hesitated a moment longer, then finally bowed his head in acceptance. "Very well." The tailor snapped his fingers, pointing at the man with the cleft lip. "Hajak, see to it. I have more important things to do."

"Of course," Hajak said, rising as the tailor returned to his desk and picked up his chalk, focusing back on his work. Hajak jumped nimbly down to the floor, taking hold of Baine's arm. "If you will kindly follow me?"

Baine allowed himself to be led into a backroom, where he found more shelves lining the walls and a slew of smaller tables, all with garments in the process of being made on them. One table contained at least forty colorful sashes and a heap of cloth scraps of all sizes and shapes. Hajak rummaged around on one of the shelves while Baine ground his teeth, expecting the House Agents to burst into the tailor shop at any moment.

"Ah," Hajak finally said triumphantly, pulling down a canvas-wrapped bundle tied with string. "Here it is."

He carried the bundle to a table, then undid the fastening, revealing two pairs of hose—one black and one yellow—two white tunics, a brown leather vest, and two doublets. Baine focused on those. Both doublets were bright, done in two colors split down the center of the garment. They both had long, slashed sleeves and integrated lacing that created a puffed-out-segmented look, allowing the tunic worn beneath to show through. One of the doublets was green and black, while the other was red and yellow. All the clothing looked like it would be three sizes too big for him.

"That one," Baine said, pointing to the red and yellow doublet as he unhooked his bow and set it on the table. He accepted Hajak's help, allowing the man to pull the garment over his head. It fell over him like a woman's dress.

Hajak stepped back afterward, examining Baine critically. "It is, unfortunately, rather large in the shoulders and arms."

Baine lifted his hands. The sleeves of the doublet extended a good six inches past them, but at least the garment had drawstring cuffs. "Can you tighten these for me so my hands are free?"

"Of course," Hajak agreed. He fussed for a few moments with the cuffs, then stepped back, nodding his head in approval. "There, that's a little better, at least."

Baine slung his bow back over his shoulders and turned to go.

"But what about the rest of the clothing?" Hajak asked.

"I'll come back for them after my performance."

"Ah, of course," Hajak agreed with a friendly smile. "I'm looking forward to watching it."

Baine glanced through the door into the main room, but there were still no signs of any House Agents. He turned back to Hajak. "You wouldn't happen to know Rupert Frake by chance, would you?"

"Sure I do," Hajak said with a shrug, folding the rest of the clothes back up in the canvas. "Why?"

"A juggler friend of mine told me I should pay him a visit if I'm ever in Crestpool. Do you know where he lives? I'd like to call on him after my performance."

Hajak wrinkled his nose as he thought. "I think over on Candle Lane. Lives with his mother and sister the last I knew, but the truth is he's rarely there. Most of the time you can find him at The Bloody Thorn."

"That's an alehouse?"

"Yes. It's also on Candle Lane."

"Thank you," Baine said. He hesitated on his way back out the door, staring at the table filled with sashes. He picked one up that was at least five feet long and closely matched the coloring of his doublet, staring at it thoughtfully. "Can I borrow this?" he asked Hajak.

"Well, I—" Hajak said uncertainly.

"I'll bring it back after I'm done, I promise," Baine lied. He pointed to the other clothes he'd bought. "Besides, you still have those if I don't return, which I will. I'm sure they're worth much more than this bit of cloth. You can hold them as collateral."

Hajak thought about that, then he smiled. "Yes, I suppose that would be acceptable."

Baine nodded in gratitude as he wrapped the sash over his head, then around his neck and the lower portion of his face. He grinned at Hajak from behind the cloth, with only his eyes and the bridge of his nose showing. "Do I look mysterious enough?"

Hajak nodded seriously. "Yes, very much so."

Baine winked. "Good."

He turned then and entered the main room, where neither the tailor nor his employees paid him any mind as he stepped back outside. Baine paused behind the canvas of the stall, adjusting the hem of the doublet that fell past his knees, ensuring his arrow bag was well hidden beneath it. He quickly unstrung his bow, tucking the string in a pocket. Baine had no intentions of leaving the curved stave behind, so he hid it as best he could, pressed against his side among the many folds of the doublet. Hopefully, no one would notice.

Several House Agents were going through the crowd watching the acrobats, Baine noticed, while others wandered around the tables beneath the hazel tree, stopping to examine each patron closely. Baine headed for the arched entrance he'd passed through earlier, keeping his head down. He was halfway to his destination when two House Agents appeared on foot, coming from the street. They paused beneath the stone arch, talking. Baine could see the Son's carriage waiting on the road behind them and he muttered a curse before turning away, heading back the way he'd come. A moment later, he almost jumped out of his skin when a heavy hand grabbed him by the shoulder, spinning him around.

"Where do you think you're going?" It was a House Agent. The man held his helmet under his arm, revealing a handsome face with blond hair and piercing blue eyes. He motioned to the acrobats in a friendly fashion. "You're a performer, aren't you? Shouldn't you be up there?"

Baine tried not to show his relief. "Yes. I just needed to get my costume fitted properly by the tailor first."

The House Agent glanced at Baine's voluminous, oversized doublet with doubt in his eyes. Finally, he snorted. "Looks to me like you were robbed, my friend. I've never seen a more ill-fitting costume in my life."

Baine lifted a hand helplessly, keeping the bowstave in his other pressed against his body as he turned away from the man to hide it. "Our regular juggler has an infected finger, so I've been asked to step in." He chuckled, gratified that his nervousness didn't show in his voice. "He's a tall, gangly bastard, that one."

"Ah," the House Agent said with a grin. "Now I understand."

"I'd best be on my way, then," Baine muttered, moving past the House Agent. He felt the man's strong hand on his shoulder again.

"You haven't seen a man dressed all in black, have you? A small fellow about your size carrying a bow over his shoulders?"

Baine's mind raced. "Actually," he said after a brief pause. "I did see someone that matches that description." He flicked his eyes around the courtyard, pausing at a belt and buckle shop across the way. He pointed towards it. "I saw him go in that shop a few minutes ago, but I don't think he ever came back out."

The House Agent's eyes lit up in anticipation, and without another word, he strode off purposefully toward the shop while putting on his helmet. Baine was disappointed the man hadn't called for any of his companions to join him, guessing the Agent was looking to collect the reward on his own. He would have liked to have had a clear path to the entranceway, but the other two House Agents remained where they were, talking as before.

Having little choice in the matter, Baine headed toward the platform, avoiding any House Agents among the crowd along the way. He'd gotten lucky with the first Agent, who'd failed to notice his bow in his eagerness to check out the belt shop. But that didn't guarantee any others Baine ran afoul of would miss it. The musicians were still playing while the acrobats continued their routine, though they looked to him like they were tired, which probably meant their act was getting near the end.

Baine could see a group of what he assumed were actors gathering behind the platform, guessing that they were up next. He headed that way, circling around the crowd until he was behind the musicians. The noise of the instruments was deafening as he made his way along the narrow corridor separating the raised platform and the stone wall behind it. A man suddenly appeared on the other side of the platform with his hands on his hips, blocking Baine's way while looking around him anxiously. Baine groaned, cursing his luck, for it was Tadley Platt's father. He hesitated midway along the corridor, which turned out to be his undoing, as something in his mannerisms must have given him away to the older man.

Gembart pointed a finger. "You!" he screamed, though his voice could barely be heard above the din.

Baine expected the bathhouse owner to shout for help then, but Gembart surprised him by rushing forward with his arms outstretched and murder in his eyes.

Thank the gods for fools, Baine thought as the older man bore down on him.

He waited calmly, already seeing in his mind how this would go. Gembart swung a balled fist for Baine's chin the moment he was in range, just as Baine had anticipated he would. The blow was a wild, looping thing that he easily ducked, the clumsy attack driven more by hatred and passion than any actual prowess. Baine allowed the older man's fist to sweep over his head harmlessly before he straightened again in one smooth motion and, using Gembart's momentum, shoved him with force toward the wall.

Baine had learned the hard way that being as small as he was usually meant being outmatched physically—which meant using your opponent's weight against him in a fight was imperative to success. It was a skill he'd become very proficient at over the years and one that had gotten him out of numerous close calls. The bathhouse owner was already off balance from the missed blow, and with Baine's opportunistic push, he was helpless to slow down, careening a moment later into the wall. The older man's head hit the stone with a sickening meaty sound, sending blood spraying as he moaned, his entire body quivering in shock before his legs gave out and he fell in a heap. Baine hurriedly bent over the motionless body, relieved to find that he was still breathing, though shallowly. His beef had been with Tadley Platt, after all, not the boy's father, who, for all Baine knew, could just be a good man grieving over his murdered son. *The innocents always suffer*, he heard Jebido say in his head.

Baine sighed and stood, glancing around, relieved to see that no one had witnessed the brief altercation. The wrap around his face had come loose during the scuffle, so he tightened it again, then hurried away, not looking left or right until he'd made it safely through the arched exit and onto the street on the other side. Once he was several blocks away from the courtyard and the ongoing festivities, Baine unwound the sash, thankful that he'd escaped the House Agents' net. He stopped the first person he saw on the street, learning that Candle Lane lay to the north of the town near the Holy House. Baine could see the House's tower from where he stood, and he smiled in anticipation as he headed toward it.

Now it was time to deal with Rupert Frake.

Chapter 15: Rupert Frake And The Spy

The main hall of The Bloody Thorn looked like a hundred alehouses Baine had seen in his life—dirty and dark, with rough plank tables supported by trestles running down the middle of the room framed by numerous worn benches. A few three-legged stools were scattered around the ends of the tables here and there, with a low ceiling dominated by thick wooden beams stained almost black. It was crowded and noisy inside the hall, with the smells of roasting meat, smoke, unwashed bodies, and ale and beer all competing for attention. Baine took in a deep breath, feeling at home and almost smiling at the familiarness of it all. He'd always loved alehouses.

Three circular metal chandeliers with flickering candles hung from the ceiling by chains, the main source of light other than a sputtering fireplace and several tiny, unshuttered windows. Baine knew a tall man like his friend Hadrack would be forced to duck to pass beneath those chandeliers, but it was hardly an issue for him. Four men sat together at one of the tables closest to the door, and they studied him with interest. One of them snickered at Baine's overly large attire, shaking his head as he muttered something to his companions, who all laughed before turning back to their mugs. Baine examined the men closely, but judging by the description the whore in Laskerly had given him, none were young enough or good-looking enough to be his quarry, Rupert Frake.

An unoccupied cut-down barrel and battered stool stood out of the way along one side of the fireplace near the hearth. Baine moved to it, unhooking his bow that he'd restrung earlier before leaning it against the wall. He sat down on the stool with his forearms braced on the barrel top, ignoring the heat from the fire while he soaked in the room's atmosphere and let his eyes and ears work for him. He estimated there were at least thirty or forty men and women in the hall, though in the uneven light, it was hard to make out many of their features clearly. Some were gambling at the far end of the room, throwing dice against the wall and laughing drunkenly. Others were drinking warm ale or beer, with the odd person eating pottage or meat pies, which Baine guessed was probably the only fare worthy of the term food in a place like this.

    A man and woman sat on a high-backed kettle bench near the door that led to the kitchens, with the man casually fondling the woman's breasts through her dress, though no one seemed to notice or care. A large wooden chest sat on the floor on the other side of the kitchen door, with the shelves above it cluttered with earthenware mugs, pewter dishes, and pitchers. Baine knew he needed to tread carefully here, not relishing another run-in with the House Agents if things went wrong for him. Some quick thinking and a lot of luck had helped him escape them the first time, but Baine knew renewing his acquaintance with fighting men of that caliber would likely result in disaster—the uncomfortable headless kind. No, if Rupert was indeed in this place, Baine needed to first identify him without revealing himself, then figure out a way to get him away from prying eyes before introducing the bastard to his knives.

    A barmaid with tawny, long brown hair piled atop her head and wearing an ankle-length green skirt and a low-cut white tunic finally noticed Baine sitting alone, tucked in by the hearth. She headed his way, and despite his purpose for being there, Baine couldn't tear his gaze away from her ample hips and overflowing bosom, marveling at how the tops of her breasts jiggled and heaved like liquid honey with every step she took. He felt lust rise in him as he pictured her naked and writhing beneath him, thrusting the thought guiltily aside a moment later. He was a recent widower, after all, though as the girl paused several feet from where he sat, Baine conceded that Flora, of all people, would be the first to say there was no harm in admiring the girl's obvious charms.

"Can I get you something?" the barmaid asked pleasantly.

She was actually rather plain-looking, almost homely even, Baine decided now that he could see her features better in the light from the fire. For obvious reasons, he hadn't given her face all that much attention at first. The barmaid's nose was much too long for her face, and her eyes were red-rimmed and set unnaturally close together. Her mouth was too small as well, with thin, cracked lips, and she had a gap you could ride a horse through between her front teeth. But despite all those flaws, Baine still found himself intrigued by the girl's unquestionable femininity, though he suspected his feelings on the matter had more to do with her straining tunic and what it barely hid than anything else.

"Uh, ale is fine," Baine said, finally tearing his gaze away from the girl's chest with a supreme effort of will. He didn't fail to notice the barmaid's knowing smirk and instead pretended to glance around the room as if searching for someone. "Have you seen Rupert Frake around by any chance? He told me to meet him here, but I don't see him."

The barmaid's smirk turned to a frown as a dark shadow crossed over her features at the boy's name. Something there, Baine guessed by the look. "Rupert left about an hour ago," the girl said in a tight voice. "Probably went off to moon over *that woman* again. As if someone like her even knows he exists."

Baine shook his head in mock commiseration, understanding immediately who she meant after what he'd learned about Rupert Frake's hopeless infatuation. "I imagine you mean Lady Elyn?"

"Who else?" the barmaid said with a snort. "That boy could have had his pick of any woman in town—fine, hard-working women that would have borne him strong sons, but instead, the fool wants that which he can never have. He's going to lose his head over Lady Elyn someday. You mark my words."

Maybe today is that day, Baine thought. *Though just not in the way you think.* He shrugged sympathetically. "Well, you know Rupert, always dreaming big."

"That I do," the girl said wearily, wearing the weight of her own obvious infatuation plastered across her face for all to see.

The barmaid shook her head sadly and turned to go just as Baine added hurriedly, "Did my old friend say where exactly he was going?"

The girl hesitated. "No, not really. But the men with him seemed just as eager as he was to leave." Baine perked up with interest at that. Men? "They were thick as thieves, those three," the girl continued without needing any prodding. She nodded her head toward the dice players. "Sat over there in the corner all alone before the gambling started, just a whispering among themselves. Every time I brought them a drink, they'd stop talking. If you ask me, they're up to no good. The only surprise is Cairn and Tad weren't along with them. Rupert and those two are usually inseparable when they're hatching one of their plots."

"Did you know the men who were with Rupert?" Baine asked, trying to appear nonchalant.

"Only one of them," the girl said with a quick nod. "Bent Holdfer. He used to live in Crestpool but moved to Collingwood a few years back. They say it was because he got Jenda Miren with child, but I—" The barmaid hesitated, taking an involuntary step backward as she looked at Baine strangely. "Are you all right?"

Baine smoothed his features, guessing he'd reacted a little too strongly after learning who Rupert's companion had turned out to be. *What incredible luck!* He forced a smile, though his insides were still tingling with excitement at the news that another of the outlaws was in town. *Could there be even more of the bastards here?* "Of course I'm fine," Baine finally said as calmly as he could muster. "Why do you ask?"

"Oh, I don't know," the barmaid said, relaxing slightly, though she continued to watch him warily. "Your face got all hard and serious there for a moment. It kind of caught me off guard." She shivered. "Felt like a ghost tickled my backside when I looked into your eyes."

"What's your name?" Baine asked to change the subject.

"Fioria."

Baine smiled disarmingly. "Well Fioria, my name is Baine. I'm sure Rupert must have told you about me?" The girl just shook her head and Baine snorted. "Same old Rupert. Everything is always about *him*." He leaned forward. "Listen, Fioria, what can you tell me about the other man with Rupert? Have you seen him around before?"

"No," the barmaid admitted. "I don't think so." She leaned forward, lowering her voice. Baine caught a whiff of onions on her breath. "But he was an ugly, mean-looking bastard, I'll tell you that much. Looked like he'd slit your throat just for the fun of it." Fioria straightened with a shrug. "Anyway, he sure didn't look like someone Rupert usually associates with." The girl glanced down at Baine, studying his attire curiously. "Course, now that I think about it, neither do you, for that matter. What's with the odd clothing?"

"It's a long story," Baine said with an exaggerated sigh. "How about I tell it to you once I have my ale and maybe some of that wonderful roast beef I smell?"

"Fair enough," Fioria replied with a musical chuckle. "I look forward to it."

"One last thing," Baine said, holding up a hand to stop her from leaving. "I know Rupert lives with his wife and brother—"

"Sister," Fioria corrected. "Rupert has a sister, little Tabina."

"Yes, of course," Baine agreed, smiling apologetically. "How silly of me to forget. Anyway, Rupert mentioned they live on Candle Lane somewhere. Do you know where that might be?"

"About five blocks down to the west of here," Fioria answered. "A three-story townhouse. Marina, Rupert's mother, is a silk weaver, and she rents the second floor from the merchant, Hectire Lent."

"Thank you," Baine said, satisfied. "You've been most helpful."

The girl nodded and headed away, and the moment she disappeared through the door that led into the kitchens, Baine jumped to his feet, grabbed his bow, and hurried outside. Dusk had just begun to fall, he realized when he reached the street. He paused on the stoop of the alehouse, hooking his bow over his shoulders and watching warily as a group of armed horsemen trotted past. They looked like Northern soldiers to his eye, but none gave him more than a perfunctory glance.

What now? Baine thought after the riders had gone. He glanced to the south, where he could just make out Lord Falmir's fork-tailed standard in the waning light—a white cross imposed over a red background—fluttering in the breeze from atop one of the turrets of the castle. Baine pursed his lips. The barmaid had said that Rupert Frake had left The Bloody Thorn with what she believed was the intention of seeing Lady Elyn. But had that just been jealousy talking, or had the boy and his companions actually gone to do just that? And if so, why? What did Bent Holdfer have to gain from such a move, or his mysterious companion for that matter?

Baine was hoping the third man with Rupert Frake and Holdfer would turn out to be the outlaw named Pater Dore. Or if not him, then at least another of the bastards who'd raided Witbridge, though he knew there was just as good a chance the man could be nothing more than a random stranger who'd had nothing to do with the killings. Holdfer's presence in Crestpool was the real question, though. Why was he here with Rupert at all? Cairn had insisted at the point of a knife that Jark Cordly had cut him, Rupert, and Tadley loose after the raid on Witbridge but had kept the rest of the men together, including Holdfer. But that information conflicted greatly with what Hanley's father had told Baine, with the miller insisting the whore Samma had overheard the entire band was planning to go their separate ways. So, had Cairn been lying or simply wrong and the whore, right? That would certainly help to explain Holdfer's presence in town and perhaps the third man's as well.

Baine took a deep breath as he glanced west, deciding his best bet right now was to find Rupert Frake's house and see if the boy had gone there. Perhaps Fioria's instincts were wrong and Rupert hadn't sought out Lady Elyn after all. Either way, there was only one way to know for certain. He set off down the street, counting off the blocks and watching warily for town wardens or House Agents.

Baine was one block shy of Rupert Frake's house, walking with his head down, when a dark form hobbled out from the shadows cast by a building and blocked his path. "Got a carver for a man who gave his all for the rightful king?"

Baine paused, examining the one-legged apparition in front of him, who was holding out a shaking hand. The man was almost as tall as Hadrack and wearing a dark cloak and hood, but he was thin and reeked of shit. He could be twenty or fifty; it was hard to tell for certain beneath the cowl.

"What's a carver?" Baine asked, wrapping his fingers warily around the knife hilt at his waist.

The beggar chuckled. "A bit of it, lad. A slice of nice. Gold for the bold. You know."

"Ah," Baine grunted, remembering now. A carver was what Afrenians called a quarter section of any coin. "You're Afrenian?"

"I'm a man without a clan. A brother with no mother. A lamb in a jam. Won't you help?"

Baine looked down at the man's missing limb. "You lost your leg fighting for the North?"

"For the rightful king, I did," the beggar muttered. "The prince of princes. The king with the ring. The man with—"

"So, Prince Tyrale, then?" Baine grunted, wondering why he was even bothering with the man.

The beggar winked in the half-light and smiled conspiratorially. "Say that, did I now? Perhaps yeah, perhaps nay, eh? A king be a king except when he's not, me thinks."

Baine frowned. Was the man mad, or was he trying to tell him something? "What do you want?"

"I told you," the beggar said. "A carver is all I ask of you—a pittance for a well-dressed man like yourself. A randy dandy you are. Sharp as a harp in them fancy clothes. Fine as shine. The best of the rest."

Baine sighed and stepped around the cripple before continuing on. He had better things to do than listen to a man who'd clearly lost his mind.

"I hear the wardens are searching the entire town for you, lad," the beggar rasped in a low voice. "Curious, that is."

Baine hesitated. He glanced around the empty street, then turned back to face the beggar. "What? What did you just say?"

The one-legged man crept forward like a spider on his crutch until they were less than three feet apart. Baine saw him wink again in the dim light. "It's a funny thing," the man whispered. "Most people barely notice a poor old bastard like me. What use am I, they say to themselves? Broken, wasted, and foul to smell and look upon as I am. An embarrassment and an abomination all at once, so they say with noses in the air. But what to do about me, ah, that's the real question." The beggar held up a long finger. "The solution to this quandary for these poor, tender souls is actually quite simple, as it turns out—most just don't bother to look at all. It's like I don't exist to them, which suits me just fine for, while it's true I only have one leg, I still have a sharp mind to go along with two eyes and two ears that are as keen as a young boy's."

"If you have something to tell me, just say it or go away," Baine growled, getting annoyed now.

"Methinks perhaps we are two birds with similar interests, no?"

Baine's eyes narrowed. "Who are you?"

The beggar shrugged. "A friend, perhaps. But the world is a dangerous place these days, and because of this, one must tread carefully—whether he be one-footed or two."

"How do you know the wardens are looking for me?" Baine asked.

"Because I saw what happened," the beggar answered with a small grin. "In the garden courtyard, I mean. A slick business, that was. There you were, dressed all in black, running like The Father was breathing down your neck. Nobody noticed you but me, but then again, noticing the unnoticeable is my business. I watched you go into the tailor shop, and I watched the House Agents as they searched for you. It was only a matter of time, says I, and then they'd have the thief, as I thought of you at the time, for there was no way out. But then, to my surprise—" The beggar snapped his fingers loudly. "Out from the shop comes a different man altogether, a performer no less, yet somehow the same man as before. A clever, clever man, it would seem." The beggar shook his head in admiration. "As I said, a slick bit of business, that, and one that piqued my curiosity. Who is this clever little man, I wonders to myself?"

"So, now what?" Baine asked, once again fingering his knife. "What are you really after? Surely all this isn't about a carver?"

The beggar smiled, glancing down at Baine's hand before shaking his head. "You won't need that, my boy. I'm no enemy of yours, I assure you. As I said before, I believe we are two similar birds, you and I. Devout followers of a cause that is more above than below, if you get my meaning."

Baine blinked, understanding now. "You're a spy for the South," he said.

"An unfortunate word, that," the beggar stated with distaste. "It sounds dirty somehow." Baine glanced at the man's filth-ridden clothing, not hiding his amazement, while the beggar grinned at the irony. "Actually, I prefer loyal servant to the House if you insist on describing me. The right side of it, anyway."

"You're one of Daughter Gernet's men," Baine guessed, knowing somehow that he was right.

"I am," the beggar confirmed. "You know her, then?"

"I do," Baine replied. He let his hand fall away from the knife, relaxing as he grinned sarcastically. "Quite a charming woman, that one. Though I think I'd prefer to fight in a shield wall stark naked than chance going up against her sharp wit and tongue."

"Indeed," the beggar agreed. "A fairer assessment I have not heard. May I ask how you know Daughter Gernet?"

"I ride with Hadrack of Corwick," Baine stated.

The beggar's eyebrows rose. "The Wolf, you say? I've heard a great deal of talk about this man. A fearsome fighter to be sure if half of it is to be believed."

"He's everything you've heard and more," Baine said proudly. "Much more."

The beggar nodded thoughtfully. "Word is he and his band of outlaws have been doing good work here in the North. Is the Wolf with you, perhaps?"

Baine's grin faded. "No, I'm alone."

"For what reason?"

"It's personal," Baine muttered. "Something that has nothing to do with Hadrack or the war."

"Everything has to do with the war," the spy grunted. He offered his hand. "Please forgive my appearance and the filth that goes with it, lad. It is, unfortunately, part of the role. My name is Chadry, Chadry Armac.

Baine hesitated for only a moment, then he took the man's hand in his. "Baine," he said.

"Ah," Chadry replied with a nod. "Well, Baine, it seems you've stirred up a real hornet's nest here. The town wardens and the Lord's men are searching for you door to door. Gembart Platt is a close personal friend of Lord Falmir's bailiff, you see." The beggar glanced at Baine's doublet. "And they know what you're wearing, by the way. They spoke with the tailor, so you should dispose of that as soon as possible. I'd also strongly consider going over the walls tonight and getting away from this place if I were you."

"My horse is stabled with—"

Chadry shook his head. "Best leave the animal where it is. Men are watching the place even as we speak. If you go back there tonight, they'll surely have you."

Baine cursed under his breath. He glanced at the one-legged man. "Thank you for the warning. I know you took a risk to tell me all this."

"Consider it professional courtesy," Chadry said with a slight bow. He pulled back his cowl, revealing a wizened face, a balding head, and a heavy silver beard. He whipped off his foul-smelling cloak, then offered it to Baine. "Take this. It's not much, but it should help throw them off the scent—no humor intended—at least for a while." Baine reluctantly took the garment as Chadry gestured toward him. "Now, give me that hideous doublet you're wearing."

"Why?" Baine asked in surprise.

Chadry grinned. "Because I know just the man who will enjoy wearing it. He's as sneaky as a rat and as fast as a cat. He'll have those wardens running around in circles all night long chasing after him." Chadry looked at Baine knowingly. "That should give you enough time to find the boy and do what you came to and get away."

Baine gaped at the one-legged man. "You know why I'm here?"

"Not for certain, but after what you just told me, I can guess," Chadry said. He ticked off a finger. "You are part of Hadrack's Wolf Pack staying at Witbridge Manor." Another finger lifted. "The place was raided not that long ago by a man posing as the Outlaw of Corwick. That man, sadly for him, didn't know he was raiding the *actual* Outlaw of Corwick's holding, which means he'll likely be dead very soon." A third finger. "Tadley Platt was one of the men who went along on that raid, and he was murdered just a few hours ago by a man dressed all in black—a man who looks just like you." A fourth finger. "Rupert Frake, who lives just a stone's throw away from where we now stand, is a close friend of Tadley Platt and was also involved in the raid." The one-legged man shrugged. "It doesn't take a lot to conclude from all that that you are here for revenge, lad." Chadry's voice softened, and his eyes filled with empathy. "I imagine they killed someone close to you?"

"My wife and son," Baine answered, swallowing emotion that threatened to rise in him.

"Ah," Chadry said. "I figured it was something like that." He sighed regretfully. "Unfortunately, this world we live in can be very cruel." Chadry motioned for Baine's doublet again. "Best get on with things, then."

Baine took off the garment, then drew on the foul-smelling cloak, wrinkling his nose. He lifted the cowl to hide his face before offering his hand to Chadry. "You have my thanks. Stay safe, and if you need a favor sometime, just get the word out and I'll be there."

Chadry took Baine's hand and shook it firmly. "It has been a pleasure, Baine. I hope you find the bastards and kill them all. But remember this. If I can figure out what you're doing here in Crestpool, others might as well, so be careful."

"I will," Baine promised.

Chadry pointed to a tall, dark house a hundred yards down the street. "That's Rupert Frake's dwelling there. Good luck." Then he turned and hobbled away.

Baine waited until Chadry had disappeared down an alleyway into the darkness, then he headed for the house the man had indicated. He paused outside the steps, looking up at the front door. The windows on the first and second floors were shuttered, but faint candlelight came from an open window on the third. Baine climbed the steps and tried the door, not surprised to find it unbarred. Fioria had said Frake and his family were renting the second floor from a merchant, which meant chances were other tenants lived above on the third. People in townhouses like this came and went all the time, so barring the door would be impracticable, and locks with multiple sets of keys were expensive.

Baine stepped inside, closing the door softly behind him. He was now in almost total darkness, so he began using his hands to probe around until he finally located an interior wall to his right. Baine knew tenement houses like this traditionally had a stairway close by in the main hall, so he shuffled forward until he found it. He began to climb, making his way stealthy upward as close to the wall as possible to avoid any creaking from the steps. He finally reached a landing, focusing on a door ahead of him where he could see a faint glow of light emanating from the crack between the door and floor. Rupert Frake's place? It seemed likely.

Baine moved forward cautiously, pressing his ear to the wood, but he could hear no sounds from inside. He carefully unlatched the door, then slowly pushed it inward, pausing in surprise at what he saw waiting for him inside. A flickering candle on a table revealed an older woman sprawled out on the wood floor, lying facedown with dark red blood pooling around her head. A dead man sat unnaturally on the floor beside the woman, propped up by a cedar chest with his head lolling back on it as he stared with unseeing eyes at the ceiling. Baine moved closer until he stood over the corpse. The dead man was young and impossibly handsome, almost too pretty to be male, with the only flaw Baine could see in his perfect features a hideous, gaping red slash across his neck.

Baine took a deep breath, knowing he'd just found Rupert Frake.

Chapter 16: A Tired Jester?

Baine wasn't sure if he should curse the fact that Rupert was dead or celebrate it. In his mind, the boy's lifeblood had belonged solely to him ever since he'd learned Frake's name, and he had to admit he felt somewhat cheated that he'd met his demise at the hands of someone else. Now all Baine could do was wonder who had wielded the knife that had ended the youth's life, and more to the point, why? Logic certainly leaned toward the culprits being Bent Holdfer and his unknown companion, though in a rough town like Crestpool, Baine knew there was an outside chance that it could have been someone else. But, if it had been the outlaws who had murdered Rupert as he believed, then that certainly satisfied the *who*, with only the *why* left to be answered. Baine decided he would ask Holdfer that very question when he caught up to the bastard, if for no other reason than he wanted to satisfy his curiosity.

Baine crouched by the body, resting his hands on his bent knees as he examined the dead boy's handsome face. He thought he could see a hint of fear and pain in Rupert's blank blue eyes, guessing that his last moments had not been pleasant. *Well, thank the gods for that, at least*, Baine thought with satisfaction. Perhaps it was just wishful thinking on his part, he conceded, and he was just seeing what he wanted to see, but even so, it made him feel better to think the boy had suffered. Baine glanced toward the dead woman on the floor, who he assumed must be Rupert's mother. He grimaced. The back of her skull was caved in by a terrible blow, the greying hair matted and streaked with dark blood, pink gore, and white flecks of bone. Had an axe done all that damage, or maybe the hilt of a sword?

Baine sighed as he let his eyes roam around the small room, which was utilitarian and sparsely furnished. A battered square table with a sputtering candle on it that he saw was almost burned down to the nub stood against one wall, surrounded on two sides by benches. He noticed three mugs and three wooden bowls also on the tabletop, with food still inside the bowls. Judging by that and the still-fresh blood on the floor, Baine figured the killings must have happened only a short time ago. A narrow cupboard built from warped oak planks rose against the end wall near a low, arched passageway, and a surprisingly new-looking rocking chair sat in the middle of the room atop a threadbare carpet. The rush-woven cushion on the chair seat was splattered with flecks of blood and gore.

A creak of a floorboard suddenly sounded from the passageway, the noise stark in the utter silence. Baine stood smoothly, dropping a hand to his knife while cursing at himself for not checking to ensure that no one else was around. He waited, listening, but the sound wasn't repeated. Baine flicked his eyes back to the table—three bowls. He'd forgotten all about Rupert Frake's younger sister. He drew his knife just in case it wasn't her and slipped forward silently on the balls of his feet, pausing at the entranceway to peer down the short passage dimly lit by the candle burning behind him. His eyes immediately locked onto those of a young girl coming stealthily toward him on her tiptoes. She froze in midstep, her mouth dropping open in surprise before she screamed in terror, turned, and ran back the way she'd come.

"Stop!" Baine shouted at the girl's retreating back. "I'm not here to hurt you."

The fugitive ignored his plea, reaching the end of the passage before disappearing as if by magic into the darkness, though Baine could still hear the sounds of her sobbing echoing outward to him. He stepped into the narrow passageway, using his left hand to guide himself along the wall as he followed after the girl cautiously. After ten steps, Baine reached the end of the corridor, finding an open space to his left leading to a second room that was as black as night. The crying was coming from in there.

"I'm not going to hurt you," Baine repeated from the entrance, trying to penetrate the gloom with his eyes. He couldn't see a thing.

"Go away!" the girl's trembling voice shot back at him between her sobs. "Leave me alone!"

Baine hesitated. The brief glimpse he'd gotten of the girl had revealed a child of around eight years old wearing a rough-spun brown linen dress with a thin build and black hair hanging down to her shoulders. Rupert Frake's sister, no doubt. *What had the barmaid told him her name was? Tarana? Turia? No, Tabina, that was it.* Baine reached out a hand, though he had no way of knowing if the child could see him or not. "Tabina, it's all right. I'm a good friend of Rupert's."

A slight gasp sounded. "You are?" she asked hopefully.

"Yes," Baine said, nodding his head. "I was with him at The Bloody Thorn not that long ago. He asked me to meet him here."

"Why would he do that?" the girl asked, her tone turning to suspicion.

Baine hesitated, thinking fast. He decided to take a chance. "Rupert confided in me he was worried about the men he was with at the alehouse. He wanted me to watch his back."

"It's too late for that," the girl said bitterly.

Baine took a deep breath. This girl was not responsible for what her brother had done in Witbridge, and if he could give her any comfort at all, he would. The innocents always pay, Jebido had warned. "Can you tell me what happened here, Tabina?" Baine asked. "Was it the men with your brother who did this?" The girl started to cry louder at that, and Baine grimaced, knowing he didn't have much time to waste here. Sooner or later, someone was bound to come and investigate. He needed answers. "Tabina?"

"Yes, it was them," the girl finally answered between sniffs.

"Do you know their names?"

"Rupert introduced one of them to my mother as Bent," the girl answered. "I don't remember what the other one was called."

She sniffed loudly. "I don't understand. Rupert said they were his friends, but then they went and—."

The girl trailed off, and Baine nodded, his suspicions confirmed. It had been the outlaws, just as he'd thought. "Do you have any idea why these men killed your family, Tabina?" he asked gently.

"No," the girl replied in a tortured voice from the darkened room. "Mama made them food, and they all sat down to eat. Rupert told Mama and me to wait here in the bedroom afterward—said they had to talk about things without any women around. They started to argue not long after that, and then we heard Rupert cry out. Mama went to see what was happening and I followed. I saw Rupert on the floor on his knees with the ugly, older man holding a knife to his throat. Mama shouted at him, and then she started hitting him with her fists before—" The girl hesitated again, sobbing louder.

"Go on," Baine prompted. "What happened next?"

"The other one, the tall one with the patch on his eye named Bent, hit her with something," the girl said between shuddering sobs. "I don't know with what. Mama fell. Blood was everywhere. I tried to run to her, but the tall man grabbed me by the hair and told me to go back to the bedroom and stay there."

Baine sighed, surprised the outlaws hadn't just killed the girl as well. "Did you hear them say anything else to each other?" he asked hopefully. "Like maybe where they were going from here?"

"No," the girl replied after a moment. She sniffed again and coughed. "Well, the man called Bent did say something about going to see a tired jester or something like that while they were eating. That's all I remember."

Baine frowned. *A tired jester? What did that mean?* He reached for his moneybag and pulled out two coins, guessing there wasn't anything else he would learn from the girl. Baine bent and set the gold by the entranceway. "I have to go now, Tabina, but I'm leaving you two Jorqs. Once I'm gone, find a town warden and tell him what happened here. They'll help you, but whatever you do, don't tell them about the money or they'll steal it from you." He hesitated. "And don't tell anyone I was here either, all right?"

"Why not?" the girl asked innocently.

Baine grimaced, deciding to tell the truth, or at least enough of it to satisfy the child and hopefully ensure her silence. "Because I'm going to find the men who murdered Rupert, and when I do, I'm going to kill them for what they did. The wardens will try to stop me from doing that. Do you understand?"

"They will?"

"Yes," Baine said gravely.

"Why?"

"Because that's how things work," Baine said evasively, feeling uncomfortable now. He was well aware that he was manipulating this child, which wasn't sitting right with him, though he knew it was necessary under the circumstances. "Do you want justice for your family or not?"

"Of course I do!" the girl said with a little steel in her voice now.

"Then you have to trust me and not say anything," Baine said. "Will you do that?"

"I guess so," Tabina said uncertainly.

"Swear to me that you won't tell," Baine said in a firm voice. "On the First Pair."

"I swear," the girl finally replied in a tiny voice. "I won't say anything about you." She hesitated. "But now you have to swear to me that you really will kill those men."

"They will die this night by my hand," Baine said. "You have my word." He turned to go, then hesitated, looking back into the blackened room. He thought suddenly of Sunna and the fate that had found her. He hadn't been able to save her or Nelsun in the end, and he knew he was failing yet another innocent child. "Good luck, Tabina," Baine said with a heavy heart. "I know this isn't fair, and I'm sorry for that. I wish I could do more."

The girl didn't reply to that and feeling miserable, Baine finally turned and made his way along the passageway, then back outside. He took a deep breath, glad to be away from the stench of blood and death in the room, knowing that Tabina was probably doomed to a life of misery without her mother to watch over her now. The chances that she'd end up on Beggar's Row or in a brothel servicing the lusts of men five times her age were a real possibility, yet there was little he could do about it at the moment. Hopefully, once his task was complete, he could return here and do something more for the girl than just give her a couple of coins.

Baine sighed, acutely aware that he was just trying to appease his conscience and that it would be far too late by the time he was in a safe enough position to help the girl. The world is a dangerous place, the spy Chadry Armac had said gravely, and he was unfortunately right. The night air had cooled since Baine had entered the house, and he pulled Chadry's soiled cloak tighter about his thin frame, barely noticing the smells wafting from it now. He looked up and down the street. A cart filled with bales of goods plodded slowly past, drawn by a chestnut-colored mule. The man leading the mule walked unsteadily ahead of it with his head down while he mumbled something unintelligible. Baine guessed he was either dead tired or dead drunk. A trio of men appeared on the next block, laughing among themselves as they headed his way.

Baine lifted his hood, then started walking rapidly away from the boisterous group as he reviewed what he'd learned. He now had a few new clues about the men he sought. First, Bent Holdfer was tall with a patch over his eye, which was valuable information that would help greatly in identifying the man. The second clue—that Holdfer's companion was ugly—was interesting, though it might prove unhelpful in the end. Crestpool was undoubtedly filled with ugly men, after all. The last clue, though, now that was a curious one, for Baine wasn't even certain it was a clue at all. Tabina had told him Bent Holdfer had mentioned going to see a tired jester, but it made little sense to him. Had she misheard the man, perhaps? Baine knew it was certainly a possibility that she had, and he wondered if he should just discount what she'd said entirely. He suddenly thought about the festival he'd witnessed in the courtyard earlier that day. Could this jester fellow have been part of the troupe of acrobats and actors that had been performing there? The idea seemed highly unlikely, yet even so, Baine knew he had to look into it further.

A dark form suddenly appeared from between two buildings, moving toward him awkwardly—a man with only one leg. Baine slowed, then stopped as he waited for the spy.

"Well, that didn't take you very long," Chadry said with a soft chuckle as he paused in front of Baine. "Nice and quiet, too. That's not always an easy thing to accomplish when you're interrogating a man. It's an art form that. I'm impressed."

"Why are you still here?" Baine asked, surprised to see the man. He noted the colorful doublet he'd given Chadry was gone, guessing he'd already handed it over to his accomplice, the rat who moved like a cat.

Chadry shrugged. "I kept a watch out just in case you ran into trouble. We birds have to stick together, after all." The spy shifted his crutch under his arm, wincing at the discomfort. "So, did you get what you wanted before you killed the bastard?"

"I didn't kill him," Baine grunted. "Turns out somebody got there ahead of me."

Chadry's eyebrows rose. "Is that a fact? Who?"

"Two men who rode with Jark Cordly," Baine answered. "Bent Holdfer and another one. I don't know that one's name yet. They also killed the mother but left Rupert's younger sister alive."

"Well, thank the gods for that small favor," Chadry said with a weary sigh.

"Listen," Baine said, putting a hand on the one-legged man's arm. "I'm glad you're here. I could use your help." He gestured behind him toward the Frake's house. "The little girl in there,

Tabina. Can you look after her or see that she's taken care of? She's all alone now."

Chadry frowned. "I don't know, Baine. I have duties to perform. I don't have time for something like—"

"Please," Baine insisted. "You and I both know what's going to happen to her if you don't."

Chadry pursed his lips and nodded. "Yes, it's a tragedy, to be sure. But we're at war, Baine. Do you know how many children have lost their families in the past year? Hundreds. It's a terrible shame, but the cold hard truth is I'm here to do a job that could save thousands of lives. I can't risk getting caught just for the sake of one poor girl. I'm sorry, but that's the way it is."

Baine looked away, knowing the spy had a valid point. He hadn't been willing to risk his life for Tabina either, so why should he expect Chadry to take that chance? He looked back at the man stubbornly. "Is there nothing you can do for her? Surely you know someone in this town you can trust?"

"I don't think—"

"All I'm asking is that you get her away from here somehow," Baine insisted, cutting the man off. "I'd do it if I could. Just send her to Witbridge Manor and have her ask for my friend, Jebido. All Tabina has to do is tell him I sent her and I promise he'll look after her. I'm begging you."

Chadry's face softened. "Why does this particular girl mean so much to you? You don't even know her."

Baine looked down at the ground. "Because she reminds me of someone else, someone I failed not that long ago. I don't want to see the same thing happen again."

Chadry rubbed his hand down his face wearily. "Well, I know a woman in town who might be willing to take her that far." He lifted a finger at Baine's hopeful look. "But I guarantee you she won't do it for free." Baine had already begun reaching for his quickly depleting moneybag as Chadry waved him off. "No, that's all right. I'll take care of the payment."

"You're sure?" Baine asked, surprised and relieved at the same time.

"The gods help me, no, I'm not," Chadry grumbled. "Not about any of this, but I'll do it anyway." He finally grinned. "You're a tough man to say no to, Baine. It's rare to come across someone with honor these days, especially in my line of work. It's a refreshing change."

"Thank you, Chadry," Baine said, meaning it. "You've taken a load off my shoulders."

The spy poked Baine playfully in the chest with his finger. "You should consider becoming a merchant, you know. With that slick tongue of yours you'd be richer than the Emperor of Cardia in no time."

Baine laughed, clapping the man on the shoulder. "Now it looks like I owe you two favors," he said.

"Three, actually," Chadry replied mysteriously. "And don't think I won't call you on them, either."

Baine's eyebrows rose in surprise. "Three?"

"I have my associates looking into Jark Cordly and the men who rode with him for you," Chadry replied. "If all goes well, I should have some names for you by morning—that is, if you can stay alive that long."

"I don't know what to say," Baine said, shaking his head in wonder. Chadry Armac was full of surprises.

"Then don't say anything," the spy replied with a shrug. He glanced toward the Frake's house. "So, any idea what happened in there?"

"No, not really," Baine answered. "Tabina said there was some kind of an argument, but she didn't know what it was about."

"Rats always turn on each other sooner or later," Chadry grunted, not looking surprised.

Baine nodded in agreement. "Is there someone in town that goes by the name of the tired jester?" he asked.

"It's not a *someone*," Chadry replied thoughtfully. "I believe it's a *something*—an inn near Town's Square. The place is actually known as The Weary Jester, though. Why do you ask?"

Baine grinned, feeling his excitement building. "Because that's where Bent Holdfer and his friend were heading next."

Chapter 17: Bent And The Ugly Merchant

Baine found The Weary Jester without much trouble. The building was situated at the crossroads where the town's two main streets met—Woodcutter's Road and Highhill Lane—and it took up most of the block. He'd spent the last half an hour watching from the shadows of a warehouse across the square from the inn, alert for any signs of wardens or House Agents while a steady stream of patrons came and went. There were no threats that Baine could see, and he was becoming more and more confident that the ongoing search for him he'd been warned about must have already occurred here. It made a certain kind of sense, actually, since his pursuers had undoubtedly checked all the inns, taverns, and alehouses first before moving on to less likely places where he might have holed up.

The Weary Jester was two-stories high and long, with a steep roof of weathered orange clay tiles and thick wattle and daub walls built over a stout timber frame. The inn was shaped like an L, with an attached stable at the shorter end leading to a small yard where guests' horses were watered and fed before being bedded down for the night inside. The main building had a series of narrow, roof-covered balconies on the second floor that extended well out over the first, with lanterns burning along every third support beam above and below. Baine watched as a man and woman appeared on one of the balconies, leaning against the railing together. The man wrapped his arm around the woman's shoulders possessively as the faint sounds of her musical laughter floated over to where he stood. The two remained that way for long minutes before finally heading back inside.

A behemoth of a man with massive shoulders and arms that were offset by an equally enormous bulging stomach stood guard outside the inn's front door, demanding a fee from anyone who wished to enter. Baine had seen more than one potential patron become indignant at the request and refuse to pay before walking stiffly away. He'd never heard of an inn demanding payment for entry before. Finally satisfied that there were no threats to be seen, Baine cut off a section of a Jorq with his knife, then crossed the square and approached The Weary Jester. The guard's dark beard and mustache were heavily oiled, Baine saw as he drew closer, finding it gave him a rather effeminate look somehow despite his intimidating size.

The guard stood with his beefy arms crossed over his chest, watching Baine as he approached with obvious distaste. "What do you want?" the man finally barked in a gruff tone when Baine paused in front of him.

Baine was forced to arch his neck back to peer up at the man's face from beneath his cowl. That face was round and fleshy, with a wide, flat nose that showed evidence of having been broken many times. The guard's eyes were small, suspicious, and mean, like a cornered pig's—not a good sign. "Why, to get in, of course," Baine answered cheerfully. He offered the sliver of coin.

The big man glanced at the gold, making no move to take it. "We don't take your kind here, so move along."

"My kind?" Baine said, taken aback slightly. He hadn't seen anyone else that had offered payment turned away during the entire time he'd watched the inn. "And what, in the name of the gods, would that kind be, exactly?"

"The beggary kind," the guard growled. He pointed to a painted sign that read, NO VAGRANTS. "This is a gentleman's establishment," the man added. He leaned forward and sniffed dramatically. "And you stink like a cesspool and clearly are not one." The guard flicked his enormous hand as if shooing away a fly. Baine noticed three ruby rings gleaming on the man's pudgy fingers. "Now, go get drunk somewhere else, or better yet, go drink your own piss back in the alley you slithered out from."

"But, I'm not here for—" Baine started to protest.

The guard put his hands on his hips, his pig eyes hardening in warning. "I said *go away*, boy, before I lose my patience and stomp on you like a roach." He gestured to the west. "The Cracked Flagon is down there about half a block or so. It's full of cut-throats, thieves, and flea-bitten whores, so you should find yourself in familiar company."

Baine hesitated, knowing he could easily slit the fat bastard's neck before the man knew what was happening, but doing so would bring him nothing but trouble, so he resisted the impulse. He turned instead and headed away in the direction the guard had said, not bothering to say anything more. There seemed no point. After a hundred paces, Baine reached the stables and looked back, pleased to see the fat man had already forgotten about him, his attention now taken up by several older men arguing over the entry fee.

Baine darted sideways into the horse yard, staying in the shadows as much as possible while he crossed the rough cobblestones. When he reached the stable entrance, he removed his foul-smelling cloak and left it on the ground near the open doors, then entered the building. Half a dozen horses stood hitched in a row down one wall inside in what were known as tie stalls. A single black mare stood alone in a stall on the opposite wall, with the only source of light a lantern hanging from a hook off a beam above her. A tall boy of twelve or so was brushing down the black mare, though he seemed disinterested in the task, while another boy with a sullen look on his face mucked horse dung from the floor into a barrow with a wooden shovel rimmed with iron.

"Yes?" the groom working the mare asked. He had a squinty, untrustworthy look around the eyes, Baine thought, with ears that stuck out from his unruly brown hair.

"I'm just checking on my horse," Baine answered for want of a better excuse.

The boy frowned, indicating the black mare with the brush he was using. "But, this is Son Adon's horse."

Baine grinned disarmingly and shrugged. "I didn't mean that one." He gestured vaguely to the other horses. "I mean that one over there, of course."

The boy flicked his eyes to the line of tethered horses, but thankfully Baine could tell by his expression that he didn't care enough to ask which one was his. "Oh," the groom muttered, returning to his task.

"What's your name, lad?"

"Fitch," the boy replied grudgingly, not looking up.

"Well, Fitch, I hope you're taking good care of my girl," Baine said. He knew some stableboys with questionable morals oftentimes skimmed grain off the top, selling it later in the town market. This weasely little bastard seemed like a prime candidate. "Giving her the proper amount of water and grain, are you?"

"Of course I am," Fitch replied in a mumble, still refusing to look at Baine. "Always do."

"Well, that's a relief," Baine said as he let his eyes roam around the stable. Most inns like this had a doorway connecting the stable to the main building, but he didn't see it. "I guess I can get back to my ale, then, knowing she's in such capable hands." The boy mucking the stalls snorted at that, but Baine ignored him. "Is there a quicker way to the main hall than going all the way back around, Fitch?"

"Why?" the groom asked suspiciously, pausing in his work to look up. "Are you trying to get past the toll?"

Baine feigned anger. "Watch your mouth, boy. I'm a well-known, paying customer of this establishment, not some worthless grifter. Now, answer the question. Is there another door?"

Fitch's features turned resentful and stubborn. "Maybe. But it's just for people who work here. Why can't you go through the front like everybody else if you've already paid?" The boy looked

Baine up and down, his lip curling in a sneer. "Perhaps because you're so far into your cups, you've forgotten the way back?"

Baine forced a smile, though inside, he was seriously tempted to thrash the little bastard and teach him a lesson in manners. "No, lad, that's not the problem. The problem is there's a beggar outside on the street that's become quite annoying and insistent. I'd rather not have to deal with him again if I can avoid it."

"Is that so?" Fitch said, looking slightly appeased. He hawked and spat into the straw beneath the mare. "I'm surprised Fat Finny hasn't cracked him over the head by now. He hates beggars, that one."

"What can I say?" Baine replied, spreading his arms. He was quickly losing his patience with this boy. "Now, is there another way in I can use or not?"

Fitch shrugged, then motioned to the rear of the stable with his chin. "Back there. Go right at the last stall. Door's at the end of the corridor. But if anyone asks, I didn't tell you about it."

"Fair enough," Baine said in agreement. He headed for the back of the stable, then paused. "One last thing, Fitch. Make sure you give my girl an extra good brushing. Not that half-assed job you're doing on the Son's mare." The groom's expression turned dark and resentful. "And if you don't, I promise you I will know, which means I'll have no choice but to speak to your employer about it." Fitch flicked his eyes to the row of tethered horses, and Baine had to keep himself from laughing out loud. Four of the six were mares, but the boy didn't actually know for sure which one Baine had claimed was his. The young groom licked his lips uncertainly, clearly about to ask for some clarity on the issue, just as Baine spun on his heel and strode away. "Remember," he said loudly, lifting one finger in the air and waving it. "Lots and lots of brushing, lad. Spare no effort and make her coat gleam like the stars. My girl deserves it!"

Baine heard Fitch curse softly under his breath just as he reached the end stall and turned down the corridor, cutting off his view of the groom. He smiled in satisfaction, knowing he'd just added several hours to the unpleasant boy's task. It seemed fitting somehow. Baine passed through a small arched doorway, following a narrow passage that eventually opened into a storage room filled with beer and wine casks as well as small crates. He could hear the sounds of a minstrel singing from behind a closed door in front of him, guessing it led to the main hall. *But should he risk going in there?*

Baine guessed that his description was all over town by now, and it probably wouldn't be long before someone noticed him if he went into the hall. Fitch had also mentioned that it was Son Adon's horse he was grooming, which meant if a priest was staying at the inn, there was a good chance a few House Agents were close by somewhere as well. Going into the hall was an even greater risk now than it had been before, Baine realized with a sinking feeling, yet how else was he going to find the two outlaws?

A door to Baine's left partially hidden by a stack of wine casks suddenly opened, revealing an older chambermaid wearing a brown apron. She looked harried and out of breath and paused in surprise when she noticed him, putting one hand on her chest. Baine could see a narrow flight of stairs going up behind her. "By The Mother, sir, you startled me!"

"Forgive me for that," Baine said, caught off guard by the woman's unexpected appearance. "I've just come from the stables—checking on my horse, you see. Fitch said it was all right for me to come this way."

"He did, eh?" the chambermaid said, frowning. "That boy is going to feel the toe of my shoe on his arse. You just see if he doesn't."

"I'm sorry if I've caused you trouble," Baine said as his mind raced. *What should he do? This woman was bound to expect him to go into the hall.* "It just seemed a shorter walk, is all," he added weakly.

"Oh, don't worry your head about it, young man," the chambermaid said, waving a hand. "No harm done." She sighed then and shook her head wearily. "My word, but it's been a busy night so far. My poor old knees can't take going up and down these stairs much more. First, that insufferable Son Adon and his retinue arrive unannounced, and now I've got to wait hand and foot on this rich merchant who's insisted on taking the entire north wing for himself." The chambermaid sniffed. "That man and his friend have already drunk two caskets of ale in the last hour and are well on their way to buggering every whore in the place, yet they still want more of both. It's shameful, really." The woman tittered, covering her mouth with a hand self-consciously to hide bad teeth. "Though I imagine, what with him being so ugly and all, the only way he ever gets any cunny is to pay for it."

Baine stiffened at that news. "An ugly merchant, you say?"

"Yes," the chambermaid said, still chuckling. "So ugly he makes the arse end of a hog look good enough to kiss." She moved past Baine and picked up a small wooden cask, which she tucked under her arm with some difficulty. Several strands of brown hair had slipped out from her wimple, and she pushed them back impatiently with her free hand. "The other one, though," the woman continued wistfully. "Now, he's not so bad to look at. Smells a bit, but then again, who doesn't? I'd give him a jump myself if I were a younger lass, but sadly those days are gone."

Baine fought to keep his expression neutral. "This man, he wouldn't happen to be tall with a patch over one eye, would he?"

The woman paused on her way back toward the stairs. "Yes, that's him. Why?"

"By the gods," Baine said with a laugh. "What a remarkable coincidence. That's my old friend Bent Holdfer. I had no idea he was in town." Baine stepped forward, reaching for the casket. "Let me take this up to him. It'll be a grand surprise when he sees it's me."

"Oh, I don't know about that," the chambermaid said hesitantly. "It's my job, you see. Hermin don't take kindly to his employees shirking their duties."

Baine put a finger to his lips. "I won't tell him, I promise." The woman seemed to be wavering, but she wasn't all the way there yet, so Baine gently took the casket from her, giving her his most earnest smile. "Besides, this way it'll save you from having to climb those horrible stairs again. You look like you could use a rest. Why not wait down here until I come back? What's the harm?"

"Well," the woman said hesitantly as Baine turned her away from the stairs, pointing her toward a crate, where he helped her to sit.

"Don't you worry about a thing—uh?" Baine added.

"Magiana," the chambermaid answered at Baine's raised eyebrow. "Magiana Frote."

"Well, don't you worry about a thing, Magiana," Baine said. He winked as he straightened. "I'll take care of everything. If I know Bent, he's bound to press an extra coin or two into your hands when he finds out you were in on our little surprise."

"Really?" the chambermaid said, looking thrilled at the idea.

"Without question," Baine assured her. "Now, how do I find him?"

The chambermaid gestured to the stairs. "Go straight down the passage when you get to the top. There's a walkway overlooking the main hall connecting the north, south, east, and west wings. Turn left from there and follow the ramp. Your friend has all three rooms on that side of the inn."

Baine smiled. "Wonderful. Now, I'm going to go up there quiet as a mouse, since I don't want to spoil the surprise." He hesitated as a thought occurred to him. "The whores you mentioned, are they still in there with Bent and the merchant?"

The woman thankfully shook her head. "No, I don't think so. They's all used up, poor lasses. Those men are wicked beasts, they are, sticking it in every hole. I heard Hermin sent for more girls from his other place, the Roasting Hog, but I don't know when they might arrive."

"That's good," Baine said, trying not to show his relief. "So, it's just them and no one else?"

Magiana nodded. "As far as I know."

Baine patted the woman's shoulder. "Then I guess that means I'll have Bent's full attention."

"I guess it does," Magiana agreed. She frowned. "But don't take too long up there, young man. I can't sit here all day, or for sure Hermin will dismiss me. If I go home without a job, my husband will beat the life from me."

"I'll be quick," Baine promised, hoping it was true as he headed for the stairs.

He took the steps two at a time, moving cat-like on the balls of his feet. Baine reached the landing above, then hurried down a wide, empty corridor until he saw the crosswalk Magiana had described. It was supported in the center by a massive carved pillar, with the ends of four narrow wooden ramps protected by short railings meeting on the gigantic column's flat top, forming an X. A sweeping staircase near the head of the southern ramp led downward into the main hall. Baine had never seen anything like it before, marveling at the engineering and ingenuity involved in building such a thing.

The noise from below became almost deafening as Baine drew closer. He could hear singing accompanied by what he thought might be a lyre-guitar, though the music was partially drowned out by the amplified sounds of many voices laughing and talking at once. From what Baine could tell, the singer had a pleasant timbre and was actually quite good, which was a huge improvement over the drunken screeching he'd unfortunately been forced to witness coming from the recently deceased Tadly Platt.

Baine paused in the center of the walkway and looked down at the merriment below. No one bothered to look up at him. But even if they had, he doubted he'd be able to see their faces clearly through the fog-like smoke given off by two massive fireplaces and hundreds of candles that rose in waves toward the ceiling above him. Baine suddenly heard footsteps coming from the north, and he turned his face away as two whores appeared, heading directly for him. One of the women was petite and young—only a few years older than Tabina—while the other was at least thirty with a sharp face made even more severe by obvious anger. The whores were walking arm and arm and seemed oblivious of Baine, with the younger girl sobbing and walking stiffly as if in discomfort.

"We'll put some honey on it, love," the older whore said soothingly. "You won't even notice the pain in a day or two. I promise."

"I hope they both rot in The Father's pits for all eternity," the young girl said fiercely.

"So do I, child," the older whore replied as they passed Baine. He saw her glance at him out of the corner of his eye before, with an angry snort, she turned back to the girl. "I hope the same fate awaits all the men in this world, the evil bastards."

Baine waited until the women were gone, then hurried along the northern ramp that led to another passage. Three doors awaited him there—one at the end and one to either side of him. He drew a knife and instinctively headed for the end door, setting the casket down in front of it. Something about this door just seemed *right* to him. Baine took a deep breath, then rapped loudly on the door. There was no sound or movement from inside. He knocked again, this time much louder.

"Dammit, Mariana, just come in!" a gruff male voice shouted. "What's the matter with you? Are you stupid or something?"

Baine knocked again, and when there was no response, he used the toe of his boot to make an urgent thumping sound. He knew a knock could always be ignored, but no one could resist seeing what that insistent thumping was all about. Baine heard a sharp curse over the noise he was making, then the sounds of heavy footfalls. He stopped kicking the door and shifted lithely to the left side of it, waiting there with his back against the wall and the knife held low at his stomach.

The door swept open on creaking hinges. "I'm going to tan your—?" Another curse as the casket was noticed, followed by drunken grumbling. "Damn lazy bitch." A head appeared in the doorway a moment later, followed by arms and burly shoulders as the man leaned down to grab the wine. Baine saw he wore a black leather patch over his right eye—Bent Holdfer. Baine moved in a blur, grabbing Holdfer by the back of the neck to steady him even as he rammed his blade into the man's right ear. The outlaw froze, his mouth working, his good eye bulging in shock before he abruptly collapsed in a heap without making a sound. The smell of fresh shit quickly filled the corridor.

"Bent?" a second man called from inside a moment later. His voice sounded far away to Baine, as if he might be in a separate room. "Is it more whores?"

Baine hesitated.

"Well?"

"No," Baine finally called out, putting his hand over his mouth while doing his best to mimic the dead man's voice. "It's just Mariana. She brought us some more wine."

"Ah, good. About time. Bring me some; that's a good fellow. I'm too tired from those last two sluts to get out of bed."

Baine sheathed his knife and unhooked his bow, notching an arrow before he stepped into a large room dimly lit by candles. He took a quick glance around, but except for some benches and chairs, two chests with cushions, and a long table, the place was empty. An open doorway stood to his left, most likely a bedchamber where he guessed the other outlaw was waiting. Baine knew he had time. Bent Holdfer lay sprawled over the door's threshold face down, wearing a white tunic and loose-fitting trousers, though his feet were surprisingly bare. Baine put the arrow back in his bag and set his bow down, then grabbed the dead man by his ankles and dragged him into the room. A thin trail of blood and excrement followed after, staining the wooden floor, but there was little Baine could do about it now. Hopefully, no one would come by and notice until his work here was done.

Once he was far enough inside the room with the body, Baine left the corpse lying on the floor in a heap and closed the door and then barred it shut. He picked up his bow, nocked it again, and then treaded softly toward the bedchamber. The room beyond the open doorway was dimly lit, with shadows dancing on the floor and along both sides of the door frame from a candle burning inside. Baine cautiously stepped to the entrance to peer inside just as the candle abruptly went out. He instinctively retreated, lifting his bow just as something came hurtling toward him from the darkness, crashing into his head with force. Baine cried out, his mind registering that the object had been a stool as he reeled from the blow and almost fell, seeing stars in his head. A big, bearded man with fierce eyes and a red-veined nose appeared from the doorway and rushed at him, growling. Baine tried to dodge aside, but he was still groggy from the blow to the head and was much too slow. The big man turned his shoulder at the last moment, using it as a battering ram against Baine's chest. He felt the wind knocked from him, losing his grip on the bow as he fell heavily to the floor.

"You little bastard!" the outlaw hissed, standing over Baine a moment later. The man flicked his gaze to Bent Holdfer's corpse, then back down at Baine. "By The Father's balls, boy, I don't know who you are, but you'll pay for this."

Baine reached for the knife at his hip, his head still ringing and his stomach roiling from nausea. The outlaw scoffed and kicked Baine in the stomach, and as Baine cried out, crumpling into a fetal position, the man snatched the knife from its sheath and tossed it contemptuously aside.

The outlaw grabbed Baine by the hair, dragging his head back painfully. "Now, boy, you're going to tell me who you are. And after you do that, I'm going to cut off those little raisins you call balls and feed them to you one at a time."

Baine glared up at the outlaw, and despite his pain, he couldn't help but grin. The man was indeed uglier than a pig's arse, just as the chambermaid had claimed. The outlaw's head was completely bald and covered by odd misshapen bumps, and he had strange, drooping ears like an elephant's. His nose was not just red-veined but crooked and hooked, with a boil at the tip seeping watery yellow pus. His eyebrows grew wildly from a thick, protruding ridge bone, and though his beard was full and long, it couldn't quite hide the livid purple scars on his neck from what Baine guessed must have been a rope. *Too bad it hadn't done its job*, he thought wryly.

"What are you smiling at, you little weasel?" the outlaw demanded.

"I'd heard you were ugly," Baine said, still smiling. He could feel blood trickling down his temple from where he'd been hit but ignored it. "But I didn't realize until now just how bad it is. It's almost like you fell from the top of the ugly tree and hit every branch on the way down."

The outlaw's eyes narrowed at the insult, and his face flushed angrily. He put his foot on Baine's chest, using his considerable weight to press him down flat on his back. "I asked you who you are," he growled as he increased the pressure. "I won't ask again, so start talking."

"I'm death for you," Baine said, his smile gone now as he stared up at one of the men who'd helped to murder his wife and son. "That's who I am, you motherless bastard."

And then Baine moved.

Chapter 18: Konway

The outlaw was a big, powerful man, weighing at least two hundred pounds or more, with most of that weight resting firmly on Baine's chest. He could feel his ribcage flexing beneath the pressure of the man's boot as he fought to draw air into his lungs, knowing bones might snap at any moment. Baine's arms were spread wide to either side of him on the floor like wings, though they felt oddly numb and unresponsive as if the blood had run out of them. He knew he had little chance to draw a knife from one of his bracers with his arms so weak, and even if he could somehow summon the strength to try, the bastard's tree trunk-like leg was in the way—which meant he needed to improvise now or die.

Baine had spent most of his life since Einhard freed him from Father's Arse practicing and perfecting warfare for hours at a time—though not the way Hadrack and Jebido did. Those two would happily spar all day with swords if you let them, but that wasn't Baine's game at all. He preferred instead to work with his knives and his bow, alternating between that and doing stretches along with a series of extensive acrobatics very similar to what the performers on stage earlier in the day had done. That training had made him not only quick and lithe but extremely flexible—which was exactly what the situation he was in now called for.

The man above Baine was strong, ridiculously so, but he also appeared overconfident—at least, Baine certainly hoped so if his plan was to work. He put that plan into motion, fighting to lift his right arm before he used his hand to slap ineffectually at the outlaw's boot to get his attention while doing his best to look like a man panicking. It wasn't all that difficult a task, actually, since the big bastard had just shifted his weight and Baine couldn't breathe at all now.

The outlaw laughed cruelly, clearly savoring the look on Baine's face, although he did ease up on the pressure somewhat, allowing him to take in a ragged breath. "Something you want to say, little bird?" the man asked with an amused chuckle.

"I have gold," Baine managed to squeeze out in a tortured voice.

"Is that so?" the outlaw grunted. The humor was gone from his ugly features, replaced with sudden interest and greed. He examined Baine's clothing curiously and smiled, revealing yellow and brown teeth. "Do tell?"

Baine used his eyes to motion toward his waist. "Moneybag. My belt. It's all yours."

"Of course it is, fool," the outlaw grunted.

He automatically leaned over to check for the bag, pawing at Baine's clothing, which was what Baine had been praying would happen. He whipped his right leg back through the narrow gap between his attacker's legs, drawing it down before lashing out and upward with all his strength, catching the man in the groin. Air exploded from the outlaw's lungs, his eyes bulging from beneath his heavy brow and his face reddening as he automatically clutched at himself. The man's ugly features were now less than a foot away from Baine, who didn't hesitate, ramming the crown of his head upward into the outlaw's nose right at the hideous boil perched on the end of it. Blood immediately sprayed as the man howled, with the excruciating pressure on Baine's chest instantly subsiding as his attacker staggered backward, pawing at his face with one hand while clutching at his manhood with the other.

Baine gratefully sucked in a deep lungful of air, then coughed harshly even as he rolled sideways, coming up a little unsteadily on his feet. He coughed again, putting a hand over the sharp pain resonating in his chest. He was hugely relieved to find that no bones were broken, knowing at worst he'd have some nasty bruising later. He could live with that.

"You little bastard," the outlaw hissed as blood streamed from his nose. He straightened with difficulty, spitting a gob of red wetness on the floor. "I'm going to spend all night making you scream, boy."

"Sorry," Baine croaked in a whisper, his voice still not his own yet. "But I think you'll find I'm not some poor, helpless whore you can abuse." He grinned, starting to feel more like himself with every intake of air. "Because, unlike them, I can hit back." The outlaw snorted, advancing a pace just as Baine whisked out the knife tucked away in his left bracer. The man paused in surprise, looking suddenly unsure of himself. Baine chuckled and lifted the knife. "I imagine you're wondering right about now just how good I might be with one of these," he said. "Maybe you think you're fast enough to take it from me, is that it? Well, let's get that silly notion out of the way right now, shall we?"

Baine didn't wait for an answer, throwing the knife sideways with a flick of his wrist, with the blade lodging a heartbeat later in the soft flesh a foot above the man's right knee, exactly where he'd aimed. The outlaw screamed in shock and staggered backward against the wall behind him, with bright red blood already seeping through his trousers. Baine rushed forward with the fingers and the thumb of his left hand extended and spread wide apart. It was something Malo had taught him onboard *Sea-Dragon*—a way to briefly incapacitate a man without necessarily killing him, depending on the force used.

Baine had never tried something like this in combat before, however, and he wasn't exactly sure how hard to hit a man this big. But considering his current circumstances, he doubted he'd lose any sleep if the outlaw died because of it. Baine rammed his hand against the base of the man's exposed throat the moment he was close enough, connecting solidly even as he used his right foot to sweep the outlaw's good leg out from under him. His opponent fell heavily to the floor with his back supported by the wall and his legs stretched out in front of him, looking dazed and shaken, the fight—at least for the moment—gone from him.

Baine dropped to his knees and put his hand on the leather grip of the knife, which had sunk into the outlaw's leg to the crossguard. "Now, you listen to me closely, you bastard," Baine growled as his adversary hacked and coughed, trying to breathe. Both the man's hands were pressed around his throat, and his eyes were glazed and unfocused. Baine gestured to the knife. "If I pull this out right now, you'll have a minute or less before you bleed out and die. Do you understand me?" The outlaw tried to speak, but nothing came from his lips except garbled wheezing. Baine shifted his grip on the knife. "You're trying my patience, you ugly bastard. I asked if you understood me?"

"Yes," the outlaw managed to say, his eyes round with fear. He kept looking at the knife with Baine's slim hand resting on it.

"Good," Baine said in satisfaction. "That's better. Now we're getting somewhere. Keep answering my questions, and maybe you'll actually live through this. What's your name?"

"Konway," the outlaw responded sullenly. Baine could tell he was regaining his senses, which meant he would no doubt try something very soon. Baine drew another knife from his boot with his right hand, pressing it to the man's chest just above his heart. The cunning look in the outlaw's eyes dampened with disappointment, and he licked his lips before adding, "Konway of Hastow."

Baine nodded, though he'd half expected the man's name to be Pater. "You rode with Jark Cordly against Witbridge Manor, yes?" Konway hesitated, and Baine twisted the knife in the outlaw's leg slowly back and forth, ignoring the man's hiss of pain as fresh blood flowed. "I won't ask again. Next time you don't answer me, the blade comes out and you can flop around like a fish out of water while I watch you die."

"You piece of—" Konway spat.

Baine leaned forward, pressing down on the second knife until blood appeared on the man's tunic. "Did you ride with Jark Cordly?" he repeated

"Yes, you little bastard!" Konway grunted. "All right? Yes."

Baine nodded, satisfied. A part of him had worried Konway hadn't been part of the raiding party and that he was torturing an innocent man. Now that fear was put to rest. "Did Cordly recruit you recently, or were you part of his original band?"

"He recruited me and a few others," Konway admitted grudgingly.

"When?"

"Last week, I think."

Baine glanced toward Bent Holdfer's corpse. "Was he one of them too?"

Konway leaned his head back against the wall wearily and nodded. "Yes."

"Why did you and Bent kill Rupert Frake and his mother?"

Konway bit his lip and Baine snorted, glancing down at the knife in the man's leg, his meaning clear. "That boy was as mad as they come," the outlaw hurried to say. "A stark raving lunatic, that one. He wanted us to help him abduct some damn noblewoman if you can imagine such a thing? Stupid, he was." Konway shook his head. "Naïve and incredibly stupid."

Baine rolled his eyes. "Let me guess. You're talking about Lady Elyn."

"That's her," Konway agreed with a sigh. "Rupert had the entire thing planned for this evening after prayers. We were going to snatch her on her way from the House. Rupert says she always takes the same route back to the castle. He promised to pay us everything Jark had given him for our help once we had her."

"And then what?"

"How should I know? I told you, that boy was daft."

"But you had no intentions of actually going through with this farce, did you?" Baine stated, understanding now.

"Of course not," Konway grunted contemptuously. "The boy might have been addled in the head, but last I looked, a crazy man's gold is just as good as anybody else's. We just needed to find out where the young fool had hidden it first."

"That's why you went to his mother's?" Baine asked.

"Yes," Konway replied. "Bent was convinced Rupert had hidden it there. Turned out he was right. The lad had stowed it away in a chest under some blankets."

"You killed Rupert's mother but not the little girl," Baine pointed out. "Why?"

"The mother's death was an accident," Konway responded with a grimace. "Bent hit her too hard." He shrugged. "He wanted to slit the daughter's throat too after that, but I've got a little girl at home around her age and I just couldn't allow it to happen."

"Honor even among thieves, eh?" Baine said, not bothering to hide his disgust.

"Something like that," Konway grumbled, looking away.

"Who else rode with Cordly?" Baine demanded. "I want names."

Konway blinked in surprise before dawning realization slowly crossed his ugly features. "So, that's what this little dance of ours is all about. You're after revenge for what we did at Witbridge Manor." Konway stabbed a finger toward Baine. "Now I get it. You're the bastard everybody has been looking for—the one who murdered Tad Platt earlier today." The outlaw dropped his hand heavily to his lap, his ugly features turning bitter. "I should have known that boy's death wasn't just a random attack like Rupert thought, but I was too focused on the bastard's gold to care."

Baine grinned and shrugged. "Well, too late for that now. And just so you know, I killed Cairn back in Laskerly, too, even though he probably would have died from his wounds anyway. He wasn't getting off that easy. None of you will."

"You got lucky with me just now," Konway said, his voice filled with derision. "If I hadn't underestimated you, you'd be dead."

"Too bad for you, I guess," Baine grunted, feeling no pity for the man. He shifted his body slightly, his grin turning to a look of fierce determination. "I'll get every last one of you who rode with Cordly before this ends. Mark my words."

"You're just as mad in the head as Rupert was, boy," Konway said with a chuckle. He finally sighed and spread his hands in a helpless gesture. "Like I said, you got lucky with me, but I'll bet that luck won't last much longer. Jark Cordly will see to that. You have no idea what you're up against. The man will snap you in half without even trying."

"We'll see," Baine muttered, unimpressed. He looked up a moment later as someone began pounding urgently on the barred door.

"Is everything all right in there? Hello? Anybody? Mister Konway, are you in there?" More banging sounded. "There's blood on the floor out here. Anybody?"

Konway grinned at Baine. "Looks like that luck of yours ran out sooner than you thought."

Baine glanced at the outlaw sourly, then back to the door. "It's fine," he called out. "I cut my hand, is all. Go away."

"Help!" Konway suddenly shouted. "It's the murderer! He's trying to kill—"

Baine cursed under his breath even as he plunged his knife into the outlaw's heart. The man gasped, his expression turning to shock before blood erupted from his mouth and he shuddered and died. Baine could hear excited shouts coming from the other side of the door, then, after a moment, the unmistakable thud of an axe. He looked around desperately, but there was nowhere to run except for the darkened room where Konway had been. Baine hesitated as the door trembled from a savage blow, followed by a second one that tore a half-inch gouge down the center panel, revealing the shining head of an axe. The axe head twisted as the wielder struggled to remove it before finally disappearing, returning moments later with force as a large chunk of wood flew off and spun into the room, almost hitting Baine.

A man's face appeared at the jagged opening—a handsome, blond-headed man. He pointed in triumph through the gap at Baine. "I've got you now, you bastard! Try to outsmart me, will you!"

Baine groaned—it was the House Agent from the courtyard that he'd sent on a wild goose chase earlier. Not having much choice, Baine snatched up his bow, then darted into the darkened room, his eyes instantly fixating on an unshuttered window ten feet away. It was his only chance. Baine ran to the window and stuck his head outside. He was facing the town square, with a balcony to either side of him, though unluckily, neither one was close enough for him to jump to easily. He could see the warehouse across the square where he'd watched the inn earlier, and there was a large group of people a hundred feet from the inn listening to a troubadour standing on a stool reciting poetry.

He looked down. The roof sloped dramatically beneath the dormered window for several treacherous feet before giving way to the eave, impossible to navigate without a long drop to the ground. That was definitely out. Baine looked up. The A-frame roof above him overhung the window by several feet, with an ornate figurehead of a boar attached to the gable near the peak. Could he reach it? Baine heard a distinct crash coming from the other room, followed by shouts. The House Agent was in. Out of time, Baine jumped lithely onto the sill and reached up for the boar, but even on his toes, he was at least three feet short. He cursed, then leaned outward, hooking his bow over the ornament's head. *Would the string hold? Only time would tell.*

Baine took a deep breath, then started to shinny up the bow's stave hand over hand, praying to The Mother not to let him fall. He could hear the excited shouts of his pursuers as they began to search the main room, knowing it would only be a matter of seconds before they figured out where he'd gone. The bow creaked and protested against his weight as he climbed, swinging back and forth, but it held, allowing Baine to reach the boar's head and grasp it securely with his left hand. He began kicking his legs while swinging his right hand wildly above him, looking for anything solid to grab. Baine almost sobbed with relief a moment later when his hand came into contact with a metal spike jutting up from the tiles along the roof's peak. He latched onto it in desperation, wrapping his fingers around the iron, then dragged himself upward until he was clear of the window and sitting awkwardly on the roof. He reached down and snagged his bow, pulling it up just in time as a blond head appeared from the window below, looking down at the ground. Baine carefully eased back along the ridge, holding his breath as he waited.

"Do you see the bastard?" someone called from inside the room.

Baine heard the blond man curse softly under his breath. "No. The roof is too steep to climb down. He couldn't have gone this way."

"Then where did he go?"

"How should I know?" the House Agent snapped harshly. "Keep looking. He's got to be here somewhere."

Baine carefully stood, balancing on the narrow peak of the ridge line as he headed away. Luckily, the slope where the edge of the dormer joined the main roof wasn't nearly as steep, and he was able to grip the edges of the thick tiles there and climb fairly easily up to the wider ridge beam of the main building. He paused at the top to catch his breath, hidden in the shadows cast by a brick chimney. *What now?* Should he attempt to lower himself to one of the balconies and try to slip out of the building or maybe make it from there down to the ground?

Baine could see in all directions from his vantage point, and he groaned in dismay when a large troop of mounted men galloped into the square and dismounted before they began to disperse at a run toward the inn. He could hear shouted commands to encircle the building echoing up to him, knowing trying to get to one of the balconies was out now. The bastards were clearly closing the noose around him, and if Baine didn't move now, they'd have him. He began to run along the ridge beam at full speed, heading south toward the stables while praying to The Mother that he didn't stumble or trip on the slippery tiles. If he could get into the horse yard unseen, maybe he could lose his pursuers in the darkness and confusion.

The stable's roof was almost ten feet lower than the inn's, Baine guessed when he reached the edge of The Weary Jester's eave, blowing hard as he peered downward on his hands and knees. He could see little definition below him, sensing rather than seeing the solidness of the roof. Baine was relieved that so far, the horse yard further out lay in almost total darkness and appeared abandoned, but he knew that wouldn't last for much longer. He thought about the stable, trying to remember what the pitch of the roof had looked like. Was it less than the inn's, or had it been sloped the same to match? Baine hadn't been focusing on anything other than getting into The Weary Jester earlier and couldn't recall enough details to be sure.

He was mulling over whether to take a chance and risk jumping anyway when a sliver of light from inside the inn appeared to his left about three feet down. He realized it was a shuttered window, with someone inside the room having lit a candle, allowing the pale orange glow to escape between two ill-fitting slats. Baine immediately shifted to his left until he was over the window. He could see the faint outlines of the stable roof beneath him now, but it was slanted enough to have made the prospect of a successful jump highly unlikely. Baine was doubly glad that he hadn't made the attempt.

He dropped to his knees again, then turned, carefully lowering himself down until his feet came into contact with the shutters. The wood was weathered, rounded at the top, and maybe half an inch thick, but it was enough to support some of his weight.

Hopefully, the hinges would hold. Baine let go of the eave with his left hand, his face pressed to the wall in front of him as he fumbled around until he felt one of the timber frames. He took a firm grip, then, mouthing a prayer, released the eave. If the shutters were to let go, this would be the moment. Baine sighed in relief a moment later. They were holding, at least for now. Sometimes there were benefits to being small.

"Hey!" a woman's voice suddenly shouted from inside the room. "Who's out there? Parver? Where are you, you drunken bastard? Parver? I need help! Someone is trying to get into my room! Parver!"

"Damnation," Baine grunted just as the shutter doors burst open.

He lost his balance immediately, his grip on the timber gone as he plummeted downward, crying out. Baine collided with the left shutter door, gasping in pain as the rounded arch slammed with force into his armpit, stunning him. He desperately clung on, draping his arm over the wood as the door swung back and forth precariously on creaking hinges.

"You thieving, stinking, no-good-for-nothing rapist! I've got you now!"

Baine looked over to see an older woman with a gnarled face and long, unbound grey hair leaning out the window with a corn broom. She jabbed it toward Baine like a spear and he cried out as the bristles cut into his face.

"Get away from there, you!" the woman cried, her face twisted in righteous indignation. "Get away, I say! You'll not be getting my virtue this night, you night-crawling sack of frog balls! I'm a lady, you bastard. So you can do your whoring somewhere else!"

Baine desperately began to lower himself down the shutter slat by slat, doing his best to ignore the repeated blows he was receiving across his head and shoulders from the broom. He finally reached the bottom frame of the shutter, hanging there as he paused to look up. The old woman was leaning out the window now that he was out of range, shaking her tiny fist at him.

"And don't you come back, you hear, or I'll give you some more to think about! See if I won't!"

Despite his dire circumstances, Baine couldn't help but grin at the woman's fierce expression. "You may have bested me this night, my love," he said with a chuckle. "But I'll be back every night hereafter until you honor me with your precious flower. You have my word as your unabashed admirer."

Baine had only a heartbeat to register the stunned look of wonder on the woman's wrinkled face before he let go of the shutter, dropping the last few feet to the stable roof. From there it was an easy climb down to the ground, though he landed awkwardly on his knees just as the sounds of hooves and the squeak of wheels filled his ears. Baine looked up, his dismay turning to overwhelming relief as a horse-drawn cart bore down on him. He stood stiffly and began dusting himself off.

"Looks to me like you owe me four favors now," Chadry the spy said with a lopsided grin from atop the cart as he brought it to a screeching halt. He gestured with a thumb behind him, his expression turning serious. "Now get in before those House Agent bastards get around here and keep your fool head down. The bees and hornets are out in full force this night, my friend, each and every one intent on stinging you to death. I've become rather fond of you for some inexplicable reason, so let's not allow that to happen, shall we? Agreed?"

"Agreed," Baine said with a laugh, needing no further encouragement. He climbed into the cart and lay down on his back. "Fifteen to go, Flora my love," he whispered to the night sky as the cart clattered quickly away from the stable. "Fifteen."

Chapter 19: The Hungry Oak

Ten minutes later, the cart came to a shuddering halt in a refuse-littered alley lit up faintly by a fat silver moon hanging over the town. Baine leaped over the sidewall to the ground and moved closer to Chadry, who remained in the driver's seat with his crutch propped up at his side. The horse snorted, shaking its head, the metallic jingle from the bit in its mouth the only sound in the eerie stillness. A dog barked somewhere to the north a moment later, followed by an answering series of high-pitched yaps to the east before silence mercifully returned. Baine noticed a tall man wearing a green cloak with the hood up waiting for them at the end of the alley, pacing back and forth on a raised flagstone stoop. The black maw of an open doorway beckoned behind him.

"Are you sure we can trust this man?" Baine said in a low tone, looking up at the spy.

"We can trust him," Chadry asserted with a firm nod. "Ancin's loyalty to the true king cannot be questioned. I'd stake my life on it."

Baine tilted his head sideways and grinned sarcastically. "Yes, but you're not, now are you? You're staking *my life on it*, which is something that I've grown rather attached to over the years."

Chadry chuckled low in his chest. "A fair point, my friend, a fair point. I promise Ancin won't let you down." The two men fell silent then until the spy finally sighed wearily. "I'll be glad when this is all over, lad. I miss my family and just want to go home."

Baine blinked in surprise. "You're not from Crestpool?"

"No," Chadry said. "I come from a town far to the south called Lestwick. That's where my wife and two boys are still. I send them money when I can, but I haven't seen them in more than eight months."

Baine frowned. "Lestwick? Isn't that part of Lord Corwick's lands?"

"Indeed it is," Chadry muttered.

"Didn't I hear he's allied himself with the North?"

"That's the rumor going around these days," Chadry agreed. "Though he denies it and claims to support Tyden." The spy snorted. "Knowing that sneaky bastard, I'm sure he's playing both ends against each other to ensure he's on the winning side when this is finally over."

Baine nodded. He hadn't thought about Hadrack's old nemesis, Lord Corwick, in many months but couldn't disagree with Chadry's assessment of him. The man was as slippery and duplicitous as they came. Baine wondered how Chadry had ended up as a spy for Daughter Gernet, sensing a good story there, though he knew this was not the right time to ask. Ancin had stopped pacing, his hands on his hips as he glared their way. It was past time to go.

Baine offered his hand up to the spy. "Thank you, my friend. I don't know where I'd be right now if not for you."

Chadry took Baine's hand in a dry, firm grip and shook it warmly. "It's been a pleasure, lad." He nodded toward the waiting man. "Ancin will get you out of town. There's a tavern about ten miles south of here—The Hungry Oak. You should make it there by morning if you hurry. Ask for the owner, Titim del Attan, and give him my name. He'll provide you with a horse and whatever supplies you need." Chadry fumbled in his clothing before pressing a thin, tightly rolled scroll held closed by an iron band into Baine's hands. "I didn't have time to get all the names you wanted, but hopefully, what's there will get you started."

Baine accepted the scroll reverently. The trail had gone cold with Konway's untimely death, and Chadry had just handed him a lifeline worth more than all the gold in the world. "I won't forget you."

"Nor I you," the spy said. "Best be going now. It looks like old Ancin is getting antsy over there." Baine nodded and turned to go. "Lad?" Baine hesitated and looked back. "Good luck," Chadry added. "You've done well so far despite all the odds stacked against you. I hope you get every last one of the bastards and make them suffer for what they did to your woman and little boy."

"I will," Baine promised, lifting the scroll in salute to the man. "Believe me, I will."

Baine helped Chadry swing the horse and cart around in the tight confines of the alley, waiting until he'd reached the cross street at the end and had disappeared around a dark building before turning away.

"About time," Ancin grunted moodily as Baine approached. "Ain't got all night for this."

Baine said nothing as he followed the tall man through the open doorway, one hand resting on the hilt of the knife at his hip. He'd lost the original during the scuffle with Konway and had replaced it with the one from his right boot. Just because Chadry trusted Ancin implicitly didn't mean Baine had to do the same.

"Close and bar the door," Ancin ordered. "Don't want no drunken fool wandering in here and pissing on the floor." Baine did as he was told while Ancin paused to light a torch, revealing a small room with rough planks on the walls and floor. A brightly colored fresco of a grape harvest dominated one wall, looking oddly out of place in the otherwise bleak room. There was no furniture, though a thin, filthy cot overstuffed with thrushes lay on the floor in one corner near a passageway.

"I'm Baine, by the way," Baine said.

"Don't care," Ancin muttered, heading toward the passage. "Just stay close to me and keep your mouth shut, and we'll get along fine."

Baine shrugged, following after the tall man, who was forced to duck to avoid hitting his head on the low ceiling of the passage. They traveled in silence for several minutes, with nothing but the sound of Ancin's ragged breathing echoing loudly in the tight confines before they passed through an archway into another room. This one was much bigger than the last, with a packed dirt floor that smelled strongly of decay. Baine noticed a small nest of grass and rags in one corner, with the fleshless skull of some rodent lying inside. A wooden cabinet missing a door stood against a wall, with what looked like a second nest spilling out from it.

"What now?" Baine whispered.

Ancin didn't answer and instead made his way to the end wall, lifting the torch. He began running his fingers along the chipped wooden paneling, clucking his tongue in annoyance. Finally, the tall man grunted in satisfaction before he pressed down hard with the palm of his hand on a section that looked no different to Baine than any of the others. An audible click sounded, followed by the panel swinging toward them on silent hinges, revealing an opening in the center of the wall three feet wide by five high.

"Get going," Ancin grunted, motioning inside with the torch.

Baine stuck his head through the opening, seeing nothing but dirt walls and pitch blackness further in. The damp, earthy smell coming from the interior was almost overwhelming. "Where does this go?"

"Down," Ancin muttered, pressing the torch into Baine's hands. "Goes under Beech Street. Comes up again about a hundred yards east of the town walls in a copse of trees."

Baine nodded. "And from there? Which way do I go?"

"There's a road about fifty feet from the trees," Ancin said, looking impatient. "Follow it south until you reach The Hungry Oak."

Baine lifted his leg and stepped through the opening, pausing half in and half out to glance back at the tall man. "Thank you. I know you've taken a big risk for me, and I appreciate it."

"Didn't do it for you," Ancin replied, his face beneath the cowl hard as stone and unreadable. "If they catch you, you never heard of me. Got it?"

"Got it," Baine agreed.

He stepped fully inside and lifted the torch, revealing a crudely rounded ceiling marred by obvious tool marks and sloping, sweating walls that were slightly wider apart than his shoulders. A large black spider on the ceiling shrunk from the flames and scurried away deeper into the tunnel. Baine took several cautious steps forward, feeling the damp earth on the floor sticking to his boots. He heard a creak behind him, not looking back as Ancin closed the panel firmly. Baine was on his own now. He took a deep breath, trying not to gag on the heady smells as he moved forward in a half crouch with the top of his head grazing the ceiling. Baine tried not to think about spiders or anything else that might be crawling around up there. The route went steadily downward, and he had to use a hand to steady himself on the wall, afraid he'd slip on the wet earth and land on his ass until, finally, the passage began to level out.

Baine paused at the bottom, once again thankful for his diminutive size. He couldn't imagine how someone like Hadrack with his mighty frame would fare trying to traverse this narrow passage. He set out again, quickly losing all track of time as he took long, slow breaths while trying not to dwell on the thought that the walls or ceiling could potentially collapse at any moment, burying him alive. He was only partially successful at it. The tunnel was surprisingly hot despite how far underground it was, and he was forced to pause every few feet, using the torch to clear away an endless array of thick spiderwebs spun from floor to ceiling. It appeared that no one had come this way in a very long time.

The tunnel finally began to rise again, and after many laborious minutes climbing upward with the damp soil working hard to impede his progress, Baine came to a dead end. He'd reached a rounded chamber that was perhaps six feet across at its widest point. A small, timber-framed trap door in the earth wall rose in front of him, bolted from the inside by a rusty iron bar. Baine cautiously lifted the bar before opening the door an inch to peer through the crack. The welcoming shine of the moon greeted him, with its bright silver rays glistening off stands of thick bushes and low-hanging tree branches, all swaying gently in a warm evening breeze. He'd made it.

Baine reached The Hungry Oak about an hour after sunrise. He'd seen very few people on the road during his journey, being careful to hide in the trees when he did until they had passed. The last thing he needed was word getting back to Crestpool about him, although he was fairly confident the House Agents had probably given up on him by now. The tavern was built at the juncture of two roads, with a monstrous oak tree towering behind it. Baine had expected to find a small, rundown building, which was typical for most of the taverns he'd visited this far out from towns. But The Hungry Oak surprised him, looking fairly new and impeccably upkeeped.

The tavern was three stories tall and built on a slight grade, with wide stone steps embedded into the earth leading up to a flagstone courtyard. A neat row of tables and chairs sat on the flagstones, and Baine was amazed to see bright red cloths covering each one, fluttering in the breeze. The tavern had two entrances on the main floor, one to the left and one to the right, which were connected by a wide wooden terrace where more tables stood. Colorful red, white, and yellow pennants hung from the banisters overlooking the terrace, with a matching pair of wooden staircases leading up to it—one to Baine's left and one to his right.

An old man with long silver hair and a broom in his hand emerged from a door on the ground floor, limping noticeably. He paused, squinting in the early morning sunshine while he watched

Baine approaching. "Morning, traveler," the man finally called out, revealing an almost toothless grin through his bushy beard. He started sweeping the flagstones free of leaves and debris, moving carefully on his bad leg. "It promises to be a fine day by the looks of things."

Baine climbed the stone steps to the courtyard, passing a huge wooden sign supported by cedar posts that read: *Welcome to The Hungry Oak—Arrive Tired and Hungry—Leave Rested and Satisfied.* "Indeed it does," he said, stopping by the closest table. "I'm looking for Titim del Attan."

"Is that right?" the old man said, pausing in his task. He flashed another smile. "Well, looks like you found him." The old man shrugged good-naturedly and resumed brooming. "Or what's left of him, at any rate. The years have not been kind, I'm sorry to say."

"Chadry Armac sent me," Baine added, lowering his voice.

The old man's eyebrows rose, and his expression turned cautious. "Is that a fact?"

"He said you'd look into giving me a horse and some supplies."

"He did, huh?" Titim muttered. The old man leaned his broom against the tavern wall, then limped toward Baine, stopping two feet away. "And why would I do that, pray tell?"

Baine hesitated, caught off guard by the question. He'd been expecting instant acceptance from this man after what the spy had told him. "Because I understand you're on the right side of this war," he finally answered carefully. "Just like Chadry is, and just like I am."

"Ah," Titim grunted, his weathered features hard to read. "And just what side might that be, lad?"

Baine took a deep breath, knowing he had little choice now but to trust the tavern owner. "The South, of course," he replied softly.

Titim glanced over his shoulder toward the building. Baine could see a barmaid cleaning tables on the terrace, but she seemed preoccupied and paid them no attention. "How is Chadry these days?" the old man asked, focusing back on Baine. "Poor bastard has never been the same since he lost his arm. Terrible shame, that."

"I think you mean since he lost his leg," Baine said with a slight smile. "Either that, or he was walking upside down on that crutch when I saw him just a few hours ago in Crestpool."

Titim chuckled, looking more relaxed. "So, how is he?"

"Doing as well as can be expected being so far from home, I suppose."

"And where is home, exactly?"

"Lestwick," Baine answered immediately. He leaned forward, lowering his voice even more. "That's where his wife and two sons are."

The old man nodded, looking satisfied. "Forgive me, lad, but you never know who to trust these days."

"I understand," Baine said.

Titim patted Baine's arm, leading him toward a table. "How do you know Chadry?"

"He got me out of some trouble last night," Baine answered. "The House Agent kind. Without him risking his neck for me, my head would most likely be on a pike right about now."

"Ah," Titim nodded knowingly. "That sounds like him. That man has a heart of gold to go along with the balls of a lion." The old man stopped them at the table and pointed. "Sit. I'll be back with food and drinks."

Baine set his bow and arrow bag on the table, then sank gratefully into a chair, feeling the fatigue washing over him from the last few days. He leaned back and closed his eyes, enjoying the morning sunlight on his face. The sounds of birds chirping merrily filled his ears, and somewhere the lonely thud of an axe echoed over and over again against a tree trunk. Baine reluctantly opened his eyes ten minutes later when Titim returned, accompanied by a boy and girl, both about fourteen years old. The boy carried a wide wooden tray filled with bowls of food, while the girl held a smaller one containing two mugs and several flasks.

"Put everything there," Titim instructed the servants, motioning to the table. He sat down facing Baine with a relieved sigh, saying nothing while the servants fussed. The girl put an empty bowl and mug in front of Baine, then added a wooden spoon and a dull knife before doing the same for Titim. Meanwhile, the boy spread out the bowls of food, the smells of which instantly set off Baine's stomach, which started rumbling in anticipation.

"You can go," Titim said to the servants. He watched them leave, waiting until they were out of earshot. "Cabbage chowder," Titim said with a smile, pointing to a steaming bowl. "Cleans out the bowels like nothing you've ever tried. At my age, there's nothing more important than that." He pointed to another bowl. "Departed creamed fish. My favorite, even though it's damn hard to eat these days without any teeth." He kissed his fingertips reverently. "Cod fillet mixed with almonds, salt, corn flour, saffron water, and ginger. Simply delicious." Titim indicated another bowl. "And here we have lamb stew with honeyed biscuits."

"I haven't seen this much food in one sitting in a long time," Baine said, amazed. He looked at the tavern owner and grinned. "You're not related to royalty to eat this well, are you?"

Titim chuckled. "No, although I've heard a noblewoman might have married a great, great uncle of mine once. Died in her sleep on their wedding night, so the story goes." The old man shrugged. "The entire thing might just be a story to impress and nothing more, though. I left Temba and my family behind forty years ago, so I guess I'll never know for certain."

"Temba?" Baine asked curiously.

"A city far to the south of here past the Tides of Mansware," Titim answered, his features taking on a faraway look.

"How did you end up here?"

Titim glanced away and waved a hand dismissively. "That is a story too long to recant, my young friend. All I'll say is I have a new family and life here, and Temba is best left in the past where it rightfully belongs." He reached for a flask, then poured dark ale into Baine's mug. "Besides, something tells me you don't have the time for it."

Baine nodded gratefully. "Unfortunately, true. Now, about that horse I mentioned. I was hoping—"

"Already taken care of," Titim grunted as he slopped chowder into his bowl. "A hearty four-year-old gelding with energy to burn. I have a boy preparing him for you now."

"Thank you," Baine said, not knowing what else to say. He couldn't believe how many people like this man had willingly helped him in the last month with no return asked. It was incredibly humbling.

"Nonsense, my boy," Titim chuckled. "A friend of Chadry's is a friend of mine. Besides, I owe the bastard more than I can ever repay."

"So do I," Baine said.

Titim lifted a mug in salute. "Then here's to us, two men—one young and one old—forever indebted to Chadry Armac."

Baine drank, downing the contents in one gulp, then used his knife to spear some fish and drop it in his bowl. He poured chowder on top, then began to eat as the tavern owner watched in amusement. "When's the last time you put anything in your belly, lad?"

Baine paused, thinking, then shrugged. "I'm actually not sure."

Chadry spun his mug in his hand, his food untouched. "So, care to tell me what this is all about?"

Baine hesitated, then, deciding there was no harm, he began reciting everything that had happened to him since he'd fallen off *Sea-Dragon*. The tavern owner listened intently, rarely commenting except to ask a pointed question.

Finally, when Baine was finished, the old man sat back in his chair. "Now that, lad, is a story worthy of the bards."

Baine sat back as well, his hunger sated. He put his hand to his straining belly. "It's not over yet," he said.

"Clearly not," Titim agreed. He shook his head. "I pity those poor bastards with someone like you on their trail."

Baine frowned, realizing he'd forgotten about the scroll Chadry had given him in his haste to escape Crestpool. He reached beneath his leather armor and withdrew it, then slipped off the small iron ring securing it.

"What's that?" Titim asked curiously.

"Chadry gave this to me," Baine explained. "I must have been more tired than I realized because I forgot all about it until now. It's the names of some of the men who rode with Jark Cordly."

Baine unraveled the scroll, which contained five names and a brief notation after each one.

Heply Boll—said to be from Thrushdale
Pit Nelly—peasant, unknown origin
Chett Lumper—ostiary, last known to have worked at the Holy House in Sheafalls
Hoop of Hillsfort—unknown
Alen Hawe—son of a farmer, local

Baine frowned. He'd recognized most of the words on the scroll, but ostiary was new to him. He glanced up at Titim. "O S T I A R Y," Baine said, spelling out the word carefully. "Do you know what that is?"

The tavern owner blinked several times while he thought. "I believe it's what you would call a guard or a doorman, lad. Someone who ensures those who wish to enter the Holy House are not inebriated, which is a sin before the First Pair, as I'm sure you know."

"Oh," Baine said, understanding now. He recalled men standing outside Holy Houses in the bigger cities before but had never really understood their role. He passed the scroll across the table. "Recognize any of these names?"

Titim accepted the scroll and glanced at it, then went still, a look of shock and dismay crossing his features. He finally glanced up at Baine, who could tell by the tavern owner's expression that he was considering lying. But then something changed in the old man's demeanor, a sense of resignation as he handed the scroll back. "Only one—the last one, Alen Hawe. Unfortunately, I know the lad and his father well. Carter Hawe has a farm about three miles south of here. He stops by the tavern regularly to play dice."

Baine could tell by the man's expression that he was far from happy. "What's wrong?" he asked.

The tavern owner shook his head sadly. "The farm has fallen on hard times since the war, and Carter has run into some sizable debt to keep it running because of it. I assume that's why the boy went with this outlaw in the first place, the damn fool."

"And?" Baine prompted, knowing there was more.

"And, lad," Titim said, bowing his head. "Alen Hawe is married to my granddaughter."

Chapter 20: Alen Hawe

Baine blinked in surprise, his eyes unconsciously shifting to his bow lying on the table as his right hand dropped to the hilt of his knife.

Titim lifted his palms up in obvious appeasement, looking deflated and somehow older and smaller than he had before he'd read the scroll. "You have nothing to fear from me, lad. You have my solemn oath that I won't stand in your way over this. The truth is, I never liked that young buck from the start. Alen is more than half wild and has an unfortunate talent for finding trouble. Sadly, my granddaughter chooses to ignore this fact, stubbornly convinced that one day he'll meld into the proper husband she imagines him to be. He will not."

The tavern owner carefully clasped his hands in front of him on the table where Baine could see them. "They say love can be blind, young man, and in this case, it's an especially apt description of Halia. That poor girl took one look at Alen, and that was it. No other man would do for her, despite overwhelming evidence of what he was. Admittedly, the boy is handsome enough, but the ugliness in him resides beneath the skin, not above." Titim clucked his tongue and shook his head sadly. "I am truly sorry this happened to you, but I honestly can't say I'm surprised Alen was involved. It was just a matter of time before the damn fool did something like this."

Baine studied Titim warily. Were his words true about not trying to stop him, or was the old man just humoring him? "You know what I plan to do to him, don't you?"

The tavern owner pursed his lips tightly together, then slowly nodded, his eyes looking pained. "I do."

"And yet, you claim you won't try to interfere? Do you really expect me to believe that?"

Titim shrugged. "Would it make any difference what I do? Will you stay your hand and ride away if I beg you to have mercy on the boy for the sake of my granddaughter?"

"No," Baine said firmly. "I'm sorry, but nothing can stop this now. A debt must be paid. My vow to my murdered family demands it."

"As I thought," Titim said with a slight nod, not looking surprised. He sighed wearily, leaning back in his chair before crossing his arms over his thin chest. "We all have debts on our souls, lad, sins that multiply over a lifetime which must be atoned for—be it in this life or the one that comes after. Today would seem to be Alen's day of atonement. All I ask is that when you kill him—which judging by your eyes, I know you will—please leave the rest of them alone. I promise they had nothing to do with what he did."

"The rest?" Baine said softly, raising an eyebrow. He slowly relaxed, removing his hand from his knife, knowing the old man was being truthful about his intentions.

"My granddaughter and the Hawe family, I mean," Titim replied. "Alen is without question a bad man—the black sheep of the family if you will. But the rest of them, from Carter on down, are good people. He has a wife and six other children, all younger than Alen. I'd hate for any innocents to get hurt over this."

"I don't hurt innocent people," Baine stated forcefully.

"Of that, I have no doubt, lad," Titim replied. "Not on purpose, at any rate. But I've lived a long time and have seen a great many things that I wish now that I hadn't. We both know accidents can and do happen despite the best of intentions. My granddaughter is pregnant with her first child, and if anything were to—"

Baine held up a hand, stopping the old man. "Nothing will happen to her. You have my word."

Titim studied Baine for several heartbeats, and then he finally nodded in acceptance. "*Casperiatii nos latte frone del fatino,*" the old man whispered, his eyes turning inward. He sighed again a moment later, focusing back on Baine, who was staring at him quizzically. "A popular saying from my homeland," the tavern owner explained. "Roughly translated, it means *fate and a man's shadow walk this life hand in hand. You can't escape either one.*"

The farm was exactly where Titim had said it would be. Baine halted the gelding on a knoll overlooking the house and outbuildings, which were still more than half a mile away. A rich field of rye stretched out beneath him, leading to the house, with a sprawling forest filling the horizon to the south on the other side of the farm. Another, larger field of golden wheat lay to Baine's left, with a rectangular, grass-covered field on his right, where a thin youth using a fire-hardened goading stick urged two oxen pulling an iron-tipped plow forward. A second, much older man stood at the back of the plow, guiding it as the blade of the tool bucked and kicked while it tore open the earth, leaving a fresh furrow in its wake.

A short woman in a blue tunic and gray skirt wearing a yellow wimple on her head worked with a group of children in one corner of the field where the plow had already passed, plucking rocks from the loosened soil and tossing them into a barrow. The woman paused as if sensing his eyes on her, straightening before wiping at her brow. She glanced his way, and Baine saw her stiffen the moment she saw him. The woman called out to the man in warning, though with the sounds of the blade scraping the ground and the wind, neither he nor the boy appeared to hear her. The woman gestured urgently to the children to join her, two of which were no more than toddlers, naked as the day they were born and filthy. Those two hid behind the woman's skirts, clinging to them while peeking out at Baine in innocent fascination. The other, older children stared up at Baine boldly, showing little fear.

"Well, here we go," Baine muttered, kicking the gelding into motion down the knoll.

He headed for the still-plodding oxen, keeping his expression friendly. The youth hesitated when he noticed Baine, looking unsure of what to do. But after a sharp command from the older man, the boy grabbed the rope harness of the nearest ox, stopping the beast and its companion. Baine didn't fail to notice the older man lift an axe from the back of the plow while the youth looked around, then stooped to pick up a fist-sized rock.

Baine halted the gelding ten feet from the pair of oxen, who stared at him with dumb indifference, then nodded to the older man. He ignored the youth and his rock completely. "Greetings. I imagine you would be Carter Hawe?"

"What of it?" the older man said. He moved around the plow, stepping in front of the boy with the axe held ready across his chest. The man wasn't tall, but the breadth of his shoulders was impressive, hinting at great strength.

Baine hooked a thumb over his shoulder toward the north. "I just came from The Hungry Oak. I've never eaten so well in my life. Titim sends his regards, by the way."

Carter's hard expression softened somewhat, though his eyes remained wary. Baine sensed the woman drawing closer in his peripheral vision, but he stayed focused on the farmer.

"That old fool sure knows how to run a fine tavern. I'll give him that," Carter Hawe said cautiously.

"That's a fact," Baine agreed. He shifted in the saddle, letting his eyes roll over the youth without making it obvious. The boy was perhaps twelve years old with a matted shag of brown hair falling down to his shoulders. He was surprisingly tall for his age, though clearly not Alen. "Titim and I got to talking," Baine continued. "And he mentioned that you and he are good friends."

"That's no secret," Carter rumbled, lowering the axe a fraction.

Encouraged, Baine pressed onward. "He also told me you have a son named Alen, who is now married to his granddaughter."

Carter's expression hardened again at the mention of his son's name. "You have a point?"

"As fate would have it, I met Alen not long ago," Baine replied. He grinned sheepishly. "Actually, Alen and I got to gambling, and—" He hesitated there when the approaching woman, now well within earshot, snorted loudly. She'd left the children behind; skirts held high as she navigated the uneven furrows toward them. Baine studied her curiously, guessing she was anywhere from thirty to forty years old, with a pinched, sunburnt face and unusually wide jawbones leading to an odd, pointed chin. Too old to be the pregnant granddaughter, he knew. Alen's mother, perhaps? Baine focused back on the farmer. "As I was saying, Alen and I were gambling recently in Laskerly at The Jolly Cock. Maybe you've heard—?"

"Listen, boy," Carter Hawe grunted impatiently. "I need to have this field plowed by sundown, and I don't have all day for mindless chatter with strangers. So, unless you're here to help, spit out your words in a timely fashion and then get going."

"Right, of course," Baine said. "How silly of me. Anyway, getting directly to the point. Alen must have had the gods watching over him that night because I swear, every roll of the dice went his way. I ended up owing him a fair sum of money, but I didn't have it all with me. Alen was good enough to take my word that I'd get the rest to him when I could." Baine spread his arms. "So, here I am."

"You sure you're talking about my brother?" the youth grunted. He grinned and glanced at his father, revealing sharp, feral teeth like a badger. "Since when does Alen ever win at dice, let alone take a man's word that he'll pay if he does?"

Baine shrugged, keeping the smile on his face. "What can I say? Maybe there's more to him than you know."

"I doubt it," the boy grumbled.

"What did you say your name was again?" Carter asked, shading his eyes to look up at Baine.

"I didn't, but people call me Baine."

Carter Hawe studied Baine critically, then finally looked away and spat. "Alen is at the house with his wife. He's leaving soon, from what I hear. Go pay him what you owe, and then ride on. I got no room for another bowl at the table. There's enough mouths to feed as it is."

"I understand," Baine said, nodding. "This won't take long. Sorry to have troubled you."

Baine guided the gelding past the woman, who he was certain now must be Alen's mother, then the children, each of whom watched him in sullen silence. The naked toddlers looked nearly identical—long unkempt hair and bronzed bodies—though one was a boy and the other a girl. The little boy made a spluttering sound with his lips, wiggling his tiny cock back and forth at Baine as he passed. Baine pretended to be afraid, making a twisted face with his tongue sticking out the side of his mouth before, a moment later, he laughed. The boy's eyes widened and he giggled, giving one last enthusiastic jiggle of his bits before he abruptly turned shy and hid behind an older sister.

Baine left the family behind, turning his entire focus on the house in the distance, with the humor quickly leaving his features, replaced by the cold face of a killer. Alen Hawe's moment of atonement was almost at hand. He followed a narrow road through the field of rye, with the plants swaying before him like rippling waves on the ocean beneath the wind's caress. A split-rail fence of weathered poles surrounded the house and outbuildings, he noted as he drew closer, with the road leading to an open gate. Baine guided the gelding through the gate and into the yard, his eyes constantly shifting to the left and right, marking everything he saw in his mind. The main house was built of limestone and unusually large, with even a second story, which Baine found surprising. Carter Hawe was clearly favored by Lord Falmir for some reason, though why the farmer was said to be in financial trouble was something of a mystery.

An outbuilding with a steeply sloped roof rose to Baine's right, with a fenced-in pen built off it where several curious pigs stared out at him. A stable stood to one side of the pen, with a goat tethered to a rope cropping sparse grass outside the open door. Numerous chickens wandered in the yard, pecking at the ground, and an anxious mother hen stood near a woodshed, watching over a brood of five clumsy yellow chicks cavorting there. A striped, orange cat sat on a fencepost near the house, its tail swishing back and forth slowly while it watched the vulnerable chicks with intense concentration.

Baine noticed a saddled black stallion standing stoically in the shade of an aspen near the stable, tied to a post beside a water trough. Carter Hawe had mentioned his son was preparing to leave, he remembered, and it looked like he'd arrived just in time to prevent that. The gelding smelled the water and snorted, pricking his ears hopefully as he headed for the trough, but Baine tugged hard on the reins, guiding him toward the house instead. He dismounted when he was close to the building, then led the gelding to the fence and wrapped the reins around the top rail.

The cat sat in the same position as before, ten feet away from Baine and the horse, watching them both with expressionless hazel eyes. It finally yawned and stretched lazily, raking its claws along the top of the fence railing before jumping down and slinking away through the grass. Baine headed for the house's front door, which, like the windows to either side of it, had been left open to catch the steady breeze coming from the north. He paused on the porch, listening to the unmistakable sounds of a woman's sobs coming from inside. A moment later, a deep male voice snapped at her to stop her blubbering.

Baine unhooked his bow and notched an arrow, then stepped through the doorway. A young man with dark hair and a trim beard sat on the end of a bench by a long table with his body turned to the side, revealing his profile. He was bent over, clearly in the process of pulling on a leather boot. A young woman wearing a light grey dress stood over him with her back to Baine and her face in her hands. The woman's narrow shoulders shook uncontrollably as she cried. Neither one had noticed Baine yet, and he took another step, pausing when a floorboard squeaked beneath him.

The man looked up, his eyes going round in astonishment before he quickly recovered his composure. "What is this?" he demanded. "Who are you?"

The woman turned and gasped when she saw Baine and his bow. She was pretty, with blue eyes and braided auburn hair that fell in a single thick strand down her right side to her waist. He noticed her protruding belly despite the loose-fitting dress she wore, guessing she was at least six or seven months into her pregnancy. This clearly was Titim's granddaughter.

Baine focused back on the man, aiming his bow at him. "I imagine you would be Alen Hawe?"

Alen took a deep breath, pausing to pull his boot on all the way before he stood. The youth was tall, standing several inches over six feet with the same wide shoulders as his father. Halia pressed herself against her husband's side fearfully, trying to take his hand in hers, but he brushed her off in irritation.

"What do you want?" Alen asked in a low voice. He flicked his gaze past Baine to the door, clearly hoping for some help from outside. There would be none.

Baine glanced at the pregnant woman. "Your grandfather says hello, Halia." The girl's eyes reflected her confusion at the mention of the tavern owner, and her mouth opened, but no words came forth. Baine shifted to his left to keep an eye on the door, his aim never wavering from Alen Hawe's chest. "I promised him that no matter what happens here, you would not be harmed," Baine added. He motioned to the door with his head. "So, please leave now. My business with your husband doesn't concern you."

Alen Hawe licked his lips, glancing again at the door while his wife made no move to leave. "This has to be some kind of mistake," the outlaw said. He spread his arms. "A misunderstanding."

"You were involved in the raid on Witbridge Manor, weren't you?" Baine hissed, trying to keep a lid on his anger. He desperately wanted to kill this man, but the girl needed to go first. "Trust me, you bastard, there's no misunderstanding."

"Witbridge Manor?" Alen said, feigning ignorance. "Where is that?"

Baine snorted. The youth was a terrible actor. "It's where you callously murdered innocent women and children just a few nights ago. Surely all the death, misery, and bloodshed you caused hasn't slipped your mind already?"

Halia looked at her husband with an expression of surprise, which quickly turned into growing horror. "What is he talking about, Alen? What have you done?"

"I've done nothing," Alen snapped. "This man has obviously gone mad. I've never even heard of this Witbridge Manor, much less been there."

A stone fireplace stood at the end of the room, recessed into the wall with a massive wooden beam above it stretching from one wall to the other. Various tools and implements hung from the beam on hooks directly over the fireplace, including a well-used bellows, three different-sized wooden ladles, two iron pans, and a pair of worn metal pincers. Baine shifted his aim slightly and released the arrow, which hissed past Alen and slapped into the bellows, quivering there as a stark warning of what was to come.

Halia started to sob again as Baine calmly nocked another arrow. He focused on the girl. "Your husband is lying to you. He rode with Jark Cordly, the imposter Outlaw of Corwick, slaughtering innocent women and children for blood-tainted gold." Baine fought hard to swallow his emotions, which threatened to overwhelm him at any moment. He forced himself to continue, his voice cracking. "Your husband and his outlaw friends killed my wife and babe,

Halia. Slaughtered them like cattle and laughed about it afterward." Baine gestured to the woman's stomach. "My son was only a few months older than that child growing inside you is right now. Think about that! This is the kind of man you are married to, Halia. This is the monster you say that you love. It's time for you to open your eyes and really see what he is. If not for your sake, then by the gods, for that of your unborn child."

"Lies!" Alen cried, looking caught and increasingly desperate as his wife regarded him with hooded eyes. "All lies, I tell you!"

The outlaw moved then, but not in a desperate, futile frontal assault like Baine was anticipating, ducking instead like a coward behind his wife. He grabbed her by the waist, ignoring her startled cry of protest as he lifted her in the air, then tossed her without hesitation directly at Baine. The pregnant woman flew through the air, her arms windmilling and mouth opened round in a circle of shock. Baine could do little in the brief time he had except turn his bow aside, terrified he'd end up impaling her or the baby on the arrowhead. Halia crashed into him a heartbeat later, and he staggered backward and fell, pinned beneath her in a gaggle of arms and legs. He watched impotently as Alen bounded for the door, disappearing outside while he fought to extricate himself from the girl.

Baine finally got to his feet and sprinted after the outlaw, only to hesitate in the entrance and look back when the girl cried out in a heart-stricken voice, "Please! Please don't kill him! I beg of you!"

Baine just stared at her sadly for a heartbeat, saying nothing, with his expression answer enough about what his intentions were. Halia started to weep even louder then as Baine dashed into the yard, sending chickens squawking in fear out of his way. He came to a shuddering stop moments later, cursing when he saw his quarry already on his horse, using the ends of the reins to frantically whip the stallion's haunches as he raced towards the forest to the south. Baine lifted his bow and drew the string back, knowing even as he did that the escaping rider was already too far away. He cursed again, ramming the arrow into his bag before running to the gelding and jumping into the saddle to give chase.

"Go get him, boy," Baine whispered, crouching low over the horse's neck as the gelding began to run.

Alen Hawe had a sizable lead and was already less than fifty yards from the forest line as he raced along a beaten path through a field of long grass. If he made it into the trees, Baine knew there was a good chance he would lose the bastard. Titim had claimed the horse Baine rode was feisty with endless energy, which he prayed was true as he urged the animal onward. The gelding responded, practically flying over the terrain as clumps of dirt and grass flew from his hooves. Alen looked back a moment later, and seeing Baine closing the distance rapidly, he began whipping his mount even harder, though it didn't seem to help much. Baine grinned triumphantly, for the gelding was everything the tavern owner had promised. That grin turned to a frown moments later, though, when Alen Hawe finally reached the treeline and disappeared into the undergrowth, leaving a burst of leaves, pine needles, and small twigs whirling in his wake.

Baine cursed, not slowing the gelding, resenting every second lost as his mount bore down on the forest. He slowed the horse when he reached the treeline, knowing if an ambush were to come, this is where it would happen. Moving at a trot now, Baine drew a knife and urged the gelding into the trees. He tensed, expecting an attack, but the forest was still and silent. A worn trail led further into the trees, with the ground torn up from the hooves of his quarry's horse. Alen had chosen flight over fight, it seemed.

Baine clucked his tongue and guided the gelding forward, following the obvious trail for a hundred more yards until he came to a bend. He paused his mount on the other side, blinking in surprise at what he saw before eventually, he started to laugh. The outlaw's black stallion stood off to one side of the path, happily nibbling at leaves, while its rider lay unmoving on the ground, spreadeagled on his back beneath a low, overhanging branch. There was blood smeared across the outlaw's forehead, but his chest was rising and falling, which meant he was still alive, at least for now.

Alen Hawe's moment of atonement had finally come.

Chapter 21: Bones Or Knots?

The outlaw was big and damn heavy, and it took Baine almost half an hour to get him onto his horse. He'd initially tried lifting the unconscious youth, but after repeated failures that only resulted in an aching back and an increasingly jittery black stallion, he'd had to resort to tying Alen's hands with rope and then using the gelding to drag him into the saddle. The outlaw now lay facedown, hands and ankles lashed firmly beneath the belly of the stallion as Baine guided the gelding further along the trail, heading deeper into the forest. He'd originally decided to wait where he was for Alen to awaken but then realized the youth's father might come looking for him. Baine had no wish to hurt the farmer, so he'd decided it would be prudent to put some distance between him and Alen's family before he and the outlaw got to know each other a little better. Besides, a man's screams can travel a long way, even when surrounded by trees.

Baine continued heading southward for an hour along the trail, then, seeing a gently sloping grade leading down to a flat hollow that looked suitable, he headed the gelding off the path, trailing the stallion's reins with its burden in his hand. The descent was softened by thick layers of leaf mold blackened by decay, with an array of brown, white, and yellow mushrooms hiding beneath the covering revealed with every plodding step of the horses' hooves. Baine reached the bottom of the hollow, which was cast in long shadows from the trees above, then continued onward, heading west now. Alen began to move sluggishly a few minutes later, groaning and pulling weakly at his bonds, but Baine paid him no mind. Where could the bastard go?

The hollow began to narrow as Baine progressed, with the tree-covered slopes to either side of him getting steeper and steeper by the minute. The forest floor appeared mostly devoid of leaves and small debris in the center of the depression as if swept neatly away by a giant's broom, though Baine guessed it had more to do with water flow during storms than anything else. He was beginning to question his choice of direction after another five minutes of travel, debating whether to turn back or not, when the ravine abruptly began to widen again, leading to an open clearing bathed in soothing sunlight. An oak tree—the trunk of which was as wide as Baine's spread arms—rose at the end of the clearing, looking both welcoming and serene. Baine knew this was the place. He halted the gelding and hopped to the ground, then did some deep knee bends to loosen his muscles.

"What about me, you little bastard? I can't breathe like this."

Baine glanced toward the outlaw splayed unceremoniously over his horse like a sack of flour. He could see only hanging feet, legs, and a trouser-covered rump from his position. Baine casually walked around the stallion, pausing to rub the horse's soft muzzle before he grabbed Alen's head by his greasy hair and yanked it savagely upwards. He bent low, so they were eye to eye. "What did you just call me?"

"Nothing," the outlaw groaned, his face filled with pain and misery. "I didn't call you anything. I swear."

"That's what I thought," Baine grunted. He let go of the outlaw's hair and circled the stallion, drawing a knife before slicing through the rope around the man's ankles. Baine retraced his steps and grabbed Alen by the scruff of his neck and seat of his pants, then yanked hard, sending him with a cry of surprise to the ground. Baine stepped back, unhooking his bow before nocking an arrow. "On your feet, murderer."

The outlaw spat blood out on the grass, shaking his head before he looked up at Baine. "Give me a moment to catch my breath, will you?"

Baine drew back the bowstring, then released, sending an arrow into Alen's left leg, three inches above the top of his boot.

The outlaw wailed in shock as the iron tip burst out the other side in a shower of flesh and blood, and he rolled onto his back, clutching at the wound with his bound hands. "If you think trying to stand on that is going to be tough," Baine growled, nocking another arrow. "Just wait until I put one in the other leg. Now get to your feet!"

Alen lifted his hands defensively, with the trailing rope tied to his wrists coiled like a snake beneath him as tears of pain streamed down his face. "All right! All right! Don't shoot." He struggled to a sitting position, equal amounts of snot, spittle, and blood dripping into his mustache. The wounded youth gingerly forced himself onto his knees, screaming in pain. He paused like that, shuddering, head lowered and chest heaving.

"Keep going," Baine grunted. He felt no pity for him—nothing but cold, all-consuming hatred.

The outlaw sobbed as he used his good leg and bound hands in tandem, pushing himself upward, where he stood wobbling unsteadily on one foot with his arrow-punctured lower leg lifted several inches off the ground.

"Not bad," Baine conceded. Alen Hawe was clearly tougher than most—not that it would do him any good in the end. Baine motioned to the oak. "Over there. Sit with your back against that tree."

"Can't we talk about this?" Alen pleaded, fighting to maintain his balance. He briefly lowered his injured leg to steady himself, then howled when his foot touched the ground.

"Is that what my wife said to you when you murdered her?" Baine asked, his voice filled with suppressed fury. He motioned to the tree again. "Now get over there, or I swear by the gods, the pain you're in now will feel like a flea bite compared to what I'll do to you next."

The outlaw sobbed in resignation, lowering his head before he began awkwardly hopping toward the tree, trailing the length of rope behind him like a long tail. Baine followed cautiously, staying back a safe distance. Alen might be wounded and his mobility severely incapacitated, but that didn't mean he wasn't still dangerous. The outlaw finally reached the tree, using the solidness of its trunk to support him as, with a hiss of pain, he sank to the ground with his feet jutting out in front of him. He automatically started to reach for the arrow embedded in his flesh with his cupped hands.

"Don't!" Baine snapped. "Leave it be." The outlaw closed his eyes, swallowing loudly as he leaned his head against the trunk. Baine lowered the bow. "If you move even one hair on your head before I get back, you die," he grunted. Baine returned to the horses, grabbing more rope from the gelding's saddlebags, grateful that Titim had provided so much. He returned to his prisoner. "Take off your boots."

"Why?" Alen asked suspiciously.

"You don't get to ask the questions, murderer," Baine said, his voice soft and deadly. "The only thing keeping you alive right now is your ability to cooperate, so I suggest you do what I said or deal with the consequences."

The outlaw blinked, then reluctantly fought to get his right boot off, tossing it aside. His face had gone white as snow from the labor, but he grit his teeth and dove in on the left boot, grunting in pain as he worked diligently to wiggle it off. Finally, with his body shuddering from the effort, the outlaw managed to slip off the boot. He leaned back afterward against the trunk looking exhausted, his chest heaving from the exertion. "Now what, you bastard?" he grunted between ragged breaths, staring at Baine with hate-filled eyes. "Do you want me to do a little dance for you next?"

Baine chuckled without humor as he cut a section of rope about two feet long from the length he carried. "We'll just have to see about that, now won't we?" He tossed the rope to the wounded man. "Tie your ankles together," he ordered. "Make sure the knots are good and tight. You know what happens if they aren't."

The outlaw glared at Baine sullenly but did as he was told, wincing and cursing under his breath as he labored to tie his feet with his bound hands. It was no easy task. When he was done, Baine approached, grabbing the trailing end of the rope still attached to Alen's wrists, careful not to get too close. He looked up, selecting a stout branch, then tossed the rope over it, with the free end now dangling by his head. Baine took his time, carefully tying one end of the rope he carried to the one over the branch using an efficient, figure-eight knot that Putt had taught him. The red-bearded outlaw had insisted there was no better or stronger knot for connecting two ropes together.

Alen watched him apprehensively, finally licking his lips. "What's all this for? What do you want from me?"

"Information," Baine grunted absently. "Now shut your mouth and let me work."

Satisfied that the knot was strong, Baine pulled down using all his weight, ignoring the outlaw's gasp of pain as the rope drew his hands up over his head. Then, careful to keep the line taught, Baine circled the tree twice before throwing the remaining rope over the original branch and tying it securely. At least fifteen feet of rope remained unused, and Baine cut it off, dropping the length to the ground near the tree. He would be needing it later. Finally, Baine stood back to survey his handiwork. Alen Hawe was now trussed up like a hog, his hands extended well over his head, his ass an inch off the ground, and his back arched painfully. It was perfect.

"You don't need to do this," the outlaw said in a pleading voice. "Please. I'll tell you whatever you want to know."

"Oh, I know you will," Baine agreed. He set his bow down, then squatted beside the bound man and drew a knife. "That was never in question, murderer." Baine placed the knife in the helpless man's lap over his groin, where the weight of the weapon and what it represented could not be ignored. He sat cross-legged, his elbows on his knees, his chin in his hands as he stared at the wounded youth. The scroll Chadry had given him with the names of the other outlaws was nestled inside his clothing, but Baine didn't need it. He knew all their names by heart. "Tell me about Heply Boll."

Alen blinked. "Uh, who is that?" Alen's acting hadn't improved in the last few hours, Baine noted as he picked up the knife without saying anything. "All right, all right," the outlaw stammered. "I'll tell you what I know."

Baine ignored him. He'd learned long ago from Einhard that you could cut a finger or two off some men and they'd barely blink or make a sound. But threatening to take a toe made even the most stubborn men quail for some reason. Baine put the blade of his knife between the little toe on Alen's right foot and the one next to it.

"I'll tell you, I said!" the outlaw called out frantically, his eyes round with horror.

Baine smiled coldly, then flicked his wrist, sending the end toe spinning away through the air. Alen screamed, his bound body twisting and writhing as dark blood welled up from the stump.

"Who is Heply Boll?" Baine repeated in a quiet voice. He put the knife blade between the next two toes.

"An outlaw!" Alen cried out in panic. "One of Jark Cordly's lieutenants."

Baine's eyebrows rose. "You mean he's not a recent recruit like you?"

Alen shook his head adamantly. "No. Hep came north with Jark. They've been together a long time."

Baine smiled, removing the knife. He set it back in the man's lap and patted him on the head like a favorite puppy. "See, now we're getting somewhere. Was that so hard? How many other men came with Jark from the north?"

"Five," Alen answered immediately. "Six if you include Hep."

"Their names?"

"Kant Reece, Pater Dore, Chett Lumper, Beney Gill, and Pit Nelly. Beney's dead, though, killed by some crippled boy—the damn fool."

Baine nodded and grinned—Hanley, no doubt. Three of the six men the outlaw had named as lieutenants were from Chadry's list, and including Jark Cordly, he now knew the names of fourteen of the men who'd raided Witbridge Manor. Six of those were already dead—seven if you included the soon-to-be Alen—leaving only six men left to be named. "I've already killed Cairn, Tadley Platt, Rupert Frake, Bent Holdfer, and Konway of Hastow," Baine said. Alen's eyes had gone wide as Baine ticked off the names on his fingers one by one. "So, who are the rest?" he asked.

"You killed all of them?" the outlaw breathed in wonder. "Even Bent and Konway?"

"I did," Baine confirmed emotionlessly. "Though admittedly, I had some help with Rupert Frake. Now enough stalling. Tell me the names of the others."

"I only know four of them, but—" the outlaw started to say. Baine reached for the knife wordlessly, and the bound man started shaking his head back and forth. "I'm telling you the truth! I swear by the gods, I can't remember the last two!"

Baine could tell by the man's expression that he was being truthful. "All right," he grunted, removing his hand from the knife. "Start talking."

"There were two brothers," Alen answered. "I remember them well. Ward and Tasker Grich. Big, mean bastards they were. I think they said once that they were deserters."

"From the North or South?"

"I'm not sure."

"Who else," Baine prompted.

"A man named Pax Colo," Alen said. He glanced at Baine. "He didn't talk much, so I don't know where he's from, but he's a small bastard like you and all twitchy and strange. I was afraid to turn my back on him."

"And the last man?"

Alen actually chuckled as he shook his head. "Vierna Alel ain't no man."

Baine blinked in surprise. "A woman?"

"Yes," the outlaw agreed. "Pretty, but just as tough as any of us. Maybe more so. Jark was humping with her, the lucky bastard. I tried, but the bitch turned me down. She turned everyone else down too but Jark and that pretty boy, though she cut him loose pretty fast." Baine nodded, guessing he meant Rupert Frake. Alen looked up at his bound hands, which had turned purple and blotchy from the constricting rope. "I've been cooperative, haven't I?" the outlaw whined. "Do you think you can loosen this a bit?"

"Maybe," Baine grunted, lying. "I heard Jark was disbanding the outlaws. Is that true?"

Alen stuck out his lower lip as he thought about that, looking puzzled. He shook his head. "No, not that I know. We were getting ready to hit another place, last I heard."

"Where?"

Alen glanced down at the knife, and he licked his lips. "I swear I don't know. We were instructed to meet Jark in Havelock next week after we'd finished celebrating—" The outlaw's features blanched at the look on Baine's face, realizing what he'd almost said.

"Keep going," Baine growled.

"That's where I was heading when you showed up," Alen said weakly. "To the meet."

"Where is Havelock?"

"About a hundred miles to the east. It's an abandoned mine near Sheafalls."

"That's where Chett Lumper comes from," Baine stated.

The outlaw looked startled. "Yes. How did you know that?"

"Never mind," Baine grunted. "So, you're saying the entire band is to meet at this mine next week?"

"Yes," Alen nodded eagerly. "That was what we were told. We're to go there and wait for Jark and his lieutenants to show up."

Baine frowned. "They stayed with Jark? All of them?"

Alen nodded his head. "They stick close to him. Sometimes the girl does, too, but she had something to do—I don't know what—and she didn't go with him. The boy did, though."

"The boy?" Baine said. "What boy?"

Alen snorted. "Just some snot-nosed outlaw wannabe. He's the one that told us about—" Alen hesitated again, swallowing before continuing, "About Witbridge Manor. Jark thinks he's some kind of good luck charm or something after how much gold we took there."

"What's this boy's name?" Baine growled.

"I don't know," Alen said. "Everybody just calls him that, Boy."

"How old is he?"

"Twelve or thirteen, maybe?"

Baine nodded. He'd been so blinded by the need for vengeance that he'd forgotten he and Jebido had determined that someone close to Hadrack must have tipped off the outlaws about the cache at Witbridge. Jebido had promised to look into the matter, though neither of them had been enthused over the idea that one of their own might be a traitor. Now that notion was put to rest, though who this *Boy* might be was a mystery—one Baine had every intention of solving. He spent the next hour interrogating Alen about the outlaws and their movements but learned little else from him that might prove useful. Finally satisfied, Baine retrieved his knife and sheathed it, then stood.

"Is that it?" Alen asked hopefully. "Will you let me go now?"

Baine chuckled, saying nothing as he fetched the rope he'd left on the ground. He returned to the outlaw, dropping to his knees by the man's feet. He tested the knots Alen had tied, tightening them until he was satisfied, then began securing one end of the rope to the bonds. "I know this fellow," Baine said as he worked. "Name's Putt. A good man, by and large." Baine paused to wink at Alen, who was staring at him in befuddlement. "Tends to cheat at dice a tad too much, and his farts would empty a pigsty, but one thing he can do is tie a damn fine knot." Baine gestured to the knot he'd just completed, tugging on the rope for emphasis. "This, for example, is one of his. Guaranteed not to fail." Baine indicated the rope tied to the branch above them. "That's one of his too. The man swears by his knots. It's almost a religion for him." He stood, holding the free end of the rope in his hand. "Now me, I'm not so certain. I mean, how do we know for sure they'll hold the way he claims, right?"

"I...I don't understand," Alen said, blinking in confusion.

"You will soon enough, murderer," Baine grunted. He dropped the rope, then retreated to the horses, returning with the outlaw's stallion. He gently turned the horse around, clucking his tongue as he urged it to slowly back up until the animal's rump was less than six feet from the bound man. Baine left the stallion's reins trailing on the ground, then whistling, returned for the rope. He wound the free end around the pommel of the stallion's saddle several times and tied it off, careful to make it tight.

"What are you doing?" Alen whispered in growing horror.

Baine glanced over at him. "Why, I thought you and I would do a little experiment, Alen. What do you say? Let's find out if my friend Putt really knows what he's talking about."

"Please," the outlaw begged, tears streaming down his cheeks. "I just want to go home. Please, I didn't know about you. It was only ever about the gold. I didn't mean to hurt your family."

"Do you know what a flight animal is, Alen?" Baine asked, ignoring the other man's pleas.

"What?" the man gasped, caught off guard by the question. "What do you mean?"

Baine shook his head, clucking his tongue in disappointment. "Growing up on a farm, I'd expect you would know, murderer. A horse is what you would call a flight animal, you see. When startled, they tend to run away as fast as possible. It's instinctive according to the greatest horsemen in the world, the Piths." Baine grinned at the look of pure horror on Alen's face. He stepped back from the stallion and picked up his bow, lifting it to strike. "I wonder which will give out first, murderer? Your bones or my friend's knots?" Baine shrugged. "Well, I guess we're about to find out, you and me." He glanced at the sobbing outlaw, then didn't hesitate, slapping the stallion's haunches with the bow.

It was a near thing in the end, but the knots won the contest by the slimmest of margins.

PART THREE

BLACK DEATH

Chapter 22: Ward Grich

It took four days for Baine to reach Sheafalls. He'd been expecting there to be, well, falls, actually, but in reality, the village had none and was really not much to look at. The buildings were all old and rundown, with a Holy House rising on a hillock overlooking the town that could have been standing there since the beginning of time. *No doubt where Chett Lumper had worked as an ostiary*, Baine thought as he studied the area with a critical eye. A sluggish river rolled slowly past the village, with the dark blue water—at least in his line of sight—measuring no more than ten feet across at best at its widest point. A crumbling stone bridge spanned the river to the north, where it joined a road heading for a series of jagged hills half a mile away. That would be where Baine would find the iron ore mine known as Havelock, he knew, although Alen had admitted that he wasn't sure of its exact location.

Which meant Baine needed to ask somebody in town for directions. He urged the gelding forward as he reflected on the last few days since Alen Hawe's rather inglorious demise. Baine had returned the dead youth's black stallion to his father's farm that same night, albeit without anyone being the wiser—at least until the next morning, anyway. He'd waited until well past midnight when the family was asleep, leaving the horse and what was left of the corpse tied up in the barn. It would be a gruesome discovery for whoever was first to walk in there, of course. But after some serious debate with himself, Baine had decided the shock of Alen's death was still better in the long run than Halia spending the next weeks, months, or possibly even years waiting in vain for her husband to come home.

The girl would be heartbroken, Baine knew, but brutal and untimely deaths were far from uncommon these days—although he conceded perhaps not to such an extent as Alen's final moments had been. In the end, Baine was hoping that with the support of her grandfather, Halia would quickly get over the bastard and find another man, one who would treat her well and be everything that Alen Hawe had not. It was the best that he could do for the soon-to-be mother.

The innocents always pay.

Baine reached the outskirts of the town, surprised by the lack of activity. The sun was well up in the sky by now, yet few people were around. An older man with one arm struggled to split firewood near a shed to his left. The man paused in his labor to regard Baine, his features cast in deep shadow from a wide-brimmed straw hat. A small group of women were crouched on their knees near the river, wringing out clothing, with several more standing further back on the bank using washing bats on dripping clothes hanging from boards. Baine could hear the women's voices echoing as they chattered to each other, overlayed by the steady, wet smack of the bats. There was no one else in view.

A large pack of mongrels came to investigate Baine once he reached the town center, chuffing and snarling, with a few of the more timid members hovering behind the main group. Those in the back alternated between yapping at him and then retreating several paces before returning to do it all again. Baine ignored the dogs, though the gelding seemed nervous at their presence, with his ears laid back and his eyes rolling uneasily.

Baine patted the horse on the shoulder. "If one of them gets too close, my friend, you have my permission to kick the damn thing into tomorrow." The gelding snorted as if he understood as Baine sat back in the saddle. He felt well-rested after the last four days and ready for almost anything. Today, he hoped, was going to be a very good day.

The tavern in Sheafalls was located at the village's center and was called The Hunter's Cup, which Baine found rather fitting considering his purpose. The place looked just as rundown as every other building in Sheafalls, though Baine had seen far worse taverns than this one before. He left the gelding in the care of a stuttering, half-wit stableboy, then made his way through a side door into the main hall. The floor inside was covered by months-old rushes that smelled of decay, and it crunched like gravel under his feet as he moved. Long tables with benches lined each wall, separated by a walkway in the center eight feet wide. Tallow candles flickered on every table, though there were few patrons; only one man sitting alone hunched over a mug with his back leaning against the wall, and three women sitting together some distance away from him. A bar stood at the far end of the room, with a woman Baine guessed to be in her fifties standing behind it.

Baine moved purposefully toward the bar, pausing after several steps when a sleek black cat darted past him underneath a table, emerging a moment later with a mouse hanging limply from its jaws. The cat trotted proudly away toward the bar, and Baine followed after it. He passed the lone man, who didn't look up, though the women stopped their conversation as he drew closer, studying him. One of them whispered something to the others, and then they all abruptly stood, shooting him several frightened looks as they hurried past him out the door. Baine watched the women leave, wondering what that was all about. He reached the bar, leaning with his hands on the oak top.

"I'm looking for Havelock," Baine said to the barmaid.

She was tall for a woman and fat, with thin grey hair pulled back severely from an oval face. Her mouth was set in a permanent frown, and her eyes were wide-set and hardened from what Baine guessed was years of disappointment. "You'd be him, then," the woman grunted in a surprisingly deep voice. "People around here have been debating whether you'd show up or not. Guess we know now."

Baine blinked in confusion. "Him? Him, who?"

The barmaid glanced at Baine's armor. "You're the one hunting those outlaws—the one they're calling *Black Death*."

Baine paused, taken aback and not sure what to say. How could this woman know anything about him?

The barmaid chuckled. "Word travels around these parts. The bards are already making up songs about your exploits. Nothing moves faster than a good song, you know." She leaned forward. "Did you really kill two men with your bare hands right under the noses of a hundred House Agents?"

Baine frowned as he thought. Could Chadry have said something about him, or Titim, maybe? It didn't seem likely, but someone somewhere was talking. "Whoever this man you're referring to is," Baine finally said, forcing a chuckle. "I assure you, it's not me. I'm just a soldier on furlough from the war."

"Sure you are," the woman said, not looking fooled. She leaned her meaty forearms on the bar, and Baine couldn't help but notice that they were twice as big as his own. "Then why are you asking about Havelock? That mine ran dry years ago. Everybody knows there's nothing up there now but wolves and bears." Baine didn't have an answer to that, and the woman laughed at his expression. "I'll tell you why. You're asking about Havelock because the Outlaw of Corwick's men are there. That's why."

"Corna!" the man at the table suddenly bellowed in a slurred, drunken voice. He motioned unsteadily with a hand, not bothering to lift his head. "More beer, woman!"

The barmaid grinned, not bothering to acknowledge the command. "Now, since you claim you're not *Black Death*," she said to Baine, leaning even closer to him and lowering her voice. She hesitated there, the dullness that had dominated her eyes until now replaced by a glow of excitement and perhaps anticipation. Baine wondered why. "Then I guess it won't mean anything to you that the man sitting over there lost in his cups is one of the outlaws, here to buy supplies. Now will it?"

Baine's entire body stiffened at the news, and the woman grinned widely in triumph at his expression. That grin slowly faded when Baine just glared at her until finally, she swallowed noisily and broke eye contact, clearly unnerved. Baine lowered his voice to match hers. "What's this man's name?"

"Grich, something like that," Corna said, all hint of humor gone from her face now.

"Which one?" Baine grunted, focused on only one thing now. He'd worry about how people had come to know about him later. "There's two of them; brothers named Ward and Tasker."

"Uh, I think now that you mention it, he said his name was Ward."

"Do the outlaws know about me?"

The woman blew out her cheeks, letting the air escape in a whoosh a moment later. Her fetid breath almost made Baine gag. "How should I know that? But if I were you, I'd assume they do. Everybody else in town knows."

"Speaking of that," Baine said. "Where is everyone? I haven't seen many people around for a town of this size."

The barmaid shrugged. "Lord Kain called up the levy three days ago. Word is a Southern force might be on the march near here. He wants to discourage them from sticking around. Not too many able-bodied men left in Sheafalls right now."

Baine nodded, understanding now. The civil war had taken a backstage to his vow in recent weeks, and he rarely thought about it anymore. He motioned to the door that led to the kitchen. "All right. I think it's time you got out of here."

"But this is my—"

"I said *out!*" Baine hissed. "I won't say it again." The barmaid hesitated, and Baine added, "The stories about me are all true—so trust me when I say you don't want to get on my bad side."

"Corna!" Ward Grich bellowed again, interrupting them. "Beer!"

"You've been warned," Baine said, pointing a finger at the woman. He picked up a full pitcher of beer sitting on the bar, giving the barmaid one final, fierce look before he turned and headed for the seated man. Baine was gratified to hear the kitchen door open and close behind him a moment later.

"About damn time," the outlaw grumbled at Baine's approach. He offered up his mug in a shaky hand, still hunched over and staring down at the rough tabletop.

Baine filled the mug, then set it on the table before sitting on the bench opposite the outlaw. He unhooked his bow and arrow bag and leaned them against the bench out of the way, waiting patiently as the man took a sip of beer. A wide leather hat hid most of the outlaw's face, revealing only a mass of red-tinged, scruffy beard covering his lower jaw. He was dressed in leather armor much like Baine's, with thick curly hair growing out from the collar.

Tired of waiting, Baine finally nudged the man's foot beneath the table with his boot. "You didn't say thank you."

Ward Grich looked up then, blinking stupidly at Baine. "You're not Corna."

"How incredibly observant of you," Baine said with a condescending smile. "What gave it away? The fact that I don't have tits or that I'm not old and fat?"

The outlaw swayed as he tried to process Baine's words. He finally gave up and glanced at the pitcher of beer instead. He drained his mug and refilled it, managing to spill a fair amount as he fought to keep his hand steady. When he was done pouring, the outlaw threw his hat on the table before taking another long drink. He wiped his mouth with the back of his hand afterward as he regarded Baine with bloodshot eyes. "You still here? Go away, little man. I'm busy."

Baine studied the drunk. The outlaw's head was shaven bald and shaped like an egg, with a high, sloping forehead and protruding blue veins at his temples. Baine shrugged, still smiling. "Unfortunately for you, I can't do that."

"Is that right?" Ward grunted. He took another drink, smacking his lips afterward as he banged the mug down. "And why is that, exactly?"

Baine's grin widened. "Because I'm here to kill you, that's why."

The outlaw chuckled, looking unconcerned as he pointed an unsteady finger at Baine. "You're amusing, little one. I'll grant you that." He cocked an eyebrow. "Are you some fat lord's pet jester, perhaps? Sent here to keep me entertained?" The man laughed again. "Personally, I would have preferred a comely whore or two, just so you know."

Baine shook his head, his expression turning serious. "No, Ward, I'm not a jester or a whore. I'm something much worse."

The outlaw scoffed, waving a hand before taking another sip of beer. "Funny man," he said. "Very funny."

"How's your brother Tasker doing?" Baine asked. "Is he waiting for you back at the mine?"

The outlaw's face instantly hardened at his brother's name, the drunken haze in his eyes clearing. *Good*, Baine thought. *Killing an inebriated man is too easy.*

"Who are you?" Ward demanded, getting angry now. He set his mug down, dropping his right hand beneath the table. That hand was hairy and large, Baine had noted, with sausage-like fingers. He doubted Ward was a knife man because of that fact, guessing he'd laid his sword down on the bench beside him where it wouldn't jab him while he drank.

"I guess you don't like bards," Baine replied. It seemed Ward Grich hadn't heard about him yet, despite what the barmaid had suggested. That was good news. "Else you would know."

"What's that supposed to mean?"

Baine interlocked his fingers and bent them outward until they cracked, feeling relaxed and at ease. "Apparently, they're making up songs about me," he said, pausing before adding, "I imagine there'll be another one soon about our little meeting here. I wonder what they'll call it? *Dead in his Cups at The Hunter's Cup*, maybe?" Ward frowned, his face reddening. "No?" Baine said. "You don't like that one? How about, *Black Death and the Drunken Fool?* That has a nice ring to it."

The outlaw stood, growling as he pounded his left fist on the table. He held a sword in his other hand. "Enough out of you!" the man hissed.

Baine read the intent in Ward Grich's eyes well before the outlaw moved. He ducked below the table, feeling warm displaced air swirling above him as the enraged man's blade missed him by a foot. Ward's momentum turned his body sideways, with his sword thudding against the solid tavern wall, sending a shower of dust and dirt falling from the rafters. Baine popped back up, snatching the knife from his hip and slashing it across the man's wrist holding the sword. The outlaw howled and dropped his weapon, blood splattering across the tabletop. His sword rebounded against the table's edge and fell, hitting the bench with a clunk before landing on the rush-covered floor.

Baine retreated before the outlaw could tip the table on top of him, moving into the open, where he waited crouched and ready. Ward Grich held his left hand clamped over his right wrist, his eyes smoldering pools of hatred as he glared at Baine. He released his wrist and slowly bent, never taking his eyes off Baine as he probed with his left hand beneath the table for his sword. Baine let him, not reacting as the wounded man finally located his weapon and stood, holding the sword awkwardly. Baine smiled when he saw that.

"Now you'll pay," the outlaw hissed as he moved out from the bench. "I'm going to cut your heart out and fry it up for dinner."

"Practiced swordplay with your left hand much, have you?" Baine asked mockingly, knowing the answer. He flicked his knife from his right hand to his left, then back again in a blur of motion. "Because I'm proficient with either one." Baine tossed the knife in the air and caught it easily, then winked at his adversary. "Not bad for a jester, eh?"

"You're an arrogant little bastard, aren't you?" Ward growled.

Baine shrugged. "I like to think of it as supreme confidence in my abilities. Something which you will soon come to appreciate."

"Bah," Ward snorted. He rushed at Baine then, lashing out with the sword.

Baine had been expecting just that, and he rolled forward in a ball, coming up on his knees beneath the enraged outlaw. He stabbed upward into the man's groin, staring into the outlaw's face as he froze in shock, his eyes bulging and the sword dropping once again from numb fingers. Baine pushed the blade deeper, twisting it as cold steel ripped through vital organs. Ward's mouth finally opened, and he screamed. The cry was choked off moments later when blood and the contents of his stomach poured out, drenching Baine in beer and half-digested, foul-smelling food.

"That's for my wife, you piece of scum," Baine grunted, ignoring the bile and blood covering him as he held the outlaw's eyes. "I'll be sure to say hello to your brother when I see him."

Baine watched the light go out of the dying man's eyes, sliding to the side just as the outlaw's legs wobbled and he fell. Baine stood, pausing to take several deep breaths before stooping and carefully cleaning his blade on the dead man's clothing. He heard a sound behind him moments later and whirled, the knife already posed to strike before he realized it was the barmaid. She stood frozen near the bar, her eyes round with shock and a porcelain water basin in her hands.

"I...I watched the entire thing from the kitchen door," the woman stammered, her deep voice shaking. "I thought you might need this."

Baine relaxed, sheathing his knife. "Thank you," he replied. The barmaid warily came closer, setting the basin on a table and dropping a cloth beside it before she backed hastily away. Baine used the cloth gratefully, dipping it in the ice-cold water repeatedly as he cleaned himself off as best he could.

"I've never seen anything like that in my life," the woman whispered in awe as he worked. "The way you moved. The way you—" She paused there, shaking her head in wonder. "The songs are true. Everything they're saying about you is true."

Baine took a deep breath and chuckled. "Don't believe everything you hear, my dear." He winked as he tossed the soiled cloth on the table. "There were only ninety-nine House Agents, not a hundred."

Chapter 23: Pax

Baine had learned from the barmaid that Havelock was located in the hills to the northwest, almost three miles from the town of Sheafalls. He'd decided to wait until dusk fell before risking approaching the mine. Corna had never been to Havelock, so she was only aware of the mine's general location from conversations overheard in the tavern. That lack of knowledge left Baine in a bind about what to expect when he got there, although he was fairly certain the outlaws would have a sentry or two posted somewhere, watching out for bears if nothing else. He would just have to improvise when the time came.

Baine had initially planned on getting himself a hot meal and some ale at The Hunter's Cup to help pass the time after he'd helped Corna clean up the mess he'd made. But unfortunately, as things turned out, neither food nor drink were forthcoming. Instead, Baine had spent the bulk of the afternoon camped outside the town in a large grove of pine and ash trees near the base of the hills, positioned so he could watch the road. If someone from Sheafalls was intent on warning the outlaws about him, he needed to know it well beforehand.

Baine peered through the sun-dappled leaves of the trees toward the fiery orange ball in the west, which was finally sinking below the horizon—though not fast enough for his liking. He thought about the reason *why* he was hiding in the grove, still chuckling about it despite his uncomfortable circumstances. It turned out the one-armed man he'd first noticed chopping wood earlier was actually the town's priest, having set aside his black robes while he worked. The Son was a fiery old man named Randers Bilk, and he'd been furious over what had happened at the tavern. The priest had been adamant that Baine leave the vicinity of Sheafalls immediately or face the consequences. What those consequences might have been were never fully stated, though Baine could certainly hazard a guess. He could still hear the old man's indignant voice in his head hours later.

"No violence!" the priest had admonished, his words hard as granite as he waggled a long, crooked finger under Baine's nose. "We are civilized people here in Sheafalls, not animals groveling in the muck! Your soul is forever tarnished now in the eyes of The Father, young man. Murder, regardless of cause, can never be tolerated in His eyes." The Son waved his only hand wildly over his head as if scaring away rabbits raiding a garden. "You must leave this place immediately before the wickedness that I see burning like a caldron inside you infects my flock!"

Baine had tried to reason with the Son after that, explaining about his murdered wife and newborn babe and the vow that he'd sworn to them. But the old bastard would have none of it. Randers Bilk had begun to preach to him then about every evil known to man—though very little of what he'd said had anything to do with Baine as far as he could tell. The priest's tirade had become increasingly unhinged as he'd warmed up, filled with thunderous words about why morality, duty, and honor were in scarce supply these days, replaced increasingly by unhealthy vices, bloodlust, and avarice. Baine had been so afraid the poor man's heart would give out before his sermon did that he'd eventually agreed to leave, if for no other reason than to get away from the mad old bastard.

A small crowd of women, old men, and children had gathered around the tavern's stoop to listen to the Son preach, nodding their heads dumbly along with his words as though they'd heard them many times—which undoubtedly they had. Other than Corna, who'd remained stone-faced throughout the entire diatribe, the crowd had cheered mightily when Baine finally rode out of town with the indignant priest's words still ringing in his ears.

Now Baine sat with his back propped up against a sturdy black ash, staring at the road through the undergrowth as the smells of wild mint, rotting wood, and pine sap filled his nostrils. A jumble of stones peeking out from a small hillock of moss-encrusted earth at the grove's edge partially blocked his view, but he could still see enough of the road to ensure that no one could slip past him. The gelding was tied further back in the trees, alternating between happily nibbling on grasses and leaves and snapping at annoying flies or other insects.

Baine had seen no one on the road the entire time he'd been there, yet even so, he was taking nothing for granted. Ward Grich had shown no indication that he'd heard about any of the *Black Death* silliness, although, to be fair, the man had been quite drunk. But just because he hadn't seemed to know, that didn't mean the rest of the outlaws weren't aware by now that they were being hunted. By Baine's calculations, he might have as many as five men waiting at the mine—six if you included the girl, Vierna Alel. An intimidating sum to most, perhaps, but Baine felt little anxiety over it. That would change, however, if Jark Cordly and his lieutenants had returned, effectively doubling the number aligned against him. It was not a very happy thought. Were the outlaws lying in wait for him even as he sat there? Baine knew it was certainly a possibility, well aware that up until now, he'd been operating in relative obscurity. But no matter how he tried to put a positive spin on things, it appeared that the cat-and-mouse game he'd been playing with the outlaws had just gotten a lot more dangerous.

Baine waited another hour until the last rays of the sun had dipped fully below the horizon, leaving the hills and lowlands cast in deep gloom as banks of thick clouds rolled in. He stood in satisfaction, stretching while thinking he could smell a hint of rain on the wind.

"Let the heavens erupt in a deluge for me, Mother," he whispered, glancing up at the sky.

Baine knew driving rain made sentries cold and miserable, inevitably making them irritable and less attentive, sometimes even retreating into shelter. It was better than nothing. He unstrung his bow just in case the rains came, then retrieved the gelding, first putting on a black cloak given to him by Titim before he mounted. He followed the road into the hills, quickly finding an overgrown offshoot of it that headed northwest—presumably to the mine. He could see little ahead of him as they traveled other than vague shapes of rocks and trees, trusting in his mount's instincts to keep them on the right path.

Thunder rumbled and rolled to the east, shaking the ground, followed by a brilliant flash of lightning to the north that lit up the skyline in harsh relief. Baine felt the first drops of rain strike his head moments later. "Here we go," he whispered, lifting the hood of his cloak as the downpour gained strength.

The gelding plodded onward, heedless of the rain, as it moved sure-footed upward along the path. The hills had closed in on both sides of them as they progressed, and Baine could only hope that the outlaws hadn't posted a man this far out from the mine since he had little choice but to stay on the road. Lightning continued to flash all around the travelers as thunder boomed and rumbled, echoing off the solid rocks and shaking the ground. Baine rode with his head down against the wind and his left hand on the reins. He clutched the collar of his cloak around his neck with the other hand in a futile attempt to keep the water out, wondering why he even bothered.

Horse and rider continued on in that fashion for an interminable amount of time, seemingly alone in a vast, inhospitable landscape lit up every few minutes by lightning cutting through swathes of roiling black clouds overhead. The brief flashes reflecting off the base of the clouds revealed nothing but inhospitable crags of wind-worn rock, dark outlines of tall pines, tufts of hardy grass growing in clumps, and walls of prickly bushes. It was as miserable a night as there could possibly be, and yet Baine had to contain himself from breaking out into happy song. The gods were watching over him. There could be no other explanation for the weather. Now all he needed was his luck to hold out a little longer by keeping the rain coming and the way ahead free of the enemy.

Baine had no sooner had that thought when a sharp whistle sounded in front of him, piercing through the rain. He halted the gelding, squinting, but could see nothing.

"Ward? Is that you?" a voice shouted a moment later. Baine thought it had come from somewhere off to his left, but with the rain and the howling wind, he wasn't certain.

Lightning flashed a moment later, revealing a brief glimpse of a man standing twenty yards away to Baine's left in the entrance to a cavern before darkness returned. Baine hadn't failed to notice the bow in the man's hands, aimed squarely at his chest.

Baine cupped his hands around his mouth. "Who's that?" he shouted, deepening his voice to mimic the dead outlaw.

"It's Pax. What took you so long?"

"Pax, you twitchy little bastard," Baine called back, adding a chuckle. He motioned with a hand even as he urged the gelding forward in a walk. "Put down that damn bow before you end up hurting someone."

Baine heard the man laugh. "Sure, all right. Did you get some cunny, Ward? Is that why you're so late?"

Baine was fifteen yards away from where the voice was coming from. He could see little of the outlaw in the darkness, praying for another flash of lightning as he slipped his right hand beneath his cloak and grasped the hilt of his knife. He carefully unsheathed the weapon, holding it by his right thigh.

"Ward?"

"What?" Baine grunted, moving closer. *Ten yards away. Come on, dammit! Where's that lightning?*

"I asked if you got some cunny in town?"

Five yards. Baine forced a laugh. "Yeah, but I'm kind of embarrassed about it."

"Not three-toed Aedith again!"

Two yards. Come on! "No," Baine said. "Worse than her."

Baine saw movement to his left, a shadow among shadows in what he guessed was the cavern's mouth. Had that been Pax or just a trick of the eyes? "What could be worse than Aedith?" the outlaw called out. "The woman has more boils on her than hot water."

Pax laughed hysterically at that, though Baine didn't get the joke. "I humped Corna," he said, sounding dejected.

"Gods, no!" Pax gasped. *One yard away now.* "That doughy, fat-assed barmaid? Are you serious?"

Baine halted the horse, having drawn even with the speaker now. He still couldn't see the outlaw, knowing he'd have no choice but to use the knife and hope. "Woman knows what she's doing," Baine said. "Nearly broke my back when she wrapped her legs around me."

Pax snickered, a high-pitched, peeling sound. "You gotta be hard up to—"

Lightning flashed without warning then, and Baine caught a quick glimpse of a small man with long, greasy brown hair dressed in brown leather armor over a grey tunic. Then the light fizzled out. It was enough. Baine moved, throwing the knife toward where he'd seen the outlaw. He heard a grunt of pain a moment later just as something tugged at the hood of his cloak, snatching it off his head. The little bastard had realized he wasn't Ward Grich and had somehow gotten an arrow off.

Baine twisted out of the saddle to the ground, landing in a crouch. Some instinct made him roll to the side just as another arrow cracked into the road where he'd been. Pax was clearly not incapacitated—yet. Baine drew another knife as he came to his feet and threw it overhand toward the cave, muttering to himself when he heard the blade clatter against solid granite. He'd missed. He dodged to the right of the opening, putting his back to the rock as he pulled another knife. Was there a way out for the outlaw, or was he trapped? There was no way to know for certain. A moment later, Baine heard the unmistakable smack of an arrow hitting flesh, followed by a shriek from the gelding and then the panicked clatter of hooves moving quickly back down the trail.

Baine cursed under his breath as his horse fled with his bowstave and arrow bag still attached to the saddle, knowing there was little he could do about it now. Hopefully, the gelding wasn't injured badly and wouldn't go far. He cocked his head, listening for any sounds that his adversary might be on the move. He thought he could hear the occasional soft grunt of pain echoing out from the cave, though there was always the chance that it was just the wind trying to fool him.

"I bet that hurts," Baine finally shouted in a taunting voice, trying to goad the man into making a move. "You're probably going to bleed out soon, you know. Want some help?"

Nothing.

"Did that knife of mine go in deep?" Baine asked. "Sever an artery, maybe?"

"Bastard!" Pax spat a moment later over the sound of the rain. Baine smiled. He was still there. "Who are you?" the outlaw demanded.

Baine chuckled. "Some people call me *Black Death*." He heard his adversary grumble, though he couldn't make out the words. "Why don't you throw down that bow and come out here so we can talk like men?" Baine added.

"Why don't you come in here and lick my sack, bastard?"

"I'd rather lie with a hundred Corna's, I think," Baine shot back. "But thanks for the offer."

"She's probably the only one desperate enough to bed you."

Baine thought he could hear the man moving around, but he wasn't certain. Had his voice been further away? He took several steps closer to the cave's mouth. "I've got all night," he called. "Do you? How's that wound doing? Bleeding a lot?"

"Pretty sure I hit your horse," Pax responded. "Got it in the shoulder—maybe nicked its heart."

"Naw, you just spooked him, is all," Baine said dismissively. "He'll be back."

The outlaw snorted. "Sure it will."

"Where's your horse, Pax?" Baine asked, worried the man's refuge might be larger than he thought. If the outlaw's mount was close and there was another way out of that cave, Baine knew sooner or later the man would try to make a run for it—assuming he could run at all. *Keep him talking. The longer he talks, the more blood he loses.*

"Like I'm going to tell you," Pax laughed. "You'll die out here in these hills, bastard."

"How many men are at the mine?" Baine asked as lightning flashed, revealing the cavern mouth in stark relief. There was no sign of Pax.

"Fifty," the outlaw responded as darkness returned. "They're going to enjoy taking turns on your ass."

"My, my, Pax," Baine said mockingly. "You certainly do have an unhealthy fixation with men. I'm no Son or Daughter, of course, but would you care to confess your sins before I send you to Judgement Day?"

"Go bugger yourself."

Baine laughed, taking another step sideways. His right boot struck something solid and he hesitated, stooping down. It was a fist-sized rock. Baine picked it up, then inched closer to the lip of the entrance. "You still there, Pax?" Nothing but silence greeted him. Baine hefted the rock in his left hand. "Cat got your tongue? Maybe you're lying there too weak to talk, eh? I can help you." Still nothing.

Knowing he had to do something, Baine leaned out and tossed the rock into the cave. He heard it bounce and skip against the stone floor a heartbeat later, but there was no reaction from the outlaw. *Was the man playing possum, dead, or had he slipped away?* Lightning flashed again, and Baine moved, rolling forward in a tight ball to come up on his feet in the cavern entrance, his knife poised to throw. The light faded out quickly again, but not before Baine had time to see a long trail of blood on the ground heading east deeper into the cave. The outlaw was gone.

Baine stepped cautiously inside the cave, glad to be out of the rain. A bank of sheet lightning flashed behind him over and over again, lighting up the interior and the western sky behind him in a frenzied barrage. Baine paused. The cave roof was low and rounded, with water dripping from a multitude of cracks caused by stubborn tree roots growing from above that had broken through the rock. Crusts of orange lichen lined the walls, and Baine could smell animal droppings and the sharp odor of stagnant water. He also saw his two knives lying on the ground—one near the cave entrance covered in blood and the other further in.

The cave suddenly returned to darkness, and Baine stooped, locating the first knife. He wiped it clean on his trousers, sheathed it, then fumbled around until he found the second one. He returned that one to his boot and then pressed onward, carefully placing one foot in front of the other while probing in front of him with his left hand. He walked that way for several minutes, certain he was heading upward, before a faint glow ahead caught his eye. He fixated on it, increasing his pace until he came to a large chamber, his mind registering three things at once; a buckskin mare tied to a metal spike jutting from a wall, a flickering torch lying on the granite floor, and a sprawled-out Pax Colo lying on his stomach ten feet from the mare.

Baine approached the prostrate man warily, circling to see his face. The mare shied away as he neared, rolling her eyes and stamping a hoof. Thunder rumbled outside, the sounds muted by the thick granite. Pax lay with his eyes closed, a pool of blood spreading beneath him. A half-full arrow bag was clipped to the man's hip, with a bow very similar to Baine's lying close by. He couldn't tell if the outlaw was still breathing, and tensing, he kicked the man's shoulder. Nothing. Baine kicked again, but there was still no reaction. More confident now, he used the toe of his boot to roll the outlaw over.

Pax's eyes popped open the moment he lay on his back. "Got you!" he cried in triumph, sweeping his right hand up.

Baine had only a moment to see the knife coming for his face, the steel blade reflecting orange in the firelight. He dodged aside, though not fast enough, feeling a burning pain sizzling along his cheek. Pax grunted, fighting to get to his feet as Baine retreated. The outlaw finally stood, holding his left side and breathing heavily.

Baine touched his cheek, his fingers coming away stained with blood. "That was pretty good," he said grudgingly.

Pax grimaced, his head moving back and forth in an unnatural twitch. "Thought I had you there, you bastard."

"Almost," Baine conceded. He gestured to the outlaw's side. "That doesn't look so good."

Pax glanced down at himself, then shrugged. "It was a fine throw. The blade went right through my armor." He snorted, twitching again. "Guess they didn't boil the leather long enough."

"It happens," Baine said. Haverty made all his armor now, claiming to have perfected the technique. The apothecary was the smartest man Baine had ever met, so he had no reason to doubt him.

"Now what?" Pax asked. He held his knife in his right hand but was weaving on his feet, looking ready to fall at any moment. Baine wasn't sure if it was real or feigned. "We going to talk all night or get on with this?" the outlaw added.

"You know you don't stand a chance of making it out of here alive," Baine said.

Pax laughed. "Of course not. I know I'm a dead man. Your blade hit something vital. But just because I'm almost done doesn't mean I can't take you with me."

"Care to answer some questions before we start?"

The outlaw's eyes narrowed. "Why should I?"

"Because Judgement Day is only minutes away," Baine answered. "Maybe unburdening your soul will help you avoid the flames."

Pax shook his head and chuckled. "Not likely. I'm going to the pits for a very long time, and nothing I say now is going to change that." The outlaw staggered then and almost fell, but Baine didn't move. There was no hurry now. Pax recovered, though barely, and he hawked before spitting a glob of blood at his feet. He wiped his mouth afterward, studying Baine with grudging respect. "So, you're the one they're calling *Black Death*, eh?"

"Not by choice," Baine said. "That's the bards' doing, not mine."

"Useless turds," the outlaw grunted. "A bunch of pretty boys that never did a day's worth of work in their lives."

"Yet, you've clearly heard the songs," Baine pointed out.

"No," Pax said. "Jark told us about you."

Baine frowned. "He's back?"

"Arrived around midday," the outlaw confirmed. He shook his head, his features turning grim as he realized what he'd said. "That's all you'll get from me, you bastard. So no more talking. Do your worst."

"Did Jark's lieutenants come with him?"

Pax paused, then chuckled smugly. "What do you think?" He twitched, then sneered. "Face it, boy, there's too many for you to handle. You'll never get them all. Even if you beat me, you're still a walking, talking dead man. It's just a matter of time before the others get you."

"Maybe," Baine replied. "But either way, you'll be long dead, now won't you?" He sighed then, willing to offer the man one last chance at some form of redemption in exchange for information. "I'm no Son, but confession might help. Are you certain you don't want to try?"

"I've said too much already," Pax muttered, swaying on his feet. He lifted the knife, gesturing with his other hand. "So come on. Let's get this over with, you bastard. I'm tired of looking at you."

"If that's what you really want," Baine said, tensing.

The outlaw might have been a formidable fighter without his wound, Baine guessed. But the tremendous amount of blood he'd lost had taken its toll. The fight—if you could call it that—lasted less than five seconds.

Baine looked down at the twisted corpse afterward. "Eleven left, Flora my love," he whispered. "Eleven left."

Chapter 24: Tasker Grich

    Baine found the gelding half an hour later lying dead in the middle of the road two hundred yards from the cave. Pax had boasted that he'd hit the animal's heart, but he'd been mistaken, Baine quickly learned after examining the horse. Instead, he found the outlaw's arrow embedded deeply in the gelding's neck, guessing it had nicked the jugular vein and the poor beast had bled to death. Baine could, unfortunately, do little for the horse now, so he worked to collect his saddle bags, bowstave, and arrow bag, cursing under his breath as he fought to extricate them from beneath the dead animal.
    Finally, when he was finished, Baine paused, taking a moment to kneel in the muck-covered road as thunder rumbled and the rain continued to fall steadily. He stroked the horse's saturated mane sadly. "I am truly sorry, my friend. You were a brave and noble steed and did not deserve this fate."
    Baine rose to his feet after a moment, heading back toward Pax's mare, who stood waiting patiently for him, her head lowered against the rain. He quickly stowed away his gear on the buckskin, then mounted, returning to the cave, where he led the horse inside by the reins. He returned to the chamber where Pax's body still lay; the enclosure lit up now by a fresh torch that Baine had jammed into a crevice in one wall. He'd initially believed Pax had entered the cave from the road, but after a quick examination of the chamber, he'd located a narrow tunnel with a high ceiling that showed fresh scuff marks made by hooves. Would that tunnel lead him to the mine? Only time would tell.
    Baine now had two bows and enough arrows to kill eleven men four times over. Hopefully, it would be enough. He took up the torch and headed out on foot, choosing to lead the mare despite the tunnel's towering height. The horse showed no hesitancy about

following him inside, which Baine considered to be a good sign. He could barely hear the storm raging outside after fifty paces, surprised when the tunnel began to widen not long after that and head downward. He hadn't been expecting that. Baine began to wonder as he progressed ever deeper if he was making a mistake, thinking in hindsight that he should have stayed on the road as he'd originally planned. He knew there was a good possibility that the tunnel would eventually lead him to the mine, but there was also an equal chance it might come out somewhere deep in the hills far from Havelock. Then what would he do in the dark and rain?

Baine wished Pax had been more forthcoming about what he knew, but he'd seen the glint in the dying man's eyes, knowing instinctively that nothing he tried—be it torture or pleading—would have made the outlaw talk. Which meant, at least for now, that Baine remained in the dark about what lay ahead, although something told him that one way or another, the end of his quest for vengeance would culminate this night. He decided his best course of action was to continue on and play this out, putting his trust in The Mother to see him through—that and his skill with a bow and knife.

The tunnel took a sharp turn to the north before it finally began to level out, then started to ascend again, which Baine hoped was a good sign. At least he was traveling in the right direction now. The tunnel floor was mostly hard granite and swept clean, with only an occasional chewed bone or pile of long-dried animal scat lying about. Baine found the slight grade going up easily manageable, with neither he nor the mare breathing hard after ten minutes of climbing. He paused at one point, cocking his head sideways as he tried to identify a faint rustling sound coming from ahead. It took him a moment to realize what he was hearing was the wind whistling through tree branches. He was close—but close to what?

The sounds of the wind and rain grew stronger as he climbed until, eventually, Baine led the mare into another chamber, this one at least ten times the size of the previous and lit by lanterns hanging off hooks embedded in the walls. A large, cavernous opening rose fifty feet opposite him, with the width protected by stout wooden walls and double gates, which were open, revealing a glimpse of a rainswept plateau outside. A second, smaller tunnel led off to Baine's left, with a corral made from thin pine logs running along the wall to his right with saddles balanced on the top railings. Five horses congregated near the gate of the enclosure, eagerly chewing on hay that a man with his back to Baine was tossing into the corral with a wooden pitchfork. None of the horses were *Pretty Girl*, though, the white mare that Jark had taken from him. There was no one else around.

Baine hastily drew his hood up, pulling the cowl down low over his eyes as the man paused in his labor, glancing his way. He was tall, with heavy shoulders and a wiry black beard twisted into braids on either side of his chin. The man wore a thick chainmail coat, knee-high black leather boots, and a longsword on his left hip. A black cloak hung over the railing near him, dripping water. Baine thought there was something vaguely familiar about his features.

"Pax?" the man grunted in surprise. "What are you doing back here? Jark told you to watch the road."

Baine shrugged and said nothing while the mare snorted eagerly, clearly smelling the fresh hay. He guided her toward the corral, keeping his head down. "Ward took my place," he muttered.

"Ward?" The man's voice sounded suspicious now. He lowered the pitchfork and leaned on it, shaking his head. "Now, why would my brother go and do that? He's already long overdue."

"Don't know," Baine grunted as he drew closer. He was happy for the sounds of the rain and wind coming through the open gates, which helped to disguise his voice. Baine indicated the smaller corral gate, motioning for the man—who Baine now knew to be Tasker Grich—to open it. He held his breath. Would the outlaw comply, or would he look closer and see through Baine's thin disguise?

Tasker hesitated for a moment, then he shook his head again as he reached for the looped rope that secured the crude gate. "Jark's not going to be happy about this, Pax," the outlaw said, turning his back as he swung the gate open. "You know he doesn't react well when his orders are disobeyed."

Baine released the mare's reins and whipped out a knife, darting behind the bigger man. He pressed the point of the blade against the outlaw's neck just below the jawline, pressing until a single drop of blood squeezed out. "Make one sound," he hissed in Tasker's ear. "And you're a dead man."

"But you're—"

"That's a sound," Baine grunted. The outlaw's eyes widened in fear, then closed again in anticipation of the pain to follow. Baine stayed his hand, not yet ready to kill. He shifted to the side to see the man's face better. Tasker looked older than his brother and wasn't quite as big, but he had the same mouth and nose. "Drop the pitchfork," Baine commanded. The outlaw opened his eyes, hesitating, and Baine pressed harder. "Do it now." Tasker Grich glared at Baine, but he did as he was told. "Good," Baine said approvingly. "You just earned another minute of life." He carefully eased the outlaw's sword out of its scabbard and tossed it to the ground, then guided the man out of the way as he used his foot to nudge the gate closed. He didn't need any of the horses inside causing a distraction. "Is this place, Havelock?" he demanded, lowering his hood.

"You're the one they call *Black Death*," the outlaw said, staring at Baine in wonder. "I can't believe you came. I thought Jark was joking about you."

Baine nodded grimly. "Trust me. I'm no joke. Now answer my question. Is this Havelock?"

"Yes, sort of."

Baine frowned. "What does that mean?"

"This is just one small part of it," Tasker said.

He tried to shift his eyes to the cavern's entrance, but Baine wouldn't let him. "Keep going," he prompted.

"The mine branches out in all directions," the outlaw explained. "With at least ten shafts in the hills around us and miles and miles of tunnels."

Baine nodded. "And your friends? Where are they hiding?" The outlaw hesitated, and Baine pressed harder with the knife. "You're trying my patience. Answer!"

"A warehouse not far from here," Tasker said through clenched teeth. "That's where they're staying."

"All of them? Jark too?"

"Yes."

Baine saw something in the man's eyes, his gut telling him that he'd just been fed a lie. He twisted his wrist sideways, clearing the blade from the man's throat, then slashed upward, slicing the outlaw's ear off. Tasker Grich howled, automatically reaching for the wound as blood sprayed. Baine grabbed the man by the throat, turning him and pushing him against the closed fence. He put the blade back under the outlaw's jaw, pushing upward, his eyes inches away from the other man's.

"Lie to me again, you bastard, and I'll cut the other one off, then start on something else. Are all your friends in that warehouse?"

"No," the outlaw gasped as blood continued to flow freely from the stump of his ear.

"Where are the others?"

"A manor house to the north," Tasker answered. "It belonged to the mine overseer once. Jark took it over."

"Who's in the warehouse?" Baine demanded. "Any of Jark's lieutenants?" The outlaw licked his lips, clearly thinking about lying again. Baine growled low in his chest in warning. "Don't."

"They're all staying with Jark," Tasker finally admitted.

Baine grinned. "So, is Hoop at the warehouse?" The outlaw blinked in surprise, then nodded. "What about that bitch, Vierna?" Baine asked. "Where is she?"

"With Jark, I imagine," Tasker answered in resignation.

Baine nodded, pleased. That left only two men unaccounted for—the only two who he didn't have names for yet. "Who else is at the warehouse?"

"Ham and Finn Lestway."

"Brothers like you and Ward?" Baine asked.

The man shook his head. "No, father and son."

"Is that it? Nobody else?"

"Yes."

"Good," Baine grunted. He thought about Alen Hawe and the last painful minutes the bastard had spent in this world. He'd dearly love to deliver a similar fate to each of the remaining outlaws, but knew that, realistically, it was no longer feasible. Speed and stealth were what mattered now. Besides, Baine had all the information he needed—which meant Tasker Grich was no longer useful. He smiled at the outlaw coldly. "You might find this amusing," he said in a soft voice. "Your brother cried like a girl when I sliced him open. Shit himself, too." Tasker's eyes widened in shock. "Make sure you say hello to the bastard when you see him in The Father's pits!"

Tasker Grich opened his mouth to say something, but Baine didn't give him time. He rammed the knife upward, pushing through soft, vulnerable flesh and cartilage until the tip punctured the man's brain. The outlaw's eyes fluttered, and he began to sag as Baine ripped his knife free and stepped back, letting the corpse drop to the cavern floor. He spit on the dead man, then glanced behind him at Pax's mare, who had her head pushed through the railings, chewing on the hay inside. She looked quite content. He hurried to the buckskin's side and retrieved both bows and his now overstuffed arrow bag, then opened the gate and ushered the mare inside the corral where she'd be safe. Next, Baine grabbed the dead man's cloak, using it to wrap the bows as best he could, hoping the garment would protect them from the rain. He took one of the lanterns off its hook near the entrance, then headed outside.

The rain was still coming down heavily, Baine noted, but at least the thunder and lightning had moved on. He carried the two bows under his right arm, lifting the lantern high with his left to look around. The plateau wasn't large—perhaps thirty feet across—with an army of tall pines rising on three sides. The wind and rain were working in tandem, trying to extinguish the lantern's flame, but so far, the oil-fed wick was resisting. The lantern was made of metal and five-sided, with the interior protected by thin panes of animal horn that had been hammered flat. Baine wasn't certain how long those panes could hold out against this kind of weather, knowing he had to move. But where? He took several paces forward, sweeping the lantern back and forth in front of him until, finally, he saw a well-worn path to his right, cutting through the trees to the north.

Baine set out along the trail at a fast walk, breathing a sigh of relief once he'd entered the trees, which dramatically cut off the wind. The rain remained, though, slicing through the branches as he forged onward. The path headed downward almost immediately, the ground littered with pebbles, shards of chipped slate, and pine needles. He smelled smoke moments later, reaching a blackened, smoldering pine tree along the edge of the trail. Baine guessed it had been struck by lightning. He took a wide berth around the tree and moved on, the overpowering smell of charred wood filling his nostrils. The trees began to thin out rapidly after only twenty paces, leading to a wide clearing. Baine paused at the tree line, listening, but all he heard was the shrieking of the wind and the patter of the rain hitting the ground.

Baine thought he could see the outlines of a large building ahead of him in the gloom, with perhaps another, smaller one standing off to the left of it. He was about to extinguish the flame of the lantern and toss it aside, then reconsidered, thinking it still might prove useful at some point. Besides, he reasoned, anyone looking outside would probably just assume he was Tasker Grich returning from feeding the horses. He hurried forward, noticing a faint glow coming from what he assumed was a window in the bigger building.

Baine made it the short distance to the building without an outcry. The window the light was coming from was shuttered against the rain and most likely barred, he guessed, with one of the slats at the top gone, allowing some light to escape. Unfortunately, the missing slat was too high for him to peer through, and the wall was covered with rain-soaked cedar shakes, impossible to climb. Baine moved on, finding a wide set of double doors near the center of the building where horse-drawn wagons could enter the warehouse easily. He tried to open them only to find the entrance barred from the inside. He located a second, much smaller door near the corner of the building and carefully tried the latch, but it was also locked. Baine found that fact surprising, since Tasker Grich was undoubtedly expected to return at some point. It appeared the outlaws were being extra careful, despite what Tasker had said about *Black Death* being nothing but a joke.

Baine circled the warehouse, finding another door at the back, but it was also locked. He thought about how he'd entered Gembart Tadley's bathhouse through an open window but didn't see any here, although even if there had been, the smooth sheathing of the walls would make any attempt at climbing virtually impossible. He needed to find another way.

Baine returned to the front of the building, staring at the double doors again as an idea began to form in his mind. He grinned, nodding to himself, then headed for the outbuilding seventy feet away, which turned out to be a combination blacksmith shop and tool shed. The floor and walls of the building were made from stout boards, with a thick thatch roof that only leaked in three or four places, leaving most of the rafters and framework inside dry. It was perfect. Baine selected the driest area, setting his weapons down. He carefully removed a pane from the lantern, then climbed the timber framework to the ceiling with the handle of the still-burning lantern clamped awkwardly between his teeth. He reached the top of the wall, then clinging onto a crossbeam with one hand, he maneuvered the lantern's open side between two of the wooden rafters supporting the thatch, which he saw was a mixture of straw and rushes rife with cobwebs. The dry underside of the thatch caught fire almost immediately and quickly began to spread.

Satisfied, Baine climbed down and retrieved his bows as the building's interior began to fill with smoke. He hefted the lantern in his hand, then threw it hard against the boarded wall opposite him. Oil splattered on the planks, followed a moment later by a whoosh before orange and blue flames ignited. Baine grinned and headed outside, selecting a spot fifteen yards back from the warehouse's side door. He grabbed six arrows, pushed their points into the ground, and then removed his bow from the cloak.

Once the outbuilding was burning briskly, Baine ran to the warehouse and banged frantically on the door. "Fire! Ham! Finn! Hoop! Get out here and help me. The toolshed is on fire!"

Satisfied that the outlaws couldn't fail to have heard him, Baine darted back to his line of arrows and snatched up a shaft, aiming his bow at the door and praying the bastards would fall for his ruse. They did. The side door was wrenched open moments later, with a shadowy body filling the entrance. The man was looking to his right at the burning outbuilding, unaware of him. Baine bided his time, waiting as the outlaw ran outside, followed by a second figure, then a third scrambling out the doorway.

"Got you!" Baine whispered.

All three men started running toward the outbuilding, shouting in alarm and confusion. Baine aimed at the last man's lower body and let fly, already nocking another arrow as the first struck the outlaw in the back of his right knee. That man howled and fell, with the two outlaws in front of him turning to look back in surprise. Baine shot again, this time taking the second man in line in the throat. The outlaw jerked from the impact and fell without a sound as Baine snatched up a third arrow. He drew, taking his time to aim while the surviving man ran directly at him, screaming and waving a sword over his head. Baine let him come, enjoying himself now. He waited until the outlaw was twenty feet away, then released, sending the arrow screeching into the man's midsection. The outlaw grunted and staggered, dropping to one knee in a puddle before, with a supreme effort of will, he forced himself to his feet, cursing Baine all the while.

Baine causally pulled another arrow from the ground, taking a moment to wipe the iron tip clean of water and muck before nocking it.

"You bastard!" the outlaw hissed, his body bent over almost double as he advanced slowly, step by treacherous step, toward Baine. The wounded man clutched at the arrow shaft protruding from his stomach with his left hand, holding his sword weakly in his right with the point dragging against the rain-soaked ground. The wind howled around the two men, helping to fuel the fire as sheeting rain cascaded down on them both. "You filthy, sheep-humping, no-good son of a bitch!"

"That's not very nice," Baine said reproachfully. He drew the arrow back and loosed, sending the shaft spinning through the rain before it slapped into the man's chest, silencing him. Baine lowered his bow as the outlaw fell with a clatter, and he nodded. "There. That's much better."

He carefully wrapped up his bow again, then moved to examine the lone survivor, who was futilely trying to drag himself through the puddles of rain toward the warehouse. The wounded man glanced over his shoulder at Baine as he approached, sobbing, then redoubled his efforts, though he was still moving at a snail's pace. Baine drew a knife as he reached the blubbering man, tossing it into the air and catching it on the way down by the handle before he stabbed the back of the man's other knee. The outlaw screamed in agony, and Baine withdrew the knife, then struck again, embedding the blade to the hilt in the man's right buttock.

"Stop!" the man sobbed, pressing his face into the muck. "By the gods, please stop! I beg of you!"

Baine left the knife in the man's ass, moving to crouch by the sobbing outlaw's head. He grabbed him by the hair, jerking his head up to stare down at his mud-splattered features. Baine felt no pity for the injured man whatsoever. "What's your name?"

The outlaw sniffed hopefully as giant tears of pain rolled down his encrusted cheeks. "Hoop, sir. They call me Hoop."

Baine nodded, gesturing to the dead men. "I take it those two were Ham and Finn, then?"

The outlaw sobbed, barely nodding. "Please...please don't kill me."

Baine smiled. "Give me one good reason why not."

Hoop blinked in confusion. "But...ugh, I—"

"Too slow," Baine grunted. He whipped a knife out from his boot and slashed open the man's neck, holding his head back as the outlaw's lifeblood gushed out onto the ground.

Baine finally released the dead man's hair once the blood had stopped flowing, closing his eyes. He took a deep, satisfied breath. *Now there are only seven of the bastards.* He heard a sudden splashing sound behind him—the pounding of running feet—and turned, having only a heartbeat for his mind to register that a young boy was barreling towards him with a shovel in his hands poised to strike—a young boy whose face he knew.

Then pain exploded across Baine's right temple, and everything went dark.

Chapter 25: Ira

Baine was awakened by freezing cold water dashed over his head. He sputtered, gasping and coughing as he blinked up at a man standing over him. The man smirked and tossed an empty bucket aside, then balled his fist and struck Baine in the face, tearing open his left cheek like an over-ripe melon that matched the cut on his right Pax had made earlier with his knife. Baine keeled over sideways from the blow, unable to stop his fall since his hands were bound securely behind his back. He hit the floor, forehead and nose cracking painfully against tightly compacted dirt, where he lay, stunned.

"Get up, you bastard," the man growled. He grabbed Baine by the hair, ignoring his cry of pain as he dragged him back to a sitting position. Baine groaned, vaguely aware that others were standing behind his tormentor, watching, though his eyes were still too unfocused to make out faces. "What's the matter?" the man standing over him asked with a sneer. "Did that hurt?" He leaned over, balling his impressively scarred fist again and thrusting it under Baine's nose. "Trust me, you turd-sucking little rat. You haven't felt anything yet."

The man was short, with broad shoulders and a bull-like neck, dressed in dark trousers and a white tunic with the sleeves rolled up, revealing beefy forearms covered in wiry black hair. His cheeks above his dark beard were pock-marked and sunken in, and he had a bulbous nose jutting out between a pair of piggish brown eyes. Baine's vision slowly began to clear and he looked around, registering that he was sitting on the floor in a large, cavernous room with a high ceiling, guessing it was the warehouse. Two men stood behind his tormentor, both staring at him with expressionless faces. Another man sat on a cot to one side, looking bored as he rolled a set of dice back and forth in his hands. Baine noticed the boy who'd struck him with the shovel standing off to one side of a closed door. He was thin as a rake with curly brown hair and an olive complexion marred by a livid purple and yellow bruise around his right eye.

"I know you," Baine croaked, his voice unsteady. The boy was Ira, the son of Ermos, the blacksmith from Witbridge Manor. With a sinking feeling, Baine now understood who the informant had been.

The outlaw standing over Baine frowned, glancing back at Ira, whose expression quickly turned apprehensive. "What's this now, Boy?" he demanded, gesturing to Baine. "You know this lump of pig shit?"

Ira nodded, chewing on his bottom lip. "Yes, Chett, I know him."

The outlaw straightened, his face turning mean as he turned on the boy, who shrank back against the wall fearfully. "Now, isn't this an interesting coincidence?" Chett took several aggressive steps toward Ira. "Maybe you'd care to—"

"That's enough," one of the other outlaws grunted calmly. This man was taller than Chett, with an athletic build and handsome features. His beard and hair were light brown and cropped close, and he wore a fine green cloak still wet from the storm. He put a hand on Chett's chest. "It's not Boy's fault, so leave him be."

"Not his fault!" Chett exploded. "By The Father's balls, Hep." The outlaw gestured to Baine. "Most of our men are dead because of this bastard, and Boy knew all along about him."

"I didn't know," Ira protested. "How could I have?"

"Boy is right," Hep said. He patted Chett on the shoulder, then stepped past him, pausing to stand over Baine. "I imagine you're from Witbridge Manor, yes? Where Boy used to live?"

Baine just glared up at Heply Boll, not hiding his hatred.

Hep sighed a moment later, then shook his head sadly. "Who did we kill that night to make you so full of bitterness, eh? A wife, mother, sister? Someone else who meant something to you?"

"My wife and son," Baine answered grudgingly. He saw Ira's eyes widen across the room. "You bastards murdered them and a lot of other good people." Baine focused on the boy, holding his gaze. "Even the town's blacksmith was killed trying to protect his family from you murderers." Ira's olive skin turned sickly white at that news, and he looked away, fighting tears with his lower lip trembling.

"What's a few less sheep in this world when weighed against that much gold?" the outlaw on the cot said with a contemptuous snort, not looking up. He was young, under twenty years old, Baine guessed, with a clean-shaven face that only helped to accent the sharp cruelness of his features.

"Have a little compassion, Pit," Hep said. He smiled at Baine, though his eyes showed little warmth. "This man's wife and son are dead because of us. Would you not seek revenge, too, if it had been you?"

"No," Pit grunted, looking unimpressed. "The only wife I ever had was a nagging bitch who never shut up. I got sick of listening to her after a month and left." The outlaw stopped tossing the dice in his hands to glare at Baine, who was shocked at the look of naked brutality shining in the man's eyes. He smiled, and Baine's blood went cold, knowing now what true evil looked like. "I remember your wife, I think. Big lass with an impressive pair of tits." Pit chuckled when Baine couldn't hide his reaction. "I bent her over a table and gave her a good time. Bitch loved every moment."

"I'll kill you!" Baine hissed, his mind exploding with rage. He somehow managed to get his feet under him and rose, barreling toward the man and screaming, only to have Heply Boll backhand him almost casually across the face, sending him tumbling back to the floor.

Pit Nelly chuckled and rose to his feet like a cat, moving to stand over Baine, who lay on his side awkwardly, staring up at him. The outlaw crouched, his unblinking, snake-like eyes holding Baine's. "Thing is, there we were, me and Lady Big Tits, humping like it was our wedding night. When out of nowhere, this babe starts bawling." Pit grinned again, looking around at the others, who were listening intently. "Seems she hid the poor thing in a cupboard and was using her cunny as a distraction." He stood, holding out his hands and gyrating his hips. "Imagine it, lads. There I was, giving Lady Big Tits all she could take, with her begging for more when that awful squalling started, ruining my rhythm. I mean, what was I to do?"

Heply Boll frowned, looking uneasy. "Please tell me you didn't hurt the babe, Pit. Please tell me that."

The younger outlaw shrugged and smiled knowingly. "Believe whatever you want."

"I'm going to make you suffer," Baine whispered, all emotion gone from his voice as he stared up at Pit Nelly. "I'm going to make you scream and beg for mercy before you die. Mark my words."

Pit's smile slowly faded, replaced with cold anger. He clamped his boot on Baine's neck, pinning him to the floor. "Is that right? And just how do you expect to do that?"

Baine said nothing, glaring up at the man.

"Well," Hep said after a moment, letting out a long breath. "The babe's death is most unfortunate, but what's done is done. Besides, we still have things to do tonight." He glanced behind him. "Kant, you and Pit take the horses up to the corral and get them into shelter. This rain doesn't look like it's going to stop anytime soon, so we'll stay here tonight. Make sure you give them water and feed, then rub them down."

Baine ticked off another name in his head—Kant Reece. The outlaw looked like he was in his late forties or early fifties and had a dull glint in his eyes like a halfwit. Part of the man's forehead was bowed in as if from a vicious blow, which might explain the dazed look. Baine wondered where Pater Dore, the last of the lieutenants, was.

"Why us?" Pit demanded belligerently, his full weight still holding Baine down.

"Because Boy, Chett, and I are going to deal with those poor bastards lying outside," Hep said in a long-suffering voice. "The last thing we need is for them to attract coyotes or wolves." He paused, his voice hard. "Unless you'd rather deal with them instead?"

"What about Tasker?" Pit asked sullenly.

Hep's lips twitched in amusement as he glanced at Baine. "Oh, I imagine you'll find his body lying somewhere around here sooner or later, courtesy of our friend here."

Pit muttered something under his breath, but he finally took his boot off Baine's neck and headed for the door, motioning for Kant to follow. "Come on, Featherhead, let's go."

Kant Reece nodded dumbly, saying nothing as he followed the younger man outside.

"My apologies," Hep said once the men were gone. He stooped to grab Baine by the shoulders, righting him again. "Pit is not exactly the friendly sort." The outlaw chuckled. "He does have his, uh, uses, though. I'll give him that." Hep stood back, hands on his hips as he regarded Baine. "So, do you have a name?" Baine said nothing. Not looking surprised, the outlaw glanced at Ira, one eyebrow raised.

"They call him Baine," the boy said.

"Ah," Hep grunted, turning back to Baine. "Good. I always like to know who it is I'm having a conversation with."

"You're having a conversation with the man who intends to kill you," Baine said.

Hep chuckled, scratching at his beard. "While I do admire you're optimism, lad, I have to say your prospects aren't looking so good at the moment."

"I've been in worse places," Baine said with a disinterested shrug. "And I'm still here." He shifted his gaze to the boy. "Your family thinks you're dead, Ira. How could you do that to them?

What will they think of you when they finally learn the truth about what you did?"

Ira swallowed and looked down, unable to meet Baine's eyes.

"Boy has a new family now," Hep said. He crossed the room to clap the youth on the shoulders. Baine didn't fail to notice that Ira flinched at the contact as though he'd just been touched by a red-hot poker. "He's a born outlaw, this one. He'll probably be running things in another year or two."

"With the weight of his father's murder hanging around his neck forever," Baine retorted. Ira flinched at his words as if he'd been whipped, but he remained silent.

"Tut, tut, my friend," Hep admonished. He returned to stand over Baine. "Life is full of hard choices. I'm sure I don't need to tell you that."

"So what happens now?" Baine challenged. "Why am I still alive?"

Hep raised his hands to his sides. "Because your life belongs to the Outlaw of Corwick now."

"The imposter, you mean," Baine spat.

"That's a matter of interpretation," Heply replied. He grinned. "If you have issues with how things stand, I'm sure you can raise the matter with Jark when you finally see him."

"Why not take me to him now? The sooner I cut his throat, the happier I'll be."

Hep laughed in delight. "My, but you certainly are a scrappy little fellow. I'll give you that."

"Untie my hands, and I'll show you scrappy," Baine growled.

"Sadly, as enjoyable as that might be," Hep said. "I have my orders. Our esteemed leader is, shall we say, occupied for the evening. He'll deal with you in the morning."

"So, you're just an obedient, faithful dog licking his master's boots then, eh?" Baine sneered. "I should have guessed."

"A faithful *friend*," Hep corrected, showing no signs of anger. "There is a difference."

Baine smiled. "I have a friend, too," he said. "A man who will go to the ends of the world to avenge me. You might want to think about that."

"Really?" Hep replied, looking intrigued. "So, tell me, Baine of Witbridge Manor. Where is this fearsome friend of yours?" The outlaw looked around the vast building in mock fear. "Is he hiding nearby, ready to pounce and rip our throats out with his bare hands?"

"Be careful what you wish for," Baine said softly.

Hep chuckled, moving to stand behind Baine. "I'll take my chances." He grabbed Baine by the shoulders, dragging him across the dirt floor to a support beam in the middle of the room. "Boy," the outlaw grunted. "Bring me some rope." Ira leaped to obey, and together, he and Hep tied Baine securely to the beam. The outlaw stepped back when they were finished. "There, that should hold you for now while we deal with that mess outside that you so ungraciously left for us."

"Dig a grave for yourself and your friend while you're at it," Baine said, glancing at Chett Lumper, who had remained surprisingly quiet during the questioning.

"Ha!" Hep laughed. "You, my friend, are really quite exceptional. I wonder if I could convince you to set aside your little vendetta and join us. We could use a man like you."

"What do you think?" Baine grunted.

"Ah," Hep nodded sadly. "I guess I can't say that I'm surprised. A pity, that." The outlaw motioned toward the door. "Come, gentlemen. Our brethren should not be left to rot in the rain like rats. After all, we owe them some dignity and recompense for their service, such as it was."

Baine put his head back against the beam when the men and boy were gone, taking solace from the silence, though he doubted it would last for long. He worked his fingers, trying to reach the ropes lashed around his wrists, but whoever had tied them had done a masterful job, and he couldn't even touch them. The outlaw and Ira had also been careful to wind the rope around the beam and his arms three times before tying it off securely, and it felt like a band of iron holding him.

Baine knew it was hopeless, but he took a deep breath anyway, letting it out until his lungs were empty, hoping to create enough slack in the rope to wriggle free. The maneuver gained him a little room but not enough to do anything practical. Baine sucked in air in frustration, trying not to let his growing despair overwhelm him. This was probably his only opportunity to be alone—such as it was—which meant it was realistically his only chance to escape. Baine glanced around, looking for inspiration, but there was nothing close by except for what looked to him like a rusty carpenter's auger lying under a cot. It was much too far away to reach, though.

Baine stretched out his leg anyway, thinking that if he could drag the cot toward him, the auger might get caught on one of the bedposts. But unfortunately, after several unsuccessful attempts, Baine conceded that it wouldn't work, for he was well short of the cot. He paused then, his heart jumping when he realized he could still feel the weight of the knife he'd hidden in his left boot. Baine had taken the blade from his right boot to replace the one on his hip he'd lost, which the outlaws had confiscated while he'd been unconscious. They'd also found the knives hidden in his bracers—presumably when they'd tied his wrists—but somehow had overlooked the blade still in his boot. But how to get it?

Baine drew his legs to his chest, then turned his left foot at an angle, using the heel of his right boot to push at the heel of the left one. The leather boot started to move down just as his toe slipped off, allowing the boot to retract to its original position. Baine cursed under his breath and tried again. He thought he heard something from outside then—a shout—and glanced up anxiously at the side door, holding his breath. The warehouse entrance remained closed, though, and after several thudding heartbeats, Baine resumed his task, finally managing to get the boot off.

He used his bare foot then, pulling the boot closer until it lay on the floor between his knees. But now what? Determined not to fail, Baine took another deep breath and exhaled. The moment he felt slack in the rope around him, Baine wriggled his body downward as far as he could, guessing he'd gained an inch or so. He inhaled, taking three sharp breaths before repeating the process, and then a third time until finally, he was lying at an awkward angle to the floor. It would have to do. Next, Baine used his toes to hook onto the top of the boot like clutching fingers, ignoring the stabbing pain in his knee as his leg bent awkwardly.

Thank the gods for all those stretches, Baine thought as he gingerly lifted the boot. He got it four inches off the ground before the boot slipped and fell back to the floor. Baine spat out another curse and tried again, this time managing to get a better grip. He lifted the boot in the air, gritting his teeth with effort as sweat broke out on his forehead, then carefully extended his foot outward. Terrified the boot would fall and he'd lose it, Baine snapped his leg toward his torso while unclenching his toes. He almost cried out with disbelief and joy when it landed with a slap on his chest, only inches away from his mouth. The boot had settled sideways, though, and Baine turned his body back and forth carefully, trying to maneuver the rim so it was facing his mouth. That's when the side door to the warehouse swung open.

"What in the name of The Mother are you doing?" Ira gasped in surprise.

"Shut the damn door!" Baine hissed.

The boy automatically obeyed, looking frightened and confused all at once. "But, what are you doing?"

"What does it look like?" Baine growled. "Trying to escape, of course."

Ira blinked, still looking as if he didn't understand. "Heply ordered me to check on you and see if you needed anything."

"How thoughtful of him," Baine said sarcastically. He motioned to the boot on his chest. "There's a knife in there. Get it and cut my bonds."

"Oh, I can't do that," Ira said, shaking his head fearfully. "They'll hurt me if I do."

"I'll hurt you if you don't!" Baine thundered, fighting to keep his voice down. "Now, do it!"

Ira took an indecisive step closer. "Is my father really dead?"

Baine took a deep breath, trying to calm his beating heart. The boy was his only chance now, and yelling at him would not help. "Yes," he finally said. "I'm sorry, but he is."

"It's my fault," Ira whispered, looking miserable.

"Yes," Baine agreed.

A single tear dripped from the boy's right eye, carving a small stream down his olive-colored cheek. "I...I just wanted to help."

"By bringing men like that to our home?" Baine said with a snort. "How was that going to help?"

"Jark promised me he'd only take the gold. He said no one would get hurt." The boy sniffed, looking very small and afraid. "He promised!"

"Promises from men like that can't be trusted," Baine said. "They care nothing for anyone but themselves."

Ira wiped at his eyes and looked at the floor, falling silent while Baine tried not to gnash his teeth in frustration. *He was running out of time*! "Your father asked about you," Baine lied. "Just before he died."

The boy looked up. "He did?"

"Yes," Baine said. "I held his hand as he took his last breath. His final thoughts were of you. He asked me to tell you that you were the man of the family now, and he charged you to take care of your mother, younger brother, and sisters. He said to tell you he was proud of you and that he loved you."

"Oh no," Ira whispered, his eyes puffy and red now as more tears cascaded down his cheeks. The boy's thin shoulders began to shake. "What have I done?" he wailed, spreading his arms wide. "I betrayed my family—for what? To be a slave to a monster? I thought with the gold they were going to pay me that my family and I could move to Gandertown. But they gave me nothing afterward but promises and beatings." Ira cupped his face in his hands, sobbing. "Now what am I going to do?"

"Redeem yourself in your father's eyes," Baine said forcefully, glancing behind the boy at the closed door. "Ermos is watching you right now, Ira. He's in the next world, sitting by The Mother's side, waiting to see what you will do. Do not fail him again."

"But I don't know what to do," Ira said weakly, lifting his head.

"Yes, you do," Baine said. "I see it in your eyes. If you want redemption for what you did, then there is only one way to get it. You must cut me free, so I can avenge what these men did to your father."

"But he'll still be dead no matter what happens!" Ira said in a choking voice. "Nothing I do now can change that."

"That's true," Baine agreed. "But at least when Judgement Day comes for you, you can hold your head up high, knowing whatever sins you committed were due to ignorance and youth, not malice." The boy looked like he was wavering, though Baine wasn't convinced yet that he'd said enough to sway him. "Listen to me, Ira. Today can be the first day of your life if you let it. A life that you can be proud of. All you have to do is take that first step by cutting me free. Everything will be easier after that. I promise."

"What about Jark and the others?"

"You leave them to me," Baine said with steel in his voice. "Get me out of this, and I swear by the gods, not one of them will live to see the sun rise in the morning."

Ira hesitated, glancing behind him at the door. Baine felt his heart sink, thinking it was over and he'd lost him, but the boy surprised him. "All right," he whispered, coming closer. "I'll do it."

"The knife is in a special compartment along the top of the boot on the inside," Baine said in relief, praying the boy wouldn't lose his nerve.

Ira nodded and squatted, thrusting his hands inside the boot. He felt around and then grunted in satisfaction, pulling out the knife a moment later. The boy moved out of eyesight, and Baine felt the ropes tighten against him soon after as Ira worked on sawing through them. A moment later, Baine was free. He jumped to his feet, automatically rubbing his wrists, thankful for the thick leather bracers he wore beneath his cloak that had at least partially protected him.

"You promise you'll kill them all?" Ira asked. His eyes were still puffy and red, though the tears had stopped.

"You have my word," Baine said, accepting the knife from the boy. He glanced around. "What did they do with my other knives and the bows I was carrying?"

"Pit and Kant kept the knives," Ira said. "Chett took the bows and arrows. He fancies himself an archer, though from what I've seen he's not very good."

"Where are they?" Baine grunted. "In here somewhere?"

Ira shook his head. "With the horses."

"Mother's Tit," Baine cursed softly as he pulled on his boot. Things had just gotten a lot harder. He headed for the door, pausing to look back at Ira. "All right, here is what I want you to do. Wait five minutes, then go find Hep and Chett and tell them that I escaped."

The boy's mouth fell open. "But why?"

"Because that way they won't suspect you had anything to do with it," Baine said, knowing if the boy hid in the warehouse, it would be the first place the outlaws would look. He didn't want to think about what would happen to Ira then. "Tell them you saw me running north."

"North?"

"That way, they'll think I've gone to kill Jark and won't be as cautious."

"Oh," Ira said. "I understand. All right."

"Good lad," Baine grunted. He opened the door a crack and peered outside, feeling the wind whistling against his face. He could tell it was still raining but could see little else despite the glow from the burning outbuilding. He glanced back at Ira. "Which way did Hep and Chett go?"

The boy pointed to the rear of the warehouse. "There's an outbuilding back there. An old chicken coop, I think. We dragged the bodies in there. Hep sent me back here after that to check on you."

"All right," Baine said with a nod. "Let's hope they're still there." He pointed at the boy. "Remember, five minutes, then go find them."

"Baine?"

Baine had already started to open the door, and he hesitated. "What?"

"I'm sorry I hit you."

"I know you are," Baine said. He touched his still-throbbing temple, guessing that he'd have a nasty bruise tomorrow—assuming he was still breathing. He shrugged and smiled. "No harm done. You're forgiven, lad."

The boy looked pleased at that. "Good luck."

Baine's smile faded. "You too," he said seriously. "Stay safe."

Then he slipped outside into the wind, rain, and darkness—a determined, silent shadow with nothing but a knife in his hand and death in his heart.

Chapter 26: Escape

Baine pulled the warehouse door closed behind him, careful not to make any noise that might alert Heply Boll or Chett Lumper. He knew they'd probably just assume it was Ira returning if they heard anything at all, yet he saw no reason to take any chances. The outbuilding was still burning in the distance, though not with the same enthusiasm he'd witnessed earlier. The roof and walls had long since collapsed, and the rain was working hard at extinguishing what stubborn pockets of fire remained, resulting in a constant hissing sound as heavy smoke rose from the ashes in swirling plumes. There was no sign of Hep or Chett that Baine could see, though he did notice a faint winking of light coming toward him along the path through the tree-covered hills fifty yards to the south. Damn the luck. It appeared that Pit Nelly and Kant Reece were already on their way back, which meant they would arrive in mere moments, and he needed to find somewhere to hide—fast.

Baine lamented the loss of his other weapons, knowing that without them, his chances of success this night were greatly reduced. He had no qualms about taking on any of the outlaws in a one-on-one fight with just his knife, but trying to do so against two or more of the bastards at the same time was just asking for trouble. His bow would have certainly evened the odds. Baine knew his best bet now was to wait things out since Hep would likely send one of the outlaws running back to the cave to recover their horses once he learned his prisoner had escaped into the hills. Baine was hoping circumstances would allow him to be waiting for that man, effectively killing two birds with one stone by eliminating him and recovering his bow at the same time. If Hep sent two men for some reason, well, at least he'd have the bow. But first, he had to make sure no one saw him.

Baine glanced around, spying a shadowy thicket of shrubs growing to his left about a hundred feet away. He dashed toward it, trying to ignore the throbbing pain in his temple and the ache in his cheek where Chett had struck him. He heard voices coming from the south, followed by the unmistakable glare of a lantern appearing at the tree line just as he reached the thicket. Baine dropped to the ground, dragging himself under cover and ignoring the odd branch that gouged at him as he wormed his way in deeper. One brushed against the knife wound on his right cheek and he hissed but kept going anyway. Finally satisfied that he was well hidden, Baine fought to turn his body around, his nose filled with the rich aroma of mountain witch alder, summersweet, and wild honeysuckle that surrounded him. He watched as Kant Reece and Pit Nelly approached the warehouse. The older man was carrying the lantern, though he was holding it at an odd angle in front of him.

"Not like that, Featherhead," Baine heard Pit say in a contemptuous voice. "I told you, you have to hold the lantern in both hands and keep your arms extended all the way." The younger man stopped, pulling Kant's arms out in front of him. "Like this, you dimwitted fool. Lock your elbows. That's a good fellow."

"But my shoulders hurt this way," Kant bemoaned, the first words Baine had heard from the man.

"Bah," Pit snorted. "We're almost there, so stop your bellyaching."

"But it don't feel good, Pit."

The younger outlaw sighed just as the rain began to lessen. Baine dearly hoped the storm wasn't over, having counted on it to help cover his retreat back to the horse cave.

"Would you look at that," Pit said, motioning to the sky. "Now it stops with us only a few paces away from having a roof over our heads again. And here I am, soaked to the skin and miserable. The gods must hate us, Featherhead."

"I'm wet too," Kant pointed out.

"Yeah, but only between the ears," Pit grumbled.

The younger outlaw looked behind him then as the shadowy forms of Heply Boll and Chett Lumper appeared around the warehouse. The rain was barely noticeable now, though the steady wind continued, rustling the leaves and plant stalks around Baine. He heard a sharp creak and bang, holding his breath as, right on time, the side door of the warehouse swung inward, revealing Ira. The boy ran toward Pit and Kant, waving his arms and shouting hysterically, but when he saw Hep and Chett, he changed directions, heading for them instead.

"He's gone! Baine is gone!"

"What?" Pit bellowed. He sprinted forward, barging into the warehouse only to reappear moments later. "The rope's been cut."

"I saw him running that way," Ira said, pointing north. Even from where he lay hidden, Baine could hear the fear and lack of conviction in his voice.

"Really?" Heply Boll said, the only outlaw to have remained calm at the news of Baine's escape. He put his hand on the boy's shoulder while the rest of the men converged around them, demanding answers. Baine swallowed, his heart thudding in his chest, matching the throbbing in his temple. Hep lifted a hand for silence, waiting until the others had stopped shouting. He focused on Ira. "I find that curious, Boy," Hep said in an even voice. "And the reason that I do is I think Chett and I would have seen him if he ran that way. Don't you?"

"He went east first," Ira said, his voice quivering as he pointed vaguely in the direction Baine was hiding. Baine realized with a sinking feeling that the youth was a terrible liar.

"And how exactly did he get free, do you suppose?"

"I don't know, Hep. Honest, I don't."

"Mother," Baine whispered, his heart in his mouth as he watched the interrogation with growing fear. "I beg of you. Please help the boy. I should never have involved him in this. I should have thought things through better, so please make those bastards believe him. Because if you don't, I'm afraid something terrible will happen to him."

"I think this whelp is lying, Hep," Pit Nelly growled. He drew a knife from a sheath at his belt—one of Baine's, he noted bitterly—and put it to Ira's neck. "Tell the truth, Boy, or I'll slit you open from ear to ear."

"But I am," Ira insisted, putting more feeling into it this time. "I swear by The Mother it's true! Why would I let him go? I'm the one who caught him in the first place, remember?"

Baine felt sudden hope, for Ira had sounded much more believable this time, with just enough outrage in his voice to make it seem real.

"You make a damn fine point, Boy," Hep rumbled in a friendly, almost fatherly voice. "Why would you, indeed? Now, tell me what you saw when you went into the building."

"Ropes, Hep," Ira said, gaining confidence. "Ropes on the floor all cut up, and Baine was gone."

"And yet, you claimed a moment ago that you saw him running away. This is the part that confuses me. If you were inside, how did you see him running? Can you explain that better for me?"

"Sure I can, Hep," Ira nodded eagerly. "As soon as I realized what had happened, I headed back outside just in time to glimpse Baine sneaking around the warehouse. He saw me and ran. I chased after him, but he was too fast for me. I gave up when I saw him make it to the hills."

"And then what did you do?" Hep asked, nodding his head in encouragement.

"Why, I came back here," Ira answered. Baine could tell by his body language that the boy was starting to believe he was out of danger. He prayed it was true.

"You came back here?" Hep said, rubbing his chin thoughtfully. He pointed to the ground. "Right here? Now, that's curious, Boy, most curious." The outlaw took a deep breath and then sighed wearily. "See, the part I still find confusing, lad, is why you didn't call out to Chett and me after Baine made it to the hills? Or better yet, why didn't you come and get us? I mean, you were already closer to us than you were to the front of the warehouse, so why return there? Why come back all this way, without saying a word to anyone, mind you, and then go back inside again? That's the part that I'm having trouble understanding. Can you help me with that, Boy?"

Baine held his breath, waiting for the answer, part of him ready to storm out there and rescue Ira, if need be, the other, wiser part holding him back. Four men were aligned against him—four heavily armed, effective fighting men who would cut him to pieces in short order if he revealed himself. To move was to die, so for now, all Baine could do was hope and pray that this would end well.

"Boy?" Hep prompted.

"I...I guess I wasn't thinking," Ira said weakly.

Baine saw Hep smile kindly in the lantern light. "No, I suppose you weren't. But who can blame you? Even the best of us lose our heads in times of stress like this." The outlaw glanced at Pit, who still held the knife to Ira's throat. He held out his hand. "Give me that, my friend. You won't be needing it."

"But Hep, he's—"

"Give me the knife, Pit. I won't ask you again."

Pit reluctantly handed the outlaw the weapon, then stood back as Heply put his arm around Ira's narrow shoulders, turning him toward the southern hills and the horse cave. He led him forward about ten paces and then stopped. "There, now that we've settled that little bit of business, Boy, I want you to do something for me. Will you do that?"

"Sure, Hep," Ira said, nodding eagerly. "Whatever you want."

"Good lad," the outlaw said. He gestured to the dark trees lining the hills. "I know Baine is out there somewhere. I can feel his eyes on me. So, what I want you to do is call out to him right now.

Tell him if he doesn't show himself in one minute, I'm going to disembowel you while he watches."

Baine groaned in despair, lowering his face to the ground. *No! No! No! What have I done?*

"But...but Hep," Ira said, sounding confused. "I told you, Baine ran north, not south."

"Yes, you did tell me that," Hep agreed. "But we both know that's a lie, now don't we?"

"I'm not—"

"Call him," Heply Boll growled in a menacing voice, the real man revealing himself. Baine realized at that moment that the outlaw was far, far smarter and more dangerous than any of the others, including Pit Nelly. Hep put his hand on the back of the boy's neck, squeezing. "Do it."

Ira licked his lips, his entire body shaking. He opened his mouth, then hesitated. Baine was certain he could see tears on the boy's cheeks.

"Just do it," Baine whispered to himself, holding his breath. "It's all right, lad. Just do what he wants and live."

"Now!" Hep said, giving the boy an impatient shake.

"Baine!" Ira called out reluctantly, his voice cracking. He glanced at the outlaw, then cleared his throat and tried again. "Baine!" he shouted much louder this time. "Run, Baine! They know! Run away!"

Heply Boll shook his head sadly, not looking surprised, then stabbed the knife deep into the boy's stomach. Baine watched in horror as the outlaw slashed sideways with the blade, then stepped nimbly back as dark blood and pink and white, slug-like entrails poured from Ira to land wetly on the ground. The boy stood frozen in shock for a heartbeat, staring down at himself in horror before he sagged to his knees, somehow remaining upright that way. He looked up at the sky, his hands stained red as he spread his arms. "I'm so sorry, Father," Ira said before he fell forward and lay still.

Baine pressed his face into the dried leaves and dirt, clamping his mouth shut to keep himself from screaming his hatred of these men. He fought back tears, knowing he'd as good as murdered Ira himself. Finally, gaining control of himself, Baine looked up as Hep casually used his foot to flip the boy's torn body over before he stooped to wipe off the knife. The outlaw casually tossed the weapon underhanded to Pit afterward, who caught it deftly.

Hep faced the hills again, cupping his hands around his mouth. "Baine!" he called out. "Boy's death is on your shoulders, my friend. It didn't need to be this way." Baine watched as Heply motioned to the other outlaws, who began to spread out and advance, all with swords drawn. "Baine, are you listening? How does it feel knowing that your selfishness and cowardice caused the death of an innocent child?"

Baine was sorely tempted to answer the bastard and damn the consequences, but then he saw the halfwit, Kant Reece, heading directly for him. The man still carried the lantern, swinging it back and forth as he drew closer. Baine hesitated in indecision, the need to avenge the boy making it hard to think. Sanity finally returned, however, as he quite rightly recognized that this was not the right time for vengeance. The outlaws would eventually pay for Ira and Baine's family, just not yet. He began retreating backward deeper into the bushes, praying Kant would turn away—but the outlaw kept coming. The halfwit finally reached the edge of the thicket and bent down with a grunt, holding up the lantern as he peered into the undergrowth.

"Do you see anything, Featherhead?" Pit called out from twenty yards away.

"Plants," the halfwit said in a serious voice.

Pit snorted and mumbled something under his breath, then added, "See any rabbits in there, Featherhead?"

"No, Pit."

"Maybe they're in deeper," the outlaw said with a snicker. "You should go look."

"You think so?"

"Pit," Hep grunted in a disapproving voice. "Stop that. We have serious business to attend to here."

"Ah, I'm just having some fun, Hep. Go ahead, Featherhead. Go get us that rabbit."

"All right," the halfwit said.

Baine couldn't believe his bad luck as the outlaw pushed his way stubbornly through the shrubs. He knew the man would see him in another moment, and having little choice, he turned on his hands and knees and began crawling away through the undergrowth as fast as he could.

"I think I hear a rabbit, Pit!" Kant Reece called out, this time with some excitement in his voice. "Sounds like a big one too!"

"Go and get 'em, Featherhead," Pit said with a laugh. "We'll have rabbit stew later once we catch this bastard."

"All right."

Baine shook his head as he crawled through the bramble on his hands and knees, lamenting the unfairness of it all. He was about to get caught because some half-witted fool was dead set on catching a rabbit. He reached the eastern side of the thicket, seeing little ahead of him in the darkness. Baine stood and started to run, hoping his bad luck was over now and he wouldn't be noticed. It wasn't and he was. He heard a shout moments later, looking back to see Kant Reece at the edge of the thicket, holding up the lantern and pointing at him with his sword. Baine heard answering shouts coming from the other outlaws, and he increased his speed, knowing they would all be converging on him now. He turned north, heading for the shrouded hills he could see rising in the distance as the sounds of pursuit rose behind him.

Baine chanced a glance over his shoulder, then to the sides. Pit and Kant were running neck and neck fifty yards behind him, with Hep and Chett racing along either flank at an angle in an effort to cut him off. Baine knew his only chance was to make it to the hills before they did and lose them in the darkness. He glanced behind him again. Kant, surprisingly, was in the lead now, less than thirty yards away, with Pit faltering and falling behind. The halfwit might be thick as mud between the ears, but the man could run like the wind despite carrying a sword and the lantern. Baine gave everything he had in one last frantic burst of energy, glancing back repeatedly as he ran for his life. He couldn't see Hep or Chett anywhere now, praying he'd lost them, while Pit had been reduced to a jog, losing ground by the moment. But Kant still remained, running with single-minded determination and looking unstoppable as he closed the distance like a wolf chasing down a hare—twenty yards away, then fifteen, then ten.

Baine took a quick glance at the hills still so far away, knowing even as he did that he wasn't going to make it. There was really only one option left. He spun around, planting his feet as Kant raced toward him. The slow-witted outlaw's face registered his surprise at the move, but he kept coming on like a charging bull anyway. Baine waited for him, his chest heaving, then when the man was five yards away, he threw the knife. The outlaw saw the blade coming at the last moment and he tried to dodge aside, but he was too slow as the point caught him in the shoulder. Kant staggered and howled, dropping the lantern, which winked out, throwing them into darkness, but not before Baine had seen Heply Boll racing toward him in his periphery vision.

Baine spun around and bolted for the hills again, expecting to be bowled over by one of his pursuers at any moment. He reached the base free of attackers and tore up the slope, reaching out blindly to use rocks, small bushes, or whatever else his questing fingers could find to help him ascend. He could hear the outlaws shouting to each other in confusion below him, but it seemed for the moment, without the lantern to help them, that they'd lost him. Baine doubted that would last long, though, for no matter how hard he tried to be careful, he was dislodging small avalanches of shale and rocks with every step upward. The outlaws were bound to hear it eventually.

Baine reached a relatively flat plateau and began running northwest, forced to skirt around an outcrop that towered above him. He glanced back as the sounds of the pursuing outlaws echoed loudly in his ears. They'd found his trail again. He reached an arroyo split by a stream swollen from the rain, splashing through it to the other side, where an imposing granite wall greeted him. He paused there to catch his breath, leaning against the stone and cocking his head to listen. Had he lost them? He could hear the outlaws calling back and forth to one another, but they seemed further away now, heading in a more northerly direction. Baine waited where he was for several minutes, panting until, finally, his racing heart began to slow. He could still hear the outlaws, but their voices were getting farther and farther away. Now what? He considered returning the way he'd come, but something told him a man like Heply Boll might anticipate that. Instead, he began working his way along the cliff wall, using his hands on the cold stone to guide the way.

Baine eventually reached a jagged gap in the cliff, and he cautiously felt around inside, seeing nothing but pitch blackness ahead of him. He sniffed but could detect no scent of animals or anything else that might signal imminent danger. Had he found an entrance to another cave, or was this just a small fissure leading nowhere? Baine decided to investigate, thinking that if it was an actual cave, it might lead him to a way out that the outlaws would never find. He stepped into the opening, waving his arms in front of him as he advanced several paces and then paused to listen. Nothing. He moved forward, cautiously placing one foot in front of the other, sensing that the space around him was getting larger as he progressed. Baine smiled in relief, convinced that his first instinct was right and he'd discovered a cave. Things were finally looking up.

That's when he stepped onto something that sagged beneath his front foot and then snapped with a loud crack, sending him tumbling downward with a cry into a dark pit.

Chapter 27: Pit Kelly And The Halfwit

Baine landed on his side against solid stone after a short fall, his hands instinctively covering his head as dirt, small rocks, and what he believed to be broken planks rained down on top of him in an avalanche of noise. Something round and solid glanced painfully off his left shoulder, followed by a jagged section of wood that cut a gouge across the back of his right hand. When the deluge was finally over, Baine began to push splintered boards and rocks off him until he was free enough to struggle to a sitting position. He coughed repeatedly, the dust swirling around him filling his lungs with every intake of air. He shook his head to clear it, then fought to extricate himself and stand, hissing at the sudden stabbing pain that arced down his right hip as he rose. He tentatively put weight on his right foot, gritting his teeth against the pain, which hurt something fierce but was still manageable.

Despite that pain, Baine felt overwhelming relief, knowing from experience if a bone or two had been broken, what he was feeling now would be a hundred times worse. "Well," he muttered, brushing himself off in the darkness and looking around. "Now what do I do?"

Baine glanced up, thinking he could just discern a rough, shadowy opening above him blending in with the blackness around it. He extended his hands over his head, hoping to find something solid to latch onto but could feel nothing but empty air. He wasn't tall enough to reach the rim. He tried jumping and missed, regretting it moments later when he landed awkwardly and white-hot fire raged along his bruised hip.

Baine bent, limping as he rummaged around blindly for some of the fallen boards, planning to stack them on top of each other beneath the hole so he could stand on them. He paused in his work. Had he just heard voices, or had it been the wind whistling inside the cave up top? Baine waited, not daring to breathe, certain that now he could make out the crunch of approaching feet from above. A moment later, he saw a faint orange glow lighting the jagged rim of the hole. Baine shrank back into the darkness, automatically grabbing one of the planks as a weapon.

"I'm telling you, I heard something from in here."

Baine recognized Pit Kelly's voice, amplified by the cave walls as the light grew steadily stronger.

"I didn't hear anything," another man responded. It was the halfwit, Kant Reece.

"That's because you've got nothing between your ears except snot, Featherhead."

"Sorry, Pit."

"How's your shoulder?"

"All right, I guess. Hurts some. Bleeding has stopped, though, thank the gods."

"Hey!" Pit grunted in surprise. "What's that up ahead there on the ground?"

"Boards," Kant replied.

Baine swore under his breath. He moved to his right, locating a cold, clammy wall, which he used to guide him as he carefully retreated away from the opening.

"Looks like some kind of mine shaft, Featherhead," Pit said, his voice echoing. "Probably leads to one of the tunnels."

"Shovels," Kant muttered.

"What?"

"There's some old shovels over there, Pit. Other tools too."

"Ah, so there are."

"Why are the boards broken, Pit?"

"Something or someone fell through here, Featherhead."

Baine heard the outlaw drop to his knees above the rim of the opening as he continued to move back slowly, praying he didn't stumble over anything while keeping his eyes fixated on the hole.

"A bear?" Kant asked, his voice quivering. "I don't like bears much, Pit."

"That hole is too small for a bear, dummy," Pit said with a mocking laugh. "But it sure is big enough for a little black rat, now isn't it? I think we found where he went, Featherhead. Here, take the torch and lean down and have a look inside. That's a good fellow."

"But I don't like rats much, neither, Pit."

"Of course, you don't, Featherhead," Pit said with a sigh. "Who in their right mind would?" The outlaw snickered again. "Oh, right. Look who I'm asking. Now stop you're talking and have a look."

"Aw—"

"Do it!"

Baine dropped into a crouch and then froze, making himself as small as possible against the wall. The area around the opening was suddenly illuminated in stark relief as a burning torch appeared, followed by an arm and then a head. The halfwit gave a slight gasp before he hastily retreated from the opening.

"What's wrong, Featherhead?"

"I burned my eyebrows, Pit. It hurts."

"You imbecile," Pit snapped. "Give me that. Now get out of the way, you damn nitwit."

The torch reappeared, this time with Pit Nelly holding it as he leaned into the hole. The outlaw swung the flame back and forth, examining the tunnel walls and the wreckage below him. "It's only about seven feet down or so," he called up to his companion. "Looks like this happened recently, Featherhead, which means it's got to be our boy. We've got the bastard now." Baine heard Kant mumble something, but he couldn't make it out with Pit's body blocking most of the hole. "What are you talking about?" Pit said with a snort. "Go back? No, we're going in there and dragging that rat out by his pointy ears." The man paused again, then took a deep breath. "Fine. You go find Hep and tell him what we found if you want. I'll go after Baine on my own. I doubt the little bastard got far."

The outlaw dropped the torch inside the tunnel, where it lay spluttering on a plank, then disappeared from view. Baine was sorely tempted to run back and get it, but he didn't want to alert Kant about his presence. Fighting one man in the tight confines of the tunnel without any weapons was feasible. Two was not.

A pair of legs appeared, dangling from the rim, and Baine turned, limping away along the tunnel as fast as he could in the almost total darkness. He heard Pit land inside the tunnel with a grunt and glanced back, realizing as he did so that it had been a mistake. He was dressed all in black and almost invisible, but the whiteness of his face was not.

"There you are, rat boy!" Pit crowed in triumph. "Featherhead! Featherhead! We've got him! Get down here!"

The outlaw didn't wait for a reply, racing after Baine as he drew his sword with a ring of steel that echoed loudly in the tight confines. Baine hefted the board in his hand, wishing for one of the few times in his life that it was a sword instead—anything that would offer him a fighting chance. The plank he held was three feet long and old, and though it felt solid enough to him, he knew it would be no match against forged steel. And so, Baine ran for his life, ignoring the protest in his hip as Pit Kelly whooped and laughed, his torch flickering wildly over his head as he gave pursuit. Baine already knew he was faster than the young outlaw, limp or not, but Pit had the advantage, able to see what was ahead of him while Baine was running almost blind, with only the weak flicker of his pursuer's torch reflecting off the walls for lighting.

He passed beneath a series of massive wooden beams embedded along the walls that supported even larger beams girding the ceiling as the tunnel began to angle downward. Baine chanced a look back. There was no sign of Kant yet, and he was pleased to see that he still had a hundred-foot lead on Pit Kelly, who had ceased his shouting to conserve energy. Now it was just a matter of who would falter first. Baine saw the wink of pooling water ahead of him as the tunnel dipped even more, leading to a flooded, rounded chamber. Having little choice, he continued until he reached the murky water and plunged in, hissing at the cold as it rose well past his knees after only a few steps.

"You can run all night, rat, but you can't hide!" Pit called out joyfully as he raced down the grade. He entered the chamber and hesitated at the water's edge, the torch lighting up the interior.

Baine saw something to his left, a tunnel branching off, and he started to wade that way only to realize that the entrance was boarded up ten feet in. He cursed and looked back, his chest heaving as the outlaw remained where he was, leaning over as he fought to breathe with less than fifty feet separating them. Baine waited, using the opportunity to suck badly needed air into his lungs.

"Why put yourself through all this, rat?" Pit Kelly finally gasped between ragged breaths. "I'm tired of running after you. Why not settle things right here and now like men?"

"I'm willing if you are," Baine said. He gestured to the man's sword with the plank he held. "Toss that thing aside, and then maybe we'll have a fair fight."

"I don't fight fair, rat," Pit said with a laugh. "Never have. But since we've become such good friends, I'll do you a favor." The outlaw sheathed his sword with a flourish. "There. If you're fast enough, you might even make it over here before I can draw it again."

"You're too kind," Baine said dryly. He glanced around, but except for the boarded-up entrance, there was nothing to see but rock walls seeping water in tiny rivulets and aged, wooden beams over his head. He glanced back at the outlaw. "I guess it's to be more running, then?"

"I guess it is," Pitt agreed casually.

Baine knew something was up by the man's voice; his instincts verified when the outlaw revealed one of Baine's knives in his right hand. He threw it without warning, and Baine twisted aside, with the spinning blade sailing past him another ten feet before falling with a splash into the water. Both Pit and Baine froze, staring at each other as they realized what had just happened at the same time. Baine finally grinned at his opponent, breaking the stalemate, then turned, desperately wading toward where the knife had disappeared.

"Oh no, you don't, rat!" Pit roared. He drew his sword again and barreled into the pool, sending spray splashing in all directions.

Baine reached the spot where he thought the knife had entered the water, but he couldn't see anything beneath the murky surface, forced to use his feet to probe around along the rock floor. Nothing. He glanced up at the outlaw, who was almost upon him, knowing he'd run out of time just as the side of his foot nudged against something. A rock? The knife? There was no way for him to know for certain.

Pit Kelly was now within striking distance, and he cried out in triumph, slashing his blade in a vicious backhand for Baine's head. Baine ducked beneath the blow, then used the plank he held to chop at the man's midriff. The board snapped in two as Pit Kelly bellowed in pain, but he still had the presence of mind to swing at Baine again. Baine did the only thing he could, letting go of the broken boards and diving beneath the water to escape while frantically searching with his hands for the knife along the floor. He felt the leather handle a moment later against his palm and wrapped his fingers around it, twisting sideways just in time as the outlaw's sword cut through the water like a harpoon, nearly impaling him. Baine felt a sharp pain burn across his lower back as he came bursting out of the water, sweeping the knife in a wide circle in front of him. He was gratified to hear the outlaw cry out as he hastily retreated, though not before he'd dropped the torch, which went out with a hiss the moment it hit the water, leaving the two men in pitch darkness.

Baine shifted three steps to his right and then crouched, trying to keep his breathing steady, afraid the outlaw would hear it. Pit Kelly seemed to be doing the same thing, making no sounds despite having taken a wound. Baine hoped that it was serious. He took a cautious step back, trying not to disturb the water. He held his empty left hand high to deflect an attack, and his knife hand positioned much lower, ready to strike at a moment's notice.

"You got lucky, rat," Pit Kelly finally spat out after several long minutes of silence. The man had backed off, Baine noted, now a good thirty feet away to his right.

"Sometimes you have to make your own luck," Baine replied. He took three steps to his left and waited, hoping the outlaw would bite and make a move, but he didn't.

"Want to talk about Lady Big Tits some more?" Pit asked mockingly. The outlaw had also changed positions, his voice now coming from Baine's left.

"Remember what I told you earlier?" Baine said before moving backward several steps. He shifted to his right as the sound of dripping water from the walls and ceiling echoed loudly. "I promised you would beg me for mercy before I killed you." Baine moved again, this time to his left.

Pit Kelly chuckled. He sounded further away now, almost as if he was retreating back to dry land. "At least I'll go to The Father's pits knowing I gave Lady Big Tits all she could handle and more. I doubt a little dwarf like you can boast the same."

Baine held his temper, aware that the man was trying to goad him into doing something stupid. "You running away?" he taunted. "Because I'm standing right over here waiting for you."

No answer. Baine pursed his lips. What was the man up to? He shifted to his right again until he came into contact with the wet wall. He paused there, certain he'd just heard a slight swishing sound off to his left. Had it been Pit or his imagination? Baine transferred his knife into his left hand, using his right to guide him along the wall as he retreated. He came into contact with a solid wooden beam, then an empty space, realizing that he'd found the boarded-up offshoot tunnel—a tunnel that he doubted Pit Kelly knew about.

Baine waited, listening, positive now that he could hear something off to his left—the slight displacement of water as someone moved furtively through it. The sound was coming closer, heading at a slight angle away from him. That wouldn't do. He deliberately raked his blade against the support beam, the sudden harsh noise ridiculously loud in the cavernous space. Baine spat out a curse under his breath, though he made sure it was high enough for the outlaw to hear him. He slipped back into the tunnel entrance and waited, leaning against the beam as the sound of displaced water changed direction, headed directly for him now. A moment later, something heavy splashed in the water ten feet to Baine's right. He grinned, knowing what Pit Kelly was doing.

"I've got you now!" Baine shouted, pretending to take the bait.

He took several steps out from the tunnel entrance, deliberately making a lot of noise as he splashed through the water toward where the sound had occurred. Then he retreated again, sliding back into the tunnel entrance as Pit Kelly roared and attacked from the left, striking where Baine had been. He heard the man's blade ring off solid stone as he hit the chamber wall, sending sparks flying in all directions.

Baine leaned his head around the entrance. "I'm here, fool," he said before ducking back.

Pit Kelly growled, and Baine heard the whoosh of air as the outlaw swung his sword in front of him wildly as he advanced toward Baine's position. Baine shrunk against the inner wall of the tunnel with his face pressed to the support beam as he waited to pounce. He heard the outlaw draw even with him, still swinging his sword. Baine held off until his adversary was three steps past the tunnel entrance, then he slipped in behind the man, focusing on the smell of sweat emanating from him. He reached up, wrapping his hand around the outlaw's lower jaw, pulling him off balance even as he stabbed upward into his back once, twice, and then again. Baine felt warm, slippery blood saturating his hand and the knife handle, knowing instinctively that he'd hit the man's liver.

He felt Pit weakening in his grip and put his lips to the dying man's ear. "I warned you what would happen, you bastard," Baine whispered. "So, you ready to beg for mercy now?"

Baine waited for a response that never came, for Pit Kelly was already dead. He let the man go, closing his eyes as the outlaw landed with a splash in the water. *I'm so tired*, he thought. *So incredibly tired.*

"Pit? Are you there? Pit?"

Baine opened his eyes at the sound of the halfwit's voice coming from the edge of the pool.

"Pit?"

He grinned wearily. "Well, why not?" he whispered to himself with a shrug. He focused on the spot the voice had come from. "That you, Featherhead?" he grunted in a low voice.

"Yes, Pit. It's me. Did you get him?"

"I did."

"Oh, that's good news, Pit. That's real good news."

"Stay where you are, Featherhead. I'll come to you."

"All right."

Baine probed around until he found Pit Kelly's body floating facedown nearby, grabbing the corpse by the collar. He started dragging it toward where Kant Reece waited.

"What are you doing, Pit?"

"Taking this rat's body to Jark," Baine grunted.

"Oh. Need some help?"

"No. But if your shoulder can hold up, you can help me carry him out of the tunnel after."

"All right. Sure is dark in here, Pit."

Baine remained silent as he drew closer to the waiting outlaw, pulling the corpse along the water's surface with his left hand, the knife in his right.

"Was it hard, Pit? Killing him, I mean."

"No," Baine muttered. He was less than three feet away now, just able to discern the halfwit's solid form in the darkness. "Grab his arms, Featherhead. I'll get his feet."

"All right."

Baine waited until Kant was bent over, grunting as he started to lift Pit Kelly's body. Then, with a quick, efficient slash of his knife, he tore open the halfwit's throat. It was almost too easy. The outlaw stiffened with a gasp, then collapsed, landing on top of the younger man's corpse.

Baine washed his knife clean in the water and sheathed it, then searched the bodies, finding another blade on Pit Kelly and a second one on the halfwit. He took them both gratefully. He debated about whether to keep Kant's sword or not before ultimately deciding against it. The weapon was heavy and would only slow him down and get in the way. He also found a leather pouch on the halfwit containing some dried meat, several apricots and dates, and the best prize of all, a flint and steel set with several pieces of char cloth.

Baine headed back toward the mine shaft, feeling reinvigorated as he consumed the halfwit's food. "Jark Cordly, Heply Boll, Pater Dore, Chett Lumper, and Vierna Alel," he said as he walked the darkened tunnel. "I'm coming for you."

Chapter 28: Heply Boll

Baine made it outside without any issues, using the broken boards to climb up out of the mineshaft just as he'd originally intended. Now he stood at the entrance to the cave studying the darkened landscape, wondering what his next move should be. The rain had stopped long ago, although a cool brisk wind still swept over the hills, adding to the chill Baine felt due to his wet clothing. He knew Heply Boll and Chett Lumper were out there somewhere hunting for him, but finding them in the dark would not be easy. The outlaws would likely be carrying torches, he guessed. But even so, there were a lot of trees, outcrops, ravines, and uneven terrain all around him, so the chances that he'd actually see his adversaries moving about were not that great. Should he forget about the two men for now and head north and go after Jark Cordly instead? It was tempting, but Baine knew that if he did, there was a good chance Hep and Chett might appear behind him at an inopportune time, which meant they needed to be eliminated first. But how to find them?

Baine looked south, thinking about the horse cave and his bow. He doubted Hep would expect him to return there after so much time had passed, but the man was smart and underestimating him could be a costly mistake. Baine's fortunes had certainly turned for the better recently, and though his odds of success had greatly improved, he knew a lot of what had happened was due to blind luck, including getting Ira's help. Without the boy, would he have been able to escape? Baine wasn't sure.

What he was sure of was the odds were still five to one against him—a vast improvement on what they'd been only recently, but still formidable. Baine's bow and arrows would make all the difference in the coming fight, but could he risk trying to get them? He fished in the leather bag for the last date as he debated what to do, his hands coming into contact with the firesteel. He drew it out after popping the date in his mouth, holding the tool in the palm of his hand. The steel was shaped like a miniature horseshoe and about a quarter of an inch thick. Baine hefted it, an idea forming. Fire had worked once before for him, so why not again?

Coming to a decision, Baine headed south, picking his way carefully across the stream again as he retraced his steps from earlier. He paused every few feet to listen, but except for the incessant chirping of crickets and the odd croak of a lonely frog, there was nothing to indicate that anyone was around. He reached the summit of the hill overlooking the warehouse and crouched behind a large boulder as he peered down. He could see the dark outline of the building rising in the distance but nothing else that indicated danger.

Convinced that he was alone, Baine started searching the ground for anything dry—not an easy task after the many hours of rain—finally finding a small copse of pine trees where he was able to collect a fair amount of pine needles, dead grass, and fallen twigs that were relatively dry. They would have to do. He carried everything back to his original position and piled it in the open near the boulder, where he knew it would be visible from both the south and the north. He returned several more times to the copse, lugging back anything that might burn until he was satisfied that he had enough material to make a decent bonfire.

Next, Baine squatted on the leeward side of the bolder, using it to break the wind. He took out the flint and steel, carefully placing a piece of char cloth on top of the flint before striking it with the edge of the firesteel. Sparks shot upward and to the side at the impact, but the fabric didn't ignite. Baine tried again, grunting in satisfaction when a tiny glow of light started on the cloth. He carefully took it in his hands, folding it like a tube as he blew carefully on the top. The char cloth began to glow even more, sending off tiny tendrils of smoke. Baine continued blowing gently until he was confident the embers wouldn't go out, then he stood, using his body to protect his burgeoning flame from the wind as he moved to his kindling. He put the cloth into a rounded depression at the bottom of the pile, then blew on it again, gratified moments later when a small orange flame appeared, licking hungrily at the needles and grasses.

    Baine sat back on his haunches, watching critically until the fire had filled the depression he'd made, smoke billowing outward from the hole and through gaps at the top. Satisfied it wouldn't go out now, he stood and hurried down the hill toward the warehouse, careful to give the building a wide birth. If the outlaws were anywhere nearby—say waiting at the horse cave to ambush him—Baine doubted they would be able to resist investigating the bonfire. He made his way to the thicket where he'd hidden earlier, grimacing when he noticed a dark form still lying sprawled out on the ground, looking small and pathetic. Poor, foolish Ira. Baine waited then, crouched by the thicket as the blaze on the hill roared into full force, stoked by the wind as long tendrils of flame and sparks leaped skyward. He knew a fire like that would be visible for miles and be impossible for the outlaws to ignore. A moment later, he heard excited voices coming from the trail to the south, just able to discern the forms of two men running from the treeline toward the warehouse. So, Heply Boll had set a trap for him after all.

    Baine waited until the outlaws had run past the building and disappeared behind it before sprinting toward the horse cave, reaching the enclosure in under a minute. The front gates were open as before, with the interior still lit up by lantern light. Baine eagerly burst through the entrance, some instinct causing him to swerve to the side just as a form suddenly appeared from behind the lefthand gate, swinging a sword. Baine rolled beneath the blow and came up on his feet in a crouch, his knife ready.

"Impressive," Heply Boll said grudgingly. The outlaw whirled his sword in his hand once, then took a defensive stance. He was carrying a shield on his left arm with the emblem of a three-headed bear on the front. The handsome outlaw smiled. "I had a feeling that you'd come back for your bows. They're an extension of a good archer's arm, after all, which I believe, my friend, you to be. I imagine their loss for you is not dissimilar to being at a king's coronation, surrounded by lords and ladies, only to realize you're not wearing any clothes."

"I've never been to a king's coronation," Baine said. "So I wouldn't know anything about that."

Heply Boll chuckled modestly. "I was being facetious, my friend. My apologies if my flair for the dramatic was a little over your head."

"Most things are," Baine responded. "I'm not a tall man, after all. But I promise I won't let that fact stop me from killing you."

"Self-deprecating humor," Hep said as he began to circle Baine warily. "You continue to astound and delight, Baine. It takes a big man to make fun of himself like that, regardless of his actual stature."

"I saw two men run past me down below just now," Baine said, matching the outlaw step for step. "Care to explain that?"

Hep smiled. "My compatriot decided to join us. Better late than never, I suppose. I hoped using him as a decoy would bring our rather bothersome fly buzzing right into my little web. I was convinced you planned some form of clever trickery to draw us out into the open, which in hindsight proved ultimately to be correct. Congratulations on being outsmarted by me my friend. Trust me, there's no shame in it."

Baine nodded, understanding now. He should have realized who the third man was right away. "That's Pater Dore out there?"

"The one and only," Hep agreed. "Pater's arrival was somewhat delayed earlier this evening due to a bout of, shall we say, indigestion? It appears he has since recovered his intestinal fortitude, luckily for me."

"But not for him," Baine grunted, keeping his eyes on the other man's feet. "Or for Pit and Kant, either, as things turned out not that long ago."

Heply Boll's eyebrows rose in surprise. "Killed them, did you?"

"Of course," Baine said casually.

The outlaw looked impressed. "I must say, Baine. You certainly are a resourceful fellow. Are you absolutely certain I can't entice you to join our merry band?"

Baine snorted. "Not so merry anymore, now is it? I'm not even sure you can call what's left a band. Are you?"

Hep shrugged. "That is easily rectified, my friend. Men come, and men go, but Jark and I, much like The Mother and The Father, are constants. Luckily for us, the world is filled with eager young fools ready and willing to jump at the chance to join our ranks. We'll return to full strength in a matter of weeks, if not days. While you, on the other hand, will, unfortunately, be dead unless you wise up and accept my offer."

"And become a slave to that bastard you serve just like poor Ira did?" Baine shook his head. "I don't think so."

"Boy was a naïve little fellow, I admit," Hep said. "But I meant what I said about him. I truly believed the lad would become a valuable addition to our group in due time." The man's face darkened. "That is if it hadn't been for you and your damn meddling, of course."

Baine nodded, barely listening now. He knew his time was limited and that he needed to put Heply Boll down now, for Chett Lumper and Pater Dore could already be on their way back to the cave. The problem was his opponent carried a shield, which could easily block a thrown knife, not to mention he wore chainmail beneath his cloak. Baine glanced around but could see nothing useful to use as a weapon. He shifted his gaze to the corral. Tasker

Grich's body was gone, he noted, and now there was a white mare milling about inside the enclosure that hadn't been there before. It was Pretty Girl!

"By the way," Baine said, gesturing to the mare. "That's my horse you've got in there."

Hep glanced toward Pretty Girl, his expression turning curious. "You mean that white one? Pater's horse? Now, how might that have come about, do you think?"

"You bastards took her from me near Laskerly a while back, remember?"

The outlaw blinked in confusion, then he shook his head and laughed. "That was you out there that night on the trail? By The Father's drooping sack, what are the chances of that happening, eh? It's a sign we're all meant to be friends, lad. I'm certain of it."

"Yes, what are the odds?" Baine growled sarcastically as he continued assessing the cavern. His eyes lit up when he noticed two bows leaning against the end post of the corral, half hidden in the shadows where the fence met the rock wall. His arrow bag lay on the ground beneath them, looking as tempting to him as an eager young virgin on her wedding night.

"Ah," Heply said, noticing where Baine's gaze was drawn. The outlaw shifted his body to block Baine's path to the bows. "I imagine you'd like to get your hands on those right about now?"

"I'm giving it some serious thought," Baine admitted. "I don't suppose you'd consider letting me go over there to get them, would you?"

"I doubt that would be beneficial to my continued health," Heply said with a cheeky grin. "Though I do appreciate the courtesy you've shown in asking politely. Perhaps another time when you and I are less inclined to kill each other?"

"Perhaps," Baine agreed. "Although we both know only one of us is leaving this cave alive."

"A fair point," Hep conceded. He spread his arms. "Then I guess we should get on with things, or would you prefer to wait until my companions return?"

"No, now seems fine," Baine replied. He leaned over and removed a knife from his boot, now with one in each hand.

Heply Boll twirled his sword again, chuckling. He turned his body sideways, presenting a smaller target behind his rectangular shield, revealing only the top of his head and feet. "Just what, exactly, do you intend to do with those toad stickers, Baine?" the outlaw asked mockingly.

"I thought I'd—" Baine moved then, whipping both knives forward in a blur of speed—one aimed for the outlaw's laughing face, the other for his extended left knee that remained hidden by the shield.

Heply Boll did what any man would do in that situation, instinctively crouching and lifting his shield to cover his head, which left his front leg unprotected. The first knife struck the top of the shield, quivering in the wood, while the second sunk deeply into the outlaw's flesh several inches below his knee in the meat of the calf muscle. Heply Boll howled and staggered backward, hopping on one leg and sweeping his sword in front of him, anticipating Baine's attack. Baine casually drew his remaining knife, choosing not to advance on the outlaw as the man hobbled backward until he'd reached the corral fence. The wounded outlaw paused there, wincing as he used the railing to support himself, panting heavily. Hep finally grit his teeth, then carefully pulled out the bloody knife before tossing it aside with a grimace of distaste.

"I guess if that was a toad sticker, then that makes you the toad," Baine said with a grin. "Does it hurt much?"

"A damn fine ploy, Baine," Heply Boll grunted, grimacing again as he looked down at his blood-soaked leg. "Damn fine." They held eyes, both men knowing what was coming next. "But I assure you, I've had splinters from firewood much worse than this little scratch."

"Now that's a splinter I'd be interested in seeing," Baine replied. "Must have been quite impressive." He darted toward the outlaw without warning, knife poised to strike as the man hastily brought up his sword and shield, crying out when his foot touched the ground.

Baine broke off the attack and stepped back, laughing. "You don't look so good, Hep," he said critically. "You sure you're feeling all right?"

The outlaw glared back at Baine, his face covered in sweat with the skin of his cheeks and forehead now the color of ash. Pretty Girl chose that moment to nuzzle the man with her nose, and he shrugged her off in annoyance. "Pater and Chett will be here any time now, Baine," the outlaw grunted. "Then you and I are going to have a little talk about all of this."

"Thanks for reminding me," Baine said. "I almost forgot about those two. I guess it's time to end this."

Baine darted to his right, ignoring the pinch in his hip as he tried to get past Hep's shield with his knife. But despite being injured, the outlaw was still fast, and he blocked the attack. Baine saw the outlaw's sword coming for his head next—which was just what he'd been hoping for. He dropped to the ground and rolled to his left as the blade hissed over him, passing beneath the bottom railing of the fence while the horses skittered away. Baine popped up to his feet again on the other side of the corral, flipping his knife into his left hand while ignoring the clumps of horse dung he'd rolled over clinging to his leather armor. Heply Boll was desperately trying to bring his shield around to protect his vulnerable flank, but fast as he was, Baine was faster. He rammed the knife into the outlaw's unprotected side, puncturing through the chainmail and into the man's kidney, twisting the blade savagely before withdrawing it. Heply Boll screamed, losing his footing as his wounded leg gave out from beneath him. He collapsed on his ass, blood on his lips as he weakly tried to stab at Baine through the railing. Baine easily avoided the blade, then stepped on it, pinning it to the ground with his boot. The outlaw tried to draw his weapon free, but his strength was gone and he quickly gave up, releasing the hilt in resignation.

He looked up at Baine through the fence. "This probably won't help much, my friend, but I didn't approve of what Pit did to your family. I would have killed him right then and there had I known about it."

"You're right," Baine growled. "It doesn't help one little bit."

Then he killed the bastard.

Chapter 29: Alone For Eternity

Baine eased into the white mare's saddle as gigantic flames roared behind him. He glanced to the east, where he could see the first faint, telltale signs that dawn was approaching. The horse snorted and shook her head uneasily, disturbed by the loud crackling, hissing, and popping from the fire only a hundred feet away. Baine glanced back at the unstoppable inferno that had once been the warehouse where the outlaws had quartered. *Perhaps I shouldn't have lit it on fire after all,* he thought, worried that a blaze of this magnitude might alert Jark Cordly. He watched as part of the western wall of the building collapsed with a rush of wind, flames, and smoke. Incredibly, the roof above it remained intact, balancing precariously on thick cross beams suspended over a network of blackened posts as tendrils of fire licked along their lengths. Baine was vividly reminded of the granary back in Springlight, where he, Hadrack, and many others had almost lost their lives not long ago.

Pretty Girl suddenly snorted and spun in a circle as heavy smoke drifted over them, indicating her impatience to be away from this place. "It's all right, girl," Baine said soothingly, patting her neck. "Just a moment longer, then we can go."

His words seemed to soothe the horse somewhat, although she still eyed the burning building warily as gigantic flames more than a hundred feet high reached for the sky, feeding on the warehouse's timber framework with ferocious energy. Someday someone might come back to this place, Baine knew, sifting through the ashes in hopes of finding some small trinket among the remains. Would they also find Ira's and the outlaws' charred bones inside as well? Or would those bones have long since been turned to dust by then?

Baine took a deep breath as he thought about the events that occurred after he'd killed Heply Boll. Chett Lumper had been the first to die; his ugly features twisted in a look of surprise when Baine's arrow caught him in the throat. The man had fallen just outside the horse cave gates without making a sound. His companion, Pater Dore, had turned and had tried to flee, which really hadn't been all that smart, as it turned out. Baine had brought the man down with a well-aimed shot to the back of the upper thigh before he'd even reached the trees, then had shot a second shaft into his shoulder to give him something to think about.

After that, Baine had cut both tendons above the man's heels with his knife, effectively crippling him. He'd left the man lying where he'd fallen, using Pretty Girl to drag Hep's and Chett's corpses to the warehouse before passing through the double doors to dump them in a heap inside. He'd also located Tasker Grich's body in one of the tunnels and had done the same for him. As an afterthought, Baine had gently picked up Ira in his arms, carrying the boy inside to place his body on one of the cots. Then, he'd returned for Pater Dore.

The outlaw had somehow managed to drag himself almost a hundred feet into the trees to the west while Baine was gone. Using a lantern from the cave, Baine had found the man hiding beneath a fallen log, half out of his mind with pain. He'd lashed the outlaw's feet together with rope, ignoring his pathetic pleas for mercy. Then, just like the others, he'd used the mare to drag the sobbing man to the warehouse, tying him in a sitting position to the same support beam Baine had been bound to earlier.

"What are you waiting for?" Pater Dore had screamed in a show of defiance when Baine was finished. "Just kill me and be done with it!" The man was thin, with dove-grey eyes, an odd overbite, sharp cheekbones, and a crooked nose.

"Tell me how to get to the manor house, and maybe you get to live," Baine had said as he'd stood over the man. He'd had the foresight to bring the lantern, which sat on a crate nearby, lighting the enormous room.

Pater had hesitated at that, hope rising in his eyes. "There's a tunnel in the horse corral, the bigger one. It leads to—"

"I know where it goes," Baine had grunted. "How far up the trail is the manor?"

"About a mile or so," the outlaw had replied.

"Who else besides Jark Cordly and the girl is at the house?"

Pater had blinked then, looking confused. "Why, no one else. Just them. They wanted time alone before dealing with you in the morning."

Baine had grinned at that. "Guess you can't always get what you want, now can you?"

Satisfied, Baine had begun moving wooden crates and empty barrels around the bound man, creating a barrier in a circle four feet high.

"What are you doing?" the outlaw had asked, sounding mystified as Baine worked.

Baine had chuckled. "You'll find out soon enough."

Once satisfied, Baine had picked up the lantern and moved away, ignoring the outlaw's continued questions. Five more empty cots stood in a row beside the one where Ira lay. Baine had moved to the nearest, ripping the canvas open with his knife before using the lantern to light the straw filling inside on fire. He'd repeated the process with the other cots, distributing them around the room against the walls where possible. Once the flames were burning briskly, he'd returned to the outlaw, leaning over a crate to peer down at him as thick black smoke began to congregate around the rafters far above, curling like menacing waves against the exposed underside of the roof's planking.

"I...I don't understand," the outlaw had said, his face livid with terror. "I thought you were going to let me live?"

Baine had shrugged at that, giving the man his best smile. "Looks like I lied, now doesn't it?" Then he'd tapped the heavy crate with his hands and winked at his victim. "These should keep you alive for a while, you bastard. Maybe deflect the flames long enough for you to repent your sins. Who knows? At any rate, I'm guessing it'll be so hot in here by the time the roof falls, you'll be cooked like a side of beef. But you never know. You might last right up until the end, fighting and gasping for one last breath." Baine had glared at the doomed man then, letting him see his hatred. "The next few minutes should give you an inclining of what eternity is going to be like for you in The Father's pits," he'd added before turning away.

Now Baine waited outside as the wind tugged at his cloak. He took a deep breath, not bothered by the smoke and heat, part of his mind certain he could smell cooking flesh. Perhaps it was just wishful thinking on his part. A moment later, one of the western support posts finally collapsed, bringing a ton of burning wood down with it. Baine thought he heard an inhuman shriek of horror and terror then as the rest of the building's roof followed, though again, perhaps that had just been wishful thinking as well.

"All right, Pretty Girl," Baine said, clucking his tongue as he nudged the mare gently in the ribs with his heels. "Let's go." He glanced back as what remained of the warehouse collapsed in on itself with a roar, sending sparks and burning embers skyward. "This is almost over. Then we can finally go home."

The horizon over the hills to the east was lit up by a bright mixture of orange, purple, and pink colors by the time Baine finally reached the manor house, which sat in shadows at the base of a towering promontory. Hadrack had described in detail what Witbridge Manor had originally looked like when he, Sim, Flora, Aenor, and Margot had first arrived there. That description closely mirrored what Baine was seeing now, although this place, rundown as it was, was much smaller than Witbridge. The house was surrounded by crumbling stone walls, with the shadier, mostly intact western side facing a cliff covered in a thick layer of climbing hydrangea. The road Baine traveled cut through a series of tree-covered hills leading to what once might have been an impressive gatehouse. Now there wasn't much left of it except for the remains of a single tower on the right side leaning precariously forward.

A crow sat perched on top of the leaning tower, turning its head back and forth curiously as it watched Baine's approach before, with a squawk, the bird leaped into the air and flapped away. Baine would have preferred coming at the manor house in stealth from a different angle, but the terrain around the building and walls worked as a natural funnel, forcing any visitors to approach head-on down the road. The manor house was well positioned from a defensive aspect, though why a mine overseer would have needed it to be was a mystery to Baine. He unhooked his bow and notched an arrow as he looked around warily for any signs of movement. Were Jark Cordly and the girl awake yet? Were they even now watching him? Baine had no way of knowing. But, even if they were, the gods had gotten him this far in one piece for a reason, so he would trust in them to keep him safe for a little while longer.

Baine guided the mare through the opening where the gatehouse had once stood, finding himself in an overgrown courtyard filled with twisting vines, tall, prickly hedges, and oddly stunted trees, all of which had somehow managed over time to break through the cobblestone with their roots. A stable missing its roof stood to Baine's left, with various other, smaller buildings—a blacksmith, a bakery, what looked like a cowhouse, and a tannery—in varying stages of disrepair attached to it in a line along the western wall. A modest-sized Holy House rose to the east, also missing a roof as well as an entire wall. The Son's and Daughter's quarters stood next to the House, attached by a narrow wooden corridor on stilts that reminded Baine of Haverty's strange house near Halhaven. Both the Son's quarters and the Daughter's looked ready to fall down at any moment.

Baine paused Pretty Girl, his ears filled with the dawn chorus of blackbirds, robins, thrushes, finches, and chipping sparrows. He focused on the house, which was two stories high with a surprisingly intact slate roof. The walls were made of stone and brick, with the outside mortar in between crumbling noticeably, especially around the lintels above the open windows and the closed double doors of the entrance. The manor had three brick chimneys—one on each of the end walls to the east and west, and one in the center, though that one was leaning precariously much like the tower at the entrance to the courtyard. Thin plumes of white smoke rose lazily from the chimney to Baine's right, possible evidence pointing to where Jark Cordly and his lady had taken up residence.

Baine dismounted, adjusting his arrow bag on his hip before he patted Pretty Girl on the shoulder affectionately. "Wait here. I'll be right back. Hopefully, this won't take long."

He walked toward the closed doors in a crouch, his roving eyes shifting from one open window above him to the next, bow nocked and ready as he stepped onto the flagstone stoop. Baine had expected the doors to be bolted, surprised when he lifted the latch and the left-hand door swung inward on creaking hinges. The interior was cast in semi-darkness, and Baine hesitated, listening intently for any sounds of movement. There were none. He cautiously stepped through the entrance, then, remembering Hep and how the sneaky bastard had hidden behind a gate, he skipped to his right as his boots shuffled loudly on the chipped tiled floor. Again, nothing but silence greeted him.

Baine took a deep breath, letting his eyes adjust to the gloom. He was standing in a long, narrow entrance hall, with a morning room on his left and a much larger main hall to his right. He entered the hall dominated by a long table at its center surrounded by carved, high-backed chairs. Most of the table was covered in thick dust and debris, though the far end was cluttered with empty bottles, flasks, and plates, some still with the remnants of a meal on them. A door to Baine's left led to a small dining room where a broken round table stood on its side, surrounded by stools. An arched entrance led Baine to a small study containing a dusty desk and rows of shelves filled with scrolls and musty leather-bound books.

Satisfied there were no threats, Baine returned to the hall, walking carefully on the plank flooring as it creaked softly beneath his weight. He passed through another door, this one leading to the servants' quarters, where he found a long row of beds stacked two high against the end wall. Several beds on the bottom looked recently used, suggesting some of the outlaws might have slept there. Baine moved on, reaching the kitchen, where he found a set of stairs leading upward. He climbed, wincing every time a step protested beneath him.

Baine made it to the landing on the first floor without hearing an outcry, then crept along the corridor in front of him, which after ten paces, branched off to his left and his right. He went right, remembering the smoking chimney, pausing at an open doorway to look inside—an empty bedroom. He moved on, checking the next room and then the next. All were empty. Only one door remained at the end of the corridor, though this one was closed. Baine advanced, creeping along the wall to mitigate any sounds of his passage. He reached the door and tried the latch, which lifted easily.

Baine pushed the door in slowly with the toe of his boot, his bow drawn. The room inside was large and well furnished, with surprisingly high ceilings painted in rich, colorful murals. A wide stone fireplace with a cracked marble mantle stood to his right, still with glowing embers inside the firebox. A four-poster bed of carved mahogany dominated the area directly opposite Baine, with a blonde-haired woman asleep on her side facing the fireplace. She had a heavy woolen blanket—the only bedclothes on the bed—draped over her body and tucked in at her armpits, revealing the soft, smooth skin of her naked shoulders. There was no sign of Jark.

Baine stepped into the room and closed the door softly behind him. He silently slid the iron bolt above the latch into its slot in the stone frame, securing the door, then advanced until he stood at the end of the bed. He studied the girl's profile, guessing she was in her early twenties at most. Vierna Alel was pretty, Baine conceded, although even in her sleep, he thought there was something cruel about the cast of her features.

"Rise and shine," Baine said, kicking the bedframe. "It's time for Judgement Day."

The girl's eyes popped open, and before Baine could register what was happening, she sat up and tossed the blanket toward him like a net. Baine had a quick glance of a slim, naked body with small breasts and wide hips, then the wool covering settled over him. He loosed his arrow anyway, which punched a neat hole in the blanket as he retreated, frantically trying to extricate himself. Had he hit the girl? Baine had his answer a heartbeat later when something solid smashed into the side of the head. He staggered, his vision blurring, then doubled up as a blow to the stomach knocked the wind from him. Baine inadvertently dropped to his knees, managing to drag the blanket aside only to see Vierna Alel standing over him holding a long staff, the butt of which was whistling toward his head with deadly intent.

Baine twisted to the side, feeling the polished, hardened wood rifle the hairs along the top of his head as it passed. He reached out with his bow, hooking it behind the girl's left ankle, then yanked her toward him. Vierna squealed in surprise and fell, landing on her naked rump on the tiled floor as Baine lashed out with his right fist, connecting with her jaw. The girl's head snapped back and she fell, the staff she held rolling away as she lay spreadeagled on the floor, her sex open and available like an overeager lover. Baine couldn't have cared less. He stood, wobbling and breathing heavily as Vierna Alel groaned, starting to stir. Baine moved, putting his boot on the girl's neck as her eyes—which were enormous and light green with tiny flecks of gold around them—

opened. Baine thought those eyes might have been mesmerizing in different circumstances, but right now, they were filled with nothing but panic and fear.

"Do you know who I am?" Baine whispered, easing up the pressure on the girl's neck slightly.

"A dead man," the girl spat. She suddenly twisted her body, bringing up a leg to try and kick Baine in the groin.

Baine had been expecting it, having used a similar ploy on Konway not long ago. He turned sideways, and the girl's bare foot struck his hip and bounced off. Baine grinned. "Nice try, bitch."

"He'll kill you," Vierna hissed. "Jark will tear you apart for this."

"Speaking of the man," Baine grunted. "Where is he?" Vierna just glared up at him, her face turning a lovely shade of blue as Baine pushed down hard with his foot. He only eased up again when the girl's eyelids began to flutter. "I asked you a question."

"Take my staff over there and shove it up your arse, you bastard," Vierna finally managed to rasp between ragged breaths.

"I'd rather not," Baine said. He applied more pressure. "Now, where is Jark?"

"You'll find out soon enough. I look forward to watching what he does to you."

"I'm afraid you're about to be disappointed over that," Baine said. "Because your time in this world is over. As for Jark, I'm sure I'll find him on my own sooner or later."

Baine snatched an arrow from his bag, removing his foot from the girl's neck at the same time. He dropped to his knees on her naked chest without warning, hearing her ribs crack as what little air remained in her lungs exploded out from her mouth in a whoosh. He didn't hesitate, using his left hand to tilt back the girl's head while he rammed the arrow point into the soft flesh beneath her jaw with his right, pushing the shaft upward as far as he could until the iron barb hit her brain. Vierna Alel spasmed uncontrollably beneath him, her eyes bulging in shock and her arms and legs flailing helplessly as saliva frothed at her mouth.

Baine waited patiently as the dying girl lost control of her bladder and the acrid stench of urine filled the room until her movements finally ceased, her body settling reluctantly into death. He lowered his head and closed his eyes when it was over, saying a prayer of thanks to The Mother for delivering the girl to him just as he heard the latch on the door behind him rattle. Baine looked up at the ceiling and smiled, knowing She wasn't done with him just yet. Jark Cordly had arrived. He stood, trying to ignore the pain and fatigue in his limbs as he drew another arrow and nocked it before turning to face the door.

One more. Just one more.

"Vierna? What's going on? Why is the door locked?"

Baine waited, drawing the string to his chin.

"Vierna?" This time the voice sounded angry as three heavy raps sounded against the wooden door, shaking it. "Dammit, Vierna! Open this door right now!"

Baine drew in deep, even breaths, knowing what was coming next. He didn't have to wait long as the door shuddered beneath a heavy kick, sending dust and small chips of stone flying. A second kick followed, this one even harder, causing one side of the iron plating holding the bolt to the wood to pop off. Baine tensed, body turned sideways, knowing the door couldn't withstand a third kick. A moment later, it crashed open, splinters flying, revealing a huge, naked hairy man with a pleated beard free of bones and a red, angry face. Jark's eyes widened at the sight of Baine standing with a drawn bow over the dead body of his lover, but instead of running as Baine had expected, the outlaw roared and charged into the room.

Baine released the arrow, striking Jark high in the meat of the shoulder near his collarbone, but the outlaw didn't seem to notice, his momentum carrying him into Baine like a two-hundred-pound battering ram. The two men staggered backward, Baine's feet getting tangled up in Vierna Alel's legs. He tripped and fell, landing on the bed with the full weight of the outlaw on top of him as the shaft sticking out of the man's shoulder poked painfully into Baine's chest.

"You bastard!" the outlaw hissed, wrapping his hands around Baine's neck. The man's fingers felt like bands of steel.

Baine pounded his bow against the outlaw's naked side and back to no avail, then let it drop, using his left hand to grasp the exposed arrow shaft. He pushed it in deeper, but all Jark Cordly did was grunt at the pain, his red face twisted in rage as he squeezed. Baine gave up on the arrow, reaching for the knife on his right hip instead. He drew it out, seeing stars in his eyes now as his lungs screamed for air. Jark Cordly seemed oblivious to the blood pouring down his hairy chest, the veins in his eyes engorged rivers of red fury. Baine plunged the knife into the man's side, relieved when the outlaw screamed, his grip relaxing. He pulled the blade free, intent on stabbing again, but this time Jark used his left arm to block him, his right strengthening around Baine's neck again. The outlaw grabbed Baine's wrist, applying pressure like a vice until the knife fell from his numb fingers, bouncing off the mattress to the floor.

Jark wrapped both hands around Baine's neck again, leaning close like a lover. "I hear they call you *Black Death*. Well, you're about to find out what that means."

Baine desperately tried to pry the man's hands away, but the outlaw's arms were like solid oak—hard, unyielding, and immovable. Knowing he was hopelessly outmatched physically, Baine did the only thing he could think of. He spread his arms to either side and cupped his hands, then struck the bigger man's ears simultaneously with all his remaining strength. The resulting effect was more than he could have ever hoped for. Jark cried out, the vise around Baine's neck receding as the outlaw shook his head, his eyes glazed and unfocused. Baine didn't hesitate, twisting his body beneath his distracted assailant until he was free before rolling off the bed to the floor. Jark Cordly tried to grab at him, but the outlaw was moving like a drunkard. He missed Baine by a wide margin and then fell facedown on the bed, where he lay moaning in pain with a trickle of blood rolling out from his left ear.

Jark Cordly fought to push himself up on his heavily muscled forearms, then to his knees. He wobbled unsteadily on the mattress, then finally stood, swaying and shaking his head. "What did you do to me, you bastard?"

Baine picked up his fallen knife, watching the naked man warily. Was this an act, or was he truly incapacitated?

The outlaw fumbled at his side, finally locating the bleeding wound there. He looked at his blood-smeared hand afterward, then shook his head again, focusing unsteadily on Baine. "I'm going to kill you now."

"You had your chance," Baine grunted.

The outlaw looked at him funny then, confusion on his face, and Baine realized in sudden understanding that Jark hadn't heard him. He laughed, realizing the blows to the ears must have burst one or both of the outlaw's eardrums.

"Laugh at me, will you!" Jark Cordly growled. "I'm the Outlaw of Corwick, damn you!" He stumbled forward, swinging his fist at Baine, who easily avoided the clumsy blow, pushing the bigger man off balance.

Jark Cordly staggered and almost fell, crying out as Baine's knife flashed, cutting a two-foot gash down the man's naked back. The outlaw bellowed in frustration like a bull, arching his back as he spun awkwardly around, only to lose his balance and fall to one knee as yellow bile erupted from his mouth.

"If you really want to pretend to be the Outlaw of Corwick," Baine said as he darted in and cut a long line down the left side of the outlaw's face with his knife from his forehead to his chin. Baine danced away again. "Then, by the gods, I'd say you need to look the part." He stood back ten feet, careful not to trip over the dead girl's body again as he examined Jark critically. "There, that's much better. But there's still something missing." Baine grinned at the murderous look on the other man's face, not caring that the outlaw probably couldn't hear a word he was saying. "You have Hadrack's scowl just right. I'll give you that. But my friend has a lot of scars on his body earned from a lifetime of fighting. How about we work on that?"

Baine didn't wait for an answer, using his advantage of speed, not to mention his intense hatred for the man in front of him as he went to work on Jark Cordly with his knife. He had no idea how long it took—ten minutes? An hour? Two? It didn't matter. By the time he was done, drenched in sweat and blood, the outlaw's dead body was barely recognizable, resembling a side of beef more than a human being.

Baine finally cleaned off his knife and sheathed it, moving slowly and painfully to pick up his bow. He made his way to the door, almost drawing it closed before pausing to look back at the pair of naked bodies lying side by side. "Well, I did hear somewhere that you two wanted to spend some time alone," he said. "I hope eternity works for you."

Baine fought to close the door, but with the broken bolt and latch, it wouldn't stay shut. He finally gave up with a shrug, knowing scavengers would find their way in there no matter what he did, anyway. He headed back outside, limping toward Pretty Girl, who tossed her head in greeting at him. It felt like every muscle in his body was protesting all at the same time as he pulled himself wearily up into the horse's saddle.

"Come on, girl," Baine said, heading the mare away from the manor. "Let's go home. I've got some friends that I'd like you to meet."

Chapter 30: Everything Has Changed

The journey back to Witbridge Manor took a week and a half, and during all that time, Baine made sure to stay away from major roads, traveling with Pretty Girl through dense, unpopulated forests and rolling hills as he headed north. He was careful to avoid contact with all people, deliberately circumventing any towns or villages he saw along the way while hunting with his bow for rabbits, squirrels, and pheasants to sustain him. Baine had needed to be alone with his thoughts after the events at Havelock, spending most of his time lost in deep reflection. As the days passed, he'd come to realize that something monumental had shifted inside him, something that he couldn't quite understand or put a name to.

Until the day he'd been swept off *Sea-Dragon*, Baine had never questioned that he was anything but a man despite his young age, especially after all he'd gone through growing up without a family. But now, thinking back to how he'd been before Nelsun Merklar and Sunna had found him on that rock, Baine knew in reality that he'd just been a naïve boy all along. Since the age of seven, he'd always had Jebido and Hadrack to look up to and lean on for support and protection. But now, after almost two months of being on his own and fighting against horrible odds, Baine knew he'd changed—still the same person he'd always been, yes—yet profoundly different at the same time. Would Hadrack and Jebido even recognize him now? Would his wife if she'd lived? Baine wasn't entirely sure, wondering after everything that had happened if he'd ever be able to smile and joke with his friends again in the same, carefree manner as before.

Pretty Girl snorted then as if trying to assuage Baine's fears, and he looked up, immediately recognizing the town that he saw rising in the distance. It was Laskerly. Baine guided the mare around the town, still not ready to see familiar faces, then across Barnwin's

Channel, heading for Thurston's Gulch. It seemed so long ago to him now that he'd been in this very spot. Baine entered the forest, pausing the mare when he reached the area where the boar had appeared, setting off a chain of events that would eventually leave a trail of blood splattered across half the north country. Baine wondered idly where that boar was and what it was doing now as he continued on his way.

An hour later, with the sun high in the sky, Baine approached the ridge overlooking Witbridge Manor. He felt a sudden lurch in his chest, remembering the fear and heartache he'd experienced the last time he'd crested that ridge only to see the village and manor house in flames.

"Don't worry, Pretty Girl," Baine said to the mare, needing to talk. "I know you haven't met Finol and young Hanley yet, but trust me when I say those two will have rebuilt Witbridge better than ever by now. In a few minutes, I promise you'll have plenty of grain to fill your belly, a nice comfortable paddock to sleep in, and maybe even—"

Baine paused as he reached the ridge and stared down at Witbridge Manor, his heart sinking. He could see no signs of activity below; no cooking fires or smoke coming from the manor's chimneys, no women washing clothing by the stream near the mill while children laughed and played around them, nor anyone moving about in the overgrown fields. There were no sheep, chickens, horses, or pigs in sight, either—everything was still and silent. Witbridge Manor looked abandoned.

"Mother Above," Baine whispered, fearing for his friends. "What happened here?"

Baine guided Pretty Girl down the slope into the valley at a gallop, following the road to what was left of the village. There was no one around and no sounds except for the mare's hooves clopping along the ground, not even the song of a bird. Where was everyone? Baine rode the mare up the hill to the manor, pausing at the closed gate, which he noted had been repaired since last he'd been there. He left the mare outside the walls, her reins trailing on the ground as he unhooked his bow and nocked an arrow, then opened the gate. He stepped inside, his heart in his throat. There was no one around, no bodies, nothing, and no evidence of an attack. The place looked neat and tidy, though it had clearly been picked clean of anything useful. Looters? Baine frowned in confusion, scratching at his beard. Looters almost always would leave a mess behind. No, this was something else.

"Oh, I thought I heard someone. Hello, Baine."

Baine glanced at the house as Putt appeared from the back, heading toward him. The burly, red-bearded outlaw was dressed in loose-fitting trousers and a white tunic with the sleeves rolled up. He held a hoe in one hand and a flask in the other.

"Putt?" Baine strode forward. "Where is everyone?"

The outlaw's creased face registered his surprise. "You mean you don't know?"

"Know what?" Baine growled. "I just got here?"

"They've all gone to Corwick Castle," Putt replied. "Set out about two weeks ago now."

Baine blinked in surprise. He would have been less surprised if the man had just told him giant turtles had floated down from the heavens to lay golden eggs on silver plates. "Why would they do that?" he asked.

"Well, Lord Hadrack told them to, of course," Putt said as if it were obvious. His eyes took on a faraway look. "Finol is to be his steward there, and apparently, I'm to be captain of—"

Baine lifted a hand, stopping the outlaw. "Lord Hadrack? What nonsense is this?"

Now it was Putt's turn to look confused. "You haven't heard about that either? King Tyden made Lord Hadrack the Lord of Corwick, granting him all the lands previously held by the traitor, Pernissy Raybold."

Baine felt his legs go weak, putting his hand on the older man's shoulder to steady himself. "Do not joke with me," he said. "I'm in no mood for games."

"It's no joke, lad," Putt replied with a frown. "Why would I do something like that? The king granted Lord Hadrack the lands for his role in ending the war."

Baine blinked again. "The war is over?"

Putt nodded. "Yes, thank the gods." He couldn't hide his puzzlement. "How could you not know this, lad? Have you been living under a rock?"

Baine looked away, still trying to process what he'd just heard. The war was over, and Hadrack was now the Lord of Corwick. It seemed impossible to be true, yet Baine instinctively knew that it was. His gaze fell on a mound of neatly trimmed grass with a wooden marker above it under a tree near the back wall of the manor. He straightened, knowing there would be plenty of time to talk to Putt after seeing his wife and son.

Baine patted Putt on his beefy shoulder. "You can tell me all about it later. Right now, I have something that I need to do."

"All right, lad," Putt said, staring at him strangely. "Whatever you want." The outlaw hesitated, clearing his throat. "Are you all right?"

Baine took a deep breath and nodded. "Yes, why?"

"No reason," Putt said, still looking at him strangely.

Baine turned and headed for the grave. He paused over it, noting that someone had placed flowers on either side of the marker, though they'd long since wilted. Baine somehow knew that it had been Jebido. He sank to his knees by the grave and put his hands on the grassy mound as he gazed at the faded words cut into the marker. It seemed like ages ago now that he'd carved them.

"It's done, my love," Baine whispered, eyes closed and head bent. "Everything I promised you and our child has been done. Those who hurt you both are no more. Sent to The Father's pits. I hope knowing this gives you and baby Hadrack some solace wherever you might be in the next world." Baine choked up then, finally letting the tears come. He remained that way for a long time, grieving for what he'd lost as the sun slowly sank in the west. Finally, as a light rain began to fall, Baine rose stiffly to his feet. "I have to go now," he said down to the grave, wiping at his tears. "I will never forget you, Flora. Nor you, little Hadrack. Someday we will all be together again. But for now, my friends need me."

Baine turned away, not surprised to see that Putt had brought Pretty Girl into the compound and had watered and fed her. He'd also taken her saddle off and was brushing her down with studious attention as Baine approached.

"She's a lovely horse," the outlaw mumbled, looking embarrassed and clearly at a loss for anything else to say. "Wonderful lines."

"That's a fact," Baine agreed, rubbing Pretty Girl's soft nose. He glanced at Putt. "Why didn't you go to Corwick Castle with the others?"

"Jebido told me to stay here," Putt answered with a shrug. "He said I was to wait for you no matter how long it took. He told me a bunch of shit-eating, halfwit outlaws didn't stand a chance against you and that you'd be back here someday. Looks like he was right."

Baine couldn't help but smile, feeling a warmth of kinship rise in his chest. Good old Jebido, always having his and Hadrack's back. Where would either of them be now if not for his steadying presence? "Do you have a horse?" Baine asked.

"I do," Putt nodded.

"Good," Baine grunted. He motioned to the mare. "After you help me saddle Pretty Girl, go get it. We've got a long ride ahead of us."

"To Corwick Castle?"

Baine laughed. "Of course, my friend. Where else? I have to bend the knee to my new lord, after all."

Corwick Castle was larger than Baine had been expecting. Built on a massive promontory, the castle overlooked a sprawling town that Putt said was named Camwick. Baine and the outlaw rode through the village filled with busy shops and well-maintained houses. People seemed to be everywhere, scurrying about on errands, shopping, or hawking their wares in an immense market square. A large Holy House rose to the west with its bell tolling, signaling to worshipers that morning prayers were about to commence.

"Did you want to pay respects to The Mother and The Father first?" Putt asked, nodding toward the House's bell tower as the ringing continued. He suddenly looked guilty. "It's been over a month since I went to confession. I imagine my soul could use a little cleansing."

Baine grimaced and shook his head. "No, you go if you want. I doubt another day or two without prayer will make much difference for me now."

Putt looked at Baine as though he wanted to say something else, then he shrugged in acceptance. "You're certain?"

"I am," Baine said. He gestured to the castle rising in the distance. "I don't want to wait any longer to see Hadrack, not even for the First Pair. It's been far too long."

"I understand," the outlaw replied. "I guess we'll talk later, then." He hesitated, grinning. "I'm glad you're back, lad. I always felt guilty about putting you on that damn rudder during a storm like that. Life just hasn't been the same without that handsome, smiling face of yours around."

Baine nodded gratefully to the outlaw, watching as he wheeled his horse around before guiding it down a side street toward the Holy House. He urged Pretty Girl onward once the man had disappeared, passing through the town before following a long sloping road to the north. The terrain on both sides of the road near the approach to Corwick Castle was littered with sharp stones of varying sizes, making travel there on foot or horseback all but impossible. With a nod of approval, Baine realized that the barrier would force any attacking party to remain exposed on the road to a barrage of arrows—a distinct advantage for the defenders. Baine finally reached the open gate, where a man who closely resembled a bear awaited him. He had a thick, heavy beard and a shaved head with looped silver rings in his ears.

"Can I help you?" the man rumbled, a scowl on his face.

Baine paused Pretty Girl. "I'm here to see Hadrack," he said.

The huge man's features darkened. "I believe you mean to say, *Lord Hadrack*."

"Baine!"

The cry had come from behind the big man, a shriek of pure joy. Baine couldn't help but smile as Lady Shana came running toward him, her skirts held high, her face flushed with happiness.

Baine dismounted, laughing as Shana threw her arms around him. "Oh, thank the gods, you're alive! I've prayed daily to The Mother and The Father to keep you safe!"

"You know this man, Lady Shana?" the huge man growled.

Shana glanced at him and laughed, the sound like fine music. "Of course I do, Ubeth! This is my betrothed's best friend."

Baine gawked. "Betrothed? You and Hadrack are to be married?"

"Yes," Shana said. "Two weeks from now, as long as—" She hesitated, and Baine saw a shadow cross her features.

"What is it?" Baine asked, knowing something was wrong. "Where is Hadrack? Is he here?" Shana took a deep breath and then shook her head, looking down at the ground. Baine put his hands on the slim woman's shoulders. "Where is he, my lady? Tell me what's happening."

Baine listened then as Shana told him about the plot to kill both Prince Tyden and Prince Tyrale, leaving the door open for Pernissy Raybold to seize the throne of Ganderland. Putt had told him some of what had happened already, of course, but Shana's version was much more informative and detailed. Baine shook his head, marveling when he heard how Hadrack had turned the tables on the former Lord of Corwick, pretending to have murdered Prince Tyden, only to have him appear at Pernissy's coronation and take the crown for himself. Pernissy was now locked up in the dungeons beneath the very castle he'd plotted on claiming, his dreams crushed while his title and all his lands now belonged to his arch-enemy, Hadrack.

"Remarkable," Baine said when Shana had finished, as always amazed by his friend's sheer tenacity, intelligence, and resourcefulness. He pursed his lips. "But why, my lady, do you look so sad and worried, then?"

"Because after the coronation, King Tyden asked Hadrack what else he could do to reward him for what he'd done," Shana said, dabbing at her eyes now with a handkerchief. She chuckled sadly and then shrugged. "You know my lord better than any of us, Baine. Not surprisingly, he wanted nothing for himself—nothing that is except Prince Tyrale's advisor."

"Do you mean that bastard Hervi Desh?" Baine whispered, his eyes narrowing.

"Yes," Shana agreed. "That's the man. Hadrack had him brought here to Corwick." She sniffed. "To the old farm where he grew up. That's where he plans to kill him—today."

"He's going to execute Desh?"

Shana shook her head regretfully. "If only that were the case. No, my love intends to fight this man barehanded to the death. No one is allowed to interfere, regardless of what happens. I couldn't bear to watch, so I came—"

"My lady," Baine said brusquely, cutting her off. "I am truly sorry, but I have to go. I hope you understand, but Hadrack might need me."

Shana smiled, her features softening with affection. She cupped his face with her hand. "Of course I understand, Baine. He's like a brother to you. I would expect nothing else."

Baine nodded, holding her eyes for a moment, both of them sharing their worry and love for Hadrack with each other before finally he turned and leaped into the saddle.

"Baine?"

"Yes, my lady?" Baine said, holding the mare back.

"There's something different about you. What is it?"

Baine hesitated. "I really don't know," he whispered honestly.

Shana nodded as if that were explanation enough. "Keep him safe, Baine. Keep my man safe for me."

"You have my word, my lady," Baine said.

Then he was off, kicking the mare into a gallop. The ride east was a blur to Baine, every emotion known to man manifesting itself at some point during the frantic race to arrive in time. Finally, with Pretty Girl covered in a sheen of perspiration and blowing hard, he saw a group of riders congregating in an overgrown field ahead of him and veered toward them. A large copse of trees arose to his left, surrounded by a wall of rocks, and Baine instinctively knew that was the bog where Hadrack had hidden as a boy to escape the nine. A lone wolf was sitting on its haunches near the wall, and it lifted its head as he galloped past, crying to the sky mournfully before loping away.

Baine reached the riders, all of whom were watching his approach, though he remained focused on only one man—Hadrack. Baine reined in the mare, locking eyes with his bare-chested friend, who looked impossibly huge and content sitting on his great black stallion, despite his face and body being bruised and battered.

"So, I missed it, then?" Baine asked, clamping down on his emotions. Inside, he wanted to rush to his friend and wrap his arms around him, but others were watching, so he just waited for the answer, his face blank and serious.

"You did," Hadrack replied with a slight smile on his lips. He looked back toward the swaying long grasses behind him, his smile growing wider as he focused on Baine again. "But it was a damn fine fight just the same." Hadrack raised an eyebrow. "And what about you? Is it done?"

Baine felt a hardness come over him as he thought about the outlaws and what he'd done to them, then he quickly shook it off and smiled at his friend. "It's done, Hadrack."

"Good," Hadrack grunted, looking pleased. He glanced around at the mounted men. "Then let's go home. I promised Shana that I wouldn't be late."

EPILOGUE

"*The Ballad of Black Death*," my granddaughter said in wonder. "That song was about Baine, my lord?"

"Indeed it was," I said wearily, having spent the last four hours retelling Baine's story to Lillia and Kather Merklar. I'd had little sleep, having written everything out the night before in a fit of energy, only to verbally repeat it almost word for word again to the two women the next morning. Now it was well past midday, and I desperately needed to get some sleep.

"I've heard that song many times, lord," Kather Merklar said, her eyes swollen and puffy from crying. "And to think that it was about my grandfather all this time. I am truly at a loss for words."

Lillia put an arm around the slim girl, hugging her tightly, her own eyes threatening tears. We were in my solar once again, and I sighed and stood, my knees popping loudly from sitting for so long. "That's the way Baine wanted it," I said. "He was always embarrassed by that song. More so as he got older."

"Whatever for, my lord?" Lillia asked, looking surprised. "Why would such a thing embarrass him? It's just a silly song, after all."

I shrugged. "Because all it did was glorify what happened, child. Portraying Baine as some kind of blood-thirsty savage who delighted in torturing his victims rather than a grieving husband and father desperate for revenge. If you recall, his wife's and son's murders are barely mentioned at all in that damn song, thrown in almost as an afterthought at the end."

I turned and looked out the window, realizing the day had turned bright and sunny. Long icicles gleaming like precious jewels dripped water from the overhang above the window where I stood as the snow from last night's storm began to melt in earnest. *Maybe an early spring will arrive soon, after all*, I thought. I heard a faint squeal of delight from beneath me, peering down into the courtyard to see my grandson, Frankin, wielding a battered wooden sword against one of my men-at-arms. The soldier was pretending to be terrified, backtracking desperately beneath Frankin's attack as the boy advanced through the wet, sloshy snow. I couldn't help but smile at the sight.

"Lord?" my granddaughter said, cutting into my thoughts. I turned to face the women. "Why didn't Baine ever marry again? My mother told me he could have had his choice of almost any woman in Corwick."

I sighed again, feeling the weight of my memories pressing down on me. "Because his love for Flora consumed him completely," I said, knowing in that, he and I had been much the same, despite my having married again after my beloved Shana. I thought about Sarrey del Fante then and grimaced, not wanting to scratch at that old wound. There would be time for that soon enough when I took up quill and paper again. Today, though, it was all about Baine.

My granddaughter was looking at me with a slight smile on her face. "But it didn't stop him from—" She glanced at her companion. "Well, you know, my lord."

I laughed then, feeling the darkness settling over me evaporate. Lillia had a way of doing that for me, thank the gods. "No, it certainly didn't stop him," I agreed.

Kather looked in confusion from Lillia to me and back again, having missed the innuendo. "I don't understand, my lady," she said.

I spread my arms and smiled, answering for my granddaughter. "I'm afraid your grandmother was just one of many, many romantic conquests that my old friend laid claim to over his life. It was in his nature, after all."

"Oh, I see," Kather replied, looking down at her hands.

"My mother once told me that Baine had bedded every pretty unwed girl in Corwick and beyond for at least a hundred miles in every direction by the time he was forty," Lillia said to me, laughter in her voice. "I was too young to understand what she meant back then, my lord, but were her words true?"

"Every pretty girl and half the homely ones as well, I'd wager," I confirmed with a smile, thinking fondly of my friend and his preoccupation with the opposite sex. "After he killed the outlaws, Baine pledged to the gods that he would never marry again," I added. "But he made no such promise to them about remaining chaste. He considered it his sworn duty to show women the appreciation and affection he believed they deserved."

"I wish I had known him better, my lord," Lillia said regretfully. "I barely remember him at all."

I smiled. "I can still see him in my mind bouncing you on his knee when you were just a babe. You were squealing so loud one of the chambermaids thought a pig had gotten into the castle."

Lillia burst out laughing, the tears in her eyes now from mirth as she pictured it. We three fell silent for a time then, each reflecting in their own way on Baine and what he'd meant to them.

"Lord?" Kather finally said tentatively. "May I ask how my grandfather died?"

I should have been prepared for it, I suppose. It's a perfectly logical question to ask, after all. Yet even so, the girl's words seared into my heart like a red-hot poker. I turned away, not answering, my black mood returning.

"My lord?" Lillia said, concern in her voice now. I heard the rustling of her dress and the scrape of the bench on the floor as she stood. "Are you all right?"

"Just tired, is all," I muttered moodily, staring out the window at nothing. "Perhaps we can talk of this later."

"Of course, my lord," Lillia said. "Forgive us."

"I'm so sorry, lord," Kather said from behind me, sounding miserable. I didn't answer her or turn around, lost in my own thoughts now.

I waited until the women were gone, aware of the tears making their way down the leathery crevasses of my face. "Oh, how I miss you, my friend," I whispered as the pane of glass in front of me fogged. "Oh, how I miss you."

I stood where I was for a time, reminiscing about Baine and Jebido and the life that was, then finally turned and limped to the door, heading down the corridor to my rooms. Thankfully, no servants were about to pester me, and I made it inside, where I lay on my bed, exhausted, as bright sunshine washed over me from a nearby window. The warmth on my face was making me sleepy as a feeling of intense contentment suddenly washed over me. Baine's story was now finished, a promise that I'd made to myself now achieved. I could only pray that I'd done it justice, for my friend had been a remarkable man and the generations coming behind us deserved to know who he'd been. It was something that I was determined to see happen before Judgement Day finally came for me.

I yawned, groaning as I rolled over onto my side with my last thought before I slipped into the world of dreams that it was time to get back to my story now. But first, I must sleep and recoup my strength, for spring was just around the corner, and tomorrow was another day.

THE END

Author's Note

As always, I want to thank you, dear reader, for your overwhelming support of this series. I've now written nine books in the last three and a half years (7 Wolf of Corwick and 2 Past Lives). Had someone told me that was going to happen when I first sat down to write The Nine, I would have laughed and called them delusional. Who knew?

Baine and the Outlaw of Corwick was a delight for me to write, though in truth when I began the story, I had in mind a novella around the fifty to sixty thousand word mark. I'd just finished the mammoth 485-page The Wolf and the Codex four days before I started this book, and honestly thought it would be a very short yet bloody companion story to Hadrack and nothing else. Well, it turned out I got the bloody part right but fell short on the short part. Oops!

Despite the book's larger-than-expected size, I debated whether to include it in the main Wolf of Corwick Castle series or keep it as a companion novel. Ultimately though, since Hadrack appears prominently in both the prologue and the epilogue, I decided that Baine's story deserved to be included in the main series, especially since there are a few hints thrown in about what's to come in following Wolf novels.

I'd also like to take this opportunity to address an Amazon reviewer of The Wolf and the Codex from the UK, who mentioned the graves Hadrack was standing over on the Watching Hill at the end of Book 5. He rightly noted that Sarrey del Fante wasn't among them and wanted to know why. Amazon does not allow comments anymore on reviews. And though I rarely responded to them before the new policy anyway, (not out of arrogance, mind you, but simply because I believe you, the reader, have the right to leave your thoughts about an author's work without being harassed if the author doesn't agree) I felt bad that I couldn't answer him. All I'll say for now, sir, is not all marriages go exactly as planned in Ganderland, just as they do here in the real world. Sarrey del Fante and what became of her will be explained in due course, I assure you.

That said, I will be taking a break from writing for a few months—no, I really mean it this time! As much as I cherish doing this for a living, writing seven days a week for months at a time takes a physical and mental toll on a person, and I need to recharge my batteries. If all goes well, the new Wolf of Corwick Castle book, The Wolf at the Door, should be out in the fall.

All the best

Terry Cloutier
April 2023